THE IMPOSSIBLE VIRGIN

Peter O'Donnell began writing at the age of sixteen, when he sold his first story. He has lost count since then but thinks the tally reaches over a thousand short stories and novels. He also writes television and film scripts.

Born in 1921, he spent two years working on juvenile periodicals and served in the Territorial Army during World War II. He began writing strip cartoons – the best known of these are probably 'Garth' in the *Daily Mirror* and 'Tug Transom' in the *Daily Sketch*. 'Modesty Blaise' took him a year to create and in 1962 she was presented as a strip-cartoon character in the *Evening Standard*. The cartoon was an immediate success, soon syndicating in over forty countries, and the 'Modesty Blaise' series of novels followed.

By the same author in Pan Books

MODESTY BLAISE
SABRE-TOOTH
PIECES OF MODESTY
A TASTE FOR DEATH

PETER O'DONNELL

THE IMPOSSIBLE VIRGIN

UNABRIDGED

PAN BOOKS LTD : LONDON

First published 1971 by Souvenir Press Ltd.
This edition published 1973 by Pan Books Ltd,
33 Tothill Street, London, SW1.

ISBN 0 330 23489 7

Printed in Great Britain by
Cox & Wyman Ltd, London, Reading and Fakenham

CHAPTER ONE

Temptation came to Novikov as suddenly, as unexpectedly, as an assassin's bullet. In nearly thirty years of adult life he had never even toyed with the shattering idea that seized him on a quiet afternoon as he sat at his bench in one of the many small laboratories housed within the grey walls of the Satellite Reconnaissance Section, in Shabolovka Street.

Mischa Novikov was a quiet, dutiful man. His dossier described him as totally reliable and without political ambition. His reliability did not stem from meekness or fear, simply from an acceptance of things as they were and had always been within the bounds of his memory.

As a young man he had served in the Red Army, and at the end of the war had been posted to the KGB. Because he spoke German well, he had operated in the Berlin Section and taken a useful part in the bloody and confused underground war there, between the agents of East and West. In that time, and under the orders of Colonel Starov, he had played his part in many intrigues, bought and sold men and information, laid traps and avoided traps, and killed two men and one woman without either pleasure or regret.

His hobby was photography, and in this he developed an expertise which came to the notice of his superiors. He was posted to a training school for a year, and then given a position in the laboratories of the High Altitude Reconnaissance Section.

Within a few years the onrush of technology made his early work seem primitive. Once he had played with mosaics of black and white photography. Now he had an armoury of remote sensors to aid him. There were satellites in orbit carrying the new detectors which operated over the entire electromagnetic spectrum.

Mischa Novikov played with the results of light-waves and sound-waves, radio and radar, heat and X-rays, magnetism and laser beam. These were his eyes. They could penetrate cloud, water, forest and even the earth itself. He had never seen a sputnik launched, never travelled in a high altitude aircraft. Novikov was concerned only with the readings on film delivered to him in his laboratory. Sometimes the readings were transmitted from space by radio, sometimes film was exposed in space and returned to earth in a parachute capsule.

Novikov was one of the interpreters. From film taken by folded optics from a height of three hundred miles he could pinpoint an object no bigger than the desk at which he worked. From film taken by side-looking radar he could penetrate thick vegetation and the earth's skin, to learn the nature of the bedrock below. With infra-red photography he could pick out diseased trees or crops, foretell volcanic activity, locate forest fires.

He played with colour filters, optical combiners and all the gadgetry that the accelerating new technology provided; and he had believed himself to be quite content until that soul-shaking moment when temptation sprang from nowhere and consumed him. It was all over in less than ten seconds. He turned the projector back and held the single frame of film on the screen, staring.

There it was, the thin orange streak. It would have been meaningless to anyone but a handful of men in the world. Mischa Novikov was one of those men. To him it meant that he could be rich and free. Strangely, he had never before thought he lacked money or freedom. Now it was as if he had always known the fierce and bitter desire which suddenly stirred in him.

Caution touched Novikov. Could there be a tiny flaw in the film? That was easily checked by comparison with the film from the second camera carried by the experimental satellite. Methodically he set up the other film and ran it. There was no flaw. A fault in his instruments, then? In his technique? He spent two hours checking his work, and was satisfied. He had made no error.

6

Carefully he snipped out the vital frames from both films. They would not be missed. Part of his job was to discard useless material before passing on his results to Head of Section. It was lunchtime. He went out and sat in Gorky Recreation Park, smoking quietly, thinking.

To defect would be easy enough. His reputation was impeccable. He and his wife, Ilona, had been cleared for the holiday cruise on the *Suvorov* in eight weeks' time. Marseilles was one of the ports of call. That would do very well. The French would give asylum without making a great noise about the affair like the Americans or the British. He had once done a six-month tour as a security man at the Embassy in Paris, ostensibly as a chauffeur. He could handle the language adequately.

Would the KGB send agents to find and kill him? After careful reflection he decided that this was unlikely. The material he handled was classified, but only part of it was for Military Intelligence. This was mainly concerned with the plotting of missile sites in the West, and clearly he had nothing to tell the West they did not already know about that. The bulk of his work lay in providing new information for the various sciences, for the geologists, the hydrographers, the agronomists and meteorologists. It was resentfully accepted that the Americans were ahead in the field of remote sensors, so there would be little he could tell them. The KGB would be extremely angry, of course, but he did not think they would take extreme action. Mischa Novikov was not quite worth it.

Tomorrow he would make a blow-up of the film and correlate it with a large-scale map. No problem there. It was part of his regular work. And there would be no problem with Ilona. Her political ideas had always been disturbingly bourgeois, though she had the wisdom never to voice them except to him. She would come with him gladly.

And then . . .

Then would come the difficult part. A thin streak of orange on a map was one thing, but to turn it into riches was quite another. The commercial complexities would be huge. But there was Brunel. That name had sounded in his mind during those few seconds when, as he first looked at the film, the world had changed and he had made his decision. Nothing was too big for that little man Brunel, not even this. And Brunel was the obvious man for quite another reason, an amusing reason. He was the man on the spot. Very much so.

Novikov smiled to himself and threw away his cigarette. He would have to be very careful with Brunel, of course. He remembered finding the still-living ruins of a man in a cellar in West Berlin, one of the Gehlen Bureau agents, who had not been very careful with Brunel. In mercy Novikov had severed the thread by which the thing in the cellar was held to life, even though it had been an enemy.

Yes. He would have to arrange his dealings with Brunel in a way which left him fully protected. Any mistake was likely to have a result initially painful and finally fatal.

In the event it was not Novikov who made the mistake. It was Brunel. The result, for Mischa Novikov, was the same. Five thousand miles from Shabolovka Street, and eight months from the day he had sat in the park making his plans, Mischa Novikov crawled from the scrub and thorn which bordered a dirt road leading to the village of Kalimba, forty miles from the western shore of Lake Victoria.

He was almost naked. For four days he had used strips from his tattered clothes to bind about his raw feet. He had sight only in one eye. His right hand was mangled as if it might have been crunched in the jaws of a leopard, except that the damage was too regular and precise to be the haphazard work of any jungle beast. His body was a mass of cuts, abrasions and suppurating wounds. Only some of them had been gathered during his flight through the jungle and in the fall he had taken down a rocky slope as he reeled under the brutal sun through volcanic hills.

He was close to death, and his mind had collapsed. He no longer thought of Ilona waiting for news of him in the small Paris flat . . . Ilona of the big firm body, the dark hair, grey eyes and warm loving mouth. He no longer thought of

Brunel, or the map, or the film with the orange streak. He no longer knew that he lived or that he was dying. Sometimes a few words rattled hoarsely from his cracked lips, always the same words. He was not conscious of speaking them, and no longer knew what they meant.

When he had crawled for a hundred yards along the dirt road he collapsed on his face for the last time. An hour passed before a battered Land Rover came juddering along. The Reverend John Mbarraha of the African Mission Society stopped the truck. He and his wife turned Novikov gently face-up. Angel Mbarraha felt for the pulse. Like her husband she was a Bantu, raised in a Mission School and later sent to England for further education.

She said, 'He is alive, John.'

'But very close to the end. We must pray for his soul.'

'Yes. But later. First we must take him to Dr Penny-feather. Our Lord will be patient.'

They put him in the back of the truck and drove on to Kalimba, to the long prefabricated hut above the village. This was called the hospital, and here Dr Giles Pennyfeather fought in his own curious way against disease in general and, at this particular moment, against the results of a crowded diesel coach, the local weekly bus, toppling off the road into a shallow ravine.

Mischa Novikov died after twenty-four hours, his nationality and identity still unknown, and was buried in the graveyard behind the small wooden church.

It was two days later that a Piper Comanche, out from England and bound for Durban, made an emergency landing just east of the Mission School, on the long flat stretch of beaten earth where John and Angel Mbarraha struggled doggedly to instruct their charges in the mysterious ways of western team-sports. The sturdy, elegant little aircraft had been caught at seven thousand feet over the Sudan by a *haboob*, a sand-storm rising from the desert like a dust-devil to towering heights and spreading its myriad particles through the upper air. Sand had found its way through the vent holes of the tanks and eventually worked through to block the fuel filter and cause loss of power.

There were no passengers on the plane. Surprisingly, the pilot was a woman. Her name was Modesty Blaise.

It was not a long job to take out the filter, wash it in petrol and replace it. She could have been on her way again the next day, but she stayed in Kalimba for twelve days, at first simply to give a pint of blood that Dr Giles Pennyfeather needed urgently, and then because he needed help even more urgently than blood.

She did not stay from any selfless urge to succour the weak and ailing, but because there was nobody else competent to help Dr Pennyfeather cope with an almost overwhelming situation, and to turn her back was impossible.

The Mbarrahas gave her a room in their small house. With Angel Mbarraha she washed filthy bandages, swept and scrubbed the floor of the hospital hut, took temperatures, carried bedpans, and helped when the onset of gangrene forced Dr Pennyfeather to amputate a limb in the little cubicle which served as a primitive operating theatre, or when some other emergency called for the use of the knife.

She had run through a whole range of emotions towards Dr Giles Pennyfeather. He was thirty but looked younger, a gangling man, all hands and feet, incredibly clumsy. She felt that in an academic sense he was probably an appalling doctor. Yet he healed his patients. Healed was the word, rather than cured. She had come to the conclusion that this was more of a psychic feat than a medical one, and that he had an extraordinary gift which stemmed perhaps from something inborn.

At first she had thought him a fool, and perhaps by worldly standards he was, but if so then he was the best kind of fool, totally without guile, optimistic, having a boundless liking for people. He was not in any way saintly. He did not exude love towards his patients. He was simply very determined to make them well and had great confidence in his ability to do so. Whatever he did was done with a kind of schoolboy cheerfulness. If he was a dedicated man he was completely unaware of it. He simply pressed on with whatever problem was thrust upon him, tackling it with clumsy optimism.

He was operating now, not on one of the bus casualties but on a woman from the village who had conceived in one of the fallopian tubes. His operating robe was a faded blue shirt and khaki shorts, well-laundered. His rather spiky fair hair rose like a great thistle-head above the sweatband round his brow, making him look like something out of a farce.

Modesty stood at the operating table, her hair capped in a silk headscarf. In the oppressive heat she would have preferred to be stripped to pants and bra, but to avoid shocking the Mbarrahas she wore an overall that Angel had contrived from a cotton housecoat.

The woman was under ether and seemed to be sustaining the operation well so far. Giles Pennyfeather had already knocked the tray of instruments on the floor, and was waiting now, unperturbed, while Modesty sterilized them anew. He hummed to himself behind his mask and peered dubiously into the abdominal cavity, held open by retractors, from which a cluster of clamps protruded.

'First time I've done this one,' he said. 'I mean the fallopian tube. All looks very confusing in there to me. Let's have another squint at that diagram, old girl.'

Modesty tried without success to think of anyone else in the world she would have allowed to call her old girl, then wondered why she did not mind it too much from Giles Pennyfeather. She used a spare scalpel to flick over the stained and dog-eared pages of the big medical book. 'I think this is it.'

Giles Pennyfeather moved to peer at the diagram, and she quickly shifted the tray of instruments to safety from under his elbow as he bent forward with gloved hands in the air, gazing at the page.

'It all looks clear enough here,' he said at last, 'but when you look in poor old Yina's tum there's just a grotty old mish-mash of bits and pieces.' He paused, reading the caption. 'Ah, trumpet-shaped. Yes, I remember now. How's young Bomutu's leg, Modesty?'

'It seems to have set pretty well. Look, is she all right for blood-pressure and respiration, Giles? I can't tell.'

'Neither can I. Black skin makes it a bit tricky to judge colour, doesn't it? Breathing sounds a bit groggy though.' He bent suddenly over the unconscious woman and said firmly, 'Now look here Yina, old girl, you just stop messing about. Keep breathing nice and easy, like a good girl, or I'll wallop your wobbly old behind when you wake up. Savvy?'

He remained bent over her, glaring at her in mock severity for several seconds, then straightened up. Modesty told herself that if Yina's breathing seemed easier it could only be her imagination. But she had heard Pennyfeather talking to his patients before, conscious and unconscious. The fact that they rarely understood a word of English did not trouble him. She had known him sit up all night holding the hand of a dying boy, talking to him in a rambling monologue. The boy had lived and was growing strong again. There was no air of mysticism about it all, and certainly Pennyfeather himself had no sense of possessing any healing power. He simply did or said whatever came into his head.

'Better splosh a few more drips of ether on her mask,' he said. She picked up the drip-bottle and obeyed. He stood gazing into the open stomach again, then gave a decisive nod. 'No good stooging around,' he said firmly, and pointed. 'There's the bit that's causing the trouble if you ask me. It just doesn't look right. I say! If it wasn't all swollen it jolly well *would* be trumpet-shaped, Modesty! Let's have a scalpel. We'll slit along a bit, get out the thingummyjig inside, then sew up the tube again.' He glanced towards the black unconscious face as Modesty put the scalpel in his hand. 'Right you are Yina, my old bosom-shaker. We'll have you all squared off in a tick.'

Modesty was certain now that in surgery he had very little experience and worked by instinct. There were moments when his clumsy hands became deft, as if they were guided by something deeper than his conscious mind, something which knew that this part of the operation was delicate and important. His sewing-up would have shamed an apprentice cobbler, but if the scars he left were not pretty his incisions seemed to heal with remarkable speed. As he worked he talked, sometimes to himself, sometimes to Modesty, sometimes to the unconscious Yina.

'Watch it now, Pennyfeather. Ahhh ... that's right. Clever lad. You can give out the pencils tomorrow. Hallo, what's this wiggly thing here? Never mind. Looks nice and healthy. You all right, Yina, my little ebony pudding? Bags of relaxation, ducky. That's the stuff. Keep the old ticker pumping nice and steady. Let's have a swab, Modesty. Once we've mopped up we can see what we're doing. That's better. Now then ...' A long pause. 'There. I think we've done the trick. Next time you make sure your egg gets down to the old womb before you let M'bolo fertilize it for you, ducky. Time for a touch of my incomparable petit-point now. Pass the needle and gut, old girl. And keep the drip going. Poor old Yina might have kittens if she wakes up in the middle of this, eh, my little liquorice stick?'

Silence while he stitched up the slit tube. Modesty thought she could detect his tongue protruding under the mask as he worked.

'There we are. Good as new.' He bent closer, addressing the interior of the cavity. 'Right, you little trumpet-shaped bugger, it's up to you now, so get fell in and start healing up on the double. One-two, one-two.' He straightened, and began to remove some swabs. 'God, those stitches are a bit rough. Never mind, at least we've got her firing on both cylinders again. I'll just make sure we've raked all the impedimenta out of her before we lash her poor old tummy up. They used to make a big point of that when I was a medical student.'

Modesty handed him forceps and he peered into the cavity. 'The trouble is, when you're training to be a GP you only do three months on surgery and most of that's just watching. Then you land a job in a place like this, where you're supposed to spend your time giving inoculations, trying to stop them drinking polluted water, and delivering a few babies, but it doesn't quite work out like that. Next thing you know you're busy with the old knife and hoping for the best. Ah well, it's all experience I suppose. And I was damn glad the AMS gave me the job. Actually I sweated through three interviews before I found out I was the only applicant.'

He began to laugh, dropped a swab he had been removing from the cavity, said, 'Sorry, ducky,' to Yina, and fished it out again. 'Right, now we'll sew the muscle-layer. I wasn't doing too well back home, really. I mean, that's why I was glad of the job. I'd picked up a bit of locum work and managed a few months as an assistant to a GP now and again, but it was always a bit tenuous. I'm not all that well up on the text-book side, you see. Stodgy stuff. And sometimes things would get broken while I was around. Poor old Doc Greeley.' He chuckled reminiscently. 'He was gardening when I told him about his microscope, and he put the fork through his foot. Nasty wound. I offered to patch it up for him but he wasn't having any. Said he'd sooner trust himself to a rabid baboon. Nice man underneath, though. I was sorry he gave me the bullet.'

When he had cobbled the incision in Yina's stomach Modesty helped to lift her down on to a crude trolley. They wheeled her into the ward and laid her on one of the paliasses which served as beds. There were twenty-two patients now, fewer than a week ago; women and children at one end, men at the other, a screen hanging between. Mary Kafoula, the local girl who had been pressed into service as ward-maid by the Mbarrahas, was plodding slowly about her work.

Several of the patients called out anxiously to Pennyfeather as soon as he appeared. They always did. He would reassure them loudly in English, and they were satisfied. Modesty they eyed warily, a little fearfully. She could attend to their needs competently enough, but that was all. She had nothing of Pennyfeather's way with them. He was talking to a young Bantu now, telling him that he had a Potts fracture and cheerfully assuring him that he would be chasing the dollies again in no time. The young Bantu understood no English but gave a wide grin of delight.

When Pennyfeather had made his rounds Modesty said, 'There's nothing else for today, Giles, only routine stuff, and I can cope with that. You go and get a few hours sleep.'

'Well, later maybe.' He squatted beside the palliasse where Yina lay. 'I'll sit with her for a bit. Want to be here when she comes round.'

She left him there, holding Yina's limp hand and chatting to her about the time he had fallen down the stairs from the top of a Number 13 bus in Oxford Street. She thought it hardly surprising if his medical colleagues considered him mad, but also a great pity. And she wondered if any of them could have done as well, out here in Kalimba, as Giles Penny-feather had done.

It was late evening when he came at last to the tiny plank bungalow where he lived, only fifty yards from the hospital hut. The village lay on one side of a small river and was the largest village in a ten-mile radius, with a population of rather more than three hundred. The beehive huts lay fairly close to the river bank. The tiny church and school, together with the Mbarrahas' house, the hospital, and the bungalow all stood on higher ground, on the western edge of the plain where Modesty had set down her Comanche.

She had prepared a cold meal for Pennyfeather and was waiting for him, smoking a cigarette, when he came from the hospital. He told her that Yina was in good shape, knocked a chair over, picked it up, and asked if John and Angel had returned from their trip to an outlying village.

'Not yet. Did you want to see them specially?'

'Oh no, it's just that . . . well, you being here with me. I mean, here in my bungalow, after dark and all that.'

'I see. Well, don't worry about my reputation, Giles.'

He blinked. 'Sorry. I hadn't thought about that, somehow. I was a bit worried about upsetting John and Angel, that's all. Awfully nice people, but a bit narrow. They're very religious, you see.'

'Missionaries often are. Never mind, I'll go up to the house as soon as I hear their truck, but I don't think they'd suspect you of trying to seduce me anyway.' She paused in the act of taking the coffee-pot from the little spirit stove and turned to look at him, suddenly curious. 'Would you, Giles?'

He ran a hand over his spiky hair and grinned a little ruefully. 'I doubt it. Hasn't been time to think about that sort of thing since you got here, and anyway I haven't had much practice at persuading dollies to let me wreak my wicked will on them. Had a frightful job getting through my exams, you see.'

'You must have got your nose out of the text-books sometimes, and I'd have thought girls would like you quite a bit.'

'Oh, they did,' he said without vanity. 'I've had a few very good times. But most of the girls who liked me weren't the going-to-bed type. They'd got this problem or that problem and just wanted someone to hold their hands and talk to them. It was much the same after I'd qualified.'

'That figures. You should have been a bit more forceful, Giles.'

'Should I? I don't know. I'm not too keen on the female hard-to-get gambit. As a matter of fact I've only ever gone with a girl when I was sure she wanted me. Expect I've missed a few chances that way.'

'I expect you have.' She turned off the stove. 'But I was wrong when I said you should be more forceful. The predators are ten-a-penny, so your kind of simplicity has its charm.' She poured coffee for him. 'And it's you, Giles, so stay with it. You may not get as many girls that way, but you'll enjoy the ones you do get a lot more.' She restrained an impulse to ruffle his hair as she passed behind his chair, with the feeling that already she had come close to patronizing him. And Giles Pennyfeather needed no patronage. He was a cheerful, undemanding man, and she had seen him do more useful work in the last ten days than she had done in the whole of her life.

'Here's your coffee,' she went on quickly. 'Come and eat now, then go to bed. You're dog-tired. I'll split the hospital duty with Angel tonight.'

'Tired? No, I'm okay, Modesty. Really.'

She brought his shaving mirror from the wash-stand and

held it in front of his hollow-cheeked face. 'Take a look. You've been knocking yourself out for over two weeks now.'

He looked at his reflection and muttered 'Christ!' in a surprised voice. She was sharply moved by the realization that he had been genuinely unaware of his own exhaustion, quite simply because he had not given a thought to it, and she found it hard to resist the impulse to put her arms about his gangling frame and draw his head down on to her shoulder. Giles Pennyfeather was probably the most unworldly man she had ever met, gauche, eccentric, sometimes irritating, always hopelessly honest. A fool by many standards. But she knew now that she admired him, and there were few men in the world of whom she could say that.

He fell asleep in his chair almost as soon as he had eaten. She managed to get him into the bedroom, supporting him as he lurched on rubbery legs, then pulled off his shoes and covered him with a blanket. While she was making the rounds in the hospital a runner arrived with a vague, half-remembered message that the Mbarrahas would not return until next morning and were talking with two policemen in the outlying village. His pidgin English was inadequate for further detail, and she knew that if she pressed him he would be driven to invent whatever he thought she wanted to hear.

She would have to be on duty in the hospital all night now, but that did not trouble her. She could cat-nap while Mary Kafoula kept watch. Mary was slow but reliable, and everything was generally much quieter now that the crisis conditions caused by the bus accident had passed.

Leaving Mary Kafoula in charge, she walked along the road and past the Mbarraha house to where the Piper Comanche stood. It was past eight PM in England now, and Willie Garvin would be listening out for her on the 20-metre band of his KW 2000A transceiver. She climbed into the cockpit and switched on her own radio mounted there beside the standard aircraft radio. It was tuned to the spot frequency they were using. Willie's voice came in against a faint background of mush. '... calling on sked. How copy?'

She spoke into the vox-operated mike. 'G3QRM, here is 5Z4QRO stroke AM answering. You're weak but clear. How copy?'

'G3QRM calling 5Z4 QRO stroke AM. Getting you fine and clear. What's new, Princess?'

'Nothing much, Willie love. My QTH is still Bedpan Alley, but things are easing a little now.' She did not ask for his QTH, his location. If he had been on the move and using the set in his car he would have announced himself as G3QRM mobile. He must be on the set in his home behind The Treadmill, the pub he owned by the Thames near Maidenhead.

He said, 'Want me to come out and 'elp a bit? I'm not doing anything special.'

'Thanks, Willie, but I think I'll be able to leave in another week, and by the time you got here it wouldn't be worth it.'

'You're not going on to Durban, then?'

'Not now. I was only running down there to spend ten days or so with John Dall, but he'll just about be leaving for the States by now. Did you cable him to say I was held up?'

'I rang 'im. He sent 'is love and said be careful.'

'His signature tune. The only thing I have to be careful of here is that Giles doesn't drop a scalpel on my foot.'

'Still leaving a trail of wreckage?'

'Yes. But still making his patients better. Most of them, anyway. It's the weirdest thing. Honestly Willie, he *talks* them better. I don't mean it's what he says, it's what he gives out.'

'Sounds impressive.'

'Oh, but he's not. Just the opposite. And so artless he sometimes makes me feel a thousand years old. I think I must be getting soft, because I'm beginning to go all maternal over him. Well, not exactly maternal.'

She heard the tail-end of Willie's chuckle, then, 'I once knew a girl who was a bit like the way this bloke sounds.

Blundered around full of goodwill like a St Bernard puppy. She was a nurse, come to think of it. I got quite paternal about 'er. Well, not exactly paternal. She was lovely to sleep with. Made you feel good, like after a sauna.'

She smiled. 'I don't suppose I'll get to check Giles for that, we're too busy, but I imagine he'd be much the same. What's new at home, Willie?'

They chatted casually for another ten minutes, then signed off. She went back to the house, took a shower, and made her way to the hospital to begin her night duty. She felt quietly happy after talking with Willie Garvin. He was always there, always the same, undemanding, content to hold the curious place in her life that few people could understand was first place.

In the morning she woke Giles at seven, gave him breakfast, then went to her room in the Mbarraha house to sleep for a few hours. She had started to undress when through the window she saw the Land Rover and another truck arrive. The second truck carried a driver and two men in police uniform. She remembered the policemen the runner had mentioned. Both trucks drove straight to Pennyfeather's bungalow. She zipped up her slacks, pulled on her shirt again and walked down the track.

Some sort of argument was going on outside the bungalow. John and Angel looked distressed. Pennyfeather was protesting, gesturing. She saw him knock the fly-whisk from the hand of a policeman with one of his uncoordinated gestures, and felt a touch of anxiety. In the new Tanzania, authority could be very touchy about its dignity.

'But look here, Sergeant, old man,' Giles was saying. 'I'm perfectly in order. Employed by the African Mission Society, got a visa, work permit, all that gubbins. Anyway, I can't leave today. Got patients to look after.' He waved an arm towards the hospital, and Angel Mbarraha stepped back to avoid the swing of his hand.

The sergeant had evidently seen a number of war films. Hands behind back, spine rigid, shoulders drawn back, he barked at Dr Giles Pennyfeather. 'Work permit is withdrawn by order of the Ministry. Do not argue with government order, please. African doctor has been sent to replace you and will arrive tomorrow.'

Giles Pennyfeather scratched his brow and blinked. 'Well, at least let me wait for him so I can hand over. I mean, I haven't actually written up many notes about the patients, so I need to see him.'

'That is not necessary. He is competent man.' The sergeant slapped the fly-whisk on the palm of his hand. 'You leave today, doctor. It is government policy. Where possible, all foreigners must be replaced by trained persons of our own people.'

Pennyfeather's dismay was turning to annoyance. 'Now look here,' he said severely, 'if your government policy means I have to leave a lot of groggy patients untended, then your government needs its arse kicked – oh, sorry Angel.'

The sergeant was glaring, and John Mbarraha broke in quickly. 'Dr Pennyfeather spoke in haste, Sergeant, he is very tired. Please allow me.' He turned to Pennyfeather. 'I am sorry. Truly I am sorry, Giles, but we have argued as much as we dare. If we make too much difficulty they might easily close the mission, the church, the school, everything we have here. Please do not worry about your patients. Angel and I can manage for a day or two, until the new doctor arrives.'

Pennyfeather stood with his big hands dangling limply, a baffled look on his face. Then he shrugged, smiled good-humouredly, and said, 'Oh, dear. I'm out of a job again.'

The police sergeant turned and stared at Modesty. 'Is this the woman, Mr Mbarraha?'

'Yes, Sergeant. She has helped us very much.'

The fly-whisk tapped against the high leather boot. 'You have no visa?' he said to Modesty.

'I'm afraid not. I didn't intend to enter the country, but I had to make an emergency landing. Mr Mbarraha has reported it.'

'Certainly he has reported it. Your aeroplane is repaired now?'

'Yes.'

'Then you will leave today. It is out of order for you to be

20

here without a visa. Very bad thing.' He pointed with the fly-whisk. 'I will return by this way tomorrow, Mr Mbarraha. I make you responsible.' He strode to the waiting truck, followed by the constable. As it roared away leaving a wake of dust, Pennyfeather said wonderingly, 'Dotty, that's what he is, you know. I can't stand chaps who chuck their weight about. Oh well, I'd better go and write up some notes for this doctor who's supposed to be coming.' He turned, then paused, struck by a thought. 'I say, John, it's all very well him saying I've got to go, but *how*? I've hardly got a bean until I can get to a bank, and then I've only got about eight weeks' salary from the AMS there. What about my fare for the passage home – will the AMS pay for me?'

John Mbarraha rubbed his tight woolly cap of hair. 'I'm sure they will, Giles, but it will take time to arrange.'

'He can come with me,' Modesty said. 'I'm going back to England.'

Pennyfeather beamed. 'I say, would you really mind? I'd be awfully grateful, Modesty.'

'Glad of the company.' She smiled. 'Now let's get the notes done. You dictate and I'll write.'

By mid-afternoon they had done all that could be done. Modesty packed her luggage and went to look for John and Angel to say goodbye. They were tending half a dozen recent graves in the little cemetery behind the tiny church.

'Giles is a good man,' said Angel, looking at the wooden crosses. 'Two were killed in the accident, and the other three could not be saved, though he tried very hard. I think no doctor could have done better.' The cross on the sixth grave bore the pokerwork legend: *An Unknown Foreign Gentleman. RIP.*

'Unknown?' Modesty said, indicating the cross.

John wiped his hands. 'He was not in the accident. He came out of the bush from the west. A white man. Angel and I found him on the road.'

'Exhaustion?'

John shook his head. 'He had been terribly hurt. Tortured.'

21

Modesty stared. 'Tortured? Some tribal thing? A leopard-man sect?'

'Not in this district, thank God. We do not know how far the man had come, but what had been done to him was deliberate, so Dr Pennyfeather said. It did not look like primitive torture. It looked . . .' he made a grimace of disgust. 'It looked sophisticated.'

She gazed down at the grave, wondering for a moment. It was very odd. But then, in Africa a thousand oddities occurred every day. It was almost certain that nobody would ever discover who the Foreign Gentleman had been.

When she had said goodbye to the Mbarrahas she took her case out to the plane, stowed it aboard, then walked down the road to the hospital to see if Giles was ready. There would be no weight problem. He had only an ancient suitcase and his medical bag. She smiled as she thought of it, for it was the most enormous medical bag she had ever seen, a vast shabby thing of scuffed leather that he could only just carry. It bulged with cases of second-hand instruments he had acquired from God-knew-where, and with an extraordinary assortment of medicines and drugs. Some of the medicines were ancient remedies long discarded by most of the profession, but Pennyfeather was not a man to be daunted by expert opinion and had great faith in their properties.

To her surprise a car stood outside the bungalow, a big Chevrolet, thick with travel-dust, but not the usual vintage jalopy of the area. She wondered if the new doctor had already arrived, complete with government-provided car, but found the idea too fanciful. When she was only ten paces from the open door of the bungalow she heard a wheezing gasp of agony. Then a cool, very cultured voice spoke in English. 'Just anything he told you, doctor, that's all we want to know. Do try to remember.'

Her pace did not change, but nerves and muscles adjusted as if a switch had been thrown, and the part of her mind that was a fighting computer assessed a score of factors, known and guessed at, between one stride and the next.

How many men were with Giles? No way of telling, but

more than one. To peer through the side window would give her sight of the situation, but if she were seen she would be at a disadvantage as far as helping Giles was concerned. And to reconnoitre would take time – not to be afforded while he was being hurt. So it would have to be the door. Not stealthily, though. That would limit her options if anyone was facing the door and saw her. Play it as if unaware, then. Make a quick appreciation and improvise accordingly. She carried no weapon, not even the kongo, the little wooden dumb-bell that was her favourite weapon for close-quarter combat.

Three paces from the door she called, 'Giles, are you nearly ready? I want to put a few hundred miles behind us while it's still daylight—'

She was in the doorway now, stopping short, giving a little gasp and widening her eyes as if in shock. Giles was sagging against the wall, grey-faced, hands clasped to his stomach. Two men. One stood over Giles, gently rubbing his chin with the knuckleduster fitted on his right hand. A compact, stocky man, bull-necked, round-faced, straight black hair cropped short. Very strong. One of those quick, heavy men. Rare. Dangerous. Full of bouncy muscle. A gun in his left hand, hanging by his side. A Colt Python, she registered, with the barrel shortened, the forepart of the trigger-guard cut away, the hammer-spur cut off. A professional's gun, modified for quick draw and quick fire. He wore a light jacket, and she knew it must hide a fast-gun harness.

The other man was taller. He wore a tailored black shirt with short sleeves, and close-fitting slacks, rust coloured. His hair was silver, carefully groomed. Beneath it, a well-bred face, a little haughty, almost impassive. A young face. Which was the true datum, old hair or young face? She checked the hands and neck. He was thirty, thirty-five. The neck and hands never lied. He might be less dangerous than the stocky man, but she would not have laid odds on it. He carried no gun. She would have seen a shoulder-holster through the shirt, and nothing dragged at the slim belt he wore. But there was a slanting pocket set rather wide on the front of his slacks. Something long and rounded protruded from it, walnut wood, close-grained. A flick-knife.

The snapshot appreciation took less than a second. Neither man had reacted sharply as she appeared. They simply looked at her, and as she gave her startled gasp the silver-haired man said casually, 'Keep her quiet, Jacko.'

The stocky man took off like a ball on the rebound. She gave a faint frightened cry, and fled, not directly away from the door but keeping close to the plank wall. He was out of the door only four yards behind her as she swung round the corner of the bungalow. In the instant that she was out of his sight she braked and turned, running three paces on the spot with stamping feet. He came round the corner fast, and she met him with knee driving into his groin, right hand read to sweep aside the gun – needlessly, for his gun-hand was outflung for balance – her left driving up with an impetus that started from her toes and gathered power from thigh, body and shoulder to explode in the heel of her hand as it took him under the jaw.

The shock of the collision sent her staggering back a pace, but she had been braced for it. His legs drawn up in involuntary reaction, the stocky man hung in the air for a second, head back, blood running down his chin from a bitten tongue. As he hit the ground and lay still, Modesty banged her shoulders hard back against the thin timber wall, scuffled her feet and gave a shrill squeak of terror, cutting it off abruptly.

And as she did so she watched the falling Colt, watched with angry foreknowledge as it curved away from his outflung hand, watched it drop with perverse exactness into the five-inch aperture of the broken pipe that projected a few inches from the ground, the pipe which had once served a soakpit below ground, long since clogged and disused. The Colt clattered faintly as it slid down the pipe. Jacko had holed out in one, and it had to happen now of all times.

She shrugged mentally and moved quickly back to the bungalow door, gathering speed as she entered. If she could get to the other man before he could pull the knife . . .

In the moment of seeing her he had, the knife was in his hand, and the blade clicked out. She braked and swerved,

24

snatching a round tin tray from the table, ready to use it as a shield if he reversed the knife for a throw. He crouched a little and edged towards her. If he had shown surprise it had passed too quickly for her to register it. His face was speculative and eager. She noted how he held the knife, how he moved, and fed into her automatic calculations the fact that this was no amateur. The knife-in-hand was his weapon, and he knew all about it. Instinct and reason combined to tell her that he was not going to throw. It was poorly designed for throwing, and she felt that this was not his technique. He was a close-quarter man.

There was no immediate chance of taking him by surprise. He knew now that she was no easy victim. She had dealt with Jacko. She must be good.

He circled her slowly, always moving to the right, following his knife-hand, and she turned with him. Three times he feinted, and once he lunged quickly, trying to slash her hand so that she would drop the tray, but he did not over-commit himself, and when the slash did not connect he jumped back smoothly to dodge the kick for his stomach. In the same moment the blade sliced down, and she swung her leg clear barely in time to avoid having the shin laid open.

He pursed his lips thoughtfully, gave a little nod as if something had been confirmed for him, and resumed his wary circling. She spared a fraction of her concentration to consider Jacko. He would not stir for five minutes, she was sure of that. Long enough. All would be over by then, one way or another. A knife-fight could never be a long drawn-out affair. It was inevitably settled within seconds of the first genuine committal by the protagonists.

From the edge of her vision she saw something move. Giles Pennyfeather. He was on hands and knees, crawling painfully towards the silver-haired man. She heard him wheeze, 'Run, old girl . . . for Christ's sake *run!*' Now he was behind her and to her right as she circled.

She snapped, 'Keep out of it, Giles – don't get in my way!' Her voice was not loud, but there was a quality in it which could well have halted a charging bull. It had no effect on Pennyfeather. He had come into her view again and was still labouring on. What he thought he could do she was unable to imagine. She only knew that with the silver-haired man as an opponent she could not afford any distraction.

She took a quick step to her right, then jumped to her left. One flickering glance to judge the distance, then she kicked sideways. He was kneeling up, trying to get to his feet. The side of her crêpe-soled boot caught him just under the heart, not too hard, but a firm blow with sufficient snap in it to send him rolling over backwards, fighting for breath. His head hit the floor with a thud, and he lay dazed.

The silver-haired man came in fast, as she had expected. She swerved, caught his high lunge on the tray, and almost had him with an ankle sweep that would have brought him down, but his jump just cleared her pivoting leg, and then he was out of range again.

It was going on too long. She knew that her most dangerous enemy was impatience, yet she could not afford unlimited patience. The silver-haired man could. He could simply continue to probe her defences, ignoring all openings except the certain one, the one that offered no risk at all of a counter ... until Jacko recovered and put the issue beyond doubt. She realized now that he had decided on this as his strategy, and she knew that no orthodox move could help her. He would be ready for them all.

So she would have to give him an opening too good to be missed. She allowed herself two minutes, and began gradually to show fear. Nothing too obvious at first, a mere hint of tautening nerves in quicker and more jerky movements. Mouth open a little now, a touch of shakiness in her breathing. She saw him register every sign, and took the pretence a step further with a darting glance towards the open door, a hesitation, a tinge of panic in her eyes. As her movements lost fluency his own became smoother and more confident.

A minute gone. Little by little she built up the impression she wanted, projecting more strongly. Twice she made almost clumsy moves and barely avoided his quick attack. But still he did not commit himself fully.

Giles was stirring. She could hear him. Suddenly she let

out a gasping sob as if her nerve had snapped, flung the tray at the silver-haired man, and turned to run for the door. He had been waiting for it and was coming after her even as he swept the tray easily aside with his free hand.

Two strides took her to the doorway. On the second stride she braked with her heel and dropped, chin to knees, curled in a ball, rolling back. Because he was committed and moving fast he inevitably over-ran her. One foot thumped against her forearms, which were wrapped about her head to protect it. Then he was above her, leaning forward at a sharp angle, falling, both arms flung forward to save himself. Her feet took him in the stomach and she unwound, putting all the strength of her body and thighs behind his own impetus as she thrust forward and up, her shoulders flat on the floor.

He made one despairing backward slash with the knife and then he was gone, rising in a great arc that carried him fifteen feet through the door before he hit the hard-baked ground. He was quick enough to keep the knife held wide as he fell, but the jarring impact smashed the breath from his body and the weapon from his hand. She was on her feet even before he hit the ground. Three long strides and her fist drove down into the neck at the base of the skull, the knuckle of her middle finger protruding. His body seemed to melt into limpness, and he lay still.

She wiped the sweat from her face and breathed deeply for a few moments, letting her nerves and muscles relax. Briefly she reviewed the fight in her mind, wondering if she had missed an easier way to win. When nothing occurred to her she was satisfied, picked up the knife and went back into the bungalow.

Pennyfeather got to his knees as she cut a piece of rope from the hank he was using to tie up his battered suitcase. He gazed at her, bewildered, slowly massaging his stomach, and said gaspingly, 'You . . . you bloody well kicked me, you know!'

'Yes, I know. But wait a minute, Giles.'

She went outside. Jacko was still unconscious. She tied his hands behind his back, performed the same service for the

27

silver-haired man, then bent to start dragging him towards the car. Pennyfeather came out of the bungalow. He seemed to be steady on his feet now, and she said, 'Give me a hand to get them in the car.'

He blinked doubtfully. 'Don't they need a bit of medical attention?'

She straightened, staring at him. 'They may well do, Giles, they may well do. But they're not going to get any. Now stop talking and help me.'

He started to speak, changed his mind, and obeyed. When the two men had been loaded in the back of the Chevrolet she got behind the wheel and started the engine. Pennyfeather said, 'Do you know them? Do you know why they came?'

'I was going to ask you that, but it can wait. I'll be back in under an hour, Giles. Don't say anything about this to John and Angel.' She drove off, taking the track which led towards the Rwanda border.

There was something warm and sticky beneath her. She felt under her buttock and found blood. The silver-haired man must have caught her with that last despairing slash of the knife as she made the throw, though she had felt nothing at the time. She pushed the car rug underneath her and drove on as fast as she dared over the ridged and broken road.

After five minutes Jacko came to his senses. She caught his eye in the mirror and said, 'Don't try anything. I really mean that.' He made no answer, but lay slumped. Pain, shock and hatred were mingled in his eyes. The silver-haired man recovered, and she gave him the same warning. There could have been no doubt in their minds that she meant it.

After twenty minutes she stopped the car near a stretch of wooded savannah and made them get out. The silver-haired man's face bore a huge graze. She said, 'I'm not wasting time with questions, I'm not even interested. Just don't come back.'

As she turned the car the silver-haired man spoke. Both his voice and his slate-coloured eyes were empty of emotion, yet there was a positive quality about the emptiness which made it more deadly than the other's naked hatred. He said,

28

'On all the evidence, I think your name must be Modesty Blaise.'

She did not answer, but tossed the open flick-knife to the ground at his feet and drove away. In the mirror she saw the two men staring after her for some seconds, then the stocky man knelt awkwardly and groped for the knife.

When she was within a mile of Kalimba she halted the car by the side of the road, on a little slope above the shallow ravine where the bus had toppled over the edge. She got out, released the handbrake, and watched the Chevrolet pitch down on top of the shattered bus, then walked on into Kalimba with one hand pressed over the wound in her buttock.

As she reached the hospital hut, Giles Pennyfeather came out, his stethoscope hanging about his neck. 'Ah, there you are,' he said sternly. 'Look here, that was a damn silly thing to do, driving off with a couple of thugs like that all on your own.'

'They weren't in any shape to make more trouble, Giles.'

'Well, I suppose not, but we ought to have called the police or something.'

'That would take days, maybe, and might get very complex.'

He walked beside her as she made for the bungalow. 'Well, yes, I can't say I liked that policeman who was here earlier. Too officious if you ask me. What did you do with them?'

She told him, and he gave a guffaw of laughter. 'Not bad! Wherever they came from they'll have a bloody long trek home. Serves them right.'

'What did they want, Giles?'

'Eh? Oh, they must have been potty. Came and asked me about that chap John and Angel found on the road, who'd been tortured. Did I tell you about him?'

'No, but John told me only today. Go on.'

'Well, when I said he'd only lived for twenty-four hours they asked me what he'd told me before he died. He hadn't told me anything, of course. When he wasn't unconscious he

29

was delirious. But these chaps must have been idiots, I couldn't seem to get it through their heads. Then the dark one started hitting me in the stomach with knuckledusters. I was pretty furious about it, I can tell you. Only an absolute sod would do that sort of thing.' He broke off, his eyes widening a little. 'I say, Modesty. You don't think *they* might have been the ones who tortured that chap?'

'Might have been? My God, do you need a second opinion on it, Giles?'

He rubbed his chin and said slowly, 'Bastards. Oh, the vicious bastards. I'd have given them a piece of my mind if I'd known. Look here, why are you clutching your behind, old girl?'

'Because it's cut. I don't think it's bad, but you'd better take a look. It's a bit un-get-atable for me.'

'Right-ho. Take your things off for a tick.'

She found a one-inch slit in her slacks, and laid them with the blood-caked seat resting in a bowl of cold water, then slipped off her pants and leaned over the table. He swabbed the drying blood away and said, 'Still bleeding a bit. Looks deepish, but it's not a long cut. Just caught you with the point of the knife by the look of it. Better have a stitch or two, though.'

She turned her head to look at him over her shoulder and said, 'Thanks very much, but I'm not offering up my behind to your idea of embroidery, Giles.'

'Eh?' He grinned at her. 'You're insulting, madam.'

'Then I'm sorry. But just give it a good swill with anti-septic and draw it together with a chunk of plaster. It'll heal. And put a thick pad on afterwards, please, I've a lot of sitting down to do for the next few days.'

'If there's one thing I hate it's a patient telling me my job. What do you know about wounds?'

'More than enough. Now just do it my way, Giles, and hate me later.'

They took off within the hour, circling the village and waving to the tiny figures gathered below. As the Comanche climbed steadily Pennyfeather said, 'I've just thought of something. I suppose we'll have to make a few stops on the

way and I haven't any money. Well, only a couple of quid.'
He began to heave about, rummaging through his pockets.
For the journey he had put on a rather thick and ill-fitting
lounge suit and a long drooping mack.

Modesty said, 'Don't worry about the money. I can stake
you.'

'Very kind of you, old girl, but God knows when I'll be
able to pay you back. Might take months to get the bit of
money I'm owed out of the country. Fishy lot, some of the
new chaps running things out here.'

'Don't worry about when you can pay me back either. I
won't dun you for it.'

He looked at her, looked around the cockpit, then shook
his head. 'Funny thing. I'd never wondered about it before,
but you must be pretty rich, having your own plane.'

'It's hired, but I'm still pretty rich. I don't think you've
wondered anything about me before, have you?'

'I suppose not.' He was mildly surprised. 'You just sort of
dropped in, and we needed help rather badly so you gave a
hand. Afraid I've taken you a bit for granted.'

'A bit. But you had more important things to think of, so
don't let it worry you.'

'All right. And many thanks for everything.' He reflected
for a moment. 'I wonder what those bastards wanted? I
mean, what they thought that dead foreign chap might have
told me?'

'It's not much use wondering.'

'No, not really. Do you think we ought to do anything
about it?'

'Like what?'

'Well . . . report it to somebody.'

'All right. If you can think of anyone who'd take any
notice.'

He brooded for a while. 'I can't, actually.'

'That's it, then. I hardly think you'll ever run into those
two men again, but if you do, don't. Stay out of their way.
It's not your kind of scene, Dr Pennyfeather.'

'Ah, that reminds me.' He pulled himself up in his seat and
turned to look at her severely. 'It was bloody silly of you,

getting into that fracas. Might have been badly hurt instead of just a cut on the behind. I mean, that sort of shemozzle's no job for a girl.'

'Never mind. I managed.'

He half closed his eyes, remembering, then opened them very wide. 'Yes. Yes, by God, you did! I can't remember too clearly, because you booted me in the wind. Don't know what you did with the stocky chap, but I came round in time to see that silver-haired wallah go for a burton.' He gave one of his sudden guffaws, then stopped short and frowned. 'Look here, it's pretty rum for a girl to manage that. I mean, he looked as if he knew what he was about.'

'They both did, Giles, very much so. You'll just have to put me down as a pretty rum girl.'

'I'm beginning to see that.' He studied her, and for the first time there was curiosity in his gaze. 'Pretty rum and pretty rich. Are you married?'

'No.'

'Affianced?'

'No. And I'm not a dike. My hormones are the right kind and work fine.'

He laughed his other laugh, the alternative to the guffaw, a breathy chuckle. 'Never doubted it, old girl. How did you get rich?'

She took her eyes from the windshield and the brown and green carpet of earth below to stare at him, but her natural impulse to freeze him faded. His question was as artless as the question of a child. She looked ahead again and smiled, wondering at herself a little, wondering why she should tell him the simple truth. 'I got rich from crime, Giles. I ran quite a big international organization. Then I retired.'

'Retired? You're not even as old as I am.'

'I started young. Younger than you'd believe.'

'And ran a gang? I say, that's jolly unusual.'

'It doesn't bother you?'

'Eh? Oh, no. I'm hardly likely to get bothered about anything you might have done.'

'Why not? Criminals can be pretty nasty people. Like those two today.'

'Oh, they're entirely different,' he said with authority. 'Bastards. I knew as soon as they showed their faces. That's why I was a bit stroppy when they started asking questions. But you're a tremendously nice person, actually, so you wouldn't do anything rotten. I can always tell. Pennyfeather's judgement is infallible.' He grinned. 'Not that my opinion would worry you much.'

She said quietly, 'You're wrong there. I value it, Giles.'

'Well, come on, tell me all about it.'

'About what?'

'Your career in crime, of course. Must have been frightfully interesting.'

'It's a very long story, even touching the ground in spots.'

'Well, we're going to be sitting up here for a very long time, aren't we? About twenty-six flying hours all told, you said. Come on, old girl, let's have it.'

She checked the compass bearing. She did not want to talk about herself, it was a practice she found wearisome. But with a touch of amusement she realized that she was going to do so because otherwise this gauche, tactless extrovert beside her would be disappointed, and she did not want him to be disappointed. How very extraordinary.

'All right, Giles,' she said. 'I'll tell you a bit about it. But do me a favour in return. Just to humour a whim, will you stop calling me old girl?'

CHAPTER TWO

The head waiter of The Legend stood by the service doors to the kitchens and made a leisurely survey of his customers. Since the restaurant was L-shaped and the service doors were set in the angle of the L, this was a good position for his surveillance.

His name was Raoul, and his salary was deservedly high.

The Legend was expensive, served very good food indeed, and made a quiet fuss of the kind of client it liked to have. Unlike most Soho restaurants, its tables were set out with plenty of space between them, and the chairs were designed to promote such comfort and well-being that the gourmet would have no distraction from his enjoyment even if he sat for three hours over his meal. The décor was skilful, designed to produce an atmosphere of tranquillity.

If you began to dine regularly at The Legend, Raoul would know your name by the third visit. He knew the names of more than half the customers present this evening, and was considering potential regulars from the rest. Some he would encourage, a few he might subtly deter. He did not want The Legend to become a fashionable haunt of personalities from the worlds of screen, fashion and photography. That kind of clientele was too fickle. One fine day you woke up and found they had decided that somewhere else was the in-place to go. Raoul wanted civilized, discriminating people. With money, of course.

His eye roamed over the regulars, and rested on the party of four at a table in the corner. Miss Blaise was back, and her escort, Mr Garvin. He was happy to see them. They were a strangely assorted pair. That Cockney accent of Mr Garvin's was quite misleading. His manners were excellent, and he had enormous style, even though he made no attempt to project it. Sometimes Miss Blaise had other escorts when she dined here, and often Mr Garvin would be there as well, but after a few weeks, or perhaps months, the new escort would disappear, and then there would just be the two of them again.

Of course, Mr Garvin was not an escort in the same intimate sense as the other gentlemen. That was puzzling in a way, but Raoul was quite sure about it. His instinct for the precise relationship between a lady and a gentleman was very acute, and he had long ago concluded that the relationship between Miss Blaise and Mr Garvin defied all classification.

Raoul considered the young man in the party. A doctor, apparently, from what he had overheard. To be honest, this was not a client he would have encouraged. The suit was cheap and fitted poorly. The voice was not loud but had a penetrating quality. And he was clumsy. He had already dropped a knife and spilt half a glass of wine. A curious companion for Miss Blaise. Not an intimate one on the face of it . . . and yet Raoul's instinct told him otherwise. Perhaps she liked him because he had no pretensions. He knew almost nothing about food and wine, but had been enthusiastic in accepting counsel from Raoul when the order was taken. Yes, that must be it. She would like a man with no pretensions, and they were very rare.

The fourth member of the party simply made no impression at all. Even Raoul could not remember whether he had seen the face before. It was a totally forgettable face, belonging to a middle-aged man of slight build, a face which seemed to wear a perpetually ingratiating expression, almost servile. A nervous little man called . . . how had Miss Blaise referred to him? Fraser. Yes, Mr Fraser. Raoul dismissed him as a subject for speculation.

If Jack Fraser had known Raoul's thoughts he would have been well satisfied. Not that it mattered what Raoul thought, but it would have confirmed to Fraser that the *persona* he had projected for so many years still made the impression he wanted. In fact Fraser had twice dined here before with his master, Sir Gerald Tarrant, who controlled an obscure department of the Foreign Office, a department whose employees operated in many parts of the world, whose work was always secret and often grim, fighting as they did in the complex underground war of intelligence and espionage.

Fraser had served as an agent in the field for many years before being posted to a desk job as Tarrant's assistant. During those years, the servile and unmemorable face he showed the world had served him well. Behind it lay a tough, unpitying man who had taken many cold risks and performed many savage necessities, balking at neither.

Raoul, with all his experience, glimpsed nothing of the reality behind the façade. His thoughts simply touched Fraser and passed him by as a nonentity. Satisfied with his appraisal of Miss Blaise's party, Raoul turned his head to view the tables in the other section of the restaurant. Quite a number of regulars with their guests, and a few new faces. Nothing that called for special consideration ... except perhaps the three men who were nearing the end of their meal, at the brandy and cigar stage.

One was very good material to be encouraged as a regular, though he was not playing host this evening. The hand-stitched suit was a hundred-guinea job, the voice and features showed excellent breeding. Strange, that silver hair. It must be premature, for the sun-tanned face was that of a much younger man. The other guest was a different matter. Stocky, with a coarse face and doubtful table manners. A gulper of wine. Foreign, but difficult to place. Tight curly hair and brown face that owed nothing to the sun. A thick-necked man with a manner slightly aggressive, slightly menacing even.

The table had been booked by the host, Mr Brunel. Nothing to fault there, at least nothing Raoul could lay his finger on, but Mr Brunel made him a little uneasy. That was odd, because in physical stature Mr Brunel was ... well, almost a midget. Four feet nine inches, perhaps? But quite in proportion. He was in his early fifties, Raoul judged. An impressive head, with thick dark hair brushed back in wings on each side. He wore his expensive clothes well. An excellent manner, quiet but assured. Not a man to argue with. Quiet, heavy-lidded eyes in a quiet face. Yet there was something ... Raoul groped for the concept ... something unhealthy about the quietness. It did not stem from serenity but from an inner deadness. Perhaps that was it. A tomb was quiet, but if you could see inside it you might well feel the same sense of unease that you felt with Mr Brunel—

Raoul jerked his thoughts away from such fanciful imagery, annoyed with himself. To assess his customers carefully was one thing, and very important, but it was absurd to become too imaginative in the practice. He assumed his warm, polite smile and began to move from table to table.

'Is everything as you wish, Miss Blaise?'

'Perfect, thank you, Raoul.'

'Then I am delighted. You have been away. Somewhere in the sun, I think?'

'Yes, I'm not long back from Tanzania.'

'I hope it was an interesting trip. It is good to see you back, madam.'

'Thank you.'

Raoul inclined his head to Willie Garvin, made a deeper bow for Modesty, and moved away.

Giles Pennyfeather looked down at the mess of fish-bones on his plate and said, 'I don't think he liked what I've done to his Dover sole.'

'At least it was dead,' Willie pointed out comfortingly. 'I mean it's not as if it was one of your patients.'

Pennyfeather grinned. 'Don't get a chance to do any surgery now I'm back here, old man. It's all right when you're out in the wilds, but here we just say, 'Ah, that's a nasty boil you've got on your neck. Take this letter along to The Middlesex and get it lanced.' Pity, really. I'd like to keep the old hand from losing its wizardry.' He looked at Modesty. 'By the way, how's your behind, darling?'

She sighed. 'Giles, you haven't asked me that for a week, and of all times you have to ask now, loud and clear.'

'Oh, sorry. But is it okay?'

'Just fine.' She looked across the table at Fraser and said, 'It got cut slightly.'

Fraser shrugged. 'That's Tanzania for you. A lot of behind-cutters if ever I saw any.'

Pennyfeather said, 'Well no, it wasn't done by a Tanzanian, actually—'

She broke in. 'Mr Fraser was just showing a polite lack of inquisitiveness, Giles.'

'Ah, I've got you now. Didn't want a general discussion about your behind, eh? Well, let's see, what were we talking about?' His eye fell on the remains of the Dover sole as a waiter cleared the plates. 'Ah, yes. Cutting up of patients. Do you know, when I was a medical student the first thing I was ever given to dissect was somebody's arm. Forearm, actually.'

'Left or right?' Willie asked.

'I never found out. What happened was that I'd got the old knife in my hand and was just going to start on the beastly thing when I passed out. Came round with my chest swathed in bandages, in a hospital bed. I'd fallen on the knife and given my ribs a three-inch gash.' He gave a bray of delight. 'I remember old Merrydew saying, "Another inch to the right, Pennyfeather, just another inch, and hundreds of future patients might well have been saved from the horror of your ministrations." He was joking, of course.' Pennyfeather turned to Fraser. 'What's your line of business, if it's not a rude question, old chap?'

'I'm a civil servant.'

'Oh, really? Pretty interesting?'

'Fascinating. Our new system of collating import/export figures is enormously exciting. Enormously.' Fraser nodded his head slowly as if awed by the thought of it.

'Well, that's jolly nice. I'm not much good at admin stuff myself,' Giles said candidly, 'but do have a go at explaining this new system to me.'

Fraser stopped nodding and stared inscrutably into space. His usually quick mind had gone suddenly blank in the face of Pennyfeather's innocent acceptance of his words at their face value. He knew that Willie and Modesty were finding some amusement in his discomfiture.

'It's – ah – rather complex,' he began, when Modesty came to his rescue, looking at her watch and saying, 'Aren't you on duty pretty soon, Giles?'

'Eh? Lord, is that the time? Yes, I must fly.' He got to his feet. 'Do excuse me. Smashing nosh. Thanks, Willie. Cheerio, Mr Fraser. Nice meeting you. Don't wait up, darling, I'll be back about four-thirty unless anything crops up, but I'll tiptoe in, quiet as a mouse.' He touched Modesty's hand, gave her a smile that lit up his rather chaotic features, then turned and marched gawkily away with arms swinging.

They watched, tensing a little as one hand missed by a fraction a huge strawberry flan on the sweets trolley, then relaxed. Willie said to Fraser, 'I took 'im to lunch at Dolly's the other day, and he got 'is cuff-link caught in a woman's 'air. Yanked 'er wig right off. I went in the loo and didn't come out for ten minutes.'

'Coward,' said Modesty, and Willie nodded unashamed agreement.

'Where's he dashing off to?' Fraser asked.

'He's got a job for a month doing some sort of locum night duty for a group practice.' Modesty shrugged. 'I say a month, but I don't know how long he'll last. As a doctor his only virtue is that he gets his patients better.'

'They probably take a fresh hold on life from wondering what's going to happen next. I gather he's staying with you at present?'

'Yes.' She beckoned a waiter and asked for coffee to be served.

Fraser said slowly, 'I suppose it would be rude of me to ask what you see in him.'

'Pretty rude, but I'll let it go since I once asked myself the same thing. The answer is, he's a nice man.'

Fraser sniffed. Perhaps because of his profession he did not suffer fools gladly, in fact he did not suffer them at all if he could help it. He decided that only the mysterious nature of woman could explain why Modesty Blaise should see anything at all in Dr Giles Pennyfeather.

'A nice man,' he echoed wonderingly. 'Could you amplify that?'

'I could, but I'm not going to. Just leave him alone, Jack, and let's get to the object of the meeting. You're being dined here at vast expense because we want something from you.'

'What sort of thing?'

'A suggestion. What can we get Sir Gerald for his birthday that would really please him?'

Fraser stared. 'Good God. You'd better have your money back. Cosy suggestions for presents aren't in my line. I didn't even know Tarrant had a birthday coming up soon.'

'Next week. He'll be back from the States by then, won't he?'

'He's due in on Wednesday.'

'That's his birthday. We've thought of all sorts of things – golf-clubs, fishing tackle, a painting, something antique. But nothing very original. So you're co-opted. After all, he's your boss so you ought to know his tastes.'

'Why the hell do you want to buy him a birthday present? All he's ever done for you is inveigle you into jobs you barely came out of alive. How many scars have you got between you that ought to have his initials on?'

Willie grinned. 'Anyone might think you 'ated old Tarrant. Fact is, you'd break your arm for 'im.'

'Balls. He just happens to be my boss.'

'If they tried to replace 'im, you'd do your nut.'

Fraser stared down at the table, his eyes suddenly bitter. 'You've touched a tender spot there,' he said slowly. 'I'll tell you something about Tarrant, something I shouldn't, but you'll know pretty soon anyway—'

He looked up and stopped short. Modesty Blaise was not listening. She was staring past him, and she said very softly, 'Willie ...' There was a quality in her voice that made Fraser's nerves go suddenly taut. Willie Garvin, lounging back in his chair, did not alter his relaxed attitude, but his eyes followed Modesty's and he edged the chair back from the table a little.

Turning his head, Fraser saw the three men who had emerged from the other section of the restaurant. They had stopped and were looking towards Modesty's table. He recognized one of them immediately, then the other two, and in his mind uttered an obscene oath even as he ventured a hesitant, ingratiating smile.

Brunel.

And the others were Adrian Chance and Jacko Muktar, Brunel's lieutenants, bodyguards and, on occasion, executioners. Chance was speaking, bending down a little to do so. Brunel listened, gave a nod, then made his way between the tables with the other two following. His lack of height in no way detracted from the ease and assurance of his manner. He halted, sketched a bow, and said, 'Miss Blaise? My name is Brunel.'

'Yes?'

Fraser saw that she kept her eyes on Brunel, not even glancing at his companions. But Willie Garvin was watching them, ignoring Brunel, and though his gaze appeared casual Fraser's highly-cultivated instinct told him that Willie was at flashpoint readiness. It was unlikely that there would be any kind of physical action here in The Legend, but not impossible. By no means. Fraser himself had once killed a man, a double-agent, in a crowded Berlin bar, with a cigarette lighter which brought a small quantity of prussic acid above its boiling point of 89 degrees and ejected the vapour into the man's face. He had then walked quietly out, long before anybody even realized that a body lay slumped over the table.

Brunel said, 'I understand you have met my colleagues.' He waved a tiny hand. 'Adrian Chance and Jacko Muktar.'

Still she did not trouble herself to look at them as she answered, 'Briefly, as I remember.'

His smile was as quiet as his eyes and his voice. 'But the meeting was not without interest, so I'm told. I find it strange that you and I have never encountered one another before, Miss Blaise, in view of our similar careers. I've heard much about you, and about Garvin, of course.' He looked at Willie, who showed no sign of having heard but continued to gaze musingly at Chance and Jacko. Brunel paused for a moment, and when nobody spoke he looked at Fraser and went on. 'An interesting gathering. I didn't expect to see you again so soon, Mr Fraser. How are you?'

Fraser fidgeted, eased a finger round his collar and said with an embarrassed smile, 'Oh, er, not too bad, really. Still a bit chesty. These winter colds drag on, don't they?'

'Do tell Sir Gerald Tarrant I look forward to an early and satisfactory meeting when he returns.'

'Yes. Yes, I'll put a memo on his desk, Mr Brunel.' Fraser twisted his thin neck and smiled meekly. Brunel eyed him for a moment, then turned back to Modesty.

'I hope this is merely a social gathering I'm interrupting,' he said, 'and not a business discussion with Mr Fraser?' His tone made the words a question.

Modesty considered him. 'I think interrupting is the significant word.'

He shook his head. 'I take your point. But the significant word is business. Always. My colleagues already feel that they are in your debt from when they last encountered you, a debt they would gladly repay. I urge you not to increase the burden of what they feel they owe you, Miss Blaise.'

'That's easy. Remind them that it wasn't by my invitation we met last time, and tell them not to have any more dealings with me.'

'Ah, if only life were so simple. But forgive me, I'm keeping you from your coffee. It's been most interesting to talk with you, Miss Blaise. I'll wish you goodnight.'

He gave a little bow and turned away. The other two men stood fast for a moment, both looking at Modesty. Jacko's face was cold and ugly. Adrian Chance wore a thoughtful, almost absent expression. He said, 'There's a long and interesting experience I hope to provide for you one day.' He spoke softly, as if to himself. For a moment a brilliant smile lit his face, and with it a dew of sweat suddenly filmed his brow. 'Oh Christ, yes,' he whispered fervently, 'I very much hope so.' They turned away together, walking quickly to catch up with Brunel.

Willie eased himself in the chair and said, 'I don't like the kind that break out in 'ot flushes. They're nasty. Is there another cup of coffee there, Princess?'

'Yes, plenty, Willie love. Pass your cup.'

Fraser said, 'I gather you've tangled with Brunel's boys in some way. What happened?'

She told him the essentials briefly. When she had finished he drew in a breath between pursed lips and said, 'You should have finished them off while you had the chance. By God you should, ducky. They reckon they're the best team in the business, and they're very touchy about their status.'

She shrugged. 'I'll walk a little carefully while they're around, but on general pattern they won't be here long. Brunel's base is that big estate he has in Rwanda, isn't it?'

Fraser nodded. 'Yes. Not all that far from the border with

Tanzania. Others get turfed out of Black Africa, but not Brunel. Quite a little princeling of his own patch out there, according to our dossier. I guess that's where your Dr Pennyfeather's mysterious tortured man escaped from.'

Willie said, 'Anything in the Brunel dossier to tie in with that?'

Fraser grimaced. 'Brunel has a finger in a dozen pies, so it's a hell of a dossier. You don't know who the man was, what he looked like, or why Brunel wanted to know what he said before he died. What do you expect me to come up with?'

'Just a thought.' Willie brooded for a moment. 'I reckon it was our silver-'aired boy who did the torture bit. He'd enjoy it.'

'Very likely. Or it could have been the girl.'

Modesty said, 'What girl?'

'Sorry. I thought you knew the Brunel set-up. Jacko Muktar and Adrian Chance are his muscle. But there's also a girl on the scene somewhere. Relationship obscure, but officially Brunel's adopted daughter. Origin unknown. She calls herself Lisa Brunel. Very beautiful, in a way.'

Willie said, 'In what way?'

'She's an albino. White hair, hardly any pigmentation. Eyes slightly pink. She wears dark glasses most of the time.' Fraser accepted a cigarette from the case Modesty offered him. 'Thank you.'

She said, 'What was Brunel getting at just now? He seemed to think you were talking business with us, and he didn't like it.'

Fraser nodded morosely. 'Yes. I know what he thought. I suppose you wouldn't consider killing him as a birthday present for Tarrant? It's not something the old man can keep on his mantelpiece, I know, but it's the thought that counts, so they say.'

Modesty sat up a little straighter. 'You were saying something about Sir Gerald when they showed up. What was it?'

'I was about to say that his head's going to roll.' Venom touched Fraser's voice. 'A political necessity.'

'Tarrant?'

'Yes.' Fraser knocked ash from his cigarette. His eyes were angry. 'Last year we organized something in Singapore to prune the Commies back a bit. A dirty little job, like most things we have to do. It had the unofficial blessing of the government there, of course, and it worked out very nicely. Except that some bureaucratic clown in their local Intelligence Department set out an appreciation of the whole thing on paper, chapter and verse, hand-written, date-stamped, everything. Brunel got hold of the papers, we don't know how, and it doesn't matter. He's got a nice cash offer for them from Moscow, and when they let the thing break there'll be a hell of a stink. We'll have all the anti-establishment mob here screaming about our Secret Service interfering in another country's affairs. The whole bit. So there has to be a scape-goat, and it can only be Tarrant.'

Modesty's eyebrows drew together. 'You said a cash offer. If that means Brunel hasn't sold yet, can't you outbid Moscow?'

'Brunel isn't interested in our cash, only in barter. He wants a list of our local agents in Prague. Moscow will pay him the earth for that.'

Willie said incredulously, 'You mean Brunel expects Tarrant to 'and over some of 'is Czech people?'

Fraser shrugged. 'You're a bit out of touch with current trends, Willie. Our game gets more like dealing in stocks and shares every day. You swap spies, you make deals. You buy and sell, if you can. Or you steal. And if you can't steal what you want, then maybe you steal something else that will give you the right leverage to get hold of what you wanted in the first place.'

'Tarrant won't play on the Czech thing,' Modesty said. It was a statement.

Fraser's grin was wolfish. 'I fancy our masters would like him to. An Intelligence scandal doesn't suit their political book just now, and a handful of Czechs are expendable. But they can't force Tarrant's hand. He expends people when he has to, but Christ, he doesn't sell them down the river.'

Willie Garvin rubbed his chin. 'I don't see it would 'elp much for us to sign Brunel off,' he said reluctantly.

'That was just a lousy joke,' Fraser said with an impatient gesture. 'I'd have him put down quick enough if it would do any good, but it won't. What we need is the papers.'

'You're sure they're genuine?'

'Genuine as the Koh-I-Nor. I've seen them.'

Willie stared. 'Say again?'

'I saw them three days ago, in a house on the corner of Welbury Square. Brunel's rented it for a month. I was given sight of the stuff so we'd know it was authentic, and it is. No photostats. They don't carry enough credence. These are the original papers. I wanted to be sick.'

Willie said, 'Why don't you frame Brunel, get 'im arrested for receiving, or 'andling drugs, then go in and grab the papers?'

Fraser sniffed. 'I'd love to, mate. But we couldn't make it stick. You'd need too many people to set up a good frame. No, it's cut and dried. When Tarrant gets back from the States he'll meet Brunel and tell him no deal. Then the Singapore papers go to Moscow, we'll get the big stink, and Tarrant takes the rap.'

'These papers. Where does Brunel keep 'em? In a safe?'

'Of course he does. In a safe at Welbury Square. I saw him take them out.'

'Then get someone to crack it. Petersen, if he's in the country. Blimey, you've used villains before.'

'Lay on a job like that with only five days to prepare? Brunel would love it. A failure would give him another fifty per cent leverage to make the stink even bigger. And don't think it wouldn't fail, Willie. That safe's a Burdach and Zeidler. It weighs half a ton, and it's the toughest thing you ever saw, built into one of the walls. That house belonged to old De Gruyle, before he died and a property company bought it. He'd sometimes have half a million quidsworth of precious stones in that safe.'

Willie drained his cup of coffee and sat back. This was bad, he reflected gloomily. He didn't like it a bit and the Princess wasn't going to like it either. He turned to look at her. She sat with her chin resting on her hand, her eyes contemplative and a little dreamy. There were two small vertical lines in the middle of her forehead, and her lower lip was pushed forward slightly. A hint of excitement stirred in him. He knew that look.

She said to Fraser, 'And this is what Brunel thinks you were talking to us about tonight?'

'I'll lay odds on it.' He laughed shortly. 'Well, at least it might keep them awake for the next few nights, waiting for you to try something. That's a small consolation.'

'It's a damn nuisance,' she said. 'Especially as we haven't very much time.'

Willie smiled happily and lifted a hand to signal for the bill. Fraser leaned forward and said in a low voice, 'Don't be a bloody fool, Modesty. You haven't a chance. That house is wired with more alarms than you've ever dreamt of. The safe's a twelve-hour job at best – and they'll be *waiting* to nail you.'

She nodded, gathering up her cigarette-case and lighter while Willie signed the bill. When Raoul had wished them goodnight and moved away she said, 'It may well be impossible, Jack, but at least let's take a look and try it for size.' She smiled, closing her handbag. 'After all, if Willie and I can pull this off it's the perfect answer to our birthday present problem.'

CHAPTER THREE

When the buzzer sounded, Brunel rose lazily from the firm warm body of the white-haired girl who lay beneath him. Without haste, he put on monogrammed pyjamas and a dressing-gown. He felt good, relaxed. Lisa had performed with the extreme and urgent passion he required of her. That it was entirely simulated held no importance for him. She lay watching him, and smiled mechanically when he looked at her.

A very satisfactory possession, Lisa, and well worth all the trouble he had taken over her. She was useful in so many ways. That she was an albino did not detract from her beauty – except in her own eyes, he thought with amusement.

Tying the belt of his dressing-gown, he said, 'I may wish you to pick up a man called Garvin. He'll probably know I've sent you, but that doesn't matter. He has a certain crude attraction, and is aware of it, so he may think he can make use of you if you encourage the idea. That would be excellent. I'll go into details later.'

He went out of her bedroom without saying goodnight. Lisa got up, went into the bathroom and turned on the shower. She felt a little sick, as she usually did after Brunel, and this troubled her. It was wrong. She stood still, listening, waiting for the voices in her head to start whispering, admonishing. When the voices did not come she relaxed gratefully, then knew a pang of guilt at her relief.

If she had dared, she would have hated the voices, but to hate them would have been the ultimate crime. It was shameful enough that she feared them, and she had tried hard to overcome it, but she was weak, too weak to wipe out her own foolish emotions entirely. She could not clearly remember when the voices first began to speak in her head, only that it was several years ago. Everything before the voices was remote and fragmented now. Sometimes they would be silent for days and even weeks, but even then they dominated her life, because she knew they would come again, usually waking her in the night, but sometimes coming to her suddenly at any hour of the day.

She had never told anybody of them, not even Brunel, for they had forbidden her to. This was strange, for the voices liked Brunel, or at least they were always pleased that she was obedient to him. She did not know who or what the voices were, and had long ceased even to wonder. They were simply there, and they did not arise from her own inner thoughts but were something apart from her. This much she knew, partly because in her weakness and wickedness she so often wanted to resist them, to disobey them, and partly

47

because the voices spoke so clearly in words, actual words to which she listened. They chanted, a tiny bell-like chorus in her head, guiding, admonishing, commanding.

When they had first come to her she had been frightened, but she had obeyed because what they wanted was simple and easy. But that had changed. Soon she had been told to do things which scared and sickened her, first with Brunel and then with others. She was inured now to the way the voices used her body, but their other demands still terrified her. She dared not show it, dared not even think what she felt, for this was wrong. The voices were always right, even when they made her kill. They were passionless and all-knowing, and they had made her understand that it was her privilege to serve their necessities, an austere and dreadful privilege that she was too stupid and unworthy to comprehend in all its fullness. If she felt revulsion, if she felt some deep-rooted desire to disobey, then this was an ugly blemish within herself, a shameful frailty.

She knew that she had satisfied Brunel, for otherwise the voices would soon have spoken their cold reprimand. On those rare occasions when she had failed them badly, their silvery tones had chanted in her head all night in passionless wrath, an unending repetition that had driven her close to collapse. But they were not displeased now, and they required nothing of her, at least nothing outside their standing commands on which she had long ceased to need reminding.

A thought touched her mind, bringing a flicker of apprehension, quickly and guiltily repressed. Brunel wanted her to pick up a man called . . . Garvin, was it? If he was a bad man, an Enemy of the voices, they might lay upon her one of those duties she dreaded so much. She shivered, remembering what they had made her do to the man in Rwanda. It had been for his own good, of course, she knew that must be so, but it had almost broken her mind. And she had been *glad* when he escaped, which was wickedness indeed. Had that been her fault? Had she in some way left him a chance he had seized upon? Surely not, for the voices would have punished her almost to destruction. And yet? . . .

She shook her head, pushing the memories away, distressed by her own weakness. Turning, she looked at her naked body in the full-length mirror with contempt. Freak. White-haired, colourless freak. Be thankful the voices condescend to use such a creature. Be glad, and obey.

She listened, hoping they had heard her thoughts and would speak their approval, but nothing came. She stepped out from under the shower, dried herself, put on a wrap, and went back into the bedroom, to the long shelves of books. If she was to be free of any duties for the moment she could relax and live her other life, the life bounded by the pages of the books.

The novels were romances, mainly historical. There were no mysteries or thrillers, no modern sex-based fiction. By far the larger proportion of books consisted of memoirs and biographies of an earlier age. It was here that she lived the serene part of her life, among the Victorians and Edwardians and their counterparts in Europe and America, with their solid confidence in a world that changed little and then slowly.

She selected *The Golden Years*, an anthology of Edwardian reflections, laid it ready on her pillow, then sat at the dressing-table and began to manicure her nails. Brunel liked her to keep her nails fairly short. She wished he did not insist on the vivid red nail varnish, it made her white hair and skin more obvious by contrast.

Brunel had not hurried when he left Lisa's room. He made his way down to the study on the first floor and pulled a curtain aside. The car parked below was Adrian Chance's. Brunel dropped the curtain, put on the lights and switched on a small portable television receiver on his desk. It relayed a picture of the porch, and the upper halves of the two men waiting there, Jacko and Chance. They had been waiting for two minutes, but showed no sign of impatience. Each man was fingering the knot of his tie with the left hand. That meant they were not acting under the threat of somebody out of sight with a gun.

Brunel pressed one of a panel of buttons to cut the front door alarm-buzzer for ten seconds, then another button which released the three locks on the door. The current for the locks and alarms was not from the mains supply, but from a bank of batteries. He watched the two men enter, saw the door close after them, then switched off the closed-circuit television and sat down. Thirty seconds later Adrian Chance knocked and entered the study followed by Jacko.

Brunel said, 'Well?'

'We waited for them to leave, and tailed them.' Chance sat down on a couch against the wall and smoothed back his silver hair. 'They drove to a block overlooking Hyde Park She has the penthouse there. Fraser took a cab and presumably went on home. Blaise and Garvin went in. A bit later lights came on in the penthouse. We waited half an hour, then came home. I fancy Garvin's staying there tonight.' His calm face twitched for a moment. 'They probably have some idea how Jacko and I feel about her.'

'What about Pennyfeather?'

'We didn't see him.'

Brunel drummed his fingers on the desk absently. 'It can't be coincidence. You saw Pennyfeather leaving The Legend, and there was a fourth place at her table where somebody had dined. Pennyfeather must have been with her.'

Jacko prowled the room, restless, saying nothing, his solid muscles moving under the tight-fitting suit. Chance shrugged and said, 'I expect so, but I don't think it's anything to do with the Novikov business.' He paused, thinking, then dabbed his forehead with a handkerchief. 'When she had us tied up in the car she didn't ask any questions, didn't search us, didn't want to know why we were interested in Pennyfeather. She's evidently brought him back to England with her, but I don't think that has any particular significance. What's important about tonight is that we saw Fraser in conference with Blaise and Garvin.'

'You believe he wants them to try for the Singapore papers?'

'I believe Fraser has nothing else on his mind at the moment, and he's a tenacious little bastard.'

'Why would they agree?'

'That I can't explain. I think they will, but I don't know

why. The word is that they've done a few things for Tarrant before. It can't be for money. The British pay chickenfeed. And it can't be just because they like him, that's absurd.'

'To us, perhaps. But there are people who act from incredible motives.' Brunel lit a cigarette. 'Whatever the reason, I share your feeling that they may well try for the papers.'

Jacko was looking at the big safe which stood against one wall of the study, its back set in the brickwork. He said in a hard, throaty voice, 'You going to put the stuff somewhere else? In a bank?'

'I can't think of anything more stupid,' Brunel said musingly. 'I very much doubt if a strongbox in a bank would be proof against the authority Tarrant's people could exert if they felt the need. I doubt if there's anywhere more secure than that safe in this house.' He looked at Chance. 'On their record, I imagine they'll try something subtle.'

'It won't be easy. They'll need twelve uninterrupted hours in the house, so they have to take care of us first. To take care of us they have to reach us. And to reach us, if we stay in the house, they have to breach the alarms. The alarms can't be cut or jammed. They can only be by-passed if we allow them to be, so that's got to be their tactic, to fool us into leaving an opening. We need to watch out for the postman, the telephone repair man, meter readers, the man sent by the council to check a faulty drain. If we suspect anybody, in any shape or form, who wants access to the house, we can hardly go wrong.'

Brunel sat in thought for some minutes. At last he said, 'Very well, Adrian. We'll operate under siege conditions for the next few days. See to everything yourself, and check every detail. From this moment I want one of you here in this study at all times. With a gun.' He looked at Chance. 'I said with a gun. You can use your knife once we've got them all sewn up.' He stubbed out his cigarette and stood up, a tiny figure behind the desk. 'You're on guard here till three AM, Jacko. Adrian takes over then. I know nothing is likely to happen tonight, that's why we'll start being careful now. They say Blaise is good at being unlikely.' He raised an eyebrow. 'You can both vouch for that, I believe?'

Adrian Chance's smile was taught and bright. 'We didn't know who she was then.'

'I'm bound to wonder if that would have made any difference,' Brunel said, and watched the sheen of moisture brought to Chance's brow by his words. Jacko flung himself sulkily on to the couch, took a gun from under his arm and checked it. As Brunel reached the door Chance said politely in a rather high voice, 'Are you using Lisa tonight?'

'No,' Brunel paused, considering. 'You can go ahead, Adrian, but don't get carried away. I may need her for a job shortly, so she's not to be marked. Understood?'

Chance looked surprised. 'A job?'

'If Blaise and Garvin don't come, I may put her to work on Garvin.'

'But why?'

Brunel said patiently, 'The Singapore papers are not my only interest, Adrian.'

'Pennyfeather?'

'Yes. He's linked with Blaise and Garvin now, so we have to move carefully. But I still think he knows something, and he's the only possibility we have left of opening up the Novikov Project again.'

Chance nodded, but without enthusiasm. Brunel said, 'Don't be downcast, Adrian. If you don't get the chance to use your little knife on Blaise in the next day or so, I'm sure we'll arrange an opportunity later.'

Lisa lay in bed on her stomach, reading a book. When the door opened and she saw that it was Adrian Chance she braced herself quickly against the involuntary tremors in the pit of her stomach, ashamed of the reluctance and apprehension that the sight of him produced in her, ashamed of her hope that he would not hurt her very much this time.

It was a month since the last occasion, and she had not expected Brunel to let him have her again so soon. To please him she must not be as she had been with Brunel. For Adrian she must resist feebly at first, then more strongly, and showing fear. When he had punished her for this, the worst would be over. There would be nothing more for her to do except remain limp and submissive, like a rag doll, while he exacted his various enjoyments on her body. Guiltily she realized her offence in thinking of his punishment of her as 'the worst'. The voices always wanted her to please Brunel, and, if he said so, to please Adrian Chance. Adrian would not have come to her unless Brunel had given permission. Therefore anything he did was by the will of the voices, and it was a fault and a blemish in her to feel as she did.

Adrian came towards her. Standing beside the bed he gazed down at her with his brilliant smile. He took the book from where it lay on the pillow and tossed it behind him, then threw the bed-covers back. She was wearing a white chiffon nightdress now, reaching only to her thighs. Still smiling down at her he began to take off his tie. She turned over and sat up, drawing up her knees and crossing her arms over her breasts, whispering, 'Please, Adrian . . . no.'

A stone's throw away, on the roof of the block of flats set on the southern side of the square, Fraser stood studying the house across the road. There had been no problem in getting to the roof. He had simply walked up the stairs to the top floor, and on up the final flight of service steps to the flat roof. It was a long block, and by moving from one end of the roof to the other he could see the front and side of Brunel's house which together formed the corner of the square where the road turned north. It was only by courtesy that Welbury Square was called a square, for in fact it was a short but very wide road.

Fraser was mildly enjoying himself, though he had little hope that his occupation would be fruitful. Leaning against the storage tank housing, he studied the situation. No windows in the side of the house, just a blank wall. In the front, a large window on the ground floor, on the right of the porch. Corresponding windows on the two floors above. Steps leading down to a basement. Railings set about six feet from the wall of the house. Wide pavement. Street lamp. He lifted night glasses to his eyes. No sign of a disused coal-chute in the pavement. He studied the windows. All curtains pulled to. A chink of light showing through the curtains of the study. He could have drawn a plan of that study from memory. It lay on the first floor, and the safe was set in the blank, windowless side-wall.

But there would be no need for him to draw a plan. There were plans of the whole house in his office, secured from the builder who had converted the interior seven years ago for De Gruyle, the diamond merchant. Fraser had got hold of them as soon as Brunel began his play with the Singapore papers, because it was a routine action.

He did not believe the plans would be any use. He did not believe that he was losing sleep now for any useful purpose, but still he was glad to be going through the motions. A part of him hoped foolishly that Modesty Blaise would come up with something. But the rest of him, the trained and analytical agent, was afraid that she might. The job simply was not on.

He moved a little and looked down into the road below. An occasional car moved east along the one-way square and turned left at the house on the corner before passing out of sight. Two men walked slowly along the opposite pavement, not talking. A little group of weirdly dressed drop-outs passed in the other direction, stopping every now and again, apparently to argue. He could hear their voices but could distinguish no words.

He looked along the road running north beside the house. Red lamps marked where a vast excavation was being started for an underground car park. Mounds of earth, trenches, piles of sewage pipes, stacks of bricks, a concrete mixer, a power-shovel. Might an engineer call at the house purporting to check on the run of cables, of water or gas? Fraser drew down the corners of his mouth in a sour grimace. That was exactly the kind of thing Brunel would be waiting for. He looked across at the roof of the corner house. Anything bigger than a pigeon would trigger the electronic alarms there. The local police had told him of two occasions during De Gruyle's time when a cat had set them off.

He looked down again. A blonde girl, long hair brazen under the lamplight, was walking slowly south from where the roadworks lay. She wore a shiny black leather suit with a very short skirt, and her hips swung in the manner of the practised tart. A man in a long mac and a trilby hat, carrying a small suitcase, was following her a little uncertainly. She turned and waited, then spoke to him as he drew near, the poise of her head and body crudely inviting. After talking together for a few moments they moved on slowly, then stopped again. The man fidgeted from foot to foot and rubbed the back of his neck.

The nervous type, Fraser thought. Not sure how much she's going to charge him. Needs encouraging. She was swinging her handbag, tossing her head archly, playing to hook him. Business was evidently slack, Fraser decided. Easy now, Irma, don't scare him off, he's new to it, this one. Make him think you're a nice warm-hearted girl and you really fancy him. Leave the money bit till after, then turn nasty, and you'll take him for everything but his bus-fare home.

She slipped her hand through the man's arm and they walked on slowly together, talking. She was kittenish now, the man still vaguely hesitant. Opposite Brunel's house was a small area where the pavement widened to take a phone booth and a pillar box, a place of shadows. She steered him towards it. Fraser leaned forward a little to watch. There was no light in the booth. Probably no phone either, Fraser reflected. Some fun-loving young scamps would have seen to that, the little sods.

The tart and the man merged into the shadows near the booth. That's right, ducky, Fraser thought approvingly. Give him a trailer. If you can't warm him up enough to forget his financial worries in five minutes, you might as well give up the game and go back to being a brain surgeon. He looked along the road running west, and wondered if Modesty was in one of the cars parked at the end. She had said she was going to case the place at ground level, and take photographs, but her camera would pick up precious little detail from that distance and angle. Fraser began to feel depressed.

In the shadows by the phone booth, her cheek against Willie Garvin's, his arms wrapped round her, Modesty gazed

55

over his shoulder at Brunel's house, the width of the road away. Willie had put down the suitcase carefully. Inside it was a powerful battery-operated spotlight. One end of the case was a filter which eliminated all visible light and allowed only infra-red to pass through. The spot was switched on now, bathing the front door of Brunel's house in infra-red light.

She fumbled under Willie's long mac and drew out the camera, a 35 mm Asahi-Pentax with a focusing spot for infra-red sensitive film. Slipping an arm round his neck so that she could hold the camera in both hands just behind his right shoulder she said, 'Lift me up a few inches, Willie.' His arms tightened, and he lifted her. She sighted over his shoulder, adjusted the telescopic lens, and took four shots of the porch and door. 'Down for a moment now.'

She moved the suitcase with her foot so that the unseen beam of the spotlight covered the ground-floor window. 'Again, Willie.' She took six shots of the big window, and said, 'Right.'

He lowered her. 'Got all you want, Princess?'

'I think so. But we'll stay clinched for a couple of minutes, just for the look of things.'

'Okay.' She felt the breath of his soundless chuckle against her cheek as they stood relaxed together. 'Strikes me as a bit unseemly, some'ow.'

On the roof of the flats, Fraser looked at the parked cars again, wondering where Modesty Blaise and Willie Garvin had got to. His watch showed half past twelve. They were to rendezvous at the penthouse at one. He shrugged, took a last glance at the square below, then turned towards the stairs bulkhead which jutted from the roof.

When the prints were dry, Willie Garvin unclipped them. With Fraser following, he went out of the darkroom, through Modesty's lapidary workshop and into the big drawing-room.

Fraser was in a sour mood which even the glass of matchless brandy he carried could not lighten. It was partly because he was tired now and partly because he was annoyed with himself. In Welbury Square he had been looking for a man and a woman and had seen them clearly without realizing that they were the couple he was looking for. He had only realized it on returning to the penthouse, when he had seen the blonde wig lying on the table and Modesty in the shiny black leather suit.

She had changed now, and was sitting on the big couch wearing a Chinese dressing-gown that lent a rich glow to her dark beauty, adding to the hint of the Eurasian given by her black hair and high cheekbones. Arms folded in the wide sleeves where golden dragons coiled against a crimson background, she sat gazing absently down at one of the glorious Isfahan rugs which lay scattered on the tiled floor. Her hair, usually drawn up in a chignon, hung loosely tied in two pigtails.

Willie Garvin stood looking at her for a moment or two, simply looking with open pleasure, then said, 'Princess'. She roused, smiled, and took the sheaf of photographs he handed her. Slowly she went through them, passing them in turn to Fraser, who studied them glumly and spread them on the couch beside her.

'They don't tell us a damn thing we didn't already know,' Fraser said. 'Can't even pick out the scanner in the porch, but it's there all right. Whoever said reconnaissance is never wasted didn't know about 28 Welbury Square.'

'Why don't you go 'ome?' Willie asked amiably.

'Because I like the brandy they serve here. It stops me worrying about what Tarrant will do to me when he comes back and finds I've told you about this and that you're both bloody well dead because you tried something idiotic.'

'We won't do that,' Modesty said thoughtfully. She indicated the photographs. 'I didn't expect to find a loop-hole. It's a matter of getting the feel of the situation. Tonight wasn't wasted.'

'And now you've got the feel, what next?' Fraser allowed another large sip of the brandy to gild his throat and looked at her angrily.

'We think,' she said. 'Let's have a run-down, Willie.'

For the next ten minutes Willie Garvin strolled back and

57

forth across the room, eyes half closed, talking. He talked slowly but rarely hesitated as he posed every possibility, from the improbable to the fantastic. He spoke of alarms and electronics, of safe-blowing, of stethoscope techniques and of thermic lances. He spoke of time and labour equations. He covered methods of entry, from the front, the rear, the roof and the basement. He spoke of sewers and cables, of disguise and deception. When he had finished he sat down, lit a cigarette, and said, 'Whichever way you look at it there's too many ifs and buts, too many areas for snags.'

Modesty nodded. She did not show any disappointment. 'Fine, Willie. That's cleared the air nicely. It always pays to get rid of the old-hat stuff before you try to think fresh. What we have to avoid is thinking a little too clever on this one, Willie love, a little too complex. Let's bear that in mind and sleep on it.'

Fraser stood up. 'It's complex because the set-up is designed to be complex, and it's not within your option to change it.' He picked up his coat. 'Well, it's been interesting, and thanks for trying.'

Modesty smiled. 'We've only just started trying, Jack.' She went with him to the doors of the private lift in the big foyer of the penthouse. 'I know there isn't much time, but if we come up with any ideas I'll give you a ring right away.'

He looked at her gloomily. 'You're a nice girl, ducky. I wish you weren't such a bloody fool. I'll probably have to emigrate.' With something of an effort he smoothed the hardness from his face, the tautness from his eyes, and allowed the humble, servile character that he habitually played to enfold him once again. Timidly he extended a limp hand. 'Well ... goodnight, Miss Blaise. It's been a pleasure. A great pleasure.'

When Fraser had gone Willie said reluctantly, 'He could be right, Princess. We got to come up with a new angle, or we don't stand a chance. I 'aven't got a glimmer of an idea meself.'

'You never see a new angle coming until it comes, Willie.

58

You know that. Just switch to receive, and forget it. Sleep well.'

'Sure.' He lifted her hand and touched the backs of her fingers to his cheek in the salutation that was peculiarly his own and for her only. 'I'll see to the locking up.'

One bedroom of the penthouse was kept permanently for Willie. Before he went to bed he checked the alarms carefully. Giles Pennyfeather would be returning sometime during the night, he remembered. Pennyfeather had his own key to the lift doors below, and had been shown the hidden switch to open them at the top. Also, the night porter knew him. But as an added precaution Willie set the control panel beside the lift doors for 160 lbs. If anybody tried to make Pennyfeather take them up with him, the lift simply would not work.

Satisfied, he went to bed. Since he did not want to think about the house in Welbury Square he thought about his current campaign to achieve a close and horizontal relationship with one Erica Nolan, aged twenty-seven, a Professor of Sociology at the LSE, whose philosophical convictions he found hilarious but whose physical parts exerted a compelling attraction on him. In five minutes he was asleep.

Modesty woke soon after four-thirty, when Pennyfeather came home. She heard him tiptoe into the bedroom and blunder about in the bathroom for a few minutes, then she called softly, 'You don't have to be quiet, Giles. I'm awake.' She sat up and put on the bedside light.

'Oh, sorry.' He came out of the bathroom, taking off his pullover. 'Did I disturb you when I knocked the bathsalts over?'

'Oh my God, you haven't done it again?'

'Well, yes, I have. I was trying to clean my teeth in the dark, you see, and I sort of bumped the jar somehow. I say, I've never tried that lemon-flavoured toothpaste before. It's quite nice but it doesn't froth much, does it?'

'That's a tube of hand cream, darling.'

'Ah, I see. That would account for it. Not frothing, I mean.'

'Yes, I suppose it would. Did you have a busy night?'

'Not very.' He pulled off his shirt. 'I just sat by the phone reading *Reader's Digest* most of the time. Got one call from that all-night garage across the road. Chap dropped a battery on his foot and smashed it up a bit, but I just sent him to hospital. It's not like in Kalimba.'

'No. Very different.' She watched him with affection as he put on a pair of Marks and Spencer pyjamas, remembering the hours in the primitive little makeshift operating theatre. 'I think Kalimba was more your style, Giles.'

'Yes, so do I. I'm writing around for something like it.' He stood with his hands on his hips, looking at her. 'You know, it's awfully good of you to let me stay here, Modesty.'

'You're welcome. Are you just going to stand there or are you coming to bed?'

'Oh, I'm coming to bed.' He got in. 'Did you have a nice evening?'

'Interesting. You feel half-frozen.'

'I am, I'm afraid. Sat in that chilly garage for half an hour, talking to the chap with the foot while he was waiting for the ambulance. Better stay away from me for a bit.'

'Don't encourage cowardice. If the man in my bed has got cold in the line of duty, he's welcome to some of my hot.'

He laughed, and manoeuvred to draw her over until she lay on top of him, his arms holding her, her head turned to rest beside his on the pillow. 'Lovely hot,' he said contentedly. 'Do you always not wear anything in bed, or is it just for me?'

'I always don't. But you're welcome to enjoy it.'

'I am. It's very nice. Yielding but not squashy. Look, I get paid on Friday. Will you accept a small contribution towards my board? I realize you're stinking rich and all that, but you know what I mean.'

'Yes, I know what you mean, darling. All right. Something for your board, then. But not your bed.'

'Oh Christ, I didn't mean that!'

'Shut up, idiot. I know. Am I crushing you?'

'A bit. It's marvellous. I hope I don't fall asleep.'

'Well, before you do, listen. Remember those two men who came and knocked you about in Kalimba, the ones who wanted to know if that unknown foreigner had said anything to you?'

'The silver-haired chap and the stocky chap? Yes, of course. What about them?'

'They were dining in The Legend tonight, with a man called Brunel. He's their boss. A very nasty man indeed.'

'They were at the same place as us tonight? I say, that's a pretty rum coincidence.'

'Oddly enough, I think it was a coincidence. I don't know whether or not they saw you there, Giles. They certainly saw me. Brunel came and spoke to me. But anyway, we need to be rather careful for a while. Willie Garvin's staying the night here, and we're all going to keep our eyes wide open.'

'Yes, I see. But why, exactly?'

She gave a little sigh. 'Well, first because the silver-haired chap and the stocky chap might try to pay me back for what I did to them. Remember?'

'Lord, yes! Look here, darling, you'd better not wander around on your own with those two about. Don't go out unless I'm with you. Or Willie.'

She pursed her lips to kiss his ear, then said, 'Darling, you haven't got it quite right. The thing is, *you* mustn't go out unless I'm with you. Or Willie. Even on your night surgery duty. Especially on your night surgery duty.'

'I don't quite follow.'

'They may also have in mind to take another crack at finding out from you if the mysterious Mr X told you anything. So one of us will keep guard on you, just in case.'

'Oh, that's ridiculous, Modesty.' He gave a muted guffaw. 'I don't need a bodyguard.'

She said carefully, 'I came in a bit useful in Kalimba, surely?'

'Yes, of course. You were bloody amazing. But I still don't take to the idea. I was pretty fed up with that chap hitting me in the stomach, and I was going to have a smack at dealing with him myself when you took over. It was awfully good of you, but after all you're a girl, and it's not really right for a chap to let a girl see to that kind of thing.'

'Unless she's a pretty rum girl, which we've agreed on. How were you going to have a smack at him, Giles?'

'Well, I thought as soon as I'd got my wind back I'd get up and kick that damn gun out of his hand to start with.'

She lifted her head and looked down at him, their noses almost touching. 'Please, Giles,' she said gently, 'please listen, and take my word for something I happen to know about. I hope you'll never face the situation again, but if you do, then never, never, *never* try to kick a gun or knife out of anyone's hand. Never. It's fine on the movies, because the man with the gun is on the same pay-roll as the man doing the kick. But it's not good for real. The hand is a very small, very mobile target. It can move a few inches much faster than your foot can move through a four-foot arc. And never try to grab a gun-hand or a knife-hand.' She shook her head slowly, her nose rubbing his. 'Understand?'

'Well, all right. But what does that leave you? I mean what *can* you do?'

'Sometimes nothing but stick your hands up, as instructed, and hope for a better chance later.'

'*You* didn't.'

'Not that time. I was able to take them by surprise, and anyway I was born sneaky and I've got a lot sneakier over the years. If you want a general rule, then you go for the man, not the weapon, and you aim to put him out of action fast.'

'I saw you do it with the silver-haired chap. What about the other one?'

'I hit him here,' she put her hand under his jaw, 'and here, with my knee.' She moved her thigh against him. 'But don't try that either, Giles, because it needs nice timing. In fact don't try anything, and let's stop talking about it. Do you feel tired or do you want to make love?'

'Both, actually.'

'Well, that can be catered for. There's all kinds.'

'You're a marvellous girl, Modesty.' He put his hand to her cheek, and the touch sent a new wave of affection through her, warm and exciting. He was not a sophisticated lover,

62

not an industrious text-book follower, but he gave a strange and healing satisfaction.

Fraser rang next morning at ten.

'They're preparing for a siege,' he said brusquely. 'I've had a man watching from an empty flat across the road. Deliveries of all kinds. They're stocking up. And nobody's left the house. They're going to sit on top of that bloody safe until you-know-who comes back from the States, and when he refuses to play they'll call in the man from you-know-whose Embassy and give him the stuff.'

Modesty said, 'All right, Jack. Thank you.'

'For the last time, don't try it.'

'I'll let you know.'

She rang off and went back to the breakfast table. Willie was reading the morning paper. Weng, her houseboy, brought in fresh coffee.

'More toast, Willie?'

'No thanks, Princess. I'm fine. How's Giles?'

'He'll sleep till noon. I told him last night that he mustn't go out unless one of us is with him, but I'm not sure it matters now. Not for a few days, anyway.'

She told him what Fraser had reported. 'If they're holed up, they can't do anything.'

Willie nodded. 'There's someone around we could use to keep an eye on Giles if we're too busy ourselves. Wee Jock Miller's in town. I forgot to tell you.'

Wee Jock Miller was a squat block of solid muscle barely topping five feet, with a razor-scarred face and only one good eye, who had been born in a Glasgow slum forty odd years ago. For four years he had been in charge of all transport matters for *The Network*, the criminal organization based in Tangier which Modesty had created and controlled. Wee Jock was a taciturn man with an inborn gift for all things mechanical. A natural engineer, he was master of anything that had wheels, tracks or a keel. He had lost the sight of his eye while serving *The Network*, and had been set up with a garage in Glasgow and a pension. *The Network* looked after its own.

Modesty remembered the indignant glare with which Wee Jock had always received her instructions, and the gloomy sniff which spoke of nameless problems and difficulties. Yet he had never failed her. On one occasion a man misled by Jock's dour attitude towards her had felt encouraged to be impudent to her in his presence. Wee Jock had promptly broken the man's nose.

'We must have him up for a drink,' she said, and cradled her coffee-cup in her hands. 'We'll ask him to look over the Rolls. I love watching him glower, and he does enjoy it so.' Neither she nor Willie had mentioned Welbury Square. They were simply waiting, hoping that something would come, knowing that it could not be forced because it would have to be a new concept.

'I like Giles,' Willie said idly, and put down the paper. 'He's got something.'

'He makes you laugh.'

'Yes, but I didn't mean that. Hard to say what it is, really. Maybe it's that 'e's the same on top as all the way through.'

She nodded. 'One of nature's innocents. He couldn't dissemble if he tried.' Her eyes sparkled with sudden humour. 'I've never known anyone who remembers so little. It appears I'm only about the fourth or fifth girl he's ever had, he's not quite sure which.'

Willie leaned back in his chair and half closed his eyes reminiscently. 'I remember my first girl all right.'

'Who was she?'

'Annie.'

'Annie who?'

'I dunno, Princess. We all just called 'er Annie the Bang at the orphanage. She was the caretaker's daughter, and 'is name was Old Creep.'

'How old were you?'

'Fourteen. It was just before I ran away. She was sixteen. Dumb as a post, but willing. It wasn't all that romantic. She was the only female around, and the big kids 'ad 'er under contract. You could buy 'alf an hour in the boiler room with Annie for a packet of snout or 'alf a dollar. They gave Annie twenty per cent, but in chocolate. Pretty fat, she was.' He looked rueful. 'I was all steamed up to get at Annie and find out what it was all about, but there was nobody to send me parcels and things, so I was always skint.'

'Don't tell me you by-passed her agents?'

'Not exactly. There was this big kid, the boss man. Dicer, we used to call 'im. A right villain, 'e was, but a sucker for a gamble. So I took 'im on at conkers, and rigged the game. Won fifteen minutes with Annie.'

'Conkers?' She gave a little snuffle of laughter and put down her coffee cup. 'Can I tell Tarrant? It's worth a lunch.'

He gestured. 'Sure.'

'How did you rig it, though? Nobble his conker?'

'No. I made mine out of lead. Cast it, painted it, drilled it, and 'ung it on a bit of string. Took me nearly a week, but it looked just like the real thing. Where I slipped up was in telling Annie afterwards. She let on to Dicer, and that was it. I 'ad to scarper.'

She cupped her chin in her hands, looking at him, her face full of laughter. 'Thanks, Willie. The punch-line gets me a champagne supper—' Her mind whirled suddenly, and she froze. Images came spinning into the receptive void.

After a few moments Willie Garvin stood up and said in soft query, 'Princess?'

Her eyes focused on him, and they were alight with excitement. 'I think you've done it, Willie. Conkers. You said Wee Jock Miller's in town, and that helps. We'll need rehearsal time and we'll need some special gear that can't be traced back to us. Fraser can fix that. It's only an admin problem, and we haven't time . . .'

She sat with her chin resting on linked fingers now, frowning a little with the intensity of her concentration. Willie Garvin did not speak. He sat down again and waited, watching her, enormously content. He loved watching her when she was thinking in over-drive. Her dark blue eyes became darker still, almost black, and there was a special little tilt to the head at the end of the long, lovely neck. Soon she would lay out the bones of the idea for him, and then they would get down to detail.

Conkers? What the hell had she come up with?

Two minutes passed. Then she said, 'Look, Willie . . .'

CHAPTER FOUR

Adrian Chance sat in the deep armchair by the curtained window of the study. A Colt .357 revolver lay on the small table at his elbow beside a half empty tumbler of weak whisky and soda, the one drink he would have during what remained of the night.

It was three-fifteen, and he had just taken over from Jacko. There were two of Jacko's girlie magazines on the table. Chance ignored them. He was bored, too bored even to make the effort of alleviating his boredom. Idly he thought about Lisa. Four days now since he had been with her. Not very long. It would be a while before Brunel gave him the okay again, but that was all right. Too much availability took the sparkle out of things. For a moment, vaguely, he half wondered what Lisa thought and felt, but he was not curious enough to pursue the question. He had used her for so long as a living toy that to consider her now as a person was beyond him.

He yawned and looked about him resentfully. For the last four days they had all been holed up in this house, waiting. Waiting for Blaise and Garvin. He was convinced now that they would not come, and was acutely disappointed. There had been promising moments. The suspect phone calls, for instance. One had been from a man purporting to sell insurance; he had made an appointment with Brunel, but failed to keep it. There had been callers at the house, too. Three men and two women in all. They were collecting for charity, or making a consumer survey, or offering to service electrical appliances. He was quite sure that none of them had been genuine, but unfortunately none of them had been either Modesty Blaise or Willie Garvin. Disguise had its limits. You could not disguise yourself to deceive somebody who knew what you looked like and was expecting deception.

It was all part of a misdirection play. That was Brunel's opinion, and Chance agreed. Probably Fraser supplied the stooges. But what was the real play? Chance thought it likely that there wasn't one any longer, that they had given up. It was a pity Brunel had taken such complete precautions. Better to have left a loop-hole, a nicely contrived loop-hole to lure Blaise and Garvin in.

He picked up his drink and sipped at it, listening to a noise outside that was familiar. Something was moving along the road, a tracked vehicle. The engine was fairly quiet, but there was a lot of rattling and crunching. Another mechanical monstrosity for the excavation up the road. They seemed to favour the night for bringing these things in. Last night there had been two bulldozers.

Chance got up and drew the curtain aside slightly, just in time to see the derrick of a mobile crane as the contraption lumbered round the corner of the house and out of view. He dropped the curtain, walked idly over to the safe and patted the smooth steel top. A beautiful safe.

Something was troubling him, nagging at his subconscious. He tried to locate it, suddenly alert. Everything was quiet. No sound except the steady throb of the mobile crane's engine outside—

That was it. The thing had stopped moving. Why?

Suddenly, impossibly, the house trembled at a giant blow as if a colossal hammer had been swung at the wall. Chance felt the floor shake beneath his feet, and a big piece of plaster fell from the ceiling. His arm felt numb, the arm he had been resting on top of the safe. That was where the blow had fallen, against the outer wall and just above the safe.

He jumped away and ran to snatch up the gun. Another dull hammer-blow made his ears sing with the reverberation, and as he turned he saw a large piece of brickwork topple to the floor, leaving a great hole beside the safe, a hole from which wide cracks radiated.

Chance's mouth was stretched in a grimace, his eyes so wide that the lids had disappeared. His brain had stopped working because for the moment it simply could not accept the inconceivable thing that was happening. The next blow shattered the wall on the other side of the safe.

Jacko was shouting from upstairs. Another massive thud, and a piece of wall, an irregular square yard of it, tumbled into the room. A lighter blow knocked away the ragged edge of brickwork near the safe, and now he saw the impossible hammer. It swung through the hole and into the room, falling. The floor shook, and there came the sound of splintering wood.

The thing was a great ball of steel two feet across, its surface pitted and scarred. Set in the ball was a heavy steel chain, and attached to this two thick wire hawsers. As Chance watched with starting eyes the hawsers tightened and the monstrous hammer was dragged back through the hole. For a moment it caught the edge of the safe, twisting it and breaking its adhesion to the weakened wall, then the hammer slid away and swung out into the darkness.

Breaking free of the shock that seemed to have locked his limbs, Chance ran towards the hole. In the road outside, the thing squatted on its tracks, a control cabin with the tall derrick rising in front of it, swinging away now, the great steel ball dangling from the hawser like a pendulum bob. It was swinging towards him again, and Chance flung himself wildly across the room. In the instant before he did so he saw that the machine was not alone. To one side, like a jackal waiting for the lion to glut himself, stood a smaller machine on caterpillar tracks, with steel arms bearing the long toothed scoop of a shovel-loader.

The hammer struck. The wall above the safe shivered and split. Bricks crumbled over the safe.

In her room, Lisa lay in bed, staring into the darkness, listening. The house shook again. She could hear Jacko's voice, shouting. Something wrong was happening. She did not try to imagine what it might be, but listened for the voices to speak in her head, telling her what she must do. The voices remained silent. She felt no surprise for it had happened this way before. The voices were never hurried. They always considered carefully before telling her what she must do.

Adrian Chance was met by Brunel and Jacko as he threw open the study door. The room was full of dust, Brunel, in a dressing-gown, slippers on his small feet, said, 'Yes?'

'Demolition thing! Hammer!' Chance jerked out, dust and sweat mingling on his face. '*They're after the whole bloody safe!* Downstairs – got to get out to them. Only way.'

He plunged down the stairs. Jacko clattered after him. Brunel followed thoughtfully, without haste.

Sitting in the cab of the ball and chain demolition crane, his feet resting on the two brakes, his hands moving on the three levers in front of him, Wee Jock Miller pursed his lips and made careful calculations in his head. Two minutes maximum for this part of the job, Willie had said. Wee Jock Miller had promised ninety seconds, and with a little luck he would even trim that time.

Willie was waiting at the controls of the cat, the front end shovel-loader. Wee Jock spared a glance in that direction, his scarred face crinkling in a grin as he let out the hoist a few feet, timing it with the swing.

The crane was a twenty-three ton Ruston Bucyrus with a fifty-five foot derrick. A lovely machine, in Wee Jock's critical opinion. You could use the ball like a pile-driver, dropping it through a reinforced concrete roof; you could slew the derrick to swing the ball like a pendulum; or you could use the horizontal dragline to draw it back for a forward swing. There was a clutch for the hoist and another for the dragline, a footbrake for each, and a slewing lever. When you juggled those controls just right, you could play with that ton of steel like a tennis ball on a string.

Wee Jock Miller chewed on the end of an unlit cigarette, watching the swing of the ball, and pushed the slewing lever forward, aiming to strike just below where the safe stood. It was there all right. He had seen the side of it after flicking the ball into the room to drag the edge of broken brickwork away. It stood in the exact position marked on the plan Modesty Blaise had produced for him. A good plan, that. A builder's plan. He did not wonder how she had come by it. He had served her for four years in the old days of *The Network*. She always got what was needed for a job, or she didn't send you in. Wee Jock Miller had trusted few men in his life, and only one woman.

The ball struck precisely where he had aimed it. Brickwork shattered and fell. Now the end of the floor joists beneath the safe had no support. He slewed the derrick smoothly, ready for another blow, but it was not needed. The joists sagged. The safe, with bits of brickwork still adhering to its back, toppled outwards and fell to the pavement with a single loud, crunching clang.

Wee Jock muttered with deep satisfaction, 'Beat that then, Wullie boy.' He switched off the engine and jumped down from the cab, watching the shovel-loader lunge towards the fallen safe.

Adrian Chance wrenched open the front door and made one stride before he managed to bring himself to a halt, his face scratched, his clothes caught in the barbs of coiled dannert wire piled high in the porch and across the narrow strip between the railings and the front window. He could see nobody, could only hear the noise of a tracked vehicle from round the corner by the windowless wall. Something fell at his feet and broke. Choking fumes rose up to sear his nose and eyes. Gasping, he tore free of the barbed wire and slammed the door shut, then cannoned painfully into Jacko as he groped his way back to the stairs, eyes streaming.

'No good,' he snarled. 'Back upstairs. Quick!'

'But you said—'

'*Back upstairs, you stupid bastard!*' Chance almost screamed the words. Brunel stood aside to let them pass, then turned and followed them, but not to the study. As they ran into the shattered room he turned the other way, to the drawing-room, put on the lights and picked up the telephone.

He had lost this one. Brunel accepted the fact coldly. Chance and Jacko were flailing about to no purpose. The coup was original in conception and could not be countered now. Whatever Chance and Jacko might think of trying, Modesty Blaise had thought of it at leisure twenty-four hours ago or more. Yes, more. And she would be ready. She would have the getaway all worked out, too. She would have the safe, complete. Not only the Singapore papers but everything else in the safe. That was very bad. Something would have to be done about her.

Brunel was dialling 999. He did not believe that calling the police would serve any purpose, but it was the necessary thing to do. The operator said, 'Emergency. Which service do you require?'

Brunel said, 'The police, please.'

In the study, Chance edged forward across the creaking floor, gun in hand. The terrible hammerblows had stopped now. The shovel-loader would be taking over, seeking to pick up the safe in its scoop. If he could get to the hole safely, he could fire down at the man on the control seat.

Something flashed through the hole and passed over his head at a steep angle, to break against the ceiling. Again his eyes began to burn and stream. He fired once, blindly, and heard glass shatter as the bullet hit a wall mirror. It was then than he knew there was nothing to be done. The fury went out of him, to be replaced by a cold and aching desire, a yearning for revenge, so all-consuming that he moaned softly as it racked him.

With one hand held to his eyes, and tears running down his dust-coated cheeks, he turned and groped his way to the door.

Willie Garvin had driven the cat hard forward, so that the great teeth of the shovel screeched on the pavement before thrusting under the scattering of rubble on which the safe lay. A shower of dust and broken bricks fell as he tilted the scoop and lifted the safe in its belly. He glanced behind him and backed towards the Morris van waiting twenty yards up the road. It looked like a big red Post Office van. The doors stood open.

The clock in Willie's head had ticked off ninety seconds only, and he was well content. Wee Jock Miller had done a beautiful job with the ball and chain. He came running past the cat now as Willie turned it and eased the shovel up to the open van, rolling the safe and broken bricks out on to the thick mattresses laid on the floor. Carefully Willie backed the cat away and killed the engine. He was not worried about interference from the house. Modesty was covering that, with the help of the dannert wire that she and Willie had off-loaded from the van and piled in the porch and across the front windows while Wee Jock was striking his first blow. Neither was he worried about anyone coming accidentally on the scene. Fraser had a man at all approaches to the square. They had set up portable 'No Entry' signs five minutes ago, and were ready to delay any passerby or policeman on the beat with the clinging persistence of the truly drunk.

A figure ran past, wearing a long mac, trousers and a beret. Modesty Blaise did not look like a woman at this moment. Cradled in one arm was the compressed-air gun, with its two-inch diameter barrel, which she had used for placing the tear-gas bombs. Willie was beside her as she climbed into the back of the van. At the wheel, Wee Jock took off as they closed the doors.

Two minutes and ten seconds. Willie Garvin gave a sigh of satisfaction. Thirty seconds ahead of schedule, perhaps a little more. The van headed out of the square, past a 'No Entry' sign and a solitary man who was fumbling his way unsteadily round the corning, clinging to the railings. He did not look up as they passed. A car pulled out ahead, a Mercedes, and they fell in fifty yards behind it. Willie moved to peer out of the small rear window. A Jaguar was following, keeping a comfortable distance. There would be two more cars lurking on the route ahead. Wee Jock Miller had brought down four drivers from his garage in Glasgow to provide interference if a chase began. Nothing obvious, of course, just a bumbling obstruction of any police car that came on the scene.

Modesty picked up the small transceiver which lay in a

padded box in one corner of the van, switched on, and said, 'Three minutes. Do you read me?'

A voice replied simply, 'Three minutes.' It was Fraser's voice.

Wee Jock was heading towards Knightsbridge at a steady speed. The lights were against him. The two cars and the van stopped. Modesty spoke into the transceiver. Thirty seconds later they moved on again. Knightsbridge now, and the approach to the Hyde Park Corner underpass. Red lights and a 'No Entry' sign for the underpass. The Mercedes kept left for the Hyde Park Corner roundabout. The van that looked like a Post Office van swerved past the sign and went on down the tunnel. The Jag followed.

Halfway along the underpass the road was blocked by a huge removal truck. The tall doors stood open, and two men were setting long steel channels to form a ramp from the roadway to the interior of the truck. One man wore a sheepskin jacket and a cap. The other was Fraser, in a black topcoat and bowler hat. The man in the sheepskin jacket turned and gave a thumbs-up sign.

Wee Jock Miller squinted balefully with his one good eye as he judged speed and distance. He was moving at fifteen mph as the front wheels met the ramp. He gunned the engine once, hard. The van took the slope smoothly, losing impetus as the front wheels reached the reinforced floor of the truck, yet keeping just enough way on her to bring the rear wheels up and over the top of the channels. It was so beautifully judged that Wee Jock scarcely had to touch the brakes to halt the van.

He cut the engine, got out of the cab and helped the sheepskinned man slide one of the channels up into the truck. Willie Garvin had opened the van doors and was helping Fraser with the other channel. As soon as they had finished Willie started to block the wheels of the van. The Jag had pulled up behind, its engine idling.

Modesty was sitting on the tail of the van now. She said, 'Jock, you're a lovely man.'

He scowled. 'We'd ha' cut it by five seconds if Wullie'd been a bit smarter wi' the cat.' He looked past her at the safe.

'Anyway, you got it, an' he laid me a fiver for every second under two minutes, Mam'selle.' He still called her by the name all men but Willie had called her in *The Network* days. His scarred face creased in a villainous grin. 'That's a hundred an' sixty quid he's doon.'

'I'll make sure he pays up. But you'll come out with a lot more than side-bets, Jock. I'll be in touch.'

'Eh?' He glowered. 'That was for auld time's sake, just.'

She smiled. 'All the same, you'll be hearing from me. You wouldn't like me to think you're sentimental would you? On your way now, Jock. And thanks again.'

He snorted, jumped down from the truck and got in beside the driver of the Jag. The man in the sheepskin coat and Fraser closed the big doors of the removal truck and moved forward to the cab. The engine roared and the truck began to lumber on its way. Eighty seconds had passed since the Post Office van had entered the underpass.

The Jag driver slipped her into gear and said, 'That's it then, Jock? All finished?'

'Aye.'

'What the hell was it all about?'

Wee Jock Miller turned a venomous glare upon him. 'All about? What the hell was *what* all about?' he growled. 'Did ye notice something, Jimmy?'

The driver pursed his lips, then shook his head slowly from side to side. 'Nothing, Jock. Not a thing.'

'Then don't ask bloody fool questions, Jimmy boy. Ever. Where's yer fags?'

In the passenger seat of the cab, Fraser took off his hat and lifted the little transceiver. He said, 'All clear now,' and waited. A voice repeated the words to him, and he switched off.

At the Knightsbridge end of the underpass a man in overalls climbed out of a Water Board van and began to take away the 'No Entry' sign.

Sitting on the safe, Willie Garvin leaned forward and held a lighter to Modesty's cigarette. In the light of the small flame he saw the tension in her eyes now. It had not been there before. For himself, he felt relaxed and wonderfully content. There was always this difference between them. His own tensions came before a caper, during the run-up to it. That was the time when she was most at ease, or seemed to be. That was when she took unexpected snags in her stride, coping so smoothly that the snags were often turned to advantage as if they had been part of the plan. Her tensions were short-lived but always came afterwards, though perhaps he alone knew her well enough to read the signs. It did not matter anyway. You had to feel the tensions sometime. They were what really made the game. They were the salt and the essence of it. And when they were past there came the sense of well-being that was already seeping into the marrow of his bones, the heady sense of having drunk nectar, of having climbed a high mountain.

He put the lighter to his own cigarette, watching her. She looked a weird sight in the shapeless mac buttoned to her neck, the male trousers and shoes, the beret hiding her hair. Only the face, the lovely composed face with the strongly arched eyebrows, declared her sex.

He patted the corner of the safe and said, 'Just like old times, Princess. I didn't 'alf enjoy that.' He saw her quick smile before the lighter clicked off.

Twenty minutes later the truck drove into a big garage on the river near Greenwich. The establishment operated as an ordinary garage, but the staff were carefully chosen men whose wages came out of Sir Gerald Tarrant's budget. At this moment the repair shop was empty. Fraser had arranged that. He trusted his people, but it was a firm principle not to let any man know more than he had to know for a particular operation.

When the doors of the garage had been closed and the safe hoisted out with block and tackle, Fraser stood gazing down at it with a dreamy look on his pinched face. Modesty Blaise was beside him. Willie and the man in the sheepskin coat were assembling a thermic lance.

Fraser said softly, 'Jesus, what a lovely job. Brunel must be spitting blood.'

'I don't think he goes in for strong emotions,' Modesty said, 'but he'll be thinking hard.'

Fraser looked at her, then smiled the most human and genuine smile she had ever seen on Jack Fraser's face. 'You look like something out of an old silent movie,' he said. 'For God's sake take that bloody beret off at least.'

She pulled off the beret and shook out her hair. 'Better?'

'Much better.' He looked at the safe, covered with dust and scratched by the shovel-loader's great steel teeth, then at Modesty again, wonderingly, as if having a mental struggle to reconcile the two. At last he prodded the safe irritably with his umbrella and said, 'I don't know. I'm trying to say thank you the right way, but I'm not much good at it. I'll tell you this, though. I've sometimes wondered just what it was that Willie Garvin felt about you, and why. Now I've got the idea.'

She looked at him, intrigued to have found a soft spot in the hard shell he wore. 'Better wait till we know what's inside before you go overboard with compliments, Jack.'

He turned away and brought a wooden chair for her to sit on. As he dumped it down he said, 'It doesn't matter what's inside. Well, it matters, but it doesn't change anything.'

Willie Garvin said, 'Gangway,' and wheeled a low trolley bearing two big oxygen cylinders past the safe. The other man followed carrying a dozen six-foot sections of thermic lance.

Fraser said, 'I've heard about these things, but I've never seen one work.'

'It's quite dramatic.' She nodded towards the lance sections as the man set them down. 'That one has a nineteen millimetre bore, and basically they're pretty simple, just a steel tube packed with steel rods burning in oxygen. You ignite the thing by pre-heating the tip with an ordinary gas cutting blowpipe. Once it's going, the oxygen reacts with the iron in the rods to produce terrific heat. You're burning up the lance all the time, of course, that's why you need plenty of sections.'

'And how long will this take?'

'About an hour.'

He stared at her. 'You're joking?'

'No. You can drill a hole through eight feet of granite in

76

less than fifteen minutes. The only snag with a thermic lance, if you're a safe-breaker, is that they can't be used very easily on the site where a safe's likely to be. All right if you're sitting in a cellar and cutting through the wall into a bank, say. But the equipment's too cumbersome for a quick in-and-out job in somebody's drawing-room.'

'Wouldn't that kind of heat destroy what's inside the safe?'

'It's so intense and cuts so fast that you get surprisingly little radiation effect. You have to be careful, of course. Willie's going to open this one by chamfering the edge where the lock is, halfway down the side. That way, the cutting flame isn't directed into the safe.'

Fraser watched the operation with sober respect. The safe, still held horizontally by the hoist, was tilted slightly with one edge of the base resting on the ground, so that the slag would fall clear rather than run into the interior. Willie, wearing a welder's mask, had ignited the lance with an oxy-acetylene blowpipe. The flame applied to the safe was almost colourless, but Fraser saw the steel surface itself change colour, and almost at once little globules of molten metal began falling to the concrete floor. He grinned suddenly and said, 'I've just realized, it wouldn't matter a damn if we did destroy what's inside. That's the whole idea.'

She glanced at him in surprise. 'Aren't you interested to see what else might be inside? This is *Brunel*'s safe.'

Fraser looked sour and stabbed inaccurately with his umbrella at a spider scuttling across the floor. 'When a chit of a girl teaches me my job, I must be getting past it,' he said gloomily.

She gave a little smile, watching the cherry-red line of the cut as the lance sliced through the toughened steel. Fraser wasn't getting past it. He was simply in a state of high excitement he had not known for quite a few years now. She said, 'There's still the most important reason for getting the Singapore papers out intact.'

'Eh? What reason?'

She turned with a touch of impatience now. 'For God's

77

sake, don't you remember why I'm here, Jack? Those papers are Tarrant's birthday present. Do you expect me to give him a handful of ashes?'

It was a wintry morning when the Daimler which had picked up Sir Gerald Tarrant at Heathrow pulled into the carpark of The Treadmill. This was the pub Willie Garvin had bought when he retired. Tarrant was not sure why Willie retained it, for he spent less than half his time here. Running a pub had quickly proved too tedious. It was a nice dream, but one achieved too early in life. Given another twenty years it might suit Willie ideally. If he lived so long.

Tarrant went in, chafing his hands, feeling tired and old. For him, this wintry day was a suitable welcome home to a wintry future. It was only a few minutes past nine. A girl was pushing a polisher over the floor, and a man was checking the array of bottles behind the bar. Tarrant knew him. He was the man Willie employed as manager, a very sound man to whom Willie thankfully delegated almost every aspect of the work. Tarrant brushed a few flakes of snow from his coat and said, 'Good morning, Mr Spurling.'

The man turned, smiled, and said, 'Why, it's you, sir. Miss Blaise said you might be coming along, but I don't think she expected you so early. She's in the workshop with Mr Garvin. You know the way, don't you, sir?'

Tarrant knew the way. He also knew that the long low building behind the pub was rather more than a workshop. Willie Garvin's workshop occupied only one end of it. The rest was a combination of gymnasium, combat dojo, pistol range, and short archery range. It contained Willie's remarkable collection of weapons, old and new, and could be entered only through double steel doors. The place was soundproof. Tarrant said, 'You'd better ring through and ask them to let me in.'

Mr Spurling glanced out of the window at the end of the bar. 'No need, sir. There's Dr Pennyfeather wandering about outside.' Tarrant's eyebrows lifted slightly but he asked no questions.

As he made his way down the brick path he saw a lean-faced gangling man with a short bush of fair hair, wearing a huge sweater which looked as if it had been woven from grey rope. He was standing with his back to the river and appeared to be doing deep-breathing exercises. As Tarrant approached, the man stopped swinging his arms and came forward. His rather unmatched features wore a smile that was oddly engaging.

'Hallo, there,' he said cheerfully. 'I expect you're Sir Gerald Tarrant.'

'That's right. How do you do?'

'I'm Pennyfeather. Giles Pennyfeather.' They shook hands. 'Just came out for a breather. Jolly nice after Africa, you know, this cold weather. They've been having a scrap in there.' He jerked his thumb towards the windowless building. 'Chucking each other all over the shop. Extraordinary business. Quite interesting, but a bit alarming if you know what I mean.'

Tarrant said, 'I do know what you mean. I believe Mr Spurling referred to you as a doctor. A friend of Willie's?'

'Well, of Modesty's really. She sort of picked me up in Tanzania when I was in a bit of a jam. She's terribly nice, you know. I've been staying at her place for a couple of weeks now, waiting for a job somewhere.'

'Yes, she's terribly nice,' Tarrant agreed. He was mildly surprised. If Pennyfeather was staying at the penthouse, then it seemed likely that he was Modesty's current ... Tarrant hesitated mentally over the word, and settled for lover. Old-fashioned, of course, but he found 'boyfriend' coy and 'young man' nauseating.

So Pennyfeather was probably that to her. Rather odd. Tarrant had known one or two of her men in the past. Hagan, the agent. John Dall, the American tycoon. Collier the urbane scholar with the pretty wit. They had all been very different, but this one was more so. None of Hagan's toughness, of Dall's immense personality, of Collier's keen intellect. He seemed a woolly-minded young man. And yet ... there was something indefinably appealing about him. No, not appealing, that made him sound like a spaniel. Engaging, perhaps?

Unexpectedly Pennyfeather said, 'Look, I really came out here to have a think about Mrs Leggett's gall-stone, if that's what it is, so don't hang on for me. You go on in. I left the doors unlocked.' He waved towards the building again.

'Thank you,' said Tarrant. 'Perhaps I'll see you again later. I hope your thoughts about the gall-stone prove satisfactory.'

'M'mm. If that's what it is,' Pennyfeather repeated pensively. 'Ah, well.'

Tarrant moved on, leaving him with hands thrust deep in his trouser pockets, great folds of the ancient sweater drooping about him like wrinkles of rhinoceros hide. The outer door had been pushed to, but swung open at Tarrant's touch. He moved on a pace and opened the inner door, suddenly eager to see Modesty again.

In the drawing-room of a suite at the Dorchester, Adrian Chance stood looking down from the window on the lines of traffic below. His arms were folded and he was very tense. Jacko was slumped in an armchair, his face sullen. Brunel sat on the couch, idly turning the pages of a morning newspaper.

'Just give us the word, that's all you have to do,' Chance said tautly. 'Give us forty-eight hours, and they're dead.'

'I see.' Brunel did not look up from the paper. 'And suppose you achieve that. What purpose will it serve?'

Chance turned, holding his anger under rigid control. 'They'd be dead,' he said between his teeth. 'Isn't that enough?'

Brunel looked up curiously. 'I don't quite follow you, Adrian. How do you visualize these things? Do you see Blaise and Garvin sitting on a cloud in heaven or a rock in hell, gnashing their teeth in eternal fury because they've been killed by you and Jacko? I can't really believe it works that way. I've always felt that death puts an end to the possibilities of revenge.'

'Then give us seventy-two hours,' Chance said urgently.

'We'll put them down slowly. Twenty-fours hours in hell before they go.'

Jacko grunted approval. Brunel returned to his newspaper. 'I've no interest in revenge as an end in itself,' he said with a touch of impatience. 'It bears no fruit. I have nothing against torture in principle, of course. It can be a very useful practice. If you could assure me that your efforts would secure the recovery of all that was in the safe, I'd be happy to give you the word. But it's too late for that. Tarrant's department will have their hands on everything. A valuable haul, but one which doesn't compromise us, fortunately.'

'But for God's sake, you can't just let Blaise and Garvin get away with it!'

Brunel put the paper aside and leaned back, half closing his eyes, steepling his fingers to touch the tips gently together. 'They've done so,' he said. 'They've already got away with it. When will you ever learn to be a realist, Adrian?'

Chance stared out of the window. 'Yes, they have,' he said. 'You insisted on keeping the stuff in the safe and you predicted they'd try something subtle. So they come along and very subtly knock a bloody great hole in the house and make off with the whole bloody safe.'

'You're confusing subtlety of execution with subtlety of conception, Adrian.' The little man opened his eyes suddenly. 'You're also speaking in a manner which is so insolent as to be dangerous. Do you understand me?'

Adrian Chance's face lost a little of its colour, and the hand he smoothed over his silver hair was not quite steady. 'I'm sorry.' He shrugged and gave a sour laugh. 'I got carried away. So do we just go home and do nothing?'

'Not at all. As you point out, Blaise has been too clever for us on this occasion. Now that intrigues me. We could use a mind as clever as that, you know.'

'Use Blaise?' Chance whipped round, gazing incredulously.

'Why not?'

'Because she'd never go into partnership with you. With

anyone.' Chance gestured helplessly, like a man trying to state a proposition that was inherently self-evident.

'I wasn't thinking of a partnership,' said Brunel. 'I was thinking what an excellent employee she might make.'

'Working for you? That's even more absurd.' Chance schooled his manner to politeness, to take any insolence from the words.

'I think not. I believe it may be possible to break into her acceptance of the idea without destroying the essential qualities I wish to retain in her. It will require a selective and nicely judged brain-washing technique, of course.'

'Brain-washing . . .' Chance murmured, and for the first time in many hours some of the tension went out of him. He stared into space, and a small hungry smile touched his eyes. 'Oh my God, yes . . . yes, I'd like that, Brunel. I want that bitch licking our hands.'

Brunel looked at him. 'I don't wish to deny you your pleasures, Adrian. But too great a degree of submissiveness might affect those qualities in her which alone interest me. So don't make the mistake of trying to achieve your objective at the expense of mine, will you?'

Jacko said, 'How you aim to get hold of her?'

'I shall begin by going to see her,' Brunel said calmly. 'She'll have to be ensnared very delicately, but I have one or two ideas which might develop admirably. We already have Pennyfeather on the scene, so perhaps I'll use the Novikov Project as bait. It's pleasant to kill two birds with one stone.'

Chance sat down, hardly listening, thinking his own anticipatory thoughts. Jacko said, 'You still reckon this Pennyfeather knows something?'

'I'm quite sure of it.' Brunel's voice was placid. 'He may not realize he knows anything, but he does. Dying men, delirious men, are babblers. Novikov babbled. And the man who heard his babbling was Dr Giles Pennyfeather.'

There was a tap on the door and Lisa entered. She wore a smart black suit with a gold brooch on the lapel, and a white blouse, a suede coat over her arm. Her face bore the usual meaningless little smile that was her customary expression when in the company of any of these three men. Perhaps only Brunel knew that it was an entirely mechanical expression, but this was not a fact which perturbed him at all.

Since they had moved to the hotel at early dawn she had made no reference to anything she had heard or seen during the night. She had long since learned never to refer to anything strange or frightening that might happen. She simply complied with Brunel's instructions, and kept that small meaningless smile. She said, 'I want to go to the shops for some make-up. Will it be all right if I go now?'

'Of course, my dear,' Brunel said pleasantly. 'We always like you to be as beautiful as possible.' He smiled. 'And especially now. Do you remember me mentioning a man called Garvin?'

'Yes. I remember.' She felt a little sickness in the pit of her stomach, but her expression did not change.

'Well, we've now discovered what we suspected, that he's a very bad man indeed. In fact, an Enemy.' His emphasis gave the word a capital letter. 'So I shall want you to become intimate with him, and when you've achieved that I shall be ready to tell you what to do next.'

She felt the prickle of goose-flesh on her skin. Brunel would tell her, and then the voices in her head would reinforce his wishes. His Enemy was always their Enemy. She might have argued, pleaded, even fought against Brunel, but she could not fight the voices. They did not hear, did not respond, only commanded. And no matter what they told her to do, no matter how terrible or humiliating, she must obey or they would drive her into madness.

Seeking an anchor of reality, she thought of the book she was reading, an historical romance; thought of the young seventeenth-century heroine with whom she was identifying, and allowed only a tiny part of her mind to deal with the unreality of Brunel. To him she said briskly, 'Do you know what this man's tastes are? What kind of thing he likes from a girl?'

'I've no information,' Brunel said, 'but I'm sure I can rely on you to be discerning in the matter, Lisa. Run along now.

I'll talk to you later about where and when you can make contact with him.'

She went out into the corridor, walked to the lift and pressed the button. As she waited, she was a girl named Jeannie, of Puritan stock, in love with a Cavalier being hunted down by Cromwell's men, torn between love and duty.

In the drawing-room of the suite Adrian Chance was saying, 'Garvin will know she's your creature. If he didn't know before, Fraser will have warned him. And you don't have to be smart to recognize an albino coming at you.'

'That's right,' Brunel said. 'I *want* Garvin to know Lisa's been put in by me.' He stood up, a small compact figure, and strolled to the window. 'You know, when we start to tame the Blaise girl we must be very careful in our timing. First we have to disorientate her. The right shock at the right moment. The right friendliness at the right moment. The right degree of brutality at the right moment. It should be an interesting exercise.'

Jacko laughed. Brunel ignored him and went on thoughtfully, 'Garvin will have to go, of course. Again, in the right way and at the right time. He's good, and I'm reluctant to discard the idea of using him, but we have to be realistic. Together they make a much too formidable team.' He lit a cigarette. 'Yes. Garvin will certainly have to go.'

CHAPTER FIVE

Standing in the inner doorway, Tarrant found himself in shadow. There was no natural light in the gymnasium. The fluorescents at the far end were switched on, lighting up that section like a stage. A radio was playing a Cole Porter selection. Modesty, wearing a leotard, was exercising on the horizontal bar.

Tarrant stood still, watching. Of all sports he liked best to watch women's gymnastics, for to him it seemed that this above all brought out perfection of the female body in form and movement. It called for perfect coordination of every muscle, and it called for strength to cope with the five g's exerted in the long circles.

He had not seen her on the horizontal bar before, and watched now with profound pleasure as she circled to a hand-stand, made a jump change to undergrip and followed with a giant back circle. As she continued, Tarrant decided that she was improving. It was a relaxed routine, lovely in its fluency and seemingly effortless in its execution. Hip circles now. A back uprise and fall turn. One movement flowed sweetly into the next. She finished with a spectacular fly-away somersault dismount, and dropped lightly to the mat, then walked over to the radio and began to turn the tuning dial.

Still Tarrant did not move, enjoying a little guiltily the pleasure of watching her unobserved. As far as he could tell she showed no signs of tension or anxiety; on the contrary she looked very relaxed, very young, as he had seen her look at times after a demanding exploit. He found this puzzling now. According to Fraser's message, which had been waiting for him at the airport, Modesty Blaise was at The Treadmill and wanted to see him urgently. Urgently was a word she would never use lightly. It could only mean she needed his help in some way, and so he had driven straight to Willie's pub. Brunel and the Singapore papers could wait. There was nothing to be done about them anyway. He owed Modesty Blaise a great deal, and was almost grateful for a chance to repay.

She had found another station on the radio, and ballet music filled the gym, the broad swinging rhythm of the *Blue Bird* movement. Willie Garvin came into view from behind the corner of the shower cubicles. He wore white slacks and a T-shirt, and was carrying two protective helmets, rather like fencing masks, and some sections of protective body padding.

He said, 'Ah, now that's the only sort of ballet I like watching, Princess. The jumping-about bit. With the rest of it, I always seem to laugh in the wrong places.'

She turned, smiled, pushed back a sweat-damp piece of hair and said, 'I'm going to buy you a soul for your next birthday.'

He put down his burden. 'How's this, then?' He sprang into the air, spinning round with each giant stride as he circled the far end of the gym, then leapt again, his legs crossing rapidly in a series of *brisés*. It was a wickedly excellent burlesque, and the look of aesthetic bliss on his craggy brown face enhanced it.

Modesty applauded. Then, as the music changed, she composed her features and came running forward on the tips of her toes. Her arms were extended backwards, her head thrust forward on the long graceful neck and turning from side to side, her feet turned out a little as she ran.

Willie said, 'Right, then!' He bounded after her in a series of passable *cabrioles*, pursuing her. She mimed fear, rolling her eyes ludicrously, whirled in a pirouette and faced him again, retreating. Willie stalked after her, miming wrath and menace as she shrank away. Their limbs and bodies made the classic movements, but always with that touch of exaggeration which brought an effect of high comedy to the performance.

Willie spun her round, took her by the waist and lifted her from behind. She adopted the straddle-legged and bent knee posture that Tarrant, a ballet-lover like herself, had always found rather incongruous. Slowly Willie lowered her. She touched down, but her knees were stuck and she could not rise. She mimed panic. Willie strutted away, performed a *fouetté*, strutted back, took her ears between finger and thumb, the little fingers curled in a refined manner, and gracefully straightened her up. Then they were off again, leaping, miming, pirouetting, recalling all the distinctive characteristics of ballet dancing with scandalous mockery.

Tarrant felt a sudden enormous sense of guilt. He was spying on them, watching them at play, and he very much doubted that any other eyes had ever seen them as he saw them now. They were playing out their high comedy not for

86

an audience but for themselves alone. The sheer exuberance of it, and the skill of their improvised mimicry, made Tarrant sigh with pleasure, and now he quite deliberately thrust aside all sense of guilt. He was enjoying himself too much to allow his pleasure to be marred by it, and he simply stood there in the shadows of the doorway, unashamed, or at least defiant of his scruples, watching Modesty Blaise and Willie Garvin at play.

The movement ended. Willie had just lifted her above his head with a hand on shoulder and thigh. They were not far from the horizontal bar. He said, 'Catch,' and threw her at it. She caught the bar, changed her grip as she swung over the top, and dropped to the floor facing him, just touching the hands ready to steady her.

Willie laughed happily and said, 'I bet Dame Margot never thought of that bit.'

'You must put it to her, Willie.' She smoothed back her hair, her face alight with the exhilaration of the romp.

'I wouldn't want to make Rudolf jealous,' he said, and walked across to where he had left the masks and the body padding. 'Well, let's 'ave a go with the sticks then.'

Tarrant drew back a pace very quietly, pulling the door to, then he banged on it with the palm of his hand, pushing it open, and walked into the gym calling, 'Good morning.'

'Good morning, Sir Gerald.' She came towards him, Willie following. 'You got here earlier than we expected, and that's nice. Would you like coffee? Something to eat?'

'Nothing at all, thank you.' He kissed her hand.

'Good to see you, Sir Gerald.' Willie helped him off with his coat. 'You got 'ere quick.'

'My plane was on time and I came straight from Heathrow,' Tarrant said. 'Fraser's message said you needed to see me urgently.'

Modesty and Willie exchanged a glance. She said, 'Fraser's a liar, but you know that. We do want to see you, but we thought you'd go to the office first and come along whenever it was convenient.'

Tarrant shrugged. 'I've always allowed Fraser plenty of

leeway for initiative, and I suppose he decided on the degree of urgency. Now, what's the trouble?'

'Trouble? Did Fraser say that?'

Tarrant frowned. 'His message certainly managed to create that impression. I thought you needed my help?'

She smiled. 'Do sit down. Willie, move those things off the locker.'

Tarrant sat, resting his hands on his knees, and looked from one to the other of them. They were smiling at him, and it came as an absurdly moving surprise to him to realize that what their smiles mainly held was affection. He fingered his moustache. They both bore scars of battles fought for him. It was extraordinary that they should like him. He said a little brusquely, 'Well, what's this all about, then?'

Modesty said, 'Just a minute.' She walked across the gym and through the door into Willie's workshop. Willie said, 'We were going to make a big deal of it. A cake, and candles and all that. But we didn't reckon on seeing you till after lunch, so you'll just 'ave to to take it as it comes.'

'Cake? What the hell are you talking about, Willie?'

'Your birthday present. The Princess 'as been on about it for the last couple of weeks now.'

'My birthday? Today?' Tarrant looked at the ceiling for a moment. 'Yes, you're right. But good God, I don't go in for celebrating birthdays at my age.'

Modesty came through from the workshop carrying a small brown-paper package, fastened with sticky tape. She said, 'That's ridiculous. I don't know when my birthday is, so I celebrate three times a year.' She put the package in his hands. 'I'm sorry it's not gift-wrapped, but never mind.' She stood beside Willie, an arm round his waist. 'From Willie and me, with love.'

Tarrant fingered the package. A book? A rare book? No. Too flexible for anything in hard covers. He said, 'When I was a great deal younger, I seem to remember I always tried to guess before opening a present.'

Willie grinned. 'I wouldn't try it with this. The Princess

88

chose it, and it's a bit special. I'll tell you one thing, though. It's genuine.'

Tarrant took out a small penknife and slipped the blade under the fold of the wrapping paper. This was very kind of them, very thoughtful indeed. With a flicker of dry humour it occurred to him that this could stand as his farewell present. No doubt the Government would give him a K when they chopped off his head, but he would value this more.

The wrapping fell away, and he held a sheaf of rather poor quality paper, feint-ruled, covered with a rounded handwriting in violet ink. As he read the first few words of the top page his pulse jumped. He had never seen these papers before, but he knew them. Fraser had described them minutely in his report, after visiting Brunel.

Tarrant sat staring at the sheaf of papers for long seconds. He was relieved to see that his hands were steady. Slowly he looked up.

'They're genuine,' Willie repeated. 'The originals.'

Tarrant said very softly, 'Jesus Christ Almighty. How much did these cost you?'

Willie laughed. Modesty said, 'That's a very rude question when somebody gives you a present. But we didn't have to buy them. We stole them.'

'It's cheaper,' Willie said sagely.

'From Brunel's place? From that safe? My dear, it wasn't possible. We examined every angle—' Tarrant broke off helplessly, looking at the papers he held. Then with a great effort he rallied his wits. Putting down the Singapore papers he rose to his feet, took Modesty's hands, and bent forward to kiss her on each cheek in turn, then gravely shook Willie's hand. 'Thank you for my present,' he said. 'Thank you both very much indeed. It's just what I wanted. May we have the ceremonial burning now?'

'The electric furnace is going,' Willie said, and led the way into the workshop. With a pair of tongs Tarrant placed the Singapore papers in the small furnace, and watched them turn to grey ash.

'I hope you have some small idea of how I feel,' he said. 'I'm afraid words won't do the trick.'

'We're glad you're pleased.' Modesty took his arm and they moved back into the gym. When Tarrant was sitting down again he said, 'Fraser put you up to this, of course?'

'No. Don't be angry with him about it. We asked him for ideas for your birthday present. Brunel happened to be there at The Legend, where we were dining, and Fraser mentioned the papers as a rather bitter joke. We took it from there.'

'But . . . how, my dear? It wasn't even a proposition.'

She said, 'I rather wondered that you didn't know about it when you arrived, but I take it you haven't seen the morning papers yet?'

'No. Fraser always sends them down with the car, but today they weren't there—' He broke off. 'Yes, I see. There's something in them which might have warned me, is there? And Fraser didn't want to spoil your surprise.'

She smiled. 'That must be why he sent a message to hustle you straight here from Heathrow. Our Jack's getting to be quite human.'

'I know you hate recounting your exploits,' Tarrant said. 'I've never had more than the sketchiest account from you. But I'd be obliged if you'd make an exception in this case. As it's my birthday.'

Willie emerged from the workshop with the morning papers and dumped them on the locker beside Tarrant. 'Read all about it,' he said. 'And don't fret about the bit that says the police are following up clues. We fixed a dead cut-off on every line they could follow. Now then, Princess.'

They left Tarrant and began to fasten protective padding on their arms, shoulders and torsos. He watched them for a moment, hardly registering what they were doing, then picked up the first of the newspapers. On the front page was a photograph of a demolition crane, and just beyond it the wall of a house with a gaping hole in the side, twenty feet up the wall. The headline screamed: *THE WRECKERS! Fantastic Robbery in Heart of London*. Tarrant drew in a quick breath of astonishment, then let it out slowly and began to read.

The reports in the different papers were much the same, but he read them all carefully before putting the papers aside. There were few questions left for him to ask, he thought. None at all, really. Fraser would have helped with the cut-offs on the hire of the equipment, and with the get-away, so he would be able to fill in the technical details of the job.

The newspapers referred to Brunel as a foreign business-man, and Brunel had issued a statement saying that there had been nothing of great value in the safe; that it had been installed by the previous occupant. He had made little use of it himself, except for keeping a small cash float of a few hundred pounds. The thieves had therefore wasted their time. That was very satisfactory, Tarrant decided, and won-dered what else the safe had in fact contained apart from the Singapore papers.

A clacking and thudding had been trying to penetrate his concentration. He looked at Modesty Blaise and Willie Garvin. They were in combat with quarter-staffs, each hold-ing a staff rather longer than six feet, an inch and a half thick at one end, and tapering slightly to one inch at the other. The clacking was the sound of wood on wood, the thudding the sound of a staff striking the body-padding.

Tarrant noticed with interest that they did not hold the staff with hands an equal distance from each end, as he had always vaguely imagined would be the technique. One hand gripped the staff only a foot down from the butt, the other in the middle. This appeared to be the basic grip, the ready position, but it was subject to swift change as the quarter-staffs whirled, parried and thrust. Yes, thrust. That was another surprise to him; which was stupid of him, he decided, for he had fenced much with the sabre and épée, and was well aware of the superior value of thrust over cut, even with so unwieldy a weapon as the quarter-staff.

Yet was it so unwieldy? It did not seem so in the hands of Willie and Modesty. She had once told him that Willie con-sidered the quarter-staff the most effective pre-firearm weapon ever devised, especially against odds, and that he had researched deeply to discover what he could of the technique used.

Watching now, Tarrant saw Willie make his staff spin in a hissing vertical circle – no, two circles, a kind of figure of eight movement, for he was not changing his grip. It formed a shield as impenetrable as the whirling spokes of a great wheel.

Modesty was trying to break through, now feinting for the juncture of the two circles, the gloved hands; now for a flank stroke at the more vulnerable waist of the figure of eight. Suddenly Willie changed the shape of the plane of his shield slightly. Modesty's staff was caught, and the end jarred to one side. A quick reverse of the staff in his hands and the butt swung down towards her helmeted head. But she had recovered, and whipped her staff up for the overhead guard, hands wide. With smooth economy of effort Willie reversed again, and the tapered end of his staff thrust forward, catching her squarely on the cane-cored padding which covered her torso.

Tarrant heard the small gasp from behind her mask as she folded forward. But still, as she fell, she brought the centre of her staff down hard on Willie's, bearing it to the floor, and she curled in a ball, drawing her feet up between her spread hands as they held the staff, then straightening her legs suddenly, so that Willie's staff was locked against the floor by her own, which was held behind her back now and had her added weight upon it.

They held the position for a moment. Then, behind his mask, Willie chuckled and said, 'You never give up, do you?' She relaxed, and he stepped back, drawing his staff away. She got to her feet, taking off the mask, and said, 'I don't fancy I was going to get anywhere much with that move. Your point, Willie.'

Tarrant applauded softly and said, 'I've never seen those things in use before. I'm inclined to have more respect for Willie's views on them now.'

She picked up a towel and wiped her face. 'I'm at least a couple of grades below Willie with them, so I rarely manage to touch him. But if you're as good as he is, then they're a formidable weapon all right.'

'Oh, consider me converted. But the opportunity for use seems limited. I mean, you can't carry one of them around with you in a handbag.'

Willie shook his head. 'I've never used one for real, and I don't s'pose I ever will. But we practise with 'em because they're good for *muga*.'

'I'm not familiar with the word.' Tarrant spoke idly. It fascinated him to hear them talk about their peculiar arts, but they had to be drawn gently. Eager questioning would make them change the subject.

'It's a Japanese word,' Modesty said. She was frowning a little, and with sudden intuition Tarrant knew that she was thinking about the climax of their recent bout, wondering what better defensive move she might have made.

'Japanese?' he said, picking up one of the newspapers and pretending to study the photograph again.

She nodded absently. 'There's *muga* in any form of close combat. It just means short-circuiting the mind so you react subconsciously, but with exactly the right move.' She towelled her neck slowly. 'Someone comes at you, and you take in a dozen things about their attitude – speed, balance, intent, committal, posture, and so on. And everything's changing every split second, so there's virtually a graph curve for every item. It's much too quick for conscious thought. You need to develop an instantaneous computer so you can feed in all the data and come up with the right counter. When you do get it right, the counter just flows. It's inevitable, so inevitable that it can sometimes look as if the opponent cooperated in throwing himself, or whatever it is that happens to him. The instantaneous computer, that's *muga*.' She flicked the towel at Willie and pulled a face. 'Mine wasn't so hot just now. What were we talking about?'

'Before *muga*? Nothing, I think. You were quarter-staffing,' said Tarrant. He felt that he had done very well. She had emerged from her reverie now, and would explain no more, but he was satisfied. 'I've much enjoyed reading the news-papers. Thank you again, and congratulations. I'm completely awed. Would it be out of order to ask if there was anything else in Brunel's safe?'

'No, that's all right.' She sat down beside him on the locker. 'There were a few bundles of papers. All rather cryptic, and they didn't mean much to us, but Fraser was pleased about one or two things. We gave him the papers and you can study them at leisure. Then there was forty thousand dollars in currency, which I thought we'd convert through safe channels and give to some charity or other. Willie wants to make it The Distressed Gentlefolk, so he can get well in with them in case he falls on hard times.'

Tarrant smiled and touched the newpapers. 'There are your expenses, of course.'

'Not too heavy, but we'll take them out first if it'll make you feel happier. There was one other thing in the safe, and we've kept it because it's an intriguing link with a Brunel operation I stumbled on not three weeks ago in Tanzania. I'll show you that now.' She looked up. 'Will you fetch it please, Willie?'

'Sure.' He made for the workshop. She said to Tarrant, 'You can have it, of course, but I'd like a copy, if you don't mind.'

'I feel that whatever it is, you have a moral right to it,' he said solemnly. 'After all, you stole it.'

Laughter sparkled in her eyes. 'We'd better not talk about morals. Not you and I.'

'Very well. Let's talk about Brunel. I was astonished to hear you say you'd crossed his path recently. Did you tangle with him?'

'With his muscle. Adrian Chance and Jacko Muktar.' She told him the story in a few brief sentences, too brief for Tarrant's liking. The two men had come to some hospital in an African village, questioned Giles Pennyfeather about a dead man, and beaten him up when he failed to supply the answers they wanted. She had come on the scene and put them out of action, then dumped them out in the bush. No reason given for her being there, no details about what she simply called putting Chance and Muktar out of action. A very nasty combination those two, Tarrant reflected. It must have been quite a scene. He sighed and held his peace, watching Willie return from the workshop.

'It was just this,' Willie said, and unfolded a canvas backed map thirty inches square. Clipped to the map was a transparency with grid lines on it, forming small squares of less than a quarter of an inch. Each horizontal line and each vertical line was numbered in the margin from one to one hundred and fifty. There were key marks on the map, and corresponding marks on the transparency. Tarrant fitted them together.

'A hand-drawn map and very well done,' he said, spreading it on his knees. 'Lakes and rivers and roads marked, but no names given. Now let me see . . . these dotted lines seem to indicate borders. There's something familiar about this neck of territory here, bordered by a lake on the east. Ah yes, that cluster of islands rings a bell. This is the area we were speaking of just now, surely?' He ran a finger along the dotted lines. 'Part of Central Africa. Lake Victoria here, a bit of Uganda to the north, then Rwanda and Burundi, with this section of Tanzania on their eastern borders.' He looked up. 'Large scale. About four miles to the inch, I'd guess.'

'Full marks,' said Modesty.

'And the transparency. That's just a coordinate grid. I presume there must be a cross-refence of two coordinates to give a particular location on this map. But where are the coordinates and what do they locate?'

'We've no idea,' Modesty said. 'But we're guessing that this is something to do with the dead man, and with Brunel sending his muscle to hit poor Giles in the stomach with a knuckleduster.'

'You're very probably right,' Tarrant agreed. 'One might go so far as to guess that Brunel knows what it is that's located somewhere on the map, but doesn't know the all important coordinates. Perhaps that's what he wanted from the dead man.'

From beyond the door there came the sound of somebody stumbling and half falling. Then Pennyfeather came in. 'I think it's gall-stones all right,' he said contentedly. 'I've been thinking about it.'

'You think what's gall-stones?' Willie asked blankly.

'Mrs Leggett.'

Modesty said, 'Never mind that now, Giles. They'll keep. Come and meet an old friend of mine, Sir Gerald Tarrant.'

'Oh, we've already met. Introduced ourselves and all that.' He gave Tarrant the friendliest of smiles. 'You looked jolly rotten when you arrived, sir. Looking much better now, though. Much.'

Tarrant said, a little taken aback, 'I've had good news since then. But was it that obvious?'

'Giles is very perceptive in his own field,' Modesty said. 'Don't worry. To anyone else you couldn't have looked more urbane.'

Pennyfeather advanced to the horizontal bar. 'I used to be able to chin myself when I was at school.' He was reaching up when Modesty said, 'Giles, come here a minute, please, and tell me if you recognize this.'

'Yes, all right. What is it?' He came across. She handed him the map and the transparency. He glanced at the transparency, shrugged, then looked at the map, holding it at arm's length and studying it with a frown of concentration. After a moment or two he said, 'It's just a map with lakes and roads marked on it. Couldn't say where though.'

'It shows part of Tanzania, including Kalimba, where we met, Giles. And some of the adjoining countries. Have you ever seen anything like that before? I mean, that map and that transparency.'

'Afraid not. Where did they come from?'

'You remember those two men who came to Kalimba and started knocking you about? The men I told you were here in London with their boss?'

'Yes, of course. You told me the other night and you've been body-guarding me ever since. Chap called Lebrun or something.'

'Brunel. Well, last night somebody pinched Brunel's safe,

96

and among other things in the safe was that map and transparency.'

'I read about that safe thing in the papers. How on earth did you get hold of this stuff, then?'

'It just fell out that way, darling, and it doesn't matter. What matters is that those people think the dying man told you something.'

Giles gave a breathy chuckle. 'I bet you and Willie pinched the safe. You can't kid me, you know.' He frowned. 'What dying man?'

'The one in Kalimba, who'd been tortured. Now did he tell you anything? Please try hard to remember, Giles dear.'

'I don't have to try hard. He didn't.' Giles passed the map to Willie.

Modesty said, 'Was he unconscious all the time?'

'Oh, lord no. He was conscious in snatches and delirious most of the time, babbling away like mad.'

'Babbling? Then he did say something!'

'Oh, yes. But he didn't *tell* me anything.'

She said gently, 'What exactly did he say?'

'That's the point. I don't know. He was a foreigner, and he babbled in foreign. Surely I told you that, Modesty?'

She put a hand to her head. 'Perhaps you did. Sometimes I get a little confused. What language was it?'

'Well, it wasn't French or Spanish or German or Italian. I don't mean I can understand those languages, but I can just about recognize them. He was a white Caucasian, if that's any help.'

'Well . . . it leaves a good few millions.'

Willie Garvin said, 'Ah, forget it. Come an' try chinning the bar, Giles.' It was an odd thing to say, Tarrant thought. He saw a flicker, not of puzzlement but of quick curiosity in Modesty's face, then it was gone. Pennyfeather took off his sweater, missed walking into one of the support wires by a fraction, and jumped for the bar. He heaved, drew himself up a few inches, legs kicking, then sagged at arm's length again, panting.

'Come on now,' Willie said encouragingly. 'You've got

more juice than that if you concentrate. Stop kicking about with your legs an' pump everything into your arms.'

'Right,' Pennyfeather panted, and tried again. This time he almost made it.

'Once more,' Willie said. 'Just 'ang there for a bit an' think 'ard about it. If that bloke was tortured, you must've made 'im jump when you were cleaning 'im up.'

'Couldn't help hurting him a bit,' Pennyfeather wheezed, glaring up at the bar with a grimace of fierce concentration.

'Breathe nice and easy. Pump the juice into your arms. What did 'e say, then?'

'Just kept saying "*nyet, nyet*".' Pennyfeather heaved, chinned the bar, gasped, 'I say!—' and lost strength suddenly, banging his chin on the bar as he fell. Sprawled on the mat, rubbing his chin, he stared up at Willie and said, 'Jesus, *that's* what he said, Willie! *Nyet*. He must have been a Russian, eh?'

Modesty stood up and said, 'Not bad, Willie love.'

Tarrant agreed. Willie's probe into Pennyfeather's subconscious memory had been a smart piece of psychology. Clearly Pennyfeather was a man who lived very much in the present, and simply forgot whatever seemed of no importance to him at the time.

'A Russian,' said Tarrant. 'That still leaves a very large field. But I have something to offer. It may be useless, but I'll tell you for what it's worth. About seven months ago a Russian named Novikov defected. He was a technician specializing in satellite photography. The French gave him and his wife asylum. I forget just where they settled in France, but I believe Novikov himself quietly left the country a few weeks later.' He looked at Modesty. 'Our friend Réné Vaubois of the Deuxième Bureau will no doubt give you chapter and verse if you want it. He owes you a favour.'

Modesty stood with arms folded across her waist, holding her elbows, head a little to one side, staring absently at the floor. It was a characteristic stance, which Tarrant recognized. The data was flimsy, but her instinct was at work. It was, Tarrant thought, like *muga* at a different level from physical combat. She would make deductions, calculations, conclusions which might seem to have little basis in logic but which in all probability would prove correct.

'Satellite photography,' she said. 'A map, and a coordinate transparency. I think you've named the dead man, Sir Gerald.'

Pennyfeather was sitting cross-legged on the mat now, lost in his own thoughts. 'I wonder what *sorok-dva* means?' he said vaguely. For a moment nobody spoke, then Willie said casually, 'What was that again, Giles?'

'*Sorok-dva, sto-odin.*' Pennyfeather repeated the syllables several times in a dirge-like chant. 'That's what the poor chap kept babbling. It's just come back to me. I sat with him all one night, you know, and he nearly drove me potty with it. *Sorok-dva, sto-odin. Sorok-dva, stod-odin.* God, I'm not likely to forget that in a hurry.'

Modesty had not moved, only turned her head, but Tarrant could almost feel the excitement in her. She said, 'It's numbers in Russian, isn't it, Willie?'

'I think so. I can only manage up to ten in Russian, but *dva* means two.'

Tarrant was mouthing the syllables under his breath. He said, 'I can give you the answer in a couple of minutes if you'll allow me to use the phone.'

'Sure, Sir G. In the workshop.'

Tarrant went through. Modesty walked to Pennyfeather, kicked his leg very gently with her bare foot, and said, 'Get up, Giles.' When he was standing she linked her hands behind his neck and said soberly, 'I think it's time you went away, darling. I don't want you to, but I've a hunch Willie and I are going to get caught up in something. The kind of thing where it's easy to get hurt, or even dead, if you're not used to it.'

'You mean what you call a caper, like you've told me about? Against those men?'

'Possibly. We're not starting anything, but I've a familiar sense of being nudged that way. So you'd better go away, Giles.'

'I haven't anywhere to go, really.'

'We can easily fix that.'

'Well, thanks very much. But no.' He was quite firm.

'Please be sensible, darling.'

'I am. I just think it's awfully wrong to run away from something that scares you, whether it's an op you've never done before or whether it's wicked bastards like those men, who go in for torture and terror and all that sort of thing. I jolly well hate it, you know. And every time someone gives in, they get stronger and worse.'

Tarrant came out of the workshop and stopped, watching the two of them as they stood in a loose embrace. He had heard Pennyfeather's last words. They were trite and could have sounded pompous, but coming from Pennyfeather they did not seem so. He was simply saying what he felt, without a trace of self-consciousness. He was not even being earnest about it.

'What I mean is,' he went on, 'if you want to chuck me out of the penthouse, well of course you have every right. And if some mission offers me a job in Timbuctu or where-ever, I'll go. But I'm not going to disappear just because some bloody bandits might do me a mischief if I stay around. Damn it all, Modesty, if everyone went on like that, we'd end up being *ruled* by horrible sods. You know, like the Mafia.'

Still with her hands behind his neck she looked at him consideringly and said, 'And what would the poor Mrs Leggetts and their gall-stones do then?'

'Well, yes, that's exactly what I mean. What would they?'

She said uneasily, 'I wish I knew how to argue with you, Giles. The trouble is you're horribly right. But people like you aren't geared to make a stand against people like Brunel. So you get chopped off.'

'I'm not making any stand. All I said was I don't intend to do a bunk.'

'Sometimes you're so thick I could hit you,' she said, then kissed him lightly on the cheek and let him go. 'Did you get the translation, Sir Gerald?'

'Russian numbers. Forty-two and one hundred and one. Following the normal map-reference system I'd say forty-two was the horizontal coordinate and one hundred and one the vertical.'

'Let's take a look.'

Pennyfeather ambled away and started trying to climb a rope that hung from a cross-beam. Willie laid the map on the locker and fitted the transparency over it. The reference fell in Rwanda, some twenty-five miles west of the Tanzanian border. After they had huddled over it for a few seconds Willie said, 'Are we expecting a genie to pop up and offer three wishes? It's a point on the map, nowhere special.'

'Not to us.' Tarrant straightened up. 'Let me take this. I'll have it checked by our own Map Section to give you a precise location and description of terrain. Assuming our guesses are right, there's *something* there which is detectable by satellite photography.'

Modesty nodded. 'Go ahead. I can't imagine that whatever it is will show up as a significant feature on any map, but at least I'd like to have it pinpointed on a fully detailed ordnance job – if the area has ever been properly surveyed.'

Five minutes later, reluctantly declining to stay for lunch, Tarrant took his leave. In the doorway, as Modesty held his coat for him to put on, he looked back along the gym to see Pennyfeather, a quarter-staff twirling in his hands, strike himself a sharp blow on the ankle. Tarrant winced. It almost made him shudder to think of Pennyfeather being on hand if Modesty and Willie got into a fight with Brunel's team.

She must have seen his expression, for he saw that she was looking at him a little challengingly, a hint of warning in her eyes. She said quietly, 'Don't ask me what I see in him, please.'

'My dear. I know I've very nearly been the death of you several times, but I hope I've never descended to impertinence.'

She laughed and relaxed. 'Sorry. I'm a little defensive

about him. But don't make judgements. You're not seeing him in his own element. He's out of place with people like us. Hard people. Judge him when you've seen him bring off a successful caesarian on a half-dead African woman, on the floor of a hut by lamplight.'

'God forbid!' Tarrant said fervently. 'I have my own inadequacies, so I'll take your word for it.'

The phone in the workshop rang. Modesty said, 'You'd better wait a second, it could be for you.' After a few moments. Willie Garvin came out of the workshop and walked down the gym, an odd look on his face, half wary, half amused. He said, 'That was Weng. He says a man called Brunel rang the pent'ouse five minutes ago and asked if 'e could call and see you this evening about six-thirty, Princess. Weng said you weren't there but he'd get in touch and ring back.'

'Well . . . that should be interesting,' Modesty said slowly. 'You told Weng to say yes?'

'Sure.'

'Why so?' Tarrant asked. 'Is it wise?'

Willie shrugged. 'I spent enough time riding ramrod for the Princess to know what she'd say without 'aving to ask.'

Modesty said, 'If Brunel wants to talk to me I'm not going to refuse. We're almost certain to learn something, and we needn't give anything away, so what can we lose?'

Tarrant frowned. 'Your heads, possibly. Brunel has just lost a great deal, and he's not used to that. I'd advise extreme caution.'

CHAPTER SIX

At six-fifteen that evening, in her bedroom of ivory and pale green and silver grey, Modesty Blaise sat at her dressing-table and touched a stray wisp of hair into place. She wore a black trouser suit, the jacket unbuttoned, and a yellow jersey blouse beneath.

Giles Pennyfeather came from the bathroom, pulling on a navy roll-neck sweater. 'You look terrific,' he said.

She got up. 'Thank you, Giles. Now listen, I want you out of the way while Brunel's here. You can pop into my workroom and amuse yourself with the lapidary equipment there if you like. Just don't touch that emerald I'm setting.'

'Why do you want me out of the way?'

'Because it's not your scene, darling.'

He grinned, and ran a hand over his spiky hair. 'Sometimes you treat me just like a child, you know.'

'No, don't feel like that.' She put her hands on his arms, half smiling, half frowning. 'Like an innocent, sometimes, perhaps. But that's what you are, and I like you that way. I'm a nasty, hard, cunning bitch, and that's just as well with my kind of scene, because otherwise I'd be dead. I can't change the scene, it's much too late. But you stay out of it, Giles.'

He laughed, and touched her brow with the tips of his fingers in a curious little gesture of affection. 'You do say bloody silly things about yourself. The fact is, you're really very sweet.'

'Sweet?' She gazed at him almost with exasperation. 'Oh, for God's sake, Giles. Look.' She half turned. He saw the black jacket flutter as her hand moved, then she was holding a small automatic. The act had been performed in the time of an eye-blink. She said, 'Sweet? I may very well inflict gunshot wounds on a man in the next half-hour.'

'Brunel? Why would you do that?'

'If he tries to kill me. Or Willie.' She slipped the automatic into the flat holster at the back of her hip.

'Then I jolly well think you'd be right. But do you truly mean he might try?'

'It's possible. I can't put it higher than that because I don't know Brunel. I don't know if he's vengeful and impulsive or if he's a cool-headed realist. So we're not taking chances. That's why I want you out of the way, Giles.'

'All right. But I'll have my medical bag ready so I can get him corked pretty quick. You don't want blood all over the rugs.'

She blinked in surprise, wondering if anything would ever shake Giles Pennyfeather, then nodded gravely. 'That's thoughtful of you, darling.'

'Good-oh.' He picked up his huge medical bag from beside the bedside cabinet and went to the door. There he paused for a moment, cogitating, then said with a touch of authority, 'And look here. Do be damn quick with that thing if you have to use it.'

'Yes, Giles.'

Two minutes later she went into the drawing-room. Willie Garvin stood there looking about him with care as he slipped two throwing-knives into the twin sheaths that lay inside the left breast of his jacket. For serious trouble, this was his weapon.

He said, 'You tooled up, Princess?'

'Yes.' She tapped her hip. 'The MAB two-five.'

He nodded, checking the free movement of the knives in their sheaths. Like Modesty's holster, the sheaths were made of skirting leather, wet-moulded to perfect shape, thin but unyielding as a board. The inside surface had been thoroughly rubbed with a paste of neatsfoot oil and graphite, to give a frictionless draw.

'We're probably being too careful,' he said, 'but I'd rather be a bit over-dramatic than a bit dead.' He looked round again and moved one of the armchairs a foot or two. 'Sit 'im 'ere Princess? With you standing in front of the fireplace and me by the couch?'

'Yes, fine. And let's keep him bracketed while he's moving.'

Brunel said, 'You're being very prudent, but you've misjudged me.' He sat in the armchair with hands resting on his knees. His small feet barely touched the floor. 'I'm not carrying a gun, drugged cigarettes, a watch that shoots cyanide darts, or anything exotic of that nature. I don't indulge in violent action myself.' He looked at Willie. 'I imagine you could put a knife through my hand before I could reach a pocket, Garvin?'

'Throat,' Willie corrected amiably. Brunel nodded without smiling, and turned his head. 'I've heard experts speak with admiration of your skill with a gun, Miss Blaise. You won't need it tonight, I assure you, so if you wish to button your jacket please do so.'

'You wanted to talk to me about something?' she said.

'Yes. But let us begin with a clear understanding. I am not an Adrian Chance or a Jacko Muktar. They are men who act on emotional drives, and would be delighted to kill you. I am a realist. I have a very natural regret for the severe loss I sustained last night, but since the situation cannot be restored I consider the incident closed. Do you believe me?'

'That hardly matters,' Modesty said. 'It would only matter to whoever robbed you. We read about it in the morning papers.'

'Of course.' Brunel smiled a quiet burnt-out smile. 'However, I wanted you to know my reaction to the incident, and I have the warmest professional admiration for the thieves. I'm quite sure I know which item in the safe they were after, but there were certain other items also, apart from a small sum of money,' he waved a hand, 'which is neither here nor there. The other items may be of marginal interest to those in whose hands I think they now rest. But there was one which I think may be of interest to you. May I take something from my inside pocket without risk?'

'If you open your jacket wide and do it slowly, yes.'

'Thank you.' Brunel opened his jacket, slipped two fingers into the inside pocket and drew out a long envelope. Lifting the unsealed flap, he slid out an oblong of stiff white paper folded several times. 'Would you care to look at this?'

Willie Garvin stepped forward, took the paper and un-folded it. No flicker of recognition touched his face as he glanced at it and passed it to Modesty. It was a black and white photocopy of the section of map they had studied earlier that day, and clipped to it was an identical trans-parency.

Brunel said, 'That is a copy, and I have several. The orig-inal was in the safe. I said just now that I bear no malice. I would like to give proof of that by offering you a partner-ship in a project of immense value.'

'I don't think we're interested.' She passed the map and transparency back to Willie, but Brunel made a little gesture inviting him to keep it, and said, 'I'm disappointed. How-ever, I'm prepared to risk telling you what that map is all about in the hope that you may be tempted to reconsider.'

She gave a shrug. 'I don't mind listening.'

'Very well. Some time ago a man named Novikov was working in a laboratory in Moscow. His job was to analyse the results obtained from satellite photography in all its various forms. One day he made an odd discovery, which he checked and double-checked. What he had found was a clear indication of a very substantial and accessible deposit of gold in an underdeveloped country of Central Africa – somewhere in the area covered by that map. The deposit extends for over a mile in terrain that has never attracted investigation. That means the easily accessible deposit, of course. There may be much more.'

Modesty said, 'Stop for a minute.' She looked at Willie, who rubbed his chin and said, 'Sounds a bit chancy. They use scintillometers for detecting different kinds of ore-bear-ing ground, but I'd say you'd 'ave to do that from an air-craft, not a stratospheric detector.'

'I'm not a scientist myself,' said Brunel, 'but I have access to the best scientific opinions, and I'm reliably informed that the Russians have developed and put into orbit satellites which can produce results previously possible only with low-flying aircraft. This was confirmation of what Novikov himself told me, of course. In any case the question no longer arises, because after Novikov defected he prospected the area secretly. The gold is there.'

Modesty said, 'If it's auriferous rock and low content, it might not be worth the cost of getting it out, especially if there are sulphides in the area.'

'This is an alluvial deposit,' Brunel said. 'Novikov was able to scratch nuggets out of the ground. He showed me samples. I believe this might be California '49 all over again. And the costs would be low.'

'Novikov came to you with this?' Modesty asked.

'Yes.'

'Why?'

'Because although costs would be low, they would only be relatively so. To secure a concession for mining this terrain, to bring in experts, take samples, build sluices and get the stuff out of the ground on a large scale, all this would be an operation for a very capable entrepreneur willing to make a large initial investment – and well able to protect that investment against all comers. Novikov felt I filled that role suitably. Also, I was on the spot, more or less. You may know that my home is in Rwanda, where I have a large estate. The authorities there are grateful for past and present favours, and anxious not to be deprived of my advice and good offices, so they allow me a free hand in my own small domain.'

'I see. Go on, if you wish to.'

Brunel sat back in his chair, steepling his fingers together. 'Novikov was too greedy. I offered to buy him out for a large sum, but he refused. He wanted a quite unwarrantable percentage of the gross as well. It's astonishing how capitalistic a communist can be when he sets his mind to it. And he insisted on a water-tight deal before he would reveal to me the precise location of the strike.'

She nodded towards the map Willie held. 'You mean he wouldn't give you the coordinates?'

'I do. He knew I couldn't find the area without them.

Prospecting fourteen thousand square miles, the area of that map, would be a lifetime's task. And to try aerial survey is out of the question. The map includes parts of four different countries, all very touchy about their rights, including over-flying.'

'So?'

Brunel spread his hands. 'I took the only possible course open to me. I had Novikov tortured in an attempt to make him tell the coordinates. Unfortunately he proved very difficult. In fact he contrived to escape in a manner that still remains a mystery to me. I would have thought the man incapable of crawling, let alone making his way through bush and desert to cross the border into Tanzania.' He looked at Modesty. 'It was several days before rumour of his where-abouts reached me. I take it he arrived in Kalimba un-aided?'

'He was dead and buried before I got there. Dr Pennyfeather told me he was picked up unconscious within a mile of the village.'

'Ah, the good Dr Pennyfeather. It is because of him that I have laid my cards on the table and offered you an interest in the project.'

'Because of him?'

'Yes. I believe Novikov must have told him something. I want to find out what it was.'

'Novikov told him nothing. I asked, after your muscle came and questioned Dr Pennyfeather with a knuckle-duster.'

'A dying man with a secret will babble, Miss Blaise.'

'In his own language. It meant nothing to Dr Penny-feather.'

'A dying man tends to babble repetitively, and about that which dominates his thoughts. It would surprise me if Novi-kov had not babbled the coordinates, it would surprise me greatly, since he had been resisting that very thing under torture. It would be almost a psychological inevi-tability, don't you think?'

'You believe Dr Pennyfeather lied to me?'

'No, not consciously. I think he may have forgotten what he heard, or failed to take note of it. But I'm sure his memory could be stimulated.'

Willie Garvin decided that Brunel made him feel ill. He wanted to pick up the manikin and throw him through the great window which filled one end of the drawing-room. Hard men and cruel men he had known in plenty. Brunel was something else. Brunel was an emotional neuter. You could perhaps feel a shred of pity for the man so twisted that he enjoyed cruelty, but not the man who simply used it as a tool.

Modesty said without expression, 'So what you want us to put into the partnership is Dr Pennyfeather? Then we help you torture him to stimulate his memory. Is that it?'

Brunel considered. 'I'm not sure that we would have to use painful methods. But yes, it might be necessary in the end. Would that distress you?' He sounded mildly surprised.

Modesty looked at Willie, then at Brunel again. She said, 'Let's put it this way. If Chance and Muktar come after Dr Pennyfeather again, if they try to lay a finger on him, I'll kill them this time. And then you. That's a promise.'

Willie Garvin said, 'I'm underwriting it, Brunel.'

The small man tapped his fingertips gently together. 'I'm afraid I've come here under a false impression,' he said at last. 'I thought you were in the same line of business as myself, broadly speaking.'

'Very broadly speaking, we used to be,' Modesty said. 'But even then there was quite a difference. We'd wipe out people like you, Brunel, if we stumbled across them.'

'I find it hard to follow you, but no matter. I take it you're rejecting my offer out of hand?'

'I did that to start with.'

'And you're not tempted by the prospect of enormous returns in due time?'

She said reflectively, 'The only temptation I have is to put you down now. I really should.' She studied him silently for several seconds, then pressed a bell-push set in the wall. 'You'd better go now.'

He stood up, his face quiet and untroubled. 'I'm disappointed, naturally. But as I said before, I'm also a man beyond the childishness of malice. You need not fear that you will have to implement your threat, Miss Blaise. To fight you over Dr Pennyfeather would be too expensive, I think.' He paused. 'However, if you try to use what I have told you about Novikov's secret, if you try to advantage yourself without me, then I would feel bound to enter the arena. You understand me?'

She looked at him with contempt. 'We haven't a grain of interest in your damned golden mile, except to hope you never locate it.'

'You're being emotional, Miss Blaise. But your hopes don't disturb me. I shall consider Dr Pennyfeather to be out of bounds, and seek some other approach, perhaps.'

'Do that.'

Weng appeared with Brunel's hat and coat, helped him on with the coat, then led the way to the foyer and the lift. There were no goodbyes. Modesty and Willie stood watching until the doors had closed behind Brunel, then they relaxed.

Willie said softly, 'There's a little charmer for you. I got a mucky taste in my mouth.'

'So have I. Open a bottle of burgundy, Willie.'

'Good thinking.' He went out of the room and returned a minute later with a bottle. She was standing by the window, looking down. He said, 'You reckon we can stop worrying about Giles, or was that clever bastard conning us?'

'I think Brunel meant what he said. That should end it as far as we're concerned, but I've a feeling it doesn't. I think he was operating on more than one level. He may have meant his offer, but he was laying trip-wires at the same time. The only trouble is, I can't see them.'

Willie opened the bottle and poured two glasses. 'I know what you mean,' he said thoughtfully. 'Whichever way you look, you feel something's coming up be'ind you. He's tricky all right, but where's the trick? I think what it is, Brunel gives us the creeps, so maybe that makes us see more in 'im than's there.'

'Could be.' She sounded doubtful. 'I still think we ought to ride shotgun on Giles for a bit. Until Brunel leaves the country, anyway.'

'I reckon so too. I'll stay on 'ere, and do night-shift at that surgery with 'im. There's probably two copies of *Reader's Digest*.'

She smiled. 'No you won't, Willie love. You'll go home and chase girls or whatever it is you were busy with before I came back with Giles.'

'But—'

'There's no need, honestly. Giles has got the sack again. Tonight is his last night in the job, and I'll sit it out with him myself.'

'The sack?'

'There was a letter waiting for him when we got back today. He tangled with one of the partners, it seems. A difference of opinion over a diagnosis. And Giles just doesn't know how to tread softly. Told the man he was talking a load of bilge. Genially enough, no doubt. But then . . .' She made a rueful face.

Giles appeared warily from the passage leading to Modesty's workroom, peered round and said, 'He's gone? My God, I didn't like him at all, you know.'

'You saw him?' Modesty took her glass of wine to Giles and gave it to him. Willie poured another for her.

'Yes, as a matter of fact I did. I was pretty intrigued, you see, so I crept along the passage and peeked round the corner. But I got down on my hands and knees first, so my face was right down on the floor. I was pretty sure he wouldn't spot me. Then when he got up to go, I sort of darted nimbly back.'

'You're a cunning little MD,' said Willie.

'Yes, I was a bit.' Pennyfeather drank half the wine in his glass and thought for a moment. 'The way he talked about torturing people was simply bloody.'

Modesty said, 'Torturing you, specifically, darling.'

'Well, yes, me. But it doesn't matter who. To tell you the truth, I kept hoping you'd shoot him. I still wish you had.' Pennyfeather nodded his head slowly with an air of regret. 'I don't usually wish people any harm, but I've never run into anyone like him before. You ought to have put that bugger down, you know.'

Willie said gravely, 'Getting rid of the body's always a bit of a problem.'

'M'mm, I suppose so.' Pennyfeather nodded judicially. 'Still, you had me on hand.'

Modesty looked at Willie, who gave a baffled shrug. She said, 'What's that to do with it, Giles?'

'Well, after all, I'm a doctor. I could have cut him up in the bath for you, or something.'

Willie Garvin choked massively on a sip of wine, blew it out in a fine spray, and staggered about thumping his chest, coughing and apologizing. Modesty sat down, staring dazedly at Pennyfeather, suppressed laughter shaking her hand so much that she had to set down her glass. She said, 'Giles . . . are you joking?'

'Eh? No, certainly not. It's nothing to joke about.'

'But . . .' She gestured helplessly.

'Well, good lord, a body's only a body, and I'd hate you to get into any trouble just for doing in a rotten swine like that. Public service, if you ask me.'

Tears in his eyes, still wheezing a little, Willie croaked, 'We could've shoved 'im down the Tweeny. You're lovely, Giles. I mean it, matey. Honest to God, you're lovely.'

'I know one thing,' Pennyfeather said with solemn conviction. 'You can laugh, but he's so bad he's dangerous, that chap. Brunel, I mean. I can tell, you know.'

Brunel was sitting in a taxi heading south down Park Lane. He was well satisfied. Despite her cleverness, Modesty Blaise had the fatal weakness he had suspected in her. She was emotionally a fool. The Singapore papers, for instance . . . she had stolen them for Tarrant's sake. Just that. Dear God, what must it be like to have such extraordinary motivations? Well, not extraordinary, perhaps. Most of the idiot human race seemed to have them. Brunel acknowledged that it was he who was extraordinary. And very glad to be so. Her reaction to his unemotional mention of torture had been typical. And Garvin was the same. That was all very good indeed. He had laid the bait, the invisible bait which would only become apparent when the catalyst was applied. And then it would be too late.

Very satisfactory. There had been one moment, though, a sharp and startling moment when she had considered killing him. He had no doubt that she had weighed the question seriously. And they could have done it without any difficulty at all, even if he had been armed. They had kept him bracketed beautifully from the moment he entered the room. He had felt no alarm at the time, but now, strangely, there was sudden dampness on his forehead. He dabbed his brow gently with a handkerchief, frowning.

Yes ... if she could be brought under control, converted into an instrument of his hand, she would be a priceless asset. It would take time, perhaps as long as a year, but it would be well worth while. To start with, Garvin would certainly have to go. Together they were far too dangerous to handle.

It was two days later when Sir Gerald Tarrant came to have tea with Modesty Blaise at the penthouse. Pennyfeather was there, rather to Tarrant's disappointment. He admitted to himself that he was capable of slight jealousy towards friends of Modesty who failed to win his entire approval. Not that he disapproved of the young doctor, but he found his innocence and woolly-mindedness more irritating than amusing. No doubt he had admirable qualities. If Modesty had taken him to herself, then that was certain. But for Tarrant it was not enough. And there, he told himself, was intolerance if you like.

She was wearing a fine woollen dress in green and white check, and rather dark sheer tights which would have enhanced her splendid legs if that had been possible. Pennyfeather was wearing a new navy sweater, cheap but in good taste. Tarrant decided that Modesty had chosen it and Pennyfeather paid for it.

As she poured tea he said, 'I have something interesting

for you, and I'd be interested myself to hear how your interview with Brunel went, if you feel free to tell me.' He glanced at Pennyfeather. 'I take it we can talk?'

'Yes, that's all right.' She had told Giles whatever he had failed to overhear during Brunel's visit. It had made little impression on him. The thought of an undiscovered deposit of gold waiting to be exploited somewhere in Central Africa was a remote conception which held no fascination for him. His only comment had been, 'You mean they cut and burned that poor Russian chap for *that*?'

Now she put Tarrant in the picture. Pennyfeather did not interrupt. It seemed to Tarrant that he paid little attention to what she was saying, but simply enjoyed watching her say it. This was a tendency Tarrant had found in himself at times, but the content of what she was saying on this occasion was more than enough to hold his attention.

When she had finished he said, 'That's really quite startling.'

'It's in confidence, please.'

'Oh, I shan't spread the secret of Novikov's golden mile around.' Tarrant gave a rueful smile. 'If any country's going to get the concession to prospect and work the area, it won't be us. Black Africa prefers the new imperialists of Moscow and Peking to the ex-colonialists. But I'm not so much startled at the facts of the matter as that Brunel made you a present of them. Can he really have believed you might go in with him?'

'I've thought about that. Maybe he looked back on my record and decided I was his type.'

'He must have looked very superficially.'

Pennyfeather said, 'I've told her. That man Brunel is an absolute shocker. A beastly man. If you want my view on it, the little swine doesn't feel anything, so there's nothing he wouldn't do. I mean nothing too loathsome.' He looked at Modesty. 'Is it all right if I take Weng down to the squash courts for a game?'

'I'd rather you waited a bit till I can come with you.'

'Oh really, darling. The courts are inside the building and I'll have Weng there. Those thick-ear merchants Brunel totes around can't possibly walk in and do anything to me there.'

'I've made mistakes like that before. Please, Giles.'

Tarrant said, 'If you're concerned about Brunel, I can tell you that he and his thugs flew out this morning to Paris. If they come back, I shall know within half an hour.'

She looked a little puzzled but said, 'Well, I'm pleased to hear that.'

'Amen,' said Pennyfeather, and stood up. 'It's quite ghastly having her for a bodyguard,' he said to Tarrant. 'I wanted to go to the loo in Oxford Street yesterday, and there was a Gents' handy, but she made me wait till we got home. Agony it was.'

He loped across the room, tripped on a rug and recovered, then disappeared in the direction of the kitchen, calling, 'Weng! Weng, my enigmatic little Asiatic! Come and get thrashed at squash.'

'Weng slaughters him,' said Modesty, and reached for a cigarette. 'You said you had something for me?'

Tarrant reached for his briefcase. From it he took a map which he unfolded. 'It's taken me a little while to get hold of this from the War Office, but it was worth waiting for. They've done a very good job.' The map showed part of Rwanda, large-scale, very fully drawn in colour, with contour lines, tracks and rivers, and with a key indicating the nature of the terrain.

'Since you told me Brunel's story just now,' Tarrant went on, 'I've been enjoying a small private joke. The late Comrade Novikov may or may not have had a sense of humour, but his sense of caution produced an amusing situation.' He moved to sit beside Modesty on the couch, spread out the map, and with a silver pencil touched an area where dotted lines marked out a shape roughly rectangular and five miles by two, according to the scale. Within the dotted boundary and close to the northern edge of it, a short thick cross had been made in red.

'The boundary shows the area of Brunel's estate in Rwanda,' Tarrant said. 'He calls it *Bonaccord*.'

'You must be joking.'

'No. I agree it sounds unlikely, but Brunel is very careful about his image in Rwanda, hence the name no doubt. You know that behind his front as a benefactor he's a little king-maker there? Or perhaps Government-maker would be more appropriate.'

She nodded. 'It wouldn't be too difficult in a very small, rather poor state. If you've got half a dozen key men in your pocket, you've got the lot.'

'True. And now here's the joke. The red cross marks the junction of Novikov's coordinates. That's presumably the centre of the golden mile, a valley according to the contour lines, as one would expect for an alluvial deposit. And my dear – *it's on Brunel's land*. Land on which he holds a forty year lease with all mineral rights. I've had that checked.'

Modesty said softly. 'My God.' She studied the map for a few seconds and laughed briefly, but when she looked up her eyes were sober. 'If Brunel hadn't killed Novikov before, he'd have killed him after, once he realized he'd been sold what he already owned.'

'I'm inclined to agree. Now there's just a little more to tell. Not important, but mildly interesting. While I was waiting for the map to come through, I cast around for somebody who knew the country well, and found a man at the Belgian Embassy who worked in Ruanda-Urundi, as it was called then, for several years before 1962, while the place was still under Belgian mandate. He'd never visited *Bonaccord*, but he'd travelled close to the area on several occasions. He'd met Brunel only once, and thought him a charming man.'

Tarrant laid his pencil on the map again. 'I asked him about the terrain all round this area, including these twin ridges here, which enclose Novikov's find. He told me they form part of a rather freakish natural feature. The native Watutsi have a name for it which I can't possibly pronounce but which means, roughly, The Impossible Virgin.'

Modesty lifted an eyebrow. 'I'm sure you asked him why.'

'I did. He explained that the two long ridges both rise to a kind of hump in the middle. They then converge, so the valley has a blind end. Beyond the juncture there's flattish ground, and then two small volcanic hills, here and here.' He pointed with the pencil. 'And finally a bigger and more rounded height here. Apparently when you see this complex from high ground to the north, it presents a rather remarkable effect.'

'Just a minute.' She took the map and studied the contour lines. 'Yes, I see. It's like an enormous woman lying on her back, legs apart and knees drawn up a little where the ridges rise in humps. These small hills are the breasts and this is her head.' She looked up. 'The way she's lying doesn't suggest virginity to me, does it to you?'

'I'm not an expert in these matters,' Tarrant said sedately.

She gave him a wicked grin. 'That's a pity. You're not old yet, and it would do you good. Why don't you find a nice attractive understanding housekeeper, about forty, and—'

'Really!' Tarrant expostulated. 'Do you mind?'

'All right. But I still don't think this looks like a virgin. And why an impossible virgin, anyway?'

'That was something he didn't know. Apparently it's an age-old joke among the natives, but he never bothered to find out why. Perhaps their language or their humour proved too obscure.'

'I'd have thought both would be crude and simple.' She looked at the map again. 'When I see Novikov's golden mile lying right between her legs, I feel I'd like to know how she got that name.'

'It's scarcely of any real importance to you,' Tarrant said with a touch of unease. 'I've only dug into this because I promised to find out anything I could for you. But I very much hope you don't intend to do anything about it.'

She looked at him with mild indignation. 'Why should you think I might? I don't want Novikov's golden mile.'

'Brunel's golden mile.'

'That makes no difference.'

'I'm relieved to hear you say so. I feared you might intervene in some way.'

'If Brunel ever finds his gold, he can keep it. I don't invite trouble.'

'Forgive me, but you do. Brunel is, to quote Dr Penny-feather, an absolute shocker. A beastly man. He indulges in torture. And I sometimes detect in you a deplorable touch of the crusading spirit, an impulse to deal with beastly men who are getting away with it because they can't be stopped officially in any way.'

She laughed and shook her head. 'God knows where you get that image of me.' She folded the map and gave it to him. 'There. So much for my crusading spirit. More tea?'

'Thank you, but no. I must go now.' He stood up. 'It's been a great pleasure to see you, as always. You look extra-ordinarily attractive in that dress.'

When Tarrant had gone, Modesty went to her workroom and set the emerald she was polishing in a dop-stick. With the jeweller's glass screwed in her eye she examined it carefully. The tiny flaw had been eliminated by the cutting. It was a smallish stone, but the quality was superb.

Sitting at her bench, she sprinkled emery flour on the wooden wheel and set it in motion. As she began to polish the gemstone she thought of Tarrant, half smiling as she remembered their first meeting, when he had set himself to blackmail her into an assignment for his department. She recalled the moment when, having shown the strength of his hand, he had suddenly changed his tactics by giving away his advantage, so placing her under an obligation he could in no way force her to repay, relying on his intuition that this would be more compelling than any other leverage.

A clever man, Tarrant. A very hard, ruthless man if need be. She had involved herself in other assignments for him, unasked. But now he would have it no more. In the silent war that he fought, his ruthlessness was of the old-fashioned kind that derived from necessity and was never an end in itself. He expended his paid agents, when he had to, but with miserly parsimony. And if his ruthlessness was of another age, so was his sense of obligation. Modesty Blaise had become his friend, and he would not put her at risk again.

She lifted the dop-stick and examined the facet she was polishing. Her thoughts turned to Brunel. That business was unfinished; she knew it in the marrow of her bones, and if she had not said as much to Tarrant it was only to avoid causing him anxiety. By a freak of chance their orbits had touched, hers and Brunel's. Whether she wished it or not they would touch again. An instinct sharpened by a lifetime of hazard was telling her so.

She felt neither eager nor apprehensive. To be drawn into strife was an inevitability for her, and she had long since accepted this as her destiny. During her lone childhood wanderings in the Middle East she had absorbed much of the fatalism of its peoples.

It is written. *In'sh' Allah.*

For a few moments she wondered idly how and when the business with Brunel would begin again, then she put the matter from her mind and re-fixed the emerald on the dopstick to polish another facet.

Six days later, in the afternoon, with light snow stippling the window against a background of grey sky, she was in bed with Giles Pennyfeather when the phone rang.

Pennyfeather cursed indignantly and waited. It rang only three times, then stopped. He gave a grunt of satisfaction, but she said, 'Help get us disentangled, darling. If I try to reach the phone like this, I'll do one of us a mischief.'

'But it's stopped.'

'It'll start again.'

'Well, maybe, I suppose, but we can ignore it.'

'Not this call.' The phone rang three times, then stopped again. She said, 'I'm frustrated too, Giles, but we can always make up for it. Come on now, let's get sorted out. That's Willie calling, and when he rings like that it's important.'

'Oh, well. All right then.'

After a few moments Pennyfeather sighed and lay back on the bed. Modesty wriggled over on her stomach, and as the phone began to ring again she picked it up. 'Yes, Willie?'

Willie's voice said, 'I thought I'd better ring you, Princess. You got a minute?'

'Of course. What is it?'

Pennyfeather was kneeling up, thoughtfully tracing the

muscles of her shoulders and back with professional interest. Willie said, 'Three days ago a girl walked into The Treadmill just on closing time. She was pretty upset, trying not to cry and all that. She was from Sweden, on 'er own, been 'ere a few months and planning to go back soon. She'd got a little car that she'd wrapped round a tree about 'alf a mile away. It caught fire and she'd lost everything. Money, papers, the lot. She was a bit dazed but not 'urt. Asked if I would put 'er up overnight and get 'er to the police station tomorrow, so they could get in touch with the embassy for 'er and fix whatever 'ad to be done. That's cutting a long cover story short.'

'Cover story?' Modesty turned on her side.

'Yes. She's very beautiful, but different. White 'air. An albino.'

Modesty stiffened. 'The one Fraser told us about?' Pennyfeather, his fingers on her inner thigh, said quietly, 'Hey, do you know your pulse rate a jumped a bit just then?'

Willie's voice said, 'I don't see who else it could be. There can't be many like 'er. Says 'er name's Christina, but that doesn't mean much.'

'So what happened?'

'I played along. Put 'er up for the night in one of the spare rooms. We 'ad a drink or two before she went to bed, and by the time she'd told me 'ow kind I was ten times over, I was telling 'er not to worry about anything, I'd see to the car in the morning, what was left of it, and she could stay a few days while she cabled 'er folks in Sweden for money and whatever she needed. She was good at it. Managed to suggest what she wanted without seeming to, so if I 'adn't known better it would've seemed like everything was my idea.'

Pennyfeather muttered, 'Fabulous stomach. I mean the musculature. I once dissected a cadaver almost as good, but yours is better. Oh my word, yes.'

Modesty said, 'And you've played along ever since, Willie?'

'Yes. Next day she insisted on making 'erself useful. We got nice and friendly. I took 'er out to dinner, and she ended up in my room that night. And every night since.'

'That was a damn fool risk to take!' There was a snap in her voice.

At the other end, Willie grinned to himself. Sometimes there was a flash of her old manner, from the days when she had run the taut, smooth organization of *The Network*. More than once, especially during his first year or two with her, she had shaken him up severely for taking unnecessary risks. He did not mind when she occasionally flared at him now. It was pleasantly nostalgic.

He said reasonably, 'She made the running, Princess, even if she managed to make it look the other way round, so if I'd locked me door she'd have known she was blown. And I was careful.' He chuckled. 'If she was going to do me in, it would've 'ad to be with poisoned toenails or something like that. She'd got nothing else in bed with 'er, and if she so much as sat up in the night I'd wake. You know I can sleep with 'alf an eye open.'

Modesty considered. Willie had an incredibly sharp nose for danger. And if he was satisfied . . .

She was vaguely aware of Giles Pennyfeather saying, 'They claim it's the most beautiful curve on the female body, and I must say—'

She said, 'Shut up a minute, Giles.' Then, into the phone, 'Yes, I suppose it's all right. You're on the spot so you're the best judge, but do watch yourself, Willie love.'

'Sure. The point is, I don't think she's been put in to sign me off.'

'Then what?'

'I can't figure. I didn't ring you before because I thought something would begin to show, and then I could give you the picture.'

'But nothing?'

'Not so far. D'you want me to prod things along a bit? I mean, give a few hints that she's blown, and see 'ow she reacts?'

Modesty said thoughtfully, 'You might well think she'd realize that you'd know whose team she's in. You don't find girls like that everywhere.'

'I wondered about it meself, but we wouldn't know except that Fraser mentioned 'er just once when we were in The Legend. Brunel keeps 'er well in the background.'

'That's true. I think you'd better jog along as you are for the time being, Willie. If you start prodding, we show our hand. Let's wait for her to show hers.'

'I was 'oping you'd say that. She's a very versatile girl. I'm enjoying meself no end.'

'Good for you. But exactly how do you read her?'

He paused a long time before answering. Then, 'I never found it 'arder to read anyone in me life, Princess. Whatever's there, I mean the real basic person, you feel it's buried so deep she can't even reach it 'erself. Sometimes it's almost like she was afraid to. But on top, she can be anything she wants to be. All I can see is the act she's putting on, and I can't tell what's underneath. You know what an android is?'

'I've read science fiction too, Willie. Someone just like a flesh-and-blood human being to look at, but a robot inside. Man-made.'

'That's it. Well, you feel with every reaction you get from 'er, it's just another circuit being switched in. Let's say almost every reaction.'

'Almost?'

'There's one thing. Look, don't think I'm shooting a line, will you?'

'Me? For God's sake, Willie.'

'All right. Well, she's 'ad plenty of men, but I don't think she's ever known what it is to really enjoy being with a man till now. And that's shaken 'er. She doesn't know 'ow to cope with it. I mean, whatever she's aiming to do, this is making it tougher.'

'It sounds as if you're being nice to her. Have you grown a little fond of her, Willie?'

He said at once, 'Yes, a bit. And sort of sorry for 'er. But don't worry, I'm watching meself.'

Pennyfeather breathed incredulously, 'I say, that cut on your behind! It's healed completely – can't even see the scar.'

She said into the phone, 'All right, Willie. Just play it by ear and keep me posted. I think that's the best idea.'

'Okay. How's Giles? I thought I 'eard 'im muttering in the background just now.'

'You may well have done. He's fine. Still waiting for a job. He's busy with a refresher course in anatomy just at the moment.'

'Blimey, I didn't think 'e was the bookish sort.'

'It's female anatomy and he's using a live subject.'

There was pause, then Willie laughed. 'I reckon 'e knows the best way to spend this sort of afternoon. Tell 'im I'm sorry I rang. 'Bye, Princess.'

She said goodbye and rang off. 'Listen, Giles. Willie's been picked up by a girl. One of Brunel's people. So I think there's going to be trouble sooner or later.'

Pennyfeather suspended his prodding inspection of her femoral muscle. 'I told you,' he said reproachfully. 'You should have shot that beastly little bugger while you had the chance.'

CHAPTER SEVEN

The voices in her head had not spoken for days now, which meant that they must be well satisfied with what she was doing. This was a relief, and she was grateful to Brunel for coaching her so carefully, more carefully even than usual. And all had happened as he had predicted. When she obeyed Brunel, the voices were always pleased.

She was coming to the belief that they must be unable to read some of the thoughts which stirred in the deeper reaches of her mind, or perhaps it was her feelings they could not read. This was strange, but it must be so, for in the last few days she had been guilty of frightful blasphemy against the voices. Lying in bed now, in the darkness of the early hours, with one arm curled across Willie Garvin's chest and her head resting on his shoulder, she shivered as she thought of her guilt.

But there was no denying it to herself. She had lost control and fallen into the grave disobedience of wanting him. It had happened the very first time they made love, and had almost shattered her, for she had never known such a thing before. It was achingly beautiful, so wonderful that it frightened her. The voices could not know, or they would be singing their cold, angry reprimands in her head, on and on and on . . .

She pressed her cheek gently against his flesh, awed by her own defiance. No voices spoke. Therefore they could not know her happiness and longing. But if she failed to obey them in carrying out their demands they would know, and the time had come now when she must make the next move, the final move, and then go.

A bitter sadness touched her at the thought of going. She tried almost angrily to thrust it aside, to be sensible. This man who lay beside her was an Enemy. He was wicked. Astonishing how completely he managed to hide his wickedness from her. Without the voices to guide her, without Brunel to guide her, she would have liked Willie Garvin in every way and believed him good. But that would be using her own judgement, which was a wickedness in itself, for she was nothing, a tool of the voices whose instrument she was privileged to be. They were wise, and knew all things.

Except . . . She hugged the thought to herself, hardly daring to formulate it. Except that they did not know her present blasphemy. And so she could pretend to herself. She could pretend Willie was what she would have believed him to be, and so cling to her happiness and her wanting a little longer. Only a very little longer.

But first there was the final thing she must do now, to prepare the way. She shuddered as she thought what that final thing might have been, though she had long since realized that it would have been hard, perhaps impossible, to kill this Enemy. In some peculiar way there had been no opportunity in all the eight days she had been with him, and she knew now that if she moved to get out of bed he would be awake at once.

No matter. It was pointless to frighten herself with what did not arise, for the final thing was very easy. It was also very strange, and beyond her understanding, but that had often been the way, and she did not dwell on it.

She stirred, stretching out a leg so that it rested across Willie's. He said in a voice that held no hint of sleepiness, 'You awake, Tina?'

'Yes. I'm sorry. I didn't mean to disturb you.'

'That's all right.' He put his other arm across and drew her a little closer. 'Nothing wrong, is there?'

'Yes.' She made her voice shake a little and spoke in a whisper. 'It's me. I'm wrong, Willie.'

'You? What you talking about, love?'

'I'm not what you think I am. Everything I've told you, it's all untrue. My name isn't Christina. It's Lisa. I'm not a Swedish girl. And the car accident wasn't an accident. It was all arranged.'

'Blimey.' He sounded more amused than startled. 'Why did you arrange it, then?'

'I'm Lisa Brunel.'

She felt his body stiffen, and said quickly, 'Keep holding me close, Willie. It's hard for me to say all this. So hard. I couldn't do it if it wasn't dark, and if you weren't holding me . . .' Tears came, and they were real. She buried her face against his shoulder, bewildered and confused, unable to remember the last time she had cried. Even when she had to be with Adrian Chance, and pretended to cry because he hurt her, there were no real tears.

Willie Garvin said, 'Well . . . don't take it that 'ard, Lisa. It's a bit of a bombshell, but I'm not going to eat you.'

'I know.' She fought to control her sobbing breath. 'I'm not afraid of that, Willie.'

'Good.' He eased round a little and wiped her cheek with the sheet. 'You're making me all wet. Just take it slow and don't worry.'

She drew in a few deep breaths, and was steadier. 'I'm spying on you for Brunel. I have to tell you.'

'Why d'you 'ave to tell me?'

'Because ... I can't bear it. I've been happy with you, Willie. So very happy.' It was easy. The truth fitted perfectly with what she had been told to do. 'I didn't know it was possible for anything to be so wonderful. You know, don't you?'

'I sort of guessed. What did Brunel put you in to find out, Lisa?'

'Not so much to find out anything. He just wanted me to keep a line on you.' She held him fiercely. 'I'm sorry.'

'Don't get worked up about it, love. Why does he want a line on me?'

'To know if you and Modesty Blaise start to do anything about the Novikov Project. He doesn't tell me everything, but there's something to do with coordinates. He thinks Pennyfeather may remember them. I'm supposed to keep my eyes and ears open for anything to confirm it.'

Willie laughed quietly. 'He's barking up the wrong tree, Lisa. Pennyfeather finds it quite a job remembering 'is own name. And we're not interested, anyway. How long were you supposed to keep this up?'

'At first it was to be for as long as I could keep my cover story going. You know, sending off cables and getting answers. Stalling. Pretending my parents had gone abroad and weren't expected back for another ten days. All the things I've been doing this last week. Brunel said as long as I was giving you a good time, you wouldn't be too quick to start wondering.'

'He was right, wasn't he?' Willie turned his head and kissed her lightly on the brow. 'You said it was to be for as long as you could make it. What's changed?'

She put a hand to run her fingers over his lips. 'Oh, Willie, Willie. It's finished. I go tomorrow.'

'Go?'

'That cable this morning. It wasn't from Sweden. It was from Brunel. He's in France. It just told me to cancel present arrangements and join him there.'

'Whereabouts in France?'

'Please. I – I can't tell you that, Willie.'

'All right. But look, if you don't want to go back to Brunel you don't 'ave to.'

'Yes, I do. I have to.'

He reached out and switched on the shaded bedside light. Propped on an elbow, he looked down at her. There were still tears in her eyes. Her short straight hair was white, yet it could as well have been ash-blonde, the near white colour of some Scandinavians. Her eyes held little colour and the whites of them were tinged with pink, but they were large and beautifully shaped eyes, set in small delightful features. Her body was perhaps too thinly fleshed on the fine bones, but her breasts were full and firm.

She said, 'Don't study me, Willie. I'm a freak.'

'That's bloody stupid, Lisa. If you were a freak to me, I'd be a freak to a Japanese or a Bantu. There's more difference. I just enjoy looking at a beautiful girl, any colour or no colour, and looking at you is something marvellous. Now you've made me forget what I was going to say.'

She said, 'That's nice,' and smiled, drawing his head down to kiss him.

'No, wait. This is important. Why do you 'ave to go back to Brunel if you don't want to?'

'Lots of reasons, Willie. Too many to explain.'

'Try me with some.'

'First, I'm tied to him. He's given me everything I have.'

'I reckon you've paid, one way or another.'

'Maybe. But I don't know any other life. It's very hard to tear up roots. And another thing, he wouldn't let me. He'd send Adrian Chance and Jacko Muktar after me.'

'To bring you back?'

'That. Or kill me. It wouldn't be revenge, Willie. He doesn't feel hate or anger, or anything much. He'd do it because I'd betrayed him. That's something he won't allow. I know. He's done the same sort of thing before.'

Willie remembered the interview with Brunel in Modesty's penthouse. Yes . . . the girl was right. Brunel would act against betrayal as a matter of cold policy. He said, 'If

Chance and Muktar try anything, they'll wish they 'adn't.'

'You mean you'd look after me?'

'That's right.'

'For how long, Willie? This year, next year? Five years time? Brunel's very patient. You really think you could act as watch-dog for me permanently?'

He was silent. She smiled, and there was as much under-standing as sadness in it. 'You don't have to answer, Willie. I know. You've enjoyed me a lot, and I'm so very glad for that. But you're never going to be permanent for any girl. You have your own ties. I've heard Brunel and the others talk about you and Modesty Blaise. They can't understand. And maybe I don't understand either, because I don't know her. But I think you have better ties than I have. You'll never want to break them, but you couldn't even if you wanted to. They're too strong now. And so are mine.'

Willie Garvin's mind was working on two levels. On one he was assessing carefully what Lisa said, trying to dis-tinguish the true from the false, and finding it hard to detect any false notes at all. On the other level he was taking her words at their face value, and they moved him strangely.

He said slowly, 'Where d'you come from, Lisa? Are you related to Brunel?'

She lay thinking for a moment. They had already moved into far deeper waters than Brunel had coached her for, and she was in an area where she had to use her own judgement. That was new and difficult. She listened for the voices to guide her, but they did not speak inside her head. So what she was doing must be satisfactory to them, even though she was simply following her own feelings and impulses. As long as she brought about the final aim of what she had to do, all would be well. It seemed that for once she need not act a part. She could simply tell the truth.

She said, 'I'm not sure where I come from. If I try to remember it makes my head hurt.' Better to put it that way. She could not tell him about the voices. 'I think I was fifteen when Brunel bought me.'

'Bought you?'

'In Morocco, I think it was. I'd been bought before, from my mother. She was a poor Arab. Very light-skinned for an Arab, a mixture, I expect. My father . . .' She shrugged in his arms. 'I never knew him and I'm not sure my mother knew who he was, but I suppose he must have been European. I hardly remember those years. I was still young when my mother sold me. It was to a pimp who ran a café somewhere, where men came to buy girls.'

'Fom the Hedjazis?'

'What are they?'

'Arabs from just east of the Red Sea. There's still a profitable line in white and black slavery goes on, and the Hedjazis are specialists from way back. They send out agents to buy for them, all over North Africa and farther south, and they'll pay till their nose bleeds for a white girl. Were you a virgin still, Lisa? I mean when the pimp finally sold you.'

'Yes. Is that important? I thought it must be, because this man kept me for a long time, years, and he never let me be touched. I just used to help in the kitchen at first, and then when I grew older I had to wear trousers and bangles and serve in the café.'

'That sounds like the routine. He was saving you up to get a big price. A fifteen-year-old white virgin would fetch some crazy bidding.'

'And I'm whiter than most,' she said, and turned her head away.

'We've gone over that already, Lisa. Stop feeling sorry for yourself. You're beautiful, and you got no right to. Come on, look at me. Now smile.' He touched her cheek and ran his fingers through her hair. 'That's better, love. Go on.'

'It's strange, I remember more since I began telling you. One night Brunel was in the café. The others, the agents I suppose, they didn't like it, but they were afraid of him. He had three other men with him, white men, but not Adrian or Jacko. I didn't see those two till a long time later, perhaps a year.'

'That was when Brunel bought you?'

'Yes. He took me away that night, and I was at his place in

Rwanda for a while, then at a school in Switzerland, for two years, a special school. Then back to Rwanda. After that he took me everywhere with him, whenever he travelled. By that time he'd adopted me legally as his daughter. I think he did that while I was at school.'

'And he uses you for this sort of thing – I mean men?'

'Yes.' Sudden fear swept her. In telling so much of the truth she had come close to lowering all her defences, close to dangerous ground. If she told some of the ways in which Brunel had used her, Willie Garvin would draw back from her as a thing of loathing. He would not understand that she was nothing, an instrument of the voices. Besides, he was an Enemy. She must remember that. She must be careful.

He said, 'You all right, love? You look a bit queasy.'

'It's nothing. Just a queasy sort of thing to talk about, I suppose.' She swallowed, and drew in a breath. 'I have to pick men up for Brunel, and find out things, and let him know what they're doing. Like now, Willie. Like now, and I'm sorry, except that it's never been like this before. The rest of the time Brunel uses me himself, or lets Adrian Chance have me. I didn't want to tell you that.'

Willie Garvin lay back. The thought of that cold-fish little manikin using her body to slake his mechanical desires was macabre. After a while he said, 'Lisa, I can't always figure what goes on in your 'ead. You know Brunel's a crook and a villain, don't you?'

The Enemy would say that, of course, and Willie Garvin was an Enemy. It was harder all the time to remember. But she must not argue with him. Brunel had been emphatic about that. She said, 'Those are just words, Willie. What he is doesn't mean anything to me.'

'Break with 'im, Lisa. Do it now. We'll work out something.'

'Don't keep on at me, Willie, please!' She said the words almost in panic. 'I'm leaving tomorrow. I can't break with him. I won't. Maybe I don't even want to. There's so much you don't understand.'

'Then tell me.'

Very slowly, her voice dragging wearily, she said, 'I can't

tell you, because it can't be said in words. It's in my head, Willie, all in my head.' It was as close to the truth as she dared to walk.

They lay in silence for several minutes. She knew he was not angry with her, for his hand kept squeezing her shoulder gently, soothingly as they lay. At last he said, 'I won't keep on. It's your life, love.'

She relaxed thankfully. It was done now, all but the final words she had to say, the important words, and they must not be said yet. They must be said only at the very end, when it would be too late for questions.

He asked, 'What time you leaving, Lisa?'

'At seven in the morning.'

'Okay. I'll drive you to the airport.'

'No, Willie. I've got a hired car coming to pick me up. I don't want airport goodbyes. I don't even want you to get up. I'll just say goodbye now, and when the time comes I'll get up and go.'

'Money?'

'I've plenty really. And luggage at Heathrow.'

'It's 'ardly worth going to sleep again. Like me to get you a cup of tea or coffee?'

'No. I want you to stay close to me. Say goodbye now, and then we won't have to say anything later.'

'Well . . . goodbye then, Lisa. And good luck. It's been nice 'aving you.'

'It's been nice being had. You want to have me now, Willie?'

'Only if it's what you want.'

'Yes. There's lots of time. I want you to make love to me for a long time in a big way.'

He turned to her, looking down at her, and began very gently to caress her face, her neck and then her body. He was unhurried, sometimes talking softly, telling her that she was beautiful and exciting, meaning it, finding the touches that gave her deepest pleasure.

There was lots of time, she knew, lots of time for the burning within her to grow steadily more fierce, rousing her until she strove demandingly with him. The anticipation of what was to come, of all that they would do together, was almost too piercing to bear.

She let go, and became herself, as a puppet by some magic might have life of its own for a brief hour. The voices were forgotten. Brunel was forgotten. She let the world fall away.

It was six-thirty when Willie roused her from sleep, gently patting her cheek. 'Time for you to get up, love. The car's coming at seven, you said.'

She tried for a few moments to cling to the wonderful unreality she had known before she had fallen asleep half an hour ago, then was frightened at her own deceit and wickedness. She prayed to nothing in particular that the voices would never know how she had abandoned them for a time to indulge her own desires. That was black blasphemy.

She said, 'All right. Stay there, Willie.' She got up, putting on the dressing-gown he had lent her, and went through into the bathroom to take a shower. As she dried herself, dressed, and made up her face, she kept her mind a blank, concentrating only on whatever she was doing at any moment. There was nothing to pack. She had only a handbag and a few toilet and make-up necessities Willie had bought for her. By five to seven she was ready. From the bathroom, by opening the window a little, she could see the approach to The Treadmill. She waited two or three minutes until she saw the car arrive, then went back into the bedroom.

Willie was sitting up, smoking a cigarette. He said, 'You look great, Lisa. Terrific.'

'The car's here, Willie. I'm going now. No goodbyes.'

'Sure.'

She went to the door, and hesitated. Slowly she said, 'I'm so glad. So glad it worked out this way.'

'What way, Lisa?'

'Brunel pulling me out. It must mean he's leaving you alone, not interested in you or Modesty Blaise or Pennyfeather any more. I'm glad of that, glad the other line he was working on has come good.' She gave a small forced smile. 'I guess I'm greedy, but the only thing I wish is that it hadn't come good for another week.'

'Me too,' Willie said, and studied the tip of his cigarette. 'I didn't know there was another line.'

She shrugged. 'Novikov's wife. He must have located her at last.' The final words, the important words she did not understand, had been said. She was pleased to have said them almost absently, as if they were of no importance at all, as Brunel had coached her. Conveniently the car hooter sounded. She looked at her watch. 'I have to go, Willie. Remember me sometimes.'

'Sure.'

She went out, closing the door. Willie Garvin muttered, '*Christ!*' and threw back the covers. From the bathroom a minute later he saw her get in the car. He watched it move off, then went back into the bedroom. Grinding out his cigarette in the ashtray, he sat on the edge of the bed and picked up the phone.

Four hours later, in the penthouse, Tarrant said curtly, 'You told me that you wouldn't look for trouble with Brunel, but that's exactly what you're doing.'

Modesty said, 'Oh, that's not fair. We didn't look for it, we've just become involved.'

Tarrant exhaled audibly. 'Involved? Why? We have a situation in which a Russian woman, Novikov's wife, who means nothing to you and whom you've never even seen, is likely to be interrogated by Brunel. Possibly in a loathsome manner, agreed. But I imagine there are hundreds of unfortunate people in the world at this moment suffering interrogation of a similar kind. One or two of my own people, perhaps.'

Modesty said, 'The Novikov woman has been thrust under my nose, the others haven't.'

Tarrant looked at her curiously. 'Do you really feel bound to intervene?'

'Feel bound? I don't know.' Her manner was impatient. 'All I know is I've done a lot of things less worthwhile than stopping Brunel getting to work on her with a red-hot knife or whatever takes his fancy.'

'The trouble with you,' Tarrant said with sudden asperity,

'is that you're developing into a blasted do-gooder, poking your nose into other people's troubles. You'll be carrying a banner next.'

Her laugh was full of delight at the absurdity, but Pennyfeather said soberly to Tarrant. 'It's all very well for you to talk, but I saw what they did to Novikov. Bastards.'

Tarrant made a gesture of resignation and sat back in his chair. The thing had begun now, and he had no chance of stopping it. Only ten minutes ago Réné Vaubois of the Deuxième Bureau had telephoned from Paris with the answer to Modesty's call made earlier that morning. He reported that soon after being granted asylum in France, Novikov had flown to Uganda, leaving his wife in a small flat in Paris. He had hired a truck and supplies in Kampala, set off for an unknown destination, and never been seen again. The Ugandan authorities had presumed his death. Madame Novikov had left the Paris flat and gone to Switzerland. Vaubois did not know why, but guessed that it was to pick up some funds there. Both the Deuxième and the CIA had paid Novikov for the technical information he had been able to supply. She had returned to France only a week ago, and rented a small farm cottage in Pelissol, a village in the Dordogne. Vaubois had been in touch with the local gendarmerie at Pelissol, and had been told that Madame Novikov was still there. And now Modesty Blaise was planning to go to Pelissol today.

Tarrant felt depressed. It was going to happen again, he could see it crystal clear. Modesty intended to tangle with Brunel, and this time it would have to be final. He said sourly, 'This damned albino girl was probably conning Willie.'

'Could be.' Willie looked up. 'I reckon there's about one per cent possibility.' He smiled. '*The lips of a strange woman drop as honeycomb, and 'er mouth is smoother than oil.* But I don't reckon so this time.'

'With Brunel, I don't like even a one per cent chance.'

Pennyfeather looked blankly at Willie. 'Where do honeycombs come into it?'

'Psalm five. Verse three.'

'Eh?'

Modesty said, 'Willie learned the psalms by heart in his youth, while he was doing a little time in the coop in Calcutta. He has quotations for all occasions.'

'Oh, I see. I was never much good at learning things by heart myself. But I've never been in clink, of course.'

'Never mind, darling, we can't all have Willie's advantages.' She looked at Tarrant. 'How could the girl be conning him? She was put in to keep tabs on us, and then pulled out. She didn't try to sell him any kind of gold-brick. In the meantime she fell for him and spilled a lot of things Brunel could never want known. He may be a cold fish but he'd hardly want to parade the fact that he lays his own adopted daughter and lets Chance have any spare rations. Where's the trick? And do you really think she could take Willie in?'

'Perhaps not.' Tarrant groped for a thought that would not quite take shape. 'But perhaps she didn't know she was taking him in.'

'What does that mean?'

'God knows,' Tarrant confessed. 'It's just that Brunel and his works frighten me.'

She said almost gently, 'We can't let that stop us.'

Willie stood up. 'You want me to try booking normal flights or a private aircraft, Princess?'

'Private, I think, Willie. See if Dave Craythorpe's available. He can put us down at the nearest airfield to Pelissol and save the journey from Paris. We don't want to lose any time.'

'Right.' Willie picked up the phone and began to dial. Modesty sat down in an armchair, leaning back, hands behind her head, legs crossed. She seemed to be studying the Paul Klee that hung on the cedar-strip wall in front of her, but Tarrant knew that with the decision made she was setting her thoughts in order. He knew, too, that there could be no half measures. She was going to stop Brunel indulging in yet another torture session, and she could only stop him by destroying him. Simply to thwart him would be to invite her own destruction at a time and in a manner of Brunel's choosing. And so she would take the initiative now. From this moment on, there was no question but that one or the other would die soon, and Tarrant feared Brunel greatly. As far as he knew, and except in the matter of the Singapore papers, Brunel was a man who had never lost, never even come close to it. He had resources of which Chance and Muktar were only the spearhead. It was true that Modesty and Willie also had never yet lost a battle in the end, but they had come very close to it several times, for they worked alone, without hirelings, and so often went in against stacked odds.

Sadly Tarrant allowed himself to enjoy the sight of her now; hair black as raven's feathers, small nose, eyes that varied from deep indigo to midnight blue, wide mouth with the lips pursed a little now as she reflected, and the long lovely neck. With her shoulders drawn back by the lift of her arms, the breasts were full and rounded against the ice-blue cashmere of the shirt-dress she wore. Very little of the slim, strong legs were hidden as she sat now, and for all their strength there was no bulge of muscle. Flat shoes on long narrow feet. Tarrant smiled wanly to himself. She always thought her feet too big, but they were right for her.

It might be the last time he would be able to enjoy looking at her, he told himself. He knew her skill and resource, knew her physical and mental strength; but all flesh and blood and bone was fragile, so easily destroyed. Brunel might be the man to destroy her.

Willie put down the phone and said, 'Dave can take us at fifteen 'undred hours.'

Tarrant got up. 'I'll be going along then,' he said.

She came out of her reverie and rose, giving him a warm smile. 'It was good of you to come round when you've no official interest in this. But it seems you've taken to spoiling me. I'm very grateful.'

'I've an official interest in anything Brunel gets up to. I'm only sorry I've been no help.'

'You can be. Could we have the map you showed me?'

'The Rwanda map? What on earth do you want it for?'

'Because Novikov's wife may have gone before we get to Pelissol. Brunel may already have taken her, or he could be at the house this minute, but he won't hold his inquisition there. He'll take her off to Rwanda. I'd guess he has a private aircraft ready for the job.'

'And if so, you propose to follow?'

'We can't just turn round and come home.'

Tarrant traced the pattern in one of the Isfahan rugs with the ferrule of his umbrella. 'When you get your teeth into something . . .' he said. 'All right. I'll send the map round to you within an hour.'

'You're a nice man.'

'Remember Brunel isn't.' He turned to look at Pennyfeather. 'Will you be staying on here, Doctor?'

'Me? Lord, no. I'm going with them. What shall I pack, Modesty?'

There was a moment of silence, then Modesty said, 'But Giles dear, you're staying here – that's if you want to. I mean, you're not coming with us.'

Pennyfeather blinked and stood up. His limbs seemed to unfold erratically, yet there was a curious touch of dignity about him. 'But I have to come,' he said, his rather penetrating voice much quieter than usual. 'You'll need me.'

'I'm sorry, Giles, I don't understand. Need you for what?'

He shook his head, vaguely puzzled. 'Well, I thought that was obvious. Sometimes you're a bit slow, darling. I suppose you've been thinking about dealing with Brunel all this time, but I've been thinking about poor old dead Novikov's wife. I mean, what are you going to do? Walk in on her and say, hallo Mrs Novikov, there's a horrible little bugger who tortured your husband to death and he's coming to get you, but don't worry, we'll protect you? Christ, do you think she'll *believe* you?'

There was another silence before Willie Garvin said slowly, 'She won't, Princess. She's Russian an' she's a defector. She'll suspect everyone and everything.'

Tarrant gave a brief laugh. He said to Modesty, 'Would you like another opinion on the doctor's verdict? I entirely agree that she'll be too suspicious to believe you or to fall in with whatever plans you may make. But *his* presence won't alter that. She won't believe him either.'

Modesty did not answer. She was looking at Pennyfeather with a touch of wry humour, like a fencing master acknowledging a hit scored by a novice, and rather proud of the prowess displayed. It was Pennyfeather who answered Tarrant. He said, 'Of course it'll make a difference if I'm there. She pretty well knows her husband must be dead, and that's all. But I was with him when he died. When I tell her about it, she'll believe me.' He turned. 'I'm sure she will, Modesty.'

'Yes, Giles. You're quite right.' She looked at Tarrant. 'He doesn't know what guile is, and it shows. Any woman would believe him. And more than that, trust him. You can take my word for it. I'm a woman, and I know.'

Pennyfeather said indignantly, 'Look here, I know perfectly well what guile is. I have to be *jolly* guileful dealing with my patients sometimes, I can tell you.'

'I know, Giles dear. I just didn't want to boast about you.'

'Oh, I see. Well, we'd better get busy. I'll take my medical bag, of course. What do you want me to pack in the way of clothes?'

'Just about everything you have will go into an airline hold-all, darling. Except your monstrous great sweater that looks like frayed rope. Leave it behind, and you can borrow a duffel coat of Willie's instead.

'We're not the same size. I'd look silly in it. I'll go and see if I can sort of roll the sweater up and strap it on outside.' He ambled away and vanished into Modesty's bedroom.

Tarrant took her hand and touched it to his lips. 'I wish you well,' he said. 'You once told me not to ask you what you saw in Dr Pennyfeather. I haven't. And now I shall never even ask myself. He's what you inaccurately called me just now.'

'What did I call you?'

'A nice man.'

CHAPTER EIGHT

Three hours had passed since the early nightfall of mid-March closed over the brown fields and the little cottage which stood alone on the slope above the village. It was warm within the thick walls of the cottage. Modesty sat on a worn couch near the ancient fireplace where dry logs crackled. She wore black slacks and shirt, her windcheater lay beside her.

A woman stood by the scrubbed table, cutting slices of crusty bread and putting them on a plate, her hands moving slowly. She was a well-built woman of forty, in a brown dress, her figure good except for the beginnings of thickness at the waist. Modesty studied her. Short dark hair with a few early threads of grey framed a strong Slavic face. The eyes were still beautiful. She moved to the range and poured boiling water into an enamel coffee jug, then wiped her hands on a tea-towel.

'Poor Mischa,' she said. 'He hoped so much. All was to be very good for us. But when he went from me, I felt it was a last going away. When he did not come back, I knew. And now you have told me.' Her English was slow and heavily accented.

Pennyfeather was unwrapping a packet of butter and putting it on a dish. It was only an hour since he had arrived at the cottage, but he was completely at home. The hired self-drive car in which they had travelled from Bordeaux was hidden in a stand of trees a quarter of a mile away. Willie Garvin was somewhere outside in the darkness, on watch. They had checked round the cottage carefully before sending Pennyfeather in on his own, and half an hour later he had emerged to tell them that all was well. Madame Novikov had accepted him and believed him. She had not wept, neither was she showing any sign of fear, only a quiet sorrow possessed her.

'Poor Mischa,' she repeated, and looked at Pennyfeather. 'I thank you for what you do for him, Doctor.'

'I just wish I could have pulled him through. I did try hard, but it was no go. I say, there's simply tons of bread here. We don't want to eat you out of house and home.'

'There is a long night, and you must eat. Also the other gentleman outside. There is cold, and some snow. I am sorry to have only a little cheese and meat, but I did not expect.'

'You mustn't trouble about us, Madame,' Modesty said. 'We may have to wait here for several days, and we want to make as little work for you as possible. Tomorrow we can arrange things better.'

'Tomorrow is tomorrow. Today you have travelled far and must eat.'

'You're very kind. Do you understand about this man Brunel? You may feel you want to run away, but I think he would find you in the end. It's better to settle things now.'

'I understand, miss. I am Russian and we know these things. I do not want to run away.'

'You're jolly brave,' said Pennyfeather.

'No. I am afraid. But for one year now I have been afraid. I become used to this.' She was cutting pieces from a cheese. 'Poor Mischa. He was so sure. He would see this man Brunel in Africa, and tell him of the gold, and then we would be rich. But always I was afraid the KGB would come to kill him. They do not let go easily.' She put down the knife and looked at Modesty. 'What will you do when Brunel comes?'

'He won't come alone, Madame. He'll have men with him. Two men, we think. We expect to intercept them before they reach the cottage, so I hope you won't know anything about it until it's all over.'

'You will kill them?'

Modesty hesitated, wondering how Madame Novikov would react. But the question had to be answered, and the Russian woman herself had put the thought into words.

'I think we have to kill them, Madame.'

The deep brooding eyes turned to Pennyfeather. 'You say this also, Doctor?'

Pennyfeather pushed his fingers through his bush of hair. 'I know it sounds a bit drastic, Madame. But honestly, they're absolute shockers, and we're terribly afraid of what they'll do to you. As this young lady explained to me, the police can't keep guard on you permanently, and they can't take any action against Brunel for *intending* to commit a crime, only after he's done it. And that's too late to help you. So really, what else can we do?'

She looked at Modesty again. 'I think the doctor does not want to. He would like to find another way. But there is not. I know. You know.' She rested her hand on the knife, looking down at it. 'I would kill them myself. I am glad they will die. My poor Mischa. In all his life he did not hurt any person except in war.'

Modesty said, 'They want the coordinates, the figures which tell where the gold-bearing land lies. Do you know them, Madame Novikov?'

'I know. Mischa told them to me. But I will not say them even to you, miss. Even to the doctor. I promised Mischa.'

'Yes, we understand. We have no interest in the gold and we don't want you to tell us.'

The woman was cutting slices from a small half-leg of lamb now. Pausing, she said to Pennyfeather, 'You do not know them? My husband did not tell you before he died?'

Modesty tried to catch Pennyfeather's eye. It was unlikely that he would understand her warning look, but an obscure instinct in her urged that nobody should be told that he had remembered the coordinates, not even Madame Novikov. The knowledge was dangerous. She failed even to draw his glance before he spoke. He gave a smiling shrug as he said, 'No, you needn't worry about that. I think he may have *tried* to tell me, but he was delirious, you see. He just kept saying things in his own language, and I'm afraid I don't know a word of Russian.'

Madame Novikov went on cutting slices of meat, slowly and methodically. Modesty kept surprise from her expression. Was Giles learning guile after all? Then she saw his eyes as he watched the Russian woman, and suddenly she understood.

Poor Mischa had died to keep his great secret. His wife was widowed now, and the secret was all that was left to her of poor Mischa. It was hardly likely that she could ever exploit it, but at least it was hers. To find that it had been discovered would bring a renewed sense of loss and distress. Giles had known that, had perceived it at once with the unexpectedly subtle instinct that was his gift, and he did not want to add to her sorrow. He had just broken cruel news to her, and for the moment he stood to her as doctor to patient. *'I have to be jolly guileful dealing with my patients sometimes . . .'* he had said less than twelve hours ago; and Modesty saw that it was true, that in this respect alone he was able to lie with all the conviction that his innocence lent him.

Madame Novikov brought the coffee-pot from the range and poured black coffee into big earthenware mugs. 'You bring the gentleman from outside now?' she said. Giles started to get up, but Modesty said, 'No, Giles.' Then, to Madame Novikov, 'He has to stay on watch, Madame. But don't worry. I'll take over from him in a little while, then he can eat.'

The Russian woman was troubled. 'It is not good,' she said. 'Very cold outside. Better he have some coffee now, to be warm. I will take to him.'

'I'll take it myself. You mustn't go outside, Madame.' Modesty picked up her windcheater. 'And I'll take my own along, if you don't mind. I want to have a few words with him.'

She was glad to get out of the cottage, and realized with a touch of shame that she did not warm to Madame Novikov. To feel sympathy for her called for an act of will. Perhaps it was the woman's stolid resignation that was oppressive. Giles seemed quite unaffected by it, but Giles of course was almost entirely selfless. She grimaced at her own inadequacy, and made her way carefully across the moonlit yard and along a thin track leading to an out-house.

Willie Garvin's voice said softly, 'Over 'ere, Princess.' He was standing where the corner of the little wooden building threw thick shadows, and was almost invisible to her until she came within four paces of him.

'Coffee, Willie love. She was worried about you getting cold, so I brought it out.'

'Thanks, Princess.' He took the mug and she stood beside him in the shadows. 'You needn't 've bothered.'

'Better to leave her with Giles for a while. He has a knack.'

'Yes.' He sipped the coffee gratefully. 'Blimey, she serves it sweet.'

'She didn't ask how many spoonfuls. We'll just have to take it as it comes. Ugh! I see what you mean.'

'Never mind. It's 'ot.'

'There's that. And she's raiding her larder. We'll have to arrange for supplies if this goes on for long, Willie.'

'M'mm. But I reckon Brunel's going to turn up pretty quick.'

'So do I. What did you make of Madame?'

'Only saw 'er for a couple of minutes. Not all that lively. Quite a looker once, maybe, but a bit slow upstairs.'

'She knows the coordinates. Novikov told her. But she's not telling. Not anyone.'

'She'd soon tell Brunel once 'e turned Chance loose on 'er. What way do we play it when they come?'

'As far as they know they've nothing to worry about, just a woman to deal with. So I can't see them making a sneak approach on foot. I should think they'll come by car, along the dirt road. We'll see them minutes before they arrive. They might ... no, wait a minute. If they come by day ... no, I mean by night—' She paused, trying to collect her thoughts, which seemed suddenly confused.

'Sorry ... wha' d'you say, Princess?'

She leaned her head back against the hut, trying to think, torpidly puzzled that Willie's voice should sound slurred. 'Listen, Willie ... I said—' But what had she been going to say? It eluded her.

Something shattered on the ground, and liquid splashed over her feet. The mug of coffee had gone from her hand.

Everything was going away from her, dwindling in perspective. Something bumped heavily against her shoulder. Willie was slithering down against the planking of the outhouse, holding his mug with great concentration, trying not to spill the coffee. She made an effort to catch him, but all strength drained out of her, and as he went down she fell sprawling across his legs.

She had one brief instant of bitter clarity, in which she saw Giles Pennyfeather drinking his coffee and sagging unconscious across the table, Madame Novikov watching him with her sad, beautiful eyes. She heard Willie say effortfully in a drunken voice, 'One per cent ... Lisa ... she conned me ...'

Then dark waves rushed upon her and drew her down.

Three minutes later the woman in the brown dress, wearing a topcoat against the cold now, walked without haste along the little footpath from the cottage. Shading the torch in her hand, she shone it down briefly on the two still figures. She switched off the torch and walked on up the slope to the low crest of the ridge. There she faced south across a shallow basin of land, pointed the torch, and flashed it slowly and deliberately six times.

Vibration. The muted roar of engines. Her head was hanging on her chest. Mouth dry and sticky. Nausea.

She lifted her head and drew in a deep breath to push down the queasiness. Willie Garvin's voice said, 'Take it easy, Princess.' He did not have to speak loudly. It was quiet inside the aircraft. Her eyes were still closed, and she kept them so while she fought with the inevitable surge of fear, absorbing it, taking hold of it and sealing it away in the dark void within her where it could not corrode her defences.

Two minutes passed. She opened her eyes, turned her head and gave Willie a little nod, then looked about her. Later she might spare time to blame herself for falling into the trap, but for the moment her mind was totally focused on assessing the situation.

A Dakota, with the seating modified, some of the seats removed to give more space and comfort. A section of the cabin partitioned off. Probably a sleeping compartment. A rich man's private aircraft, well appointed. She was in a double seat. Giles Pennyfeather was beside her, still unconscious. Instead of a normal seat-belt, two crossed straps held him upright in his seat. She was held in the same way herself. To her left was Willie Garvin. They were all three secured in strait-jackets. Willie was not in one of the normal seats. Straps across his lap and at his ankles held him to a plain wooden chair, its four legs set in steel collars with flanges which slotted into sockets bolted to the deck. There were signs that this was a makeshift job, and she did not understand it, for there were empty seats available. Through the window beyond Willie she could see thin grey cloud and a line of gold on the horizon. So it was nearly dawn, and they were flying south. Rwanda seemed the likely destination.

In the double seat facing her sat Brunel, beside a pale girl wearing dark glasses. She had fine features and short hair, ash-blonde. No, white. This was Lisa, then. On the port side she saw Adrian Chance, alone, and when she turned her head she could see Jacko Muktar farther aft. Jacko was looking out of a window. Chance was reading a magazine.

They ignored her. When Jacko glanced round for a moment, when Chance looked up from the magazine, their eyes passed over her as if her seat had been empty. This was out of character. It must be a tactic of some sort. She put it aside to consider later.

No sign of Madame Novikov. But the woman in the cottage, the woman who had served them with drugged coffee, was not Mischa Novikov's wife. That was shatteringly obvious now. No untrained Russian housewife could have brought off such a skilful deception. She had certainly been one of Brunel's contacts, hired for the job, and she had played the part superbly. Brunel knew where to find whatever kind of talent he wanted.

It had been the subtlest trap imaginable, yet simple in essence. First, offer Blaise and Garvin a partnership and use the opportunity to test their reaction to the concept of severe torture. Then set up Novikov's wife as a victim and use Lisa to leak the fact to Willie Garvin. But meanwhile replace Novikov's wife with someone clever enough to act the part. Then simply wait for the expected reaction. Blaise and Garvin come hotfoot on the scene, ready for trouble from any quarter but one – from the supposed victim. And without any trouble at all she serves them drugged coffee. No fuss, no violent action, no problems.

And the real Madame Novikov? Impossible to be sure when the switch had taken place, but the woman who had returned from Switzerland to France a week ago must have been the fake. Yes ... that would be at about the same time that Brunel had put Lisa in to float the lure for Willie Garvin, to drop the last-minute hint that Brunel had located Novikov's wife. Probably Brunel had located the woman as soon as Novikov escaped, had questioned her and killed her. If so, she could not have known the answer to his questions.

It had all been planned with immaculate precision. The one very small bright spot on the whole horizon was that for his own reasons Giles had denied knowing the co-ordinates when the fake Madame Novikov had asked him. Modesty realized now that her own instinct had been true in that moment; but she should have given more thought to it, wondered why something deeper than reason was warning her. Well ... it was too late now.

Cautiously she tested the strait-jacket, not for strength, that was a waste of time, but for the amount of give in the canvas sleeves and the straps which ran from the sealed cuffs to buckle in the middle of her back, holding her arms wrapped round her body.

Strait-jackets were for restraining people who had lost their reason. You could get out of one if you knew how, and given a little time; perhaps two minutes if you were strong and supple, and if there was enough give in the sleeves and traps. You gained as much slack as the material would yield, then worked the upper of your crossed arms higher until you could bring the hand over the opposite shoulder. It was easier if you could lie on the floor on your back and slither along feet-first; this helped to push the securing strap up your back. Then, when you got one hand over the point of your shoulder, you forced your head through the crook of you arm, and you were nearly there. With your arms hanging in front of you it was simply a matter of getting a foot on the strap that linked the two sleeves, and drawing the jacket straight off over your head.

But you didn't escape from a strait-jacket while under surveillance, and the twin diagonal seatbelts holding her would prove a hindrance, perhaps an unsurmountable one. Willie could make it, though. The lap-straps holding him to the chair would not hinder him. He would need one foot free, but the straps holding his ankles were only of half-inch leather. He could break one by twisting it against the chair-leg.

She saw now that he must have been working at the task, for the strap across his back was far higher than it should have been. There was no sign of movement from him. His face was still pale from the effects of the drug and he sat a little slumped, gazing absently at the back of the magazine that Adrian Chance was reading, *Autocar*.

She spared a moment from her assessment of the situation to feel sympathy for Willie. His self-recrimination would be merciless. From the moment Lisa walked into The Treadmill he had been expecting a con, expecting deception, but in spite of this the albino girl had sold him a gold-brick. It was an incredible achievement, a shattering one. He would never forgive himself ... even if he had the chance, her mind added bleakly.

She looked again at Brunel and the girl, at Chance and Jacko Muktar. Nobody spoke. Nobody gave any sign of noticing that she had come round. Beside her, Pennyfeather stirred and groaned faintly. Jacko appeared to be dozing now. Adrian Chance had taken out a pencil and was making calculations in the margin of the magazine. Brunel was reading a hard-cover book. She saw from the dust-jacket that it was a volume of General de Gaulle's memoirs.

Lisa was doing nothing. There was a strained expression on her face, no sign of triumph. She sat gazing out of the window, not as if watching the clouds or the ground below, but as if listening for something. The overall impression was peculiar, a little eerie. Occasionally she turned her head, looking about the cabin of the aircraft, perhaps looking at Modesty for a moment, but with no more interest than if they had both been passengers on a scheduled flight. Not once did the eyes behind the dark glasses turn towards Willie Garvin.

Modesty registered the fact that Lisa Brunel was not enjoying her achievement. That was puzzling, but worth remembering. It might be useful. Brunel turned a page of his book. As he did so he lifted his head for a moment, and his eyes rested on Modesty, without interest or curiosity. Then he looked down at the new page and continued reading.

There was nothing to be done for the moment, nothing at all. The present set-up offered no possibilities. She fought down another wave of nausea and began to review the larger situation. They were in a very bad spot. If she had dared to let herself feel frightened she would have felt very frightened indeed. But they were alive still, and looked like staying alive for a while at least. Bad spots she had known before in plenty, but there had always proved to be a way out. It might not always be so, might not be so this time, but that was not for thinking about. You learned to think only about what might be fruitful in helping you when the moment came, the moment of opportunity.

Brunel's motives were important. If this was for revenge, they would surely have been dead by now. So he had ensnared them for some other reason. The Novikov coordinates? Possibly, but there must be more to it than that. Brunel could not have known for sure that they would bring Giles Pennyfeather to France with them. So what else?

She thought of the interview with Brunel in the penthouse. He had said he was not interested in revenge as such, and that he was a realist. She still believed him. It showed in the man. He must have a purpose in taking them to Rwanda, perhaps more than one purpose. She thought carefully, but could find no answer, and this disturbed her deeply. To deal with an enemy whose motives you could not fathom took away all power of anticipation. It was like trying to fight blindfold.

She looked around her again, showing as little interest as Brunel had displayed in her. What was the aim of this present tactic? Chance and Muktar should have been gloating. The albino girl should have been either glowing or smug with her success. And Brunel? She did not know. She only knew that he had the initiative now, totally, and that he would use it to achieve whatever his aim might be, with all the proven cunning and passionless savagery of his nature.

His aim. She kept coming back to that, and the enigma made her nerves crawl. Again she steadied them, using all the mental tricks she had learned since childhood. This was when it was hardest to hold back the natural thrusts of fear, when speculation could go no further and when positive planning of a move was impossible. There was no basis on which to plan. A chance might come when they landed, or even before, but more probably later. She could only be alert and ready to seize it, as Willie Garvin would be.

She looked at Willie again. He was sitting to her left and a little forward of her. He seemed not to have moved a muscle, but she saw that the buckle at the back of the strait-jacket was perhaps another inch higher. It was just above the chair-back now, and he could use that to help push it up still farther. As she watched she saw the canvas of the sleeves and shoulders grow very gradually more taut until she could almost fancy she heard the material creak under the strain. He was seeking a fraction more play before continuing his infinitesimally slow task. It might be pointless, for the final act of escape from the strait-jacket would take seconds at least, and he would never be allowed to make it. But somewhere along the line a chance might offer, and he was preparing for that.

Thankfulness rose like a sudden warm wave within her. She was not alone. She had Willie Garvin, and he would not give up. There was not much to be done, but he had set himself patiently to it. Remembering years gone by, she acknowledged that this was something she herself had taught him in the days when she had found him and, by some alchemy she had never understood, changed him from a

149

dangerous gutter-thug to the cheerful and matchless companion who had in turn changed her own life.

The comfort of his tenacity in so many times of danger was beyond all price. Her heart rose a little. With his strength and skill, Willie was worth a battle-platoon. And he would keep going. With a gun-barrel at his head and the hammer falling on the cartridge, he would still be scheming and fighting to find a way out.

He had not spoken to her since those first words as she came to her senses. That was sound. It was unlikely that he understood the tactic of silence adopted by Brunel and his entourage any more than she did, but he had realized that to ask questions of them, or even to exchange words with her, would in some way be an act of weakness, a submissive acknowledgement of their mastery. Willie had decided to play them at their own game, unless she gave him a different lead.

Beside her, Giles Pennyfeather lifted his head and muttered, 'God, I feel sick . . .'

She said, as Willie had said to her, 'Take it easy, Giles.'

'Eh? Christ, we're up in the air!' He shook his head, winced, tried to move his arms, stared blankly down at the strait-jacket securing him, then saw Brunel and the albino girl sitting opposite. The girl was gazing out of the window. Brunel turned a page of his book without looking up.

Pennyfeather turned to stare at Modesty. His hair was standing on end and his eyes were round and huge in the pallor of his lean face. 'What happened?' he said hoarsely. 'I was drinking some coffee and—' He craned his neck round. 'Where's Madame Novikov?'

'She wasn't Madame Novikov. We made a little mistake, Giles. Now don't talk any more.'

'Don't *talk?*' He jerked about furiously, tugging against the straps that held him, then relaxed, panting. 'Why the hell not?'

'Because there's nothing to talk about, and you'll disturb the other passengers. I'm going to sleep for a bit. You might as well do the same.'

'But look here—!'

'No, Giles.' She closed her eyes.

Pennyfeather stared at her in total bewilderment, a jumble of half-formed questions flitting across his mind. He twisted his head to look all about him with the vague hope of finding some reason for her odd behaviour.

Ah! There were those two bastards Modesty had seen off in Kalimba. And this white-haired girl must be the one Willie had talked about. There was Willie himself, strapped to a chair. Pretty weird, that. The whole thing was weird, everybody just sitting and saying nothing, ignoring everybody else. Christ, this was a nasty business! Modesty and Willie had slipped up somewhere. Still, knowing the sort of sod Brunel was, it was lucky they weren't all dead by now. Why had Modesty shut him up like that? Pennyfeather pondered the enigma. Yes, it made sense in a way. You couldn't very well ask Brunel what was going to happen next. It wouldn't do any good and it would seem like being scared. Well, he *was* scared, of course. The whole thing was pretty scary. Still, much better not to let on. Yes, he could see that. He'd sometimes felt pretty damn scared facing up to a job of surgery he wasn't too sure about, out in Kalimba. But you didn't show it. You didn't even show it to yourself. This was much the same sort of thing in a way, when you came to think about it. Well all right, then.

Pennyfeather yawned deliberately and settled back in his seat. He did not think he could pretend to sleep, but decided to find something to occupy his mind. Very pretty, the albino girl. A bit skinny, but she wore clothes well. Must be a tricky piece of work if she'd managed to fool Willie Garvin. Didn't look tricky, though. Looked like a girl on the verge of a breakdown. Much too tense. There were all the little signs. Might have a complex about being an albino. Ah, albinoism. Now what did he remember about it from the medical books? That would do to keep him occupied . . .

The plane droned on. It was some time later that Brunel put down his book and picked up the small mike attached to his arm-rest, speaking into it so quietly that Pennyfeather could barely hear, though he fancied the language was

French. He nudged Modesty, who opened her eyes. Brunel put down the mike and looked out of the window.

Modesty glanced at Willie. He had gone as far as he could go in preparing to escape from the strait-jacket. Because he was using the maximum give of the material, she knew it must be uncomfortable trying to breathe with his arms wrapped so tightly across his chest, but he showed no signs of stress.

The Dakota was losing height, and she wondered why. Impossible to know at what hour they had taken off. Brunel had had to get their three unconscious bodies to an airfield somewhere – or more likely to a disused landing strip. That would have taken time. She had an uncanny instinct for location, and when she first woke it had told her that they were still over France. She thought they might be crossing the south coast now, or at least drawing near to it. If they were heading for Rwanda they would have to put down to refuel at least twice, even if the plane carried extra tanks, but they would surely reach North Africa on the first leg of the flight. Yet the plane was descending.

They broke through cloud, and Brunel murmured into the mike again. The plane banked and changed course. They were turning east. No, coming round still more, making a long east-west elipse, and holding altitude now. She could look through one of the windows on the far side of the cabin, down through the dawn light to grey and brown hills below. She saw irregular patches of green. A small village there, at the end of a narrow ribbon of track. To her right now she saw thin white streaks reaching up to merge with the mountain snows. Provence, where the spurs from the Maritime Alps ran south. She was sure of it.

Was Brunel waiting for some sort of signal from below? No possible landing place there, just rugged country with a few cultivated patches at the foot of the hills between ridges of rock. The plane turned again, banking steeply, and the straps that held her grew taut. Brunel sat holding the mike, looking across the cabin and down through one of the port windows, his face as quiet as a deserted house. He turned his head and nodded to Adrian Chance, who got up and slid open the door set in the port side. A blast of air plucked at his silver hair.

Now Modesty saw that Chance wore a belt attached to a nylon safety-line anchored to his seat. She turned her head and saw that Jacko was standing now, bracing himself against the tilt of the deck, wearing a similar safety-line. There was an expectant grin on his face. The grin made her nerves burn with sudden alarm, and in the same moment Brunel lifted his voice and spoke directly to her above the roar of the wind. He said, 'It's time for Garvin to go now.'

Shock hit her like a blow from a club. She heard Giles Pennyfeather say, 'What—?'

Then Jacko was gripping the back of Willie's chair, kicking the releases of the clips that held the legs. A forward shove slid the flanges from the deck sockets. She saw Willie start to struggle, and suddenly there was frost in her blood as shock turned to raw fear.

The chair slid across the deck, and she heard the creak of the strait-jacket's canvas and leather as it was tortured under the stress of Willie's huge and desperate strength. Then, as the chair cannoned into the side of the cabin only a foot from the door, he forced his head through the crook of his upper arm, unwinding the strap across his back.

She was fighting now herself, straining madly against the grip of the strait-jacket. Beside her, Giles was struggling too, cursing in a wild, cracked voice.

Willie's back was towards her, his knees against the side of the cabin. He could use his arms to some extent now, but they were still encased in the sealed sleeves of the jacket, with the long strap joining them, and there was no freedom yet for his hands. Chance and Jacko were behind the chair, pulling it back so that it could be thrust sideways and then forward through the open door.

She was screaming silently inside her head as she fought like a trapped animal against the strait-jacket. The diagonal seatbelts were thwarting her, and she could not even begin to shift the securing buckle at her back. Through the door she could see the ground below, the cruel stony spurs.

Somewhere in her mind, somewhere beneath the horror and fury, a tiny piece of mental machinery continued to register data. They were at three thousand feet, perhaps a little more, cruising over the mid-slope of the mountains where grey spurs interlocked with narrow green valleys, a thousand feet below the snows.

It was perhaps only ten or fifteen seconds since Brunel had spoken, but the scene for her seemed to be taking place in slow motion. Still held to the chair by the straps at thighs and ankles, Willie had little power to manoeuvre. Adrian Chance and Jacko had pulled the chair back and were edging it sideways now, to line it up with the door.

Willie swung his arms up and back, twisting his body. The strap linking the sealed cuffs looped over and caught Jacko round the neck. Using the purchase, Willie jerked the chair round, crossing the strap, and in the same moment yacked Jacko's head down to butt him viciously between the eyes.

With a great aching agony she saw the look on Willie's face. She had seen it many times before, when she had fought him in practice, a look of total concentration, eyes a little narrowed, appraising, calculating. At this moment action engulfed the fear that would otherwise grip him. The whole of his being was absorbed in the process of finding the best of the limited moves available to him. Jacko was on his knees at Willie's feet now, choking in the grip of the strap looped about his neck. Chance slammed a fist at Willie's face.

Muga. Willie's head flicked sideways, and as the first grazed his cheek he turned and snapped, setting his teeth in the wrist. Chance made a shrill, strangled sound and swung his other fist. Willie took it on the top of the head, still holding the grip with his teeth. Then he leaned back and heaved with his arms.

She thought wildly, '*God, he's going to make it!*' She knew his next move. He would heave the choking Jacko against Chance and send him sprawling. Three seconds and he could be out of the strait-jacket, still held to the chair but with hands and arms free. Jacko carried a gun, Chance a knife. If Willie could get a hand on one or the other . . .

There was Brunel, still. He sat with an elbow on the arm-rest, chin on hand, watching quietly. The girl, Lisa, seemed frozen, her lips bloodless. Then her hands began fumbling feebly with her seatbelt. Her mouth was beginning to open. She was going to scream.

Modesty stopped struggling vainly against the straps and sagged down hard in her seat, estimating the distance between her and Brunel. She might, she might just reach his knee-cap with her booted toe. Enough to cripple him for a few seconds.

She saw Willie heave Jacko's body up and round, slamming it against Chance to send him reeling aft. In the same moment he hooked the toe of his right boot behind the chair-leg and leaned forward, thrusting outwards with his knee. The narrow leather strap holding his ankle snapped like paper. Chance tripped and fell as the safety-line brought him up short. Willie let Jacko drop to his feet, and put his free right foot on the man's neck, on the strap that was looped around it. But as he bent forward in the chair for the final heave to draw the strait-jacket over his head, the plane banked steeply to turn across the mountain spurs again.

The chair toppled over sideways. Then, feet-first, neatly and precisely, it slid across the tilted deck and out through the exact centre of the open door.

The albino girl screamed. There was a gleam of per-spiration on Brunel's brow, but without heat he swung a small arm and hit her across the mouth with his open hand. Modesty sat with locked muscles, staring, her flesh crawling. For still Willie had not gone. Not quite. Jacko's safety-line was stretched to its limit and he lay with his head a foot from the door. His face was almost black, his tongue bulging from his mouth. The doubled strap was still looped about his neck. It passed over the threshold and out of sight, rigid as a bar of iron. Willie, still secured to the chair, must be hanging below.

Adrian Chance crawled forward. There was a knife in his hand now, and murderous fury in his face. He reached out to cut the leather a few inches from the threshold, but before the blade could touch it the strap went suddenly limp.

Modesty sat quite still. The sweat on her face felt like beads of ice. She knew what had happened. There had been nothing for Willie to grip inside the sealed sleeves. After a few split seconds the strait-jacket, secured from above by the strap round Jacko's neck, had simply been dragged off Willie's body.

In the moment that he fell the plane had banked again. Through the window she saw the falling shape, the four chair-legs jutting from it incongruously. It was five hundred feet below now, and dwindling as it flashed away in a long parabola towards the slopes of grey rock. Then the tiny shape that was Willie Garvin falling to his death was gone from her blurring vision, lost against the background.

Brunel spoke into the microphone. The aircraft's wing came up. They were climbing again, coming round to head south once more. Very slowly she turned her head away from the window.

Adrian Chance was unwinding the strap from Jacko's thick neck. He drew in the empty straight-jacket, slid the door shut, bent over the stocky man for a moment, then looked up and said to Brunel, 'It's all right. He's breathing.' His voice, rising and falling unevenly, sounded very loud in the new quietness of the cabin now that the door was closed.

Brunel said drily, 'He can hardly take any credit for being alive. Neither can you, Adrian. When I remember that you wanted me to let you take on Garvin in a straight fight with your little knife . . .' He shook his head, then looked at Modesty. 'I see now why you've been so successful in the past.'

Pennyfeather said in a shaking voice, very loudly, 'Oh, you bastard! You stinking, animal, murdering *bastard*!'

'We're all animals, Dr Pennyfeather. The trouble with most men is that they're for ever aspiring to be something more. I've never fallen into that foolish error. It was necessary for me to dispose of Garvin, and I've done so.' He picked up his book. 'In case you're wondering about it, neither of you is going the same way. As a doctor, would you care to attend to my unconscious colleague if you were freed from that strait-jacket for a few minutes? We have your medical bag with us, and you are under the obligation of the Hippocratic Oath, are you not?'

Grey-faced, Pennyfeather said, 'If I could get at you, I'd have a good try at killing you, Brunel.'

'As you please.' Brunel turned his head and said, 'Do your best for him, Adrian.' He opened his book and began to read. Beside him, the girl sat with her hands pressed to her face, her body trembling.

Modesty had been only dimly conscious of the exchange. Her eyes were closed, her face might have been chiselled from white marble. There was the salt taste of blood on her tongue. At some time during the struggle she had bitten through her lip. Willie Garvin was dead, and the grief in her was the greatest pain she had ever known. She slowed her breathing, letting the pain wash through her, not fighting it because she knew that if she tried to resist she would break down, and she could not let Brunel see her break. For Willie's sake she could not do that.

At last her mind was still, suspended in an unmoving sea of pain. She held it so for long minutes, then began warily to let the little burning daggers of thought penetrate her awareness, the thoughts which must be faced and absorbed.

Willie was dead, and she was alone again, not only now, in this moment, but for all the future. If there was to be any future. Alone. There would not be another Willie Garvin. No use to close her mind to it. She must face it now, must think of him, of Willie and herself through all the years.

She forced herself to go back to the beginning, and remember the early days, the days before Willie Garvin, when at barely twenty she had been running an expanding organization of hard men, criminals of every kind. Looking back now, it was difficult to recognize herself. She had been harder than any of the men who worked for her, or else she could never have ruled them. Because she made her own rules, and would not tolerate certain profitable but vicious areas of crime, there were some who had seen this as weakness, and she had found it necessary to teach them otherwise. With increasing success, the task had become easier. To be employed by *The Network* came to carry its own special cachet. The old hands were quick to slap down or throw out any who did not want to conform to the ways she had established. They were in a winning game, and they did not want the wheel put out of balance. She had found a few good lieutenants, but there had never been one who understood her, whose mind could mesh smoothly and easily with hers. Not until the coming of Willie Garvin.

Pain stabbed into her, but she forced herself to go on remembering. She had taken him from a Saigon jail, the twisted gutter-rat with a sour grudge against the world; the man of so many skills and such tremendous potential, all blanketed by the grey lethargy that a harsh childhood and a life of nomadic crime had laid upon him.

She had taken him from jail, told him that she had no interest in the kind of rat he had been in the past, and given him a particular job to do, a delivery job, alone. She was playing a hunch. The job involved trusting him with ten thousand dollars in gold, to be delivered in Hong Kong, and that money she gambled as coldly as a professional poker player, for she had glimpsed something of what lay deep within Willie Garvin. The potential.

The simple delivery job had gone hopelessly wrong, through no fault of his. But what he had risked and achieved, on his own initiative, to pick up the pieces and make it go right, was a story that took her breath away when at last he returned to tell it. The man who returned was different from the old Willie Garvin, and had grown more different week by week and month by month until, like a butterfly from a chrysalis, the new Willie Garvin emerged, the blandly cheerful man with a personality that dominated even the hard and jealous lieutenants of *The Network*'s inner circle.

In less than a year he was her second in command, and the others accepted this as entirely natural. She had found a perfect right arm. But more than that, much more, she was no longer alone. His mind engaged with hers as smoothly as the cogs of a precision watch, and his dedication to her was total. She knew that by some freak of mental chemistry he quite simply adored her. Yes, she could acknowledge the word now. It was not a blind adoration. He knew her faults and encompassed them as being a part of her, not wishing her different. It was also on a level above and beyond physical desire. That did not arise, was not a part of what grew slowly between them, even though he was always fully aware of her as a woman, proud of her as a woman.

And when they had split up *The Network* and retired, there had been yet another shift of relationship, for now he was no longer in her employ. Because she thought it was best, she had reluctantly tried to make him go his own way. It had not worked for Willie Garvin. He was lost without his talisman, Modesty Blaise. And the tides of fate would not allow this. There had been Tarrant, and the first of the new kind of caper, quickly followed by others. When Tarrant made no call on them, involvement came from other directions, often by the slightest quirk of circumstance. They did not seek trouble, but it found them, and they came to be content that this should be so, for the sharp spice of occasional danger had become something close to an addiction.

But now ...

Now Willie Garvin was dead, and for the moment her world had fallen apart. They had never been fools, never failed to recognize that one day, perhaps this time, perhaps next time, a caper would go against them, and that one or both would die. It was part of the game they had chosen, as others choose to climb a mountain and to risk making the notorious traverse that has killed a dozen men before them.

Now it had happened, and it was Willie who had gone. Better that way, perhaps. She knew he would have wished it so himself, for she could more easily sustain the loss than he. Easily? God, if this was easy—

She caught at herself, pinching out the dangerous spark of self-pity. No tears. Willie Garvin is dead. Absorb it. Accept it.

Sleep well, Willie love. They were good years. You were always there when I needed you. A shoulder to cry on after a rough caper. Yours was the only shoulder I ever cried on. You liked that. Thank you for everything, Willie. You always made me feel I was something special.

She called up the remembered voice, the gravelly voice and the grin that went with it. *'You look terrific, Princess. Let's 'ang around in the foyer before we go in, so I'll get all the men 'ating my guts.'*

You taught me to laugh, Willie. All those stories about the girls you'd known. Did you sometimes want me? I never tried to make you feel that way. It's not everything, not even the most important thing. We had so much more. I always felt you didn't want to change anything because it might spoil what we had, break the pattern. And it might. It has to make a difference. I'd have been sad to lose the big thing for the small. I think that's how you felt.

Sleep well, Willie love. I led you into this, but I'm not going to start feeling guilty. How you'd hate that. I don't know if you're able to worry about me, but please don't. If they manage to sign me off, it won't be because I didn't try, you know that. I'll take a little time to get my balance. It's going to be hard to go solo after all this time, but I won't quit. And there's poor Giles. I have to get him out of this if I can. Not easy. I'll need a better chance than you got. Keep your fingers crossed for me.

Sleep well, Willie love . . .

The acceptance was made, the reality absorbed, even though the pain was still raw and would never be completely wiped away.

Gently she coaxed her mind to stillness. Her nerves were quiet again now. Slowing her breathing still more, she sought and found the trance-like yoga state of being which is like a small hibernation, the mental and physical processes virtually halted. And there she rested.

When she opened her eyes again the sun was past its zenith, and ahead she could see the coast of North Africa. The seats opposite were empty. On the port side, Jacko sat with his head resting gingerly on a pillow, a wet towel wrapped round his neck, or rather between his head and massive shoulders for he had hardly any neck. Lucky to be alive, she thought, a little bitterly. Most men's necks would have snapped when Willie went over the threshold.

Adrian Chance, his wrist bandaged, looked at her with murderous blue eyes, hating her. She knew why. With everything against him, Willie had almost beaten them both, Chance and Muktar. It was a savage humiliation. Adrian Chance had to hate somebody for it, and since Willie was dead she was now the most natural substitute. The girl, Lisa, lay curled up on a double seat, forward on the port side, asleep.

Modesty turned her head to find Giles Pennyfeather looking at her wonderingly. His face was tired and drawn, but he was quite calm. She saw that the weariness in him was from shock, not fear or despair. That was good. She lifted an eyebrow, glancing at the empty seat opposite, asking where Brunel was.

Pennyfeather said very quietly, almost whispering so that the words would not reach Chance, 'He's in the cockpit, or whatever you call where the pilot is.' He looked down at his strait-jacketed arms, then at her face again. 'I'm sorry. I mean about Willie. I wish I could hold your hand.'

She nodded, acknowledging her understanding of all that lay behind his words, all that could not be said. After a moment he went on, 'You've been asleep for ages. Do you feel a bit better now?'

'Yes. And you?'

'I'm all right. Do you want to go to the loo?'

'No. I wasn't just asleep. I went away for a while.'

'Like that yoga stuff? Sort of trance?'

'In a way.'

'I didn't know you could do that.'

'An old man called Sivaji taught me. In the Thar desert, north of Jodhpur. Later I sent Willie to him—' She broke off. 'It doesn't matter. Has anything happened?'

'Not much. They unfastened me and let me go to the loo about an hour ago. That silver-haired bastard was holding a gun at the back of your head all the time until they strapped me up again. Do you know where we are?'

'Just crossing the North African coast. We'll probably refuel at some small airfield, then press on for Rwanda.'

'Do you think we'll find a chance to get these buggers down?'

'Not for a while yet. They'll keep us strapped up till we get to Rwanda. After that – well, maybe something will offer. We'll have to be ready, and snap at it.'

He said, as if confessing to a defect, 'Look, I'm a bit out of my depth, Modesty. I mean, you'll have to tell me what to do. I'm not a Willie Garvin, but I'll have a good try.'

'Yes, I know you will.'

He brooded for a moment. His eyes rested on Jacko, across the aisle, and a grimace that was half grin and half snarl touched his thin, tired face as he said, 'They bloody well had to work for it, didn't they? Willie hadn't a ghost of a chance, all strapped up against the two of them. But by Christ, he nearly got them just the same. I bet you're proud of him, and that's something.'

Yes, it was something. She would think of it again in time to come, perhaps, if she had any time to come. But for the moment it hurt too much.

Brunel came through from the flight compartment. He glanced at Lisa, at Chance and Jacko, then sat down facing Modesty, looking at her. She met his gaze, her face impassive. He did not stare, but simply looked, and she looked back. For perhaps two minutes they held the steady gaze, then Brunel smiled quietly and picked up his book. Turning to Chance he said, 'Our guest has blood on her chin. Wake Lisa and tell her to clean it up.'

When the girl was roused she moved like an automaton, her eyes blank. She had taken off the dark glasses now. She brought cotton-wool and a little bottle of antiseptic from a first-aid box. The liquid was cold and stinging as she wiped the dry blood from Modesty's chin and lip. When she had finished she stood looking down at Modesty with dull eyes until Brunel said, 'Go and sit down.'

He stood up and bent to look at Modesty's face. 'There, that's better,' he said. The note of sympathy in his voice bewildered her. She looked back at him without expression. 'It's stopped bleeding,' he said. 'More comfortable now, I hope.' He smiled, swung his arm, and hit her across the mouth hard with the spine of the book that he still held. It was so utterly unexpected that she had no time to ride the blow. Her head sang, and she felt fresh blood run from the split lip.

Pennyfeather lunged against his straps, calling Brunel a vile name. Brunel ignored him and sat down. Opening the book, he began to read.

Modesty clawed at her scattered wits, fighting to collect them. The blow, the hurt, was nothing. But her inability to understand the purpose of the whole performance, to grasp Brunel's motive, hit her hard and deep. That he had a motive she was very sure, but she could not decipher it. She knew that in all contests the will is the crucial factor. She had learned to feed her own will, to focus it so intensely that it would release power to the physical and mental springs of her being when she called upon it. But to overcome an enemy demanded an understanding of him, a recognition of cause and effect in his make-up. In this, Brunel confounded her. She did not know why he had killed Willie Garvin in such a way and at such a time, did not know why he had ordered Lisa to tend her minor hurt and then struck her. He was unfathomable, and she had never faced an un-fathomable opponent before. A thread of panic sparked within her and she quelled it sharply, aware that she was in the subtlest kind of danger, the danger of self-doubt and lost confidence.

It was bad. She smiled at Giles and gave a little shake of head, telling him not to worry. Closing her eyes she began slowly and with infinite patience to rebuild her inner strength, to repair her shaken defences.

Sooner or later you had to lose. But it must never be this time. Especially not this time, against Brunel. This one had to be won, for Willie's sake if for nothing else. Yes, make it for Willie. That's what he'd like more than anything. In remembrance, instead of a posy.

CHAPTER NINE

Adrian Chance put his hands round Lisa's neck and squeezed gently. One of his wrists still bore the marks of Willie's teeth under a two-inch bandage. She was lying on her back across the bed, her head hanging awkwardly over the edge, and he was sprawled across her. Their moist flesh clung in the humid air. Thin blades of sunlight penetrated the slats of the blind at the big window.

'Come on. Talk to me, Lisa,' Chance said, watching the strained perplexity in her face, enjoying it.

'Please . . . I can hardly breathe.' She struggled a little, and he allowed her to edge round until her head was supported on the bed. He could feel her trembling, and had the pleasurable satisfaction of knowing that it was not assumed.

She said, a little desperately, 'I'm sorry – I'm trying, but I don't know what you want me to do, Adrian. You seem different.'

'You must learn to cope with my whims, darling. I've told you what to do. Talk to me.'

'But . . . what about?'

'Oh, let's see now. Tell me what Willie Garvin was like.'

'I can't. I forget.' She closed her eyes.

'What a pity. Tell me how you enjoyed seeing him thrown out of the plane. I'm sure you remember that. You screamed at the time.'

'I was frightened.'

'For him?'

'No!' She cried out the denial urgently, praying that the voices would hear and would believe the lie. 'I was frightened he – he might get away and hurt me.'

It was four days since the Dakota had landed on the airstrip at Kigali, fifty miles to the north of *Bonaccord*. For the first two nights the voices had never let her rest. They had known the evil in her, known how she had been shattered by the death of an Enemy. In the moment when she saw him go down to his death she had screamed not only in fear for him but in horror and protest. The voices had punished her for it, their passionless reproaches whispering in her head all through the night hours until she had felt her mind would collapse, and had almost longed for that release.

But for the last two nights they had let her rest. It seemed that the punishment was over. She did not want to think about Willie Garvin again, for to do so might revive the displeasure of the voices.

'A falling body,' said Adrian Chance, caressing her, 'accelerates at thirty-two feet per second, per second. At fifteen hundred feet it reaches a terminal speed of roughly one hundred and twenty miles per hour. I'm not too good at mental arithmetic, but if he went out at three thousand feet I think it must have taken more than twenty seconds for him to get down and make a hole in the ground. Or bounce, as the case may be. I wonder what he thought about all that time?'

She began to shake with dry, soundless sobs. Again he knew that this was not her usual compliant pretence, and elation at his success ran like threads of fire through his veins. When she was quiet again he said, 'What do you think of Modesty Blaise?'

'I don't know.' Her voice was a whisper. 'She doesn't say anything, doesn't do anything.'

'That's right.' Anger touched his voice. 'But Brunel still thinks she's some sort of superwoman he can put to work for him.'

'Well, I expect so, then. He always is right—' She gasped in sudden pain as Chance hurt her. 'I'm sorry, Adrian. Was it wrong to say that?'

For a moment he did not answer, was unable to speak for the rage which had exploded within him. He hated Modesty Blaise as he had never hated anyone or anything in his life before. The knowledge that Brunel was working to make her a willing lieutenant was unbearable to Adrian Chance,

165

for he knew now that she was not to be another Lisa, a plaything. If Brunel's brain-washing worked, then she would stand as an equal to Jacko and himself. The thought was as painful as raw acid on the skin. His hatred expanded to encompass Brunel, and the sweat broke out on his body.

He drew a deep breath and said, 'Are you listening? Brunel told me to tell you what the scene is for tonight.'

'Yes, I'm listening.'

'All right. She has dinner with us. You and Brunel, me and Jacko. We talk. At least, the three of us do, Jacko isn't exactly an Oscar Wilde. All very civilized and amiable. As usual, she'll only speak when spoken to, and then as little as possible. She doesn't know what's going on, but she's not going to ask. Have you got it so far?'

'Yes, Adrian.'

'Just when coffee is served, van Pienaar and Camacho walk in. They don't say a word. They grab her, rip the dress off her back, pin her across the couch and beat her with a strap.' A sour note entered his voice. 'Not the buckle-end. Brunel doesn't want her hurt much, just humiliated. The point is, darling, and listen *bloody* carefully now,' he pinched her thigh brutally, 'The point is that the rest of us go on talking and having our coffee and smoking, just as if it wasn't happening. We don't register it *at all*. Is that clear?'

He felt her shoulders move as she said, 'I don't understand, but I know what you want me to do. Won't she make trouble? I mean, fight and struggle.'

Chance smiled very brightly. 'No, she won't. She'll only fight if she thinks we're going to kill her. She knows that somewhere in *Bonaccord* we've got Pennyfeather tucked away, and we've told her we'll kill him slowly if she tries anything at all out of line. So she's completely hog-tied. Do you see?'

'Yes, Adrian, I see.'

'All right. That's enough talking. Now . . .'

When he left her she lay limply on the bed, her muscles aching from the painful contortions he had compelled from her. The other pain, the burning pain in her side, had started again, and she felt feverish. Perhaps it would go, as it had

166

done before. Perhaps it would get worse. She did not care. She would not speak of it to Brunel. If it got worse, and she died, then at least she would be free of all this.

Willie Garvin had been an Enemy, but in those few days spent together he had changed everything for her. Now he was dead, and in the depths of her mind where she prayed the voices could not hear, she mourned him, and was filled with self-loathing because it was she who had trapped him so that he could be killed. Nausea stirred suddenly within her, and she lurched at a stumbling run to the bathroom.

Modesty Blaise woke at dawn in the small bedroom on the upper floor. She threw back the sheet, got up, moved to the narrow window, and looked through the slats of the blind. On the flagged patio, one of Brunel's overseers, an Angolan, sat on a bench with a hunting rifle resting across his knees. There was always an armed man there.

Standing naked with her back to the dressing-table she looked over her shoulder into the mirror. The flesh of her back and buttocks was slightly swollen, the skin still red. She moved her shoulders. The muscles felt a little stiff, but that was all. There was soreness but no damage. Camacho had used a broad leather belt to beat her, and he had not cut the skin.

Automatically she went to the door and found it locked, as she had known it would be. Adjoining the bedroom was a small cubicle with a shower and lavatory. When she had showered and dried herself she put on a dressing-gown and sat in front of the mirror to do her hair. Brunel had provided the dressing-gown, together with three or four dresses belonging to Lisa. They were too tight and too short, but it did not matter.

For a moment she began to wonder what would happen to her today, but then quickly blocked the speculation. Whatever happened, it would seem to have no basis in reason. Brunel might treat her with all the courtesy of a guest, and perhaps take her round the estate. Or she might be shut in the sweat-box beyond the gardens for a few hours, as she had been on the second day.

She knew now that this erratic treatment had purpose. The seeming lack of logic was in itself a logical policy. Brunel was out to break her, but not simply to break her. It was to be done in a very special way, so that in the end she would be psychologically bound to him in a master-servant relationship. The alternation of harsh and kindly treatment was the first stage of the campaign, calculated to create disorientation in her, to alter her own image of herself.

Her throat was dry, and she went to the bedside table to pour herself a glass of water from the tall jug there. At least that was something which remained predictable. They always provided her with water. Once they had left her locked in her room all day and night without food, but they had not denied her water.

She took a hairgrip from the dressing-table and turned back the rug beside the bed. On the polished wooden boards were scratched faint lines, her attempt to make a plan of *Bonaccord*. She had been driven round the big estate once, on the morning they had arrived, with Brunel pointing out and explaining this or that feature as if she had been a houseguest. It seemed a dreamlike fantasy to her at the time, and it still seemed so.

There had been no chance to make a move when they landed at Kigali. Giles Pennyfeather, free from his straitjacket, had been taken off the plane first. They had told him quite simply that if he attempted anything foolish then Modesty Blaise would die. And when Pennyfeather had been taken away in a car, they had told her that he would die if she gave any hint of trouble. She had not seen him since, and had not asked about him. To ask anything, for food or rest or relief, or for Giles Pennyfeather, would gain nothing and would be the beginning of submission.

She had to find Giles, to know where he was, before she could dare to make any move towards an escape. And in five days she had not been able to pick up the slenderest clue to help her.

She closed her eyes and tried to visualize all that she had seen of *Bonaccord*. It was a well planned estate. The house faced a little south of east, a long building of two storeys with a wing or sprig at each end. Her own room was at the end of the southern sprig. Timber-built, the house held something of the style of a Bavarian chalet, with a low-pitched roof overhanging the long balconies. The rustic exterior was deceptive. Inside, the house was quietly palatial and had been constructed with every modern facility. The walls were insulated, there was air conditioning and a deep-freeze store room. The furnishing and appointments spoke of design experts and unlimited expense. It stood at the top of a very gentle rise, looking out across several miles of grassy savannah to a rocky ridge beyond which there lay a great marsh covered with papyrus. The area between the two sprigs formed a huge patio, and beyond this were green lawns and flowerbeds fed by underground water-pipes.

South of the savannah was the farming area of *Bonaccord*, bordering a small river which fed Lake Rweru, and with a village of prefabricated huts as its centre. The *Bonaccord* farms were something rare in this region, as she had seen on the journey from the airfield at Kigali. The area had once been barren from over-stocking and periodic bushfires, but by irrigation and drainage Brunel had made the land fertile. His people grew a variety of crops, mainly manioc and groundnuts, sorghum and coffee.

'All supplied free to the grateful authorities for export,' he had said during the guided tour. 'I am considered a great benefactor. We also grow sufficient basic crops to be self-supporting, and we manage to graze some sheep and goats.'

She had estimated that in the village huts in the farm area Brunel had about eighty workers. They were all Bantu families imported from farther south. Also imported were a dozen Kikuyu who seemed to act in some kind of watchdog capacity. The cook and the four house-servants were all male Chinese, with quarters on the ground floor of the south wing, beyond the kitchens. Brunel and his entourage occupied the north wing. There were five white overseers, two from Angola, two from South Africa, and an Englishman. Their quarters were in the central span of the house, upstairs.

'Useful fellows,' Brunel had said. 'I've managed to instil a reasonably paternalistic attitude in them towards the natives. They were rather too fond of cracking the whip at first. Of course, it doesn't matter too much what happens to imported labour, that's why I use it, but I like to preserve a good image here as far as possible.'

She had since learned that all five overseers were wanted men in their own countries. Camacho and Mesquita for rape, Loeb for murder. She did not know about van Pienaar or Selby, but assessed the South African as a thug and the Englishman as a psychopath. It was Mesquita who was sitting on the patio below now, a rifle across his knees.

She made a scratch on the floor to mark the position of the big workshop and garage beside the fuel store, a few hundred yards south-east of the house, then frowned, troubled by the realization that the generator house was also in that complex and that she had forgotten about it until now. Normally she would have been able to sketch a rough plan of the whole estate after that single tour with Brunel, quickly and without hesitation, but her mind seemed to be struggling against a torpor she had not known before.

Behind the house, to the north-west, lay a belt of wooded savannah which gave way to an area of arid twisting valleys and ridges, confusing and without pattern. It came to her that there would be one pattern at least, for it was out there, near the edge of the estate, that the configuration of The Impossible Virgin lay. She had not seen the area beyond the wooded savannah, but knew its nature because she had overheard Pienaar talking with Brunel. One of the Kikuyu who patrolled the estate as guards had found the spoor of a lion only half a mile from the house, and van Pienaar was eager to organize a hunt. There was game in plenty away to the east, around the marshes, but apparently it was rare for a lone cat to roam into the estate.

Looking down at a small circular scratch on her map she thought of the gorilla, Ozymandias. Brunel had taken her to see him at the end of the tour, on that first day. A hundred yards from the house, where the belt of trees began, there was a wide dell surrounded by acacias, and here a huge circular cage some forty feet in diameter had been built. In it lived Ozymandias, a silver-backed mountain gorilla.

She remembered the sharp stink of ammonia, the sullen eyes glaring from beneath the great ridged brows; the huge hands gripping the bars, and the silvery sheen on the fur of the back as Ozymandias snarled at them and turned away, rolling across the cage on feet and knuckles. But above all she remembered the look on Brunel's face, the tiny spark in the red eyes.

'I keep him as an object lesson in the superiority of brains over muscle, Miss Blaise,' he said musingly. 'Look at that terrifying creature. When Ozymandias stands up, he measures nearly six feet – the height of a man, no more. He weighs 360 pounds, perhaps twice the weight of a man. His chest is big, sixty-two inches; his shoulders huge, three feet across. But his strength is fantastic in comparison, more than a dozen times greater than any human's. Put the strongest man in the world in that cage, and Ozymandias will simply pull him apart as if he were made of cardboard.'

Brunel glanced towards the car, where Adrian Chance and Jacko Muktar were waiting, Jacko leaned against the bonnet. He had a gun in his hand.

'Jacko is a strong man,' said Brunel. 'You managed to hurt him. But you couldn't hurt Ozymandias. No man who ever lived could hurt Ozymandias with his bare hands. Would you like to try, Miss Blaise?'

She said, 'No,' and considered killing Brunel now, quickly, while the chance offered. She could probably outrun Jacko and Chance through the trees. But there was Giles Pennyfeather. To kill Brunel now was to kill Giles.

Brunel said idly, 'Adrian wants to put you in the cage with Ozymandias. It's almost a burning ambition in him.' She made no answer, and after a little silence Brunel went on, 'Perhaps Ozymandias is my one vanity. I am a small man, lacking in physical strength. And there he stands, the epitome of raw muscle-power, a creature to inspire terror, capable of destroying even a lion if truly roused.' He spread his hand, and she saw that it was no bigger than a child's. He smiled. 'Yet Ozymandias is a prisoner in a cage, and I am free. He belongs to me.' Brunel glanced towards the car. His manner was careless and with no shred of drama in it. 'As those two men belong to me, and others like them. Strong and violent men.' He looked at her again, and added without emphasis, 'As you will belong to me. Shall we continue our tour now?'

The impact of his words had been small at the time. She had known many enemies, heard many threats. But now it was daily growing harder to kill the sense of helplessness that was eroding her defences. She knew that if the mental shield crumbled, fear would break through and she would be lost. Throughout a life of many dangers, the key to her survival had been a total refusal to acknowledge defeat. It was a mental attitude she took for granted, but now it was in question, and this in itself was frightening.

Staring down at the pattern of scratches on the floor, she tried to analyse her loss of confidence. Five days now . . . in five days she had achieved nothing at all. This was bad beyond belief, and she could not understand it. When all the factors of her situation were taken into account, there had to be some loop-hole she could exploit, some plan which at least offered a chance of success. But her mind seemed to have lost a vital element, the essential driving power which had always carried her through.

She had discarded half a dozen vague ideas because they would not come into focus. And why was that? There was Willie's death . . . yes, that had hit her harder than she had ever been hit before. But she would not accept that it could destroy abilities which had always been hers, the ability to think, to plan, and to act decisively when the moment came. All this had been a part of her since childhood, long before Willie came. Even in recent years she had often worked solo, to bring Willie himself out of trouble on more than one occasion. And there was no lack of compelling motive to drive her into action now. Apart from herself, there was Giles Pennyfeather to be saved. Above all, she ached to win this one for Willie.

But the muscles of her mind would not respond. When she drove them hard, seeking for ideas, she found her thoughts going round in circles. When she gave up conscious effort and simply made her mind an expectant void, no spark of inspiration came.

Five days now.

She drew in a deep breath and said softly, savagely to herself, 'Don't panic, you stupid bitch. Now ... take it step by step. First thing, find Giles. How?' The impetus of her thoughts faltered. Then, 'Go and look for him, for God's sake! You can handle the lock on that door. Go and look for him tonight. Just don't get caught, that's all. And if you are ...'

A dozen vague, shadowy doubts began to flit through her mind. She fought them down, groping for the fine focus of concentration and for the hard confidence she had always been able to command until now, trying to stimulate them by anger.

'Do something you thick-headed cow!' she whispered. 'Five days ... and all you've done is find reasons for not doing anything. Think what could be happening to Giles, and for God's sake make a move. Good or bad, you do *something* in the next twenty-four hours!'

Brunel sat on the big veranda taking breakfast with Adrian Chance and Lisa. Jacko had gone into Kigali with the refrigerated truck which collected supplies flown in monthly to the airfield. The strap burn on his neck had almost healed now.

'I thought that affair last night went very well,' Chance said. 'Did you, Lisa?'

She brought her thoughts back from elsewhere. 'Last night?'

'When the Blaise girl took a strapping.'

'Oh ... yes.'

'What do you mean – yes?'

Brunel broke in. 'You look rather flushed this morning, my dear. Are you unwell?'

'No. No, I'm quite all right, thank you.'

'All the same, perhaps Dr Leborde had better have a look at you. I can radio Kigali.'

'Leborde's away for a month,' said Chance, and grinned. 'Maybe Dr Pennyfeather would do.'

'Really, I'm quite all right,' Lisa repeated mechanically. It was untrue. The pain in her stomach was worse. She was almost glad.

Brunel studied her for a moment, then said, 'Well, we'll see. Now take your coffee inside. I want to talk to Adrian for a while.'

Chance watched the girl go. She walked a little stiffly, and he recalled with pleasure his activities of the previous day with her. Pouring himself a fresh cup of coffee he smiled and said, 'It's a pity Blaise didn't put up a fight when they started beating her. Might have proved interesting. I hoped she would.'

Brunel said, 'She believes herself to be waiting for the most promising moment, Adrian. A more intelligent attitude than yours would be in similar circumstances, I fancy.'

The smile remained on Chance's face, but it had become fixed and meaningless. 'Perhaps so. But are you sure you don't overestimate her?'

'Quite sure. This is a slow business, of course, but even so far her resistance is astonishing. It's also very gratifying. When she's fully conditioned, she'll be invaluable.'

Chance was stirring his coffee. His movements slowed, and he stopped, still holding the spoon. 'When you say invaluable . . . I'm not really sure what you mean.'

'I mean that she will eventually become a tower of strength to me, if you must have it in cliché form, Adrian.'

'I hope—' Chance seemed to have difficulty in speaking, and his face was pale. 'I hope you don't mean that her position will be superior to mine and Jacko's?'

Brunel lit a cigarette. 'If this works out as I expect, then in the end you'll be taking orders from her, naturally. You might as well get that firmly into your head now.' He watched for the beads of perspiration to spring on Chance's brow, and saw them appear.

'You *can't!*' Chance said in a frightful whisper. 'We hate her guts!'

Brunel nodded. 'That's because she's better than you are. You hate my guts too, Adrian, if you care to think about it. Perhaps you have. It's quite unimportant and doesn't affect the human logic of the situation at all.'

'But I thought Blaise was going to be—'

'You thought she was going to be another Lisa. A plaything. You were wrong. I warned you at the time. Listen to me carefully, Adrian. You're an excellent hatchet-man. You'll never be anything more. Blaise also is superior to you in your own line, and also has many other considerable qualities. I advise you to be realistic and accept that as a fact of life. It's quite unalterable.'

In the searing fury that gripped him Chance forgot all caution. '*Suppose I don't?*'

Brunel surveyed him without interest. 'Then you'd have to go, Adrian.'

'And who'll see to that for you? Jacko?'

'No, it might upset him briefly. But there's Loeb, Selby and the rest. Any or all of them. They don't like you and they'd jump at the opportunity. That's the way I arrange these things. Or I could use the Kikuyu, with those machetes they handle so well. Now do try to control yourself, Adrian. This kind of conversation only distresses you. Hating me is a waste of energy, because you can never do anything about it. If you tried, successfully or otherwise, you would die slowly, I promise you. You know it, and you won't try.' Without pausing for any reaction Brunel went on calmly, 'And now tell me how you're getting along with Dr Pennyfeather.'

Adrian Chance sat still for several seconds, looking past Brunel to the distant ridge. His face beneath the silver hair was rigid and wet. The pupils of his eyes had shrunk to black pinpoints. He made a strange sighing sound, then said in a faraway voice, 'Pennyfeather? I haven't got anything out of him yet.'

'You've hurt him considerably. Perhaps your methods are too direct?'

'Perhaps he never even heard the coordinates. Or if he did he can't remember them.'

'He heard them,' Brunel said. 'He told me Novikov babbled a great deal in Russian, and kept saying the same thing over and over again. All right. Part of what he babbled was the coordinates. You can take that as a fact. Penny-feather says he can't recall the words, which he wouldn't understand anyway, or even the sound of them. I'm not sure he isn't lying on that point. I gained a distinct impression that he wasn't being entirely frank.'

'I've been taking it slowly so far. He'll be entirely frank before I've finished with him.' Chance had regain some of his colour now, and the shock was fading from his eyes.

Brunel thought for a while. 'You're to cease treatment for the time being,' he said at last. 'The suspense of wondering when it's going to start again will work on him. Then you can recommence. I want him brought to a state where he's genuinely trying to tell all he knows, has a burning desire to do so, one might say. Then, if that doesn't produce the coordinates, we'll try hypno-narcosis to dredge them out of his subconscious. They're there all right.'

Chance emptied his coffee cup and stood up. 'How long do you want me to suspend treatment?'

'A few days. I'll let you know. And this afternoon we'll try an experiment. We'll let Blaise and Pennyfeather meet for a while.'

'Let them meet? What for?'

'To see what the result is. They'll interact upon one another, and I can't think it will be to their benefit, but it may well be to ours. Neither of them is likely to produce much hope in the other.'

Chance shrugged. 'All right. I suppose you know what you're doing.'

Brunel nodded. 'Be very sure of that, Adrian.'

She wore a white linen shift dress of Lisa's. It was an hour since lunch and the ground was steaming after a light rain shower when she saw Giles Pennyfeather shuffling towards her as she stood near the gorilla's cage. Brunel had said,

'Why don't you take a stroll to see Ozymandias? You might run into an old friend.'

She had thought it the start of another deliberately confusing project, and had expected anything but to see Giles. Now she moved towards him, not hurrying because she was sure they would be watched from the house. He seemed to be limping along aimlessly, but then he saw her and increased his shuffling gait.

With an effort she kept her face impassive as he came closer. He was carrying his shoes, and his feet were wrapped in strips torn from the legs of his trousers, which now reached only to just below his knees. His lean face was hollow, his eyes sunken, the spiky hair matted with grime. Despair swept her at the realization that he had been viciously hurt and that she had nothing to offer him, had conceived no plan that might even provide a spark of hope.

He waved a shoe, and a great grin of pleasure split his gaunt, dirty face as they came together. She saw the abrasions on his wrists, the rope-marks.

'Christ, I thought they were having me on!' he said, and dropped the shoes to grip her hands. 'Are you all right?'

'Yes. I'm all right, Giles. Look, I want to kiss you hallo, but I guess they're watching and I don't want them to see a big scene. Just let's walk up and down here. They can't have peppered the ground with bugs, and the house is too far away for anyone to hear us.'

'Right-ho.' He slipped his hand under her arm. 'I'm a bit slow on the old pins, I'm afraid.'

'Yes. I saw. But I mustn't show I care, not while they're watching. What have they done?'

'Well, a bit of hefty slapping about every day. Makes you damn dizzy, that does. And pretty long spells without water, but that's not too bad. I don't like being kept in the dark all day and night, though. Makes the time pass a bit slowly, you know.' He looked down at his crudely swathed feet. 'Then there's the toenails. That silver-haired sod comes and yanks one off every day. A sort of finale to the slapping about. It doesn't half bloody well hurt.'

At the banality of his comment she felt a sob of aching laughter rise in her throat, but managed to swallow it down, her nerves quivering as she fought against the thrust of hysteria. She said, 'Oh my God, I wonder you don't hate me for getting you into this.'

'Eh? It wasn't your doing. I mean, we couldn't just sit on our backsides. It's just a pity something went wrong. Have they been giving you a bad time?'

'Not like you. They've hardly touched me.'

'Well, that's something.'

'Not very much. I've been trying to work out what to do, but ...' She shook her head. 'I don't know what's wrong with me. This is my kind of business and I ought to have got us out of it long ago, but ... I'm not doing very well.'

'Don't be bloody silly, you can't expect to work miracles.'

'It doesn't need a miracle, Giles. It just needs hard thinking and a bit of fire in the belly. I seem to have run out of both just now.' She could hear the hint of desperation in her own voice, and drew in a long breath, trying to concentrate. 'Listen, I don't know how long we have together, so tell me where they're holding you. That's the important thing. Once I know, maybe I can do something.'

'Oh, there's a little sort of brick building behind that power-house place, next to the fuel store. They keep me locked up in there.'

'I see. Have you told them anything?'

'You mean the coordinates? Not likely! Oh, I'm not being terribly heroic or anything like that.' He gave a little bray of laughter. 'I fairly screech my head off when they do a toenail. It's a wonder you haven't heard me, but I suppose the generator noise muffles things. No, I decided I'd better not tell them the coordinates because once I do that they'll kill me, and I'm not too keen on that.'

'But ... how long can you hold out, Giles?'

'I haven't actually thought about that. I've only got five toenails left, but when they're gone I suppose that silver-haired sod will start on something else. So far, I just take each day as it comes, and hope something will turn up.'

She felt sick with hatred for herself. He must have sensed it, for he gave her arm a little squeeze and said, 'Don't you worry about it, old girl – oh, sorry, I didn't mean to call you that. We'll just keep soldiering on until you think of something, eh? I was a bit worried they might get the idea I absolutely couldn't remember *anything* poor old Novikov jabbered, and then they'd give me the chop anyway. But I've been terrifically cunning about that. I managed to give that little bastard Brunel a sort of impression that I might just vaguely remember something if only I could pin it down. Keeps them hoping, see? Now, how are things going with you, old darling?'

'I've got the soft option, Giles. They're out to break me, but with fairly painless brain-washing.'

'Yes . . . look at me for a minute, Modesty.' There was a note of authority in his voice, a note she had heard when he was dealing with a patient. She turned her head, and had to press her lips tightly together as she looked into his haggard face. Though the eyes were sunken, they were still Giles Pennyfeather's eyes, outward-looking from a quite unquenchable spirit of whose quality he was completely ignorant. A wave of humility and affection coursed through her, and with it she felt the awakening of a fiery spark of will.

He was frowning, lips pursed as if trying to pin down a thought that flickered in the shadows of his mind. At last he said, 'Have you been feeling a bit confused? I mean, I know the whole situation's pretty grotty, and most people wouldn't know whether to suck it or blow it. But you've been tangled up in the same sort of thing quite a bit before. Doesn't it usually sort of sharpen you up? Clear the mind, and all that?'

'Usually, yes. That's what scares me, Giles. I don't seem to have what it takes any more.'

He gave a short laugh. 'I wouldn't wonder. Come on, let's keep walking. Look, there aren't any obvious symptoms you could find listed in a medical book, but there's something about the way you look, darling. I'm bloody sure they've been feeding you one of the thymoleptic drugs.'

'*What?*' His words hit her like a douche of cold water in the face, startling yet stimulating.

'Thymoleptic. There are several kinds, but it's basically a drug that would make a healthy person confused, unable to concentrate.'

She forced herself to match his hobbling pace, but her fingers were digging into his arm as excitement and relief swept headily through her. She said in a whisper, 'The water. Could it be given in water, Giles?'

'Oh lord, yes. It can be administered orally.'

The jug of water in her bedroom. She knew it now with absolute certainty. The jug was always there, always kept filled. The mere knowledge that her lack of power was caused by an outside source acted upon her like an elixir. She said, 'How long will it take to wear off, Giles?'

'Well, it varies a lot as between individuals. I think you'd shake off anything pretty quickly. Say three or four days, once you stop being dosed of course.'

'I can stop that without their knowing it. They dose the water-jug in my room. I can empty that at about the usual rate, and drink from the washbasin. Don't let them see you looking pleased, Giles. If you can't look deadpan, look miserable.'

'Righty-ho.' He composed his features into a lugubrious expression.

With the adrenalin effect of what he had told her, her mind seemed to be racing now, but she knew this would be short-lived. To make hasty decisions, to take hasty action in the euphoria created by his mental shot in the arm, would be to court disaster.

She said, 'Let's make it three days, then. From tomorrow.' Her stomach tightened. Three more toenails for Giles. Or rather, three less. 'Can you hang on for that long, darling? It makes me sick to ask, but I swear I'll come for you by then, by the fourth night. And before then if I really feel I'm back on form. But not a minute later anyway. Then we'll make our break, win or lose.'

'That's marvellous,' he said simply. 'It makes something to look forward to.'

She glimpsed a movement from the corner of her eye and said, 'I think they're coming for us.'

He turned his head. 'Yes, they are, Brunel and Jacko. I wonder why they let us meet?'

'So we could each see how helpless the other was. A morale-breaker. Don't say anything, just look listless.'

They waited in silence, watching Brunel and Jacko approach. Brunel said, 'It's nice to have a gossip with one's friends, but I'm afraid I must break it up now. Have you enjoyed yourselves?'

Modesty gave a tired shrug and looked at him with dull eyes. Giles rubbed his forehead with a grimy hand. When neither of them spoke Brunel said, 'All right, Jacko, take Dr Pennyfeather back to his suite.'

Jacko jerked his head. Pennyfeather picked up his shoes and hobbled away. Brunel watched them go, then looked at Modesty. 'Aren't you going to ask me to spare him Adrian's attentions?'

Again the small shrug. 'What difference would it make?'

'You can never tell.' Brunel was watching her closely. 'You haven't asked anything of me so far, you know, and there have been several occasions. But when you learn to do so, when you accept that asking *me* for what you want is the only way open to you, then you'll find it will make a lot of difference.'

She studied him without interest for a few seconds, then moved past him towards the house, heading towards the veranda along the south wing, so that she would be able briefly to have a sight of the fuel store and garage complex beyond, where the small brick building that was Giles Pennyfeather's prison lay.

She wished now that she had thought to ask him what kind of lock was on the door.

CHAPTER TEN

Lying in a lounging chair under the warmth of the late morning sun, his squat hairy legs bulging against the shorts he wore, Jacko Muktar grunted, 'You not talking much. You mad because Brunel don't let you work on that doctor these last couple days?'

Adrian Chance did not open his eyes. He said lazily, 'No, I'm not mad about anything, Jacko. Just thinking. Have you ever wondered how it is that Lisa always does whatever Brunel says, no matter what? I mean, really no matter what. She hates most of it like hell, especially a killing, but she does it just the same. Have you ever wondered why?'

Jacko shrugged massive shoulders. 'Because he's Brunel.'

Chance laughed. The excitement in him was so intense that for a moment or two he was on the verge of blurting out the tremendous discovery he had made, but with an effort he crushed down the impulse and said, 'Yes, I guess you're right.'

'Blaise is tougher,' said Jacko sleepily. 'Tougher than Lisa. But he'll get her, Brunel will. Different, though. He'll make her carry a hatchet for him, same as us.'

No he won't, by Christ! Chance said to himself with almost prayerful passion. *Not now!*

He thought of his discovery. Even now, nearly twenty-four hours later, his mind was still scarcely able to encompass it. And he had come upon it quite by accident, by a million to one chance.

Yesterday. Brunel's study. Only the third time in six years that he had been in that study on his own. The radio telephone was causing trouble, and Brunel had told him to look at it and check for a loose connexion.

The study seemed to have absorbed the aura of Brunel's presence, and he felt uneasy there, an intruder. Perhaps for this reason his hands had been a little clumsy. There was a small plastic card with a circuit diagram, fixed in a slot in the chassis of the radio telephone. He had put it on the desk to study it as he worked, and knocked it off the edge with his cuff. Incredibly, after falling on to his knee the card had fluttered down and caught the air in such a way as to swoop suddenly against the drawers in the right-hand pedestal of the desk, slotting neatly through the thin crack between the top of the lowest drawer and the cross-brace above it – and disappearing. It was just like a conjuring trick, and he had given a startled, nervous laugh. A million to one chance.

The drawer was locked when he tried it. He did not want to go and tell Brunel. It would only mean suffering under Brunel's cool, ironic tongue. He tried the drawer above, and it came out easily. With relief he reached in and down into the deep bottom drawer. It was then he made the discovery, though at first it roused only a vague and furtive curiosity in him.

Why would Brunel keep this portable tape-recorder? He did not use it for dictation. Chance had never seen him use it at all. And it was not simply a tape-recorder. There was a radio transmitter bolted to the back of it, with an extending rod aerial. Very puzzling. Chance looked at the spool of tape set on one of the spindles, and his face broke out in sweat as temptation grew within him.

It was mid-afternoon. Brunel was out of the house, making an inspection of the farms. He would be gone for a full hour, and nobody else would come to the study. There was ample time to listen to a little of what was on the tape. Still Chance hesitated. Perhaps what broke the spell was the bitterness which had seethed and burned within him since the moment on the veranda when Brunel had coolly told him that one day he would make way for Blaise and take orders from her.

Chance swore vilely under his breath, plugged the ear-piece into his ear with a hand that shook, and switched on the recorder. There was a second switch which apparently linked the recording to the radio-circuit, but he was careful not to touch this. The thought of broadcasting his offence, to no matter where, was chilling.

Ten minutes later, when the tape had run only a quarter of its length, he switched off. For another five minutes he sat as if in a daze, remembering what he had heard, trying to assess the possibilities presented to him by this fantastic discovery. He knew that something huge lay within his grasp, but reason had yet to catch up with instinct.

Fantastic was the word . . .

He came to himself with a start, reeled the tape back on fast rewind, thrust the machine into the drawer, and slid the upper drawer back into place. That night he lay awake until the early hours, feverish with excitement as the tendrils of his thoughts touched a concept which had seeded within him, touched it and were snatched away at first, as a woman might warily test the heat of an iron.

Gradually the doubts faded and his confidence grew. He let his thoughts enfold the idea, examining it calmly. It could be done. It *could* be done . . .

Temptation shook him as a terrier shakes a rat, and when the spasm was past he lay with blurred and delightful images floating through the darkness of his mind. It was all being offered to him. Everything . . .

He slept, and when he woke his mind was clear and cool. He would have to listen carefully to the whole of the tape, and to any others he could find, before doing what he had decided upon. Today, in the afternoon, Brunel was driving into Kigali with Jacko. Apart from Lisa, he would have the whole north wing of the house to himself, and Lisa would be no problem, would never come near the study. He would have the afternoon alone there. That was time enough and to spare.

Even within twenty-four hours of her meeting with Giles Pennyfeather, it was clear to Modesty that there was a marked difference in her. She could feel the cogs of her mind beginning to mesh more smoothly again, her ability to concentrate was improving, and her sense of purpose was hardening.

After forty-eight hours the urge to take action had become almost overpowering, and seemed to hum like a dynamo within her. The sense of becoming herself again brought fierce exhilaration, and she sometimes spoke to Willie Garvin in her thoughts.

It's going to be all right, Willie love. He's relying on the drugs to keep me from doing anything, and he'd be right if Giles hadn't guessed. The confusion . . . it's a horrible feeling and it brings on a sort of inertia. But that's all over now. I don't even think it's going to be very difficult, Willie. All I have to do is reach Giles, get him out, then run for the border in one of the cars. I'll head for Kalimba. John and Angel are there, those missionaries I told you about. They'll take care of Giles. And when he's safe, I'll come back here and deal this bunch out of the game – Brunel, Chance, Muktar, and anyone else who gets in the way. Don't worry though, Willie. I'll be careful. I only wish I could finish them off before we make the getaway, but it's an extra risk. Getting Giles clear is the main thing. Different if you were with me. We could . . . no, I won't think about that. I'm all right, but I do miss you so. Sleep well, Willie love.

Over the last two days the system of alternating civilized treatment with sudden and irrational harshness or humiliation had continued as before, but there had been nothing major, only constant pinpricks. Today she was free even of those, for Brunel was away for the afternoon with Jacko, and she had realized now that Brunel did not trust Adrian Chance to carry on the campaign alone.

She had been given nothing to eat since breakfast, and was locked in her room. It suited her very well. Since learning of the thymoleptic drugs, she had spent many hours in trance, linked to physical reality by only a thread of consciousness, reaching down into the cool depths of the psyche as she had been taught, and directing the unfathomable energies there to the end of cleansing her body from the subtle enemy that lingered in her bloodstream. And for two hours each night she soundlessly performed a whole range of exercises to bring every muscle up to perfect pitch.

On the third night she tested herself. The lock on her door

yielded to a short piece of stiff wire broken from the bed-spring and shaped to her purpose. Wearing the black slacks and shirt that were the only clothes of her own she possessed, she spent two hours moving about the sleeping house like a shadow.

In the kitchen she found a flash-lamp. With kitchen scissors she cut a small patch from the bottom of her shirt, made a hole in the centre, and tied it over the lens so that the flash-lamp produced only a thin pencil of light. There were several kitchen knives in a drawer, and she took one with a six-inch blade, tucking it down inside her boot. For half an hour she examined doors and windows, checking them for alarms but finding none. When the time came tomorrow night, she would be able to leave the house without difficulty.

As she prowled, she looked for anything which might be of use to her but which would not soon be missed if she took it. She did not think the missing kitchen knife and flash-lamp would rouse any suspicion. In a cupboard of the sideboard she found an empty cruet she had never seen in use. It was made of close-grained wood, and the salt-cellar mushroomed at the top. When she fitted it into her fist the ends protruded an inch on each side. It would make a good improvised kongo, and she slipped it into the pocket of her slacks.

Checking her reactions as she stood in the darkness with the flash-lamp switched off, she found that her nerves were steady and that confidence was flowing smoothly through her. This was the mental attitude she had always known, and the comfort of rediscovering the old pattern brought relief beyond all words.

Ten minutes later she found that the upper floor of the north wing of the house was sealed off. This was where Brunel and Lisa, Chance and Jacko, had their bedrooms. The sealed section could be approached only by way of the long corridor which ran north and south from the top of the stairs, and halfway along the northern arm of the corridor was a solid door. It was locked, and she squatted on her haunches in the darkness for long minutes, deciding whether or not to try picking the lock. It was very tempting. If she

could get to Brunel and his entourage while they slept ...
but no.

Opportunism was a strong element in her make-up. She
had often used it to turn a setback to advantage. But instinct
warned her that this was not the right opportunity. Brunel
was not the man to set up a standing defence which would
easily yield. Though she could see no signs of it on this side
of the door, she felt certain that it was wired to an alarm
system. Their bedroom windows would be similarly wired.
This was the fortress section of the house, and to be treated
with the greatest caution.

She put the wire probe back in her pocket and moved
away down the corridor. There were doors on each side, and
these were the bedrooms of the five overseers. She had seen
them occasionally, coming or going from their rooms.

Camacho was snoring. She listened outside his door for a
while, making up her mind, then eased the latch back and
edged inside. For five minutes she waited, until she could
make out his sleeping figure. He was sprawled on his face,
one arm hanging down. Switching on the flash-lamp she
moved the pencil beam slowly round the walls of the room,
ready to flick it off if his breathing changed. There was a
hunting rifle in a rack on one wall, and a holstered Webley
revolver hanging over the back of a chair.

Again she was sorely tempted, but the moment was not
right. Tomorrow night before she left to get Giles – that was
the time to pick up the gun.

Silently she withdrew and closed the door, then moved
along the passage to the south wing and her own small
room. When she had locked the door behind her with the
probe, she hid her few trophies behind the cistern in the
shower cubicle and undressed. Her spirits were high now,
tempered only by the underlying ache that marked her grief
for Willie Garvin. And this, she knew, was something she
would always have to live with.

It's pretty good, Willie, she told him, lying in bed and
watching the slits of moonlight from the lowered blind.
There are three cars and a Land-Rover. I've seen them

coming and going, and I'm damn sure they don't immobilize them. I'll take the Land-Rover and short out the ignition. That track to the border might be pretty rugged for a car. It runs over a high ridge. I can remember now, from the map Tarrant gave us. But at least it's a marked track, so the Land-Rover should be able to cope. Better disable the rest of the cars. They may have some other transport down in the farm area, but it'll take longer to get on the road. I was all right tonight. I had to make a dry run to try myself out, but I was all right. Must have got that muck out of my system. So it's tomorrow night for go. Wish me luck, Willie love.

No answer came to her out of the darkness.

Lisa was awake. The pain in her stomach had become sharper, more fiery, but this alone was not what kept her awake. The burning seemed remote, as if it were happening to some shadowy counterpart of her.

Eyes tightly closed, body rigid, she was listening to the voices, and her whole being was racked by terror and doubt. For an hour they had spoken to her last night, chanting repetitively, emotionlessly, as she had once heard a Greek chorus chant its message in the ancient theatre at Epidaurus.

The whispering instructions that the voices had for her, their exhortation and their command, were frightening beyond anything she could ever have imagined. There was a difference in the voices, too. The choice of words, the style of delivery and the phrasing were the same, or almost the same, but there was a harsher timbre, a sense of urgency tinging their measured coolness. Yet this was understandable, for their sing-song message shattered a pattern she had believed changeless.

... *Brunel must die, Lisa. You are chosen. Brunel has become an Enemy. You are our child and our disciple. Brunel must die and you are chosen. This is your privilege and your honour. This is your path to peace. All frailty of the past will be forgiven, all sins lifted from you. Brunel has become an Enemy. Brunel must die. Evil has entered his mind. He gives thought to your destruction. But you are our*

child and we your protectors. He must die by the knife and
you are chosen. In obedience to us you will find peace. There
is no other way but through us. Brunel must die by the knife.
The knife lies under your sleeping head. The time to strike
has been chosen. It shall not be of your choosing but of our
choosing. It shall not be done under the sky but between
walls. The moment shall be when next he lies upon you.
When next Brunel lies upon you he must die by the knife in
your hand. Let no fear or question enter your heart. Brunel
has become an Enemy and must die, Lisa. You are chosen . . .

Though she paced the room, though she pressed her hands
over her ears, the voices chanted on in her head until their
words were carved into her mind. For an hour they had
spoken to her last night, and now again. She had looked for
the knife and found it, under the mattress beneath her
pillow, a stiletto with a long needle-pointed blade.

She had dreaded that Brunel might come to her during the
day just past, or tonight, yet when he did not come her
torment had grown greater in the knowledge that this was
only a postponement, that the moment was still moving
towards her on the stream of time. She had put the knife
ready under her pillow, waiting in dread for the High Priest
of the voices who had now, incredibly, become an Enemy.
But in all the hours since the voices had first spoken, Brunel
had not come to her room to lie upon her. There were only
the voices, whispering the same terrible message in her head,
stamping it into her brain.

It was ten minutes before breakfast when Adrian Chance
strolled into Jacko's room. The window which led to the
balcony stood open. Beside it there was a small teak table
which Jacko used as a work-bench. His four hand-guns hung
on the wall above the table. Below them stood a compact
rack of tools. A vice was attached to one end of the table.

Jacko was not checking his guns when Chance entered, he
was studying a map spread out on the table. Chance threw
him a cigarette and sat down in an armchair, stretching out
his legs. Jacko grunted a greeting.

189

'Today's charade for Blaise,' said Chance. 'Are you listening, Jacko?'

'Sure. I could make a good charade putting a bullet in her gut.'

'I've a much better idea myself, but this isn't the moment for it.' Chance smiled. He was very relaxed. 'Today we play it Brunel's way.'

'Every day.'

'You can never tell. Let's just stick to today. The morning she's brought down to breakfast and she gets the olde-worlde courtesy. We stand up when she comes in the room. We treat her like a lady. If she takes a cigarette, we compete to light it. Later Brunel takes her for a drive round *Bonaccord*. This gets her jumpy, because she wonders what's coming next.'

'So what comes?'

'Nothing yet. The soft treatment continues through lunch. It's gone on long enough for her to start relaxing. Brunel leaves. Then suddenly she doesn't exist for us any more. She's not there. You know what I mean?'

'I know. Like before.'

'Yes. Then two of the boys walk in, Selby and Loeb. They rope her up. We just go on chatting. They take her down to the farms, strip her and strap her over an oil-drum, all set up for a gang-bang by the natives.'

Jacko's head jerked round. His stare was incredulous but hopeful. 'Brunel wants it *real?*'

'Not quite.' Chance's smile was twisted. 'At the last minute, or rather at the last second, our hero appears on the scene.'

'Our hero?'

'Brunel, you dumb bastard. He stops the performance. No big scene. He just stops it, and our dark beauty is taken home to the safety of her little room, undefiled. Don't ask me who our dark beauty is.'

'Blaise,' said Jacko, and nodded his big head. 'But what's the idea?'

Chance sighed. 'If you were a woman, Jacko, and if about fifty Bantu were lined up to screw you, and if someone came along and stopped it, wouldn't you be a little bit glad? A little bit thankful? Even if you hated his guts?'

Jacko pondered. 'But she knows he wants that. Wants her thankful. She's going to know he set it up.'

Chance stubbed out his cigarette. 'She hardly knows the time of day, Jacko. She's full of dope and confused as hell. He's increased the dose these last two days. Look, you don't have to understand it. Do you know what you have to do?'

'Sure I know. Light her cigarettes. Then when Brunel goes, she's not there. I don't see her no more. Then the boys come and take her.' He scratched his chest and leered. 'Do we get to see them set her up?'

'Yes. We can go and watch. Brunel has to be her only saviour. You'd better take a cold shower first, you randy bastard.'

Jacko grinned. Chance stood up, his eyes on two throwing knives which lay on the cabinet beside Jacko's bed. He said, 'Are those Garvin's?'

'Uh? The knives? Sure. In sheaths under the jacket. You know. We took it off before we put the strait-jacket on him.'

Chance moved across and picked up one of the knives, examining it closely. It was the most superbly balanced knife he had ever touched, and the hilt nestled sweetly into his hand. 'They're beautiful,' he said impressed. 'You want them, Jacko?'

'No good to me.' Jacko glanced at the rack over the table. 'A gun for me. Every time.'

'Thanks. I might try my hand at throwing.'

'A bullet throws easier.' Jacko returned to his map.

Chance crouched, the knife in his hand. His feet danced and the blade glittered as he cut and stabbed at the air, shadow-fighting.

A marvellous knife. He had heard somewhere that Garvin made them himself. In that case no more would ever be made. These two would be rarities. Chance smiled to himself at the thought. He wandered across the room to Jacko and said, 'What's that?'

'A map.'

Chance laughed. He was in very good humour. 'I can see it's a map, you thick ape. What of?'

'Around here.' Jacko gestured vaguely. 'It's good.'

'Where did you get it?'

'Found it in Garvin's jacket.'

Chance looked over Jacko's shoulder, only mildly curious. Odd that Garvin should have been carrying a map of this area. Large-scale, too. It covered the whole of *Bonaccord* and some of the surrounding territory. Jacko should have shown it to Brunel, the fool. It might be important—

The small red cross near the north-western boundary suddenly hit his eye like a bullet. *Christ! This was a detailed blow-up of part of Novikov's map!* No coordinates marked, but . . .

The cross. The little red cross. As surely as he could hear the thudding of his own heart, Chance knew that he had the answer Brunel had been seeking. The gold was there, between those two long ridges. By God, it had lain under Brunel's hand all this time, not just in Rwanda but within the boundaries of *Bonaccord* itself. So Pennyfeather had been stalling. Even with the nails ripped from his toes he had kept it up. Tough boy. Astonishing. Pennyfeather had known all the time. Blaise had known.

Now Adrian Chance knew.

Jacko jabbed a finger on the map and said, 'I always figure there's got to be a track here. Make a short cut to Kigali. Save going round the lake. Next time I take the Land-Rover, I try.'

Chance tore his eyes away from the small red cross. He would not tell Jacko. Not yet. He looked where Jacko was pointing, then at the map key. It was hard to breathe evenly, and he took his time before he said, 'You'll end up in a marsh, you silly bugger.'

'Marsh?' Jacko peered, then gave a deep chuckle. He never resented Chance's insults. 'No goddam good.' He pushed the map aside and stood up. 'Breakfast, hey? We go light Blaise's cigarettes.'

'That's right. But leave the chat to Brunel and me. It's not your line. Can I borrow this?'

'The map? Sure. Take it. I just figured there was a track.'

'Never mind. I might find something interesting myself.' Chance folded the map and slipped it into his pocket. An enormous and almost unbearable excitement was throbbing within him. It seemed that once you started to reach out and make things happen the luck began to flow.

It was all coming to him now.

At three o'clock in the afternoon Brunel sat in his study reviewing the day's main event and acknowledging to himself that it had not produced the impact he had hoped for.

As soon as Selby and Loeb had set up the Blaise girl for the gang-bang in the village she had simply passed out. Brunel did not think it was involuntary, from shock or fear. He believed it had been a deliberate and self-induced loss of consciousness. That was interesting, an unusual accomplishment. It was also a little disturbing. He would not have thought Blaise could manage such a trick when her mind was confused by drugs.

Certainly it had weakened the effect of his own appearance on the scene. She was unconscious when he arrived, and the charade was completely lost upon the one person it had been devised for. At his orders, Selby and Loeb had cut the ropes lashing her to the oil-drum, wrapped a blanket about her limp naked body, and put her in the car with him. They were almost back at the house before she opened her eyes. And then Brunel could only tell her with cool reassurance that she had not been violated, that he had arrived in time to put a stop to the affair. It was not the same. The impact had been much diluted. She had listened without any apparent reaction, her eyes dull and uncaring.

A disappointing outcome, yet something of a challenge, Brunel decided. He felt he had struck the right note in his manner towards her, in being amiable but not too solicitous. She was in her room now. She could rest for a few hours, he had told her. A light meal would be sent up later. She need not fear that anybody would attempt such a crude jest with her again. Not without his orders, certainly.

Remaking Blaise in the way he wanted was going to be more difficult than he had anticipated, Brunel concluded. Not impossible, just more demanding. He would have to give closer attention to it.

The sight of her when he had come upon the scene that afternoon, her naked body spread-eagled over the big oil-drum, lingered in his memory, and he realized now that it had roused a need in him. He put away the files and reports which lay on his desk, and went out of the study. Adrian Chance and Jacko Muktar were in the billiard room.

'Where's Lisa?' he asked.

Adrian Chance, in the act of chalking the cue, paused for a moment, not looking up, gazing at the tip of his cue as if it suddenly held great interest for him. 'In her room,' he said at last.

'I'll be with her for the next half hour,' Brunel said. 'See that we're not disturbed, Adrian.'

Chance nodded. 'Yes, of course.'

Brunel went out. Chance studied the table, chose his shot and moved round behind the cue-ball. As he bent for the stroke he felt utterly confident. The ball flashed down the table, came off the cushion, kissed the red and the white. When the balls had finished rolling they were gathered in a tight group which offered a long break.

Jacko whistled. 'Jesus! That's the best shot you ever made.'

Chance straightened up, his smile cool and bright. He cocked his head to look at the ceiling. 'Not quite the best,' he said.

Lisa was lying on her bed when Brunel entered, and for a moment she stopped breathing. He said, 'You look feverish. Is anything wrong?'

'No. It's just the weather.' Her voice sounded strange to her. 'There's nothing wrong.'

'Good. Undress, please.' He began to take off the pale blue shirt he wore.

She stood up, slipped the dress from her shoulders and let it fall. Her eyes were closed as she unclipped her bra. She was listening for the voices. They did not speak to her now, but the message they had burned into her mind ran on and on, like the sound of the sea heard in a shell held to the ear.

There was never any variation in Brunel's union with her. It was quite mechanical and rather slow. She lay down on her back. He knelt beside her, then moved on top of her, seeking her. She kept her eyes closed. Her right hand was under the pillow, gripping the hilt of the stiletto. She did not wait, did not dare to wait. She brought her hand down beside her hip, then up, with the knife poised above his back, angled towards her.

She struck, and though she could put little force behind the awkward thrust, the blade went home as if against no resistance at all. Brunel jerked once, and gasped. She heard him say in a shocked, unbelieving voice, 'But . . .'

And that was all. His body went slack. She rolled sideways, pushing against him in panic as nausea surged within her. There came a soft thud as his small body hit the floor beside the bed.

It was five minutes before the spasms of retching passed and she could drag herself back from the bathroom, clutching at a chair as her legs threatened to fold beneath her. The pain in her stomach had focused to a red-hot skewer point now, as if the killing of Brunel had unleashed it.

He lay on his side, the hilt of the knife jutting from between his shoulder-blades. There was only a trickle of blood. Dazedly she wondered what she should do. Three times before this the voices had made her strike down an Enemy, but then there had always been Brunel to give instructions. Now Brunel was the Enemy she had struck down, and the voices were silent, offering no guidance.

She dragged a forearm across her sweating face and doubled up with pain. She could not stay, could not stay here with Brunel lying dead. There was a dressing-gown lying across the chair. She managed to straighten herself and pull it on, then lurched to the door, dragging it open, stumbling into the passage, falling to her hands and knees.

Almost fifteen seconds passed before she could draw
enough breath into her lungs to scream for help.

In the far wing of the house, Modesty did not hear the
scream. She was asleep, gathering her energies for the night's
work that lay ahead. She had not enjoyed the ordeal laid
upon her by Brunel during the afternoon, but neither had it
shattered her.

For most of the time she had believed that the threatened
performance would not be carried through. When it seemed
that her belief was wrong, when she had been roped across
the oil-drum and the jabbering natives were being herded
into line, then she had used deep respiration combined with
muscle tension to drive the blood from her head and bring
unconsciousness. If the gang-bang went through, at least she
would not know about it, would not have the immediacy of
memory and sensation to overcome later.

In the event, Brunel had appeared only a few seconds
after she had put herself under. That was a pleasant relief to
be greeted by on awakening, when she had probed with the
first tiny thread of awareness and found there was no need
to sink into oblivion again.

When she had been locked in her room, she took the jug
of drugged water and carefully poured another half pint of
it down the lavatory before settling to sleep.

It was less than an hour later that something roused her.
She sat up, eyes narrowed and she tried to interpret the
bustle of footsteps and muffled sound of raised voices from
the main corridor. A voice shouted from the patio below.
She got off the bed and moved to the window. The slats of
the blind were half closed. Peering between them, she saw
Camacho with his rifle. He had been on guard there when
she was returned to her room, and he seemed to be calling a
question across the length of the patio, to somebody at an
upstairs window in the north wing.

She held her breath and turned her head to listen, cupping
a hand behind her ear. Something unexpected had certainly
happened. An atmosphere of bustling alarm seemed to per-

196

vade the house. She heard Jacko Muktar's voice shouting from the far end of the patio.

'. . . gone crazy! She killed him – killed *Brunel*! An' she's sick in the gut, swallow poison maybe! Chance says to bring that doctor quick!'

Camacho called, 'You drunk, man! Killed Brunel? You drunk as hell.'

'Chris'sake, she *killed* him I tell you! Knife in the back! Go get that goddam Pennyfeather quick, Camacho!'

Modesty stood still, her mind racing as she tried to re-assess the situation. Lisa had killed Brunel. That was incredible, but she could not doubt the note of urgency in Jacko's voice. The why and the how of what Lisa had done did not matter. It was done. Brunel was dead. And that changed everything. She went to the wardrobe and began to put on shirt and slacks.

Giles Pennyfeather was being brought here to the house. If she could find or create an opportunity now, with everything in chaos, it would be well to do so, for otherwise Brunel's death might prove to have altered the situation for the worse. Presumably Chance would take charge, at least for the time being. He could never replace Brunel, could never take over Brunel's operations, but he would surely aspire to it. Vanity would not let him recognize his inadequacy.

And with Chance in command, she would not live very long. His hatred for her had grown during the days since their arrival here. She had seen it in his eyes. Giles would go too, and painfully. Chance would never continue Brunel's patient campaign of trying to force Giles' memory by moderate torture well-spaced. He would try to tear the coordinates from Giles, working as he had worked on Novikov, perhaps only half believing that Giles knew them.

She brought the kitchen knife, the wire probe and the make-shift kongo from their hiding place, hesitating for a few seconds before putting them near at hand under the mattress. It was tempting to have them on her, but better to wait until she was ready to make a move. At present the situation was confused, unpredictable.

The thought came to her that with Camacho gone she might climb down to the empty patio. If she could cross the patio unseen, she could follow Camacho, put him out, free Giles, and take one of the cars . . .

She pulled on her boots and moved to check that the patio was still empty. As she reached the window a small truck roared round the north wing of the house and came to a halt. Van Pienaar was driving, Selby beside him. There were two Kikuyu in the back, each with a rifle. She had seen a dozen of them down in the village that afternoon, keeping the Bantu in order. It seemed that the handful of Kikuyu had been imported to form a private police force of Brunel's little empire, under command of the overseers. They had the look of city natives rather than villagers, and handled their rifles with trained familiarity.

Van Pienaar spoke to them, pointing at the window of her room, then he and Selby moved off into the house, almost running. No chance of going through the window yet. She would have to wait. Perhaps in a general upheaval Chance would forget about her until tomorrow, or at least postpone dealing with her in the confidence that she was heavily doped and could give no trouble.

Perhaps. Her mouth twisted at the corner in bleak mockery of herself for entertaining the hope. If she had read Chance rightly he would not sleep on his hatred. It was too consuming.

She considered using her probe to open the door, but discarded the idea. There were people coming and going, on the stairs and in the main corridor. Without a gun, she could never get through them. Looking out of the window, past the corner of the south wing, she saw Giles Pennyfeather. Camacho was urging him along with an occasional shove from behind. He was hobbling still, but seemed to be moving less painfully than when she had last seen him, three days ago. That was strange. Had Brunel suspended the torture? . . .

They disappeared from her sight, and a minute later she heard Camacho's voice shouting on the stairs. Then the sound of voices and footsteps gradually faded away, and there was silence. After a little while she went and sat down on the bed, watching the door, waiting.

They assembled in the lounge. Camacho and van Pienaar, Loeb, Mesquita and Selby. Only Jacko was absent, upstairs watching Pennyfeather attend to Lisa.

Chance took up his position behind the chair Brunel had always used, resting his arms on the back of it. He said crisply, 'All right, let's get this sorted out. Brunel's dead and Lisa killed him. Now I'll tell you where we go from here.'

'Kill that white-hair bitch first,' said Loeb. He was angry and spoke in a deep, growling voice. He was also frightened. For six years now he had lived under Brunel's protection, and he felt suddenly exposed. With Brunel you were okay. He was a little man but he had big brains. A big man inside. When Brunel said the word you jumped, by God, and that was fine. You did the job, you got plenty of money and three months leave every year, any place you wanted, any place the police couldn't touch you. It was good. But now Brunel was gone. Loeb shook his head. It was hard to believe it, hard to believe anyone could kill Brunel.

'Kill that bitch,' he said again.

'No,' Chance said coolly. 'That's asking for trouble, and there's no need for it anyway. Pennyfeather says she's got acute appendicitis. Needs an emergency operation. So we can just let her die. Then we'll have a nice natural death for the police doctor from Kigali.'

Selby, a sandy-haired Englishman with faded blue eyes and a seemingly lipless mouth, said, 'And Brunel? There's going to be questions.'

Chance spread his hands. 'We tell the truth. She killed him, and we don't know why. It's simple.'

'There's us,' said Camacho. 'What happens to us afterwards?'

'We just go on as before,' said Chance. 'We inherit this place. I'll bring in a penman to fix a Will, and since there's nobody to challenge it there won't be any problems. Don't worry, I'll take good care of you boys.'

'You?' Camacho lifted an eyebrow. 'Somebody put you in charge?'

'Jacko and I did. Anybody want to argue?' Chance could feel the power within him and it was wonderful. These men were thick-headed fools, lost without Brunel. If it had been his own hand that struck down Brunel they would have torn him apart in animal fury, as they had wanted to kill Lisa. As it was, they were frightened and desperate. Desperate for a new leader. His own personality would bend them like reeds. He could feel it. The whole thing came down to confidence. That was what Brunel had had, above all else. Now he had found and unleashed it in himself, and was almost stupefied by its power.

The men looked at one another uncertainly, and Chance laughed. 'You bloody fools,' he said. 'All you do is run *Bonaccord*. This is where Brunel chose to live, not where he made his money. He was big-time, with a dozen smart operations going. I know them all.' It was a lie, but it was said with total conviction. Brunel kept meticulous files in his study, and Chance was sure he could learn all he needed from them. 'I'm the only one who can keep the organization running, the only one who can keep the loot coming in. If you don't want a piece of it, you can always quit. I can replace you in a week, any one of you.'

Selby said, 'Hold it. Nobody talked about quitting. You reckon you can take over and keep things going like Brunel?'

'I'll do better, Selby,' Chance said softly, and ran a hand over his silver hair. 'Brunel was getting a little over the hill. There's been dust collecting on three or four projects for months now.' He looked round upon the men, gathering them under his dominance, knowing they were his. So this must have been the way it was for Brunel. God, it was so easy . . .

Loeb said, 'Okay. What happens now?'

'Normal routine.' Chance sat down in Brunel's chair and stretched out his legs. 'You go down to the village, Loeb, and tell them Brunel's dead. It won't mean a lot to them, but make it casual and keep everything cool. The work goes on as before.'

'What happens to Brunel?' Selby jerked his head towards the ceiling.

'We'll delay reporting on that until Lisa's as good as dead. That won't be long. You and van Pienaar get Brunel boxed up and put in the refrigerator truck. Leave the rest to me. I should think I'll be able to call Kigali some time tomorrow. We'll unfreeze Brunel ready for the police doctor. I'll handle the police myself. There won't be anything for them to do except make a report.'

'Okay.' Loeb put his hands on his knees and stood up. He was thinking that maybe Chance could make a job of filling Brunel's shoes. He'd been closer to Brunel than anyone else, he had brains, and he wasn't squeamish. Yes, it might work out pretty good.

Van Pienaar said, 'There's the Blaise woman and that Pennyfeather, don't forget. They better be out of the way.'

Chance leaned back in the chair, chin on chest, gently tapping the tips of his steepled fingers together. He did not realize that this had been one of Brunel's mannerisms, nor that his voice held something of the flatness with which Brunel had always made his pronouncements.

He said, 'I don't forget anything, van Pienaar. Blaise and Pennyfeather will be gone before sunset. Just go and get on with what you have to do.'

CHAPTER ELEVEN

Modesty watched the truck pull out of the patio. Mesquita was on guard there now, a Belgian FN light automatic rifle slung on one shoulder. Quietness had settled upon the house again after an exodus of the overseers. Two of them had carried away towards the garage a small blanket-covered form on a stretcher.

She frowned, her lower lip caught in her teeth. Indecision plagued her, but it was not the indecision of a confused mind. Choosing the best moment to make a move depended on factors unknown to her and not readily guessed at. It depended mainly on what Chance had in mind. If she broke out now, it might be too early; if she delayed, it might be too late. There was no way of judging. A glance at the sky told her that there was half an hour to sunset. Here, just south of the equator, nightfall was swift. Better to wait for that.

She was wondering what had happened to Giles Penny-feather when she heard his voice in the passage that led to her room. It was raised in angry indignation. 'Now look here, you bastard! I'm not just going to let that girl die—' His voice broke off with a grunt on the last word. She heard Chance say something she could not catch, then Jacko laughed.

They were outside the door now. A key turned in the lock and the door was throw open. Jacko was there, standing back, gun in hand. Beyond him, across the passage, Chance gripped Giles Pennyfeather by the hair from behind, drawing his head back, holding a knife to his throat.

Jacko motioned with the gun and said, 'Out.' He stepped aside. She walked out of the room, watching Chance. A nerve twisted painfully inside her as she saw that the knife he held was one of Willie's knives. There was an aura about Chance, the feverish glow of a man seeing visions of glory. He gave her a glittering smile and said, 'All dressed up in your working clothes, I see. I wonder if you're as heavily doped as Brunel thought? Never mind, I rather hope not. We want you to appreciate what we've arranged for you. Hands on top of the head, please. Face the wall and keep quite still. One little wrong move and Dr Pennyfeather gets a quick tracheotomy. Now, make sure she's clean, Jacko.'

Jacko was very thorough, his rough hands probing every inch of her body and clothing. At last he said, 'Okay.'

'We're going downstairs and out of the house now,' Chance said. 'Through the dining-room and out at the back.

Jacko's behind you with a gun. I'm behind him with Penny-feather. You understand the arrangement?'

She nodded.

'Right, let's go.'

As she turned, Pennyfeather said in a strangled voice, 'Can't you get it through your stupid bloody head, Chance? That girl's going to *die* if you don't let me operate on her pretty quick!' She saw that his feet were still bound in rags, but he looked less haggard than before. The only emotion on his face was one of fury.

'You're repeating yourself, you silly man,' Chance said, and drew a bead of blood with the knife-point. 'Move along, please.'

'No! She's my patient now!'

Chance laughed incredulously. 'Your patient! Jesus, you're out of this world, Pennyfeather. It's almost a pity to lose you. Now move along, or your friend gets a bullet right through her liver.'

After a moment Pennyfeather said bitterly, 'My God, you're an evil bastard . . .'

They moved down the stairs and out through the big french windows of the dining-room. Jacko kept a steady three paces from Modesty, his gun aimed at her back. Chance herded Pennyfeather along ten paces behind. They crossed the open ground to the fringe of trees and came to the ring of acacias where the cage stood. Ozymandias was dozing in the shade on his bed of grass in the small central section of the great cage. This was circular and had a door which opened or closed from outside by a pulley and chain, so that Ozymandias could be confined while the cage was cleaned.

The door of the main cage stood open. Jacko said, 'Get in.'

Modesty stood still. If Chance was going through with this, she might as well try something now. Anything. It could be no more hopeless than being caged in with the gorilla.

Chance said briskly, 'Get in. Or I'll start cutting pieces off Pennyfeather for every five seconds you wait.'

Did they mean to go through with it? Or was this a continuation of Brunel's campaign, intensified? She half turned her head. Six feet away, Jacko's finger was on the trigger. He was tense and ready. Chance said, 'I'll begin now.'

She moved forward and into the cage. As she turned, Jacko took Giles Pennyfeather by the shoulder and gave a thrust which sent him stumbling against her. The door clanged shut. Jacko picked up the two big padlocks and slipped them through the hasps.

Chance gave a laugh of sheer delight, his eyes sparkling. He moved round the cage and hauled on the chain. The door of the inner compartment slid up. Chance secured the chain. Ozymandias lifted his great head and blinked. Then slowly he got to his feet.

Modesty moved to the outer bars, schooling herself not to hurry. There was one sure way to win a brief respite, to gain time for a final throw, however desperate. She said, 'Listen, Chance. We know the coordinates.'

His eyes widened in mock surprise. 'That's very interesting.'

'You'd better believe me, and get us out quick. Once we're dead you can say goodbye to a bankful of gold.'

'The coordinates. Now let me see if I can guess. Forty-two and one hundred and one. Right? The valley's only about two miles away, isn't it? I haven't had time to take a look yet, but I'll get around to it very soon.'

Jacko said, staring, 'Is that right? That really *right*? You *know* them?'

Chance was looking past Modesty at the gorilla. It had shuffled out of the inner cage now and was staring at Pennyfeather, grunting deep in its throat. Chance said, 'You didn't hear her argue, did you, Jacko? Yes, I know the coordinates. I've already got what Brunel couldn't get. As I told the boys, they'll do better with me than with him.'

Modesty absorbed the shock. Her last card, her only card that might win a reprieve, had fallen under Chance's ace. She turned away. Ozymandias was shuffling back and forth, keeping his head turned to watch Pennyfeather all the time. His grunts were growing louder, more angry. Giles Pennyfeather stood a little hunched, arms wrapped about his middle, a curious look on his face, as if he were trying to remember something.

Modesty forgot about Chance and Jacko, concentrating all her attention on the gorilla. It might take him seconds or minutes to make up his mind, she guessed, but sooner or later he would charge these invaders of his domain. Like all wild animals he feared the man-smell, but he would overcome that.

She edged round slowly until Ozymandias was between her and Giles. When he charged at Giles she would go in from behind and try ... what? She had no weapon. You might divert a gorilla for a few moments, but that was all. A dozen powerful men could not hold him, for though their united strength might almost match his own it could not be brought to bear within the unity of one mind and one body. They would be destroyed piecemeal.

Ozymandias stood upright and pounded his stomach, bellowing. The drumlike sound was louder and far more frightful than she had ever imagined.

Jacko had sat down on a pile of empty sacks near the small corrugated iron shelter where the gorilla's feed was kept. He said, grinning, 'How about I get a few stones an' throw at him, huh? Make him mad.'

Before Chance could reply there came a sound, a big soft sound from a little way off. It was only when Modesty heard Chance's shocked curse that she turned her head for a quick glance. A quarter of a mile away, beyond the house, a long spear of flame and smoke pierced the air.

Jacko was on his feet. 'Jesus! It's the fuel store! Some goddam fool – we got to get the foam wagon, quick!'

Chance stood as if frozen, his head twisted to glare over his shoulder. Jacko caught at his arm and shook him. 'Chris'sake, Adrian! The transport!'

Chance turned his head. The fury in him was close to madness, and perspiration ran in rivulets down his distorted face. He slammed an open hand against one of the bars and said in a shrill voice, 'I want to see her die!'

Jacko dragged him round. 'The generator!' he yelled.

'That goes, we got no power! You gone *crazy*?'

Chance pressed his knuckles to his head and seemed to make an enormous effort, then he wiped his hands down his dripping face and said flatly, 'Call the village and get the boys up with the foam wagon. I'll start moving the transport clear.' He took one last glance at the cage, then turned and began to run hard with Jacko on his heels.

Modesty pressed a shoulder between two of the bars, then tested hips and head. Not enough space, not enough by a good two inches. Flesh could give, but not bone. She turned. Ozymandias had stopped bellowing. He was hunched with knuckles on the ground, poised. Abruptly he gave an ear-splitting scream and rushed at Giles. Modesty had started to launch herself after him when, incredibly, she saw Giles hop forward a pace, his arms still folded round his body, crouched low now.

Ozymandias halted only ten feet away, then turned and lurched back and forth on all fours, gibbering angrily. She saw the shiny leather of his enormous chest, the colossal arms and shoulders, the nightmare face and the great thews of the bowed legs.

Giles was jerking his head sideways, winking at her hugely, urgently. She moved towards the bars, then round a little. He hopped over to her, still crouched. Ozymandias halted his pacing and watched them, glaring and scolding. Giles whispered, 'Look, crouch down, darling! Now fold your arms like this. And *don't* run if he charges. They bluff at first. Might make a dummy rush two or three times before he comes in for real, and maybe we can calm him down before then.'

She squatted like Giles, her mind half numb with unbelief, wondering how in God's name he knew anything about the attacking-ritual of gorillas.

'Ah, that's jolly good,' he breathed. 'Looks a bit weird, I know, but this is the posture of submission. It means we're not threatening him. I read an article in *Reader's Digest* by some woman. You know, in that London surgery when I was on night duty. She got on very well with a gorilla tribe up in the Virunga Range. The thing is, you've got to *act* like a gorilla, she said. Hold on, I've just remembered something.'

He crawled spiderlike across the cage, a grotesque figure in his ragged trousers and swathed feet, picked up a stump of wild celery from the ground, nibbled it, then tossed it at the grumbling gorilla's feet. 'Naoom! Naoom!' he said ingratiatingly in a deep voice.

Ozymandias surveyed him, then picked up the stalk and began to gnaw it, but the deep-sunk eyes in the great head were still suspicious and hostile. Pennyfeather rolled back to Modesty, knuckles to the ground, legs bowed.

'That's their word for food, so this woman said,' he whispered. 'She actually spent about three years with them, so she ought to know. Says they're not aggressive if you don't alarm them, especially if you act monkey-like. We'd better do that.' He began to scratch his chest vigorously with both hands, paused, frowned, and said, 'No, wait a minute though. It wasn't *Reader's Digest*. It was the *National Geographic*, now I come to think of it.'

It was an insane moment for laughter, but she had to swallow a great hiccup of it. Ozymandias threw the stump of celery away and stood on all fours watching them, growling a little. Giles muttered, 'Do it again, Modesty.'

'Do what?'

'That sort of belch you did just now. But nice and deep this time. They do that a lot.'

She swallowed air, and let forth the deepest eructation she could manage. Giles gazed at her admiringly. 'Christ, that was marvellous! I wish I could do it, but I've never got hold of the knack. Better move about a bit. He might think we're rather rum monkeys if we just squat here.'

Pennyfeather went lurching away round the cage, grunting and whimpering, arms folded submissively across his stomach. Modesty watched for a moment, then copied him. This was the stuff of farce, but she knew that in seconds it might turn to bloody destruction. Ozymandias rose, drummed on his great belly, and squatted down again. His belligerence seemed to have waned, but this could be no more than a reprieve. A casual buffet, a single clutch from one great hand, would mean the beginning of the end.

Pennyfeather rolled back to her and whispered, 'Is there any way we can get out? I mean, once Chance and that stocky sod come back it'll be too late.'

She said, 'Give me a minute to think.' Without a probe, there was no hope of opening the two great padlocks. The vertical bars of the cage were set in a massive ring of concrete bedded in the ground; the bars of the roof sloped up slightly in a shallow cone, and were no wider apart than the verticals. Giles was sitting down now, fixing a strip of rag that had come loose from his foot. She saw Ozymandias thump down on his haunches and begin to pluck at his own foot. She looked at the bars again, and the germ of an idea took shape in her mind.

Knuckling her way across the cage she picked up a bunch of long grass, then moved to the bars. Dividing the grass, she knotted one bunch of it round the foot of the bar, the other at shoulder height round the same bar. Giles joined her and muttered, 'What's that for?'

'It's a pretty wild idea, but we might as well try.' She gripped the marked bar with both hands, braced her feet against the bars on each side, then began to jerk back rhythmically.

Giles said, 'You'll never bend *that*!'

'I know. But Ozymandias might. He was imitating you just now. So if I can get him to imitate *me* . . .'

'God!' he beamed at her. 'I hope so. That woman didn't say. In the article, I mean.'

She kept it up for a full minute, then rolled away, with Giles lurching after her. Ozymandias watched them, still squatting. For the moment he did not seem dangerous. They waited, but he made no move.

'Stupid bugger,' Giles muttered angrily. 'That was a jolly good idea, but he's got no bloody sense.'

She said, 'Look. You're scratching your head and he's doing the same. I think you're the one who attracts him. Go and give it a try.'

He gave her a pallid grin from a face made gaunt by long

days of pain and stress. 'A gorilla queer? All right, let's see.'

He had braced himself and tugged at the bar for thirty seconds when Ozymandias lumbered forward, grunting menacingly. Giles lurched out of the way, then watched with open mouth as Ozymandias gripped the bar, clutched the adjoining bars with prehensile feet, and flung his great bulk backwards.

The first jerk made the bars of the roof rattle and vibrate. Pleased with the effect, Ozymandias threw himself back and forth, jerking harder. Pennyfeather breathed, 'My God, he's doing it!'

Modesty watched, trying to detect any yielding in the bar. It was an inch and a quarter in diameter. Ozymandias could never tear it free from the concrete below or from the great iron collar at the top, but he might well bend it before he became too bored with the performance. And if he could bend it only a couple of inches the gap would be enough for them to squeeze through.

The gorilla dropped to the ground and shambled away, satisfied that he had demonstrated his dominance. After a pause, Modesty knuckled her way across to the bars. The one marked by the twists of grass was nearly bent, and so were the two adjoining bars which had taken the purchase of his feet. But still the gap was not enough. For the first time she became aware of the smoky haze and the smell of burnt oil. Chance and the others were fighting the fire at the fuel store. When they had it under control, or when it was burnt out, Chance would return.

She wiped the sweat from her face and said, 'Once more, Giles.'

He had scarcely begun when Ozymandias came lumbering over, roaring his jealousy. This new game was his, and his alone. He grasped the bar. The cage shook and rattled. This time a full two minutes passed before Ozymandias grew bored. Then he squatted down in front of the bent bar, scolding and glowering.

Giles ran a hand through his filthy hair and said, 'He's not going to let us near it!'

Modesty stood up. 'I think he's made enough space. It's got to be enough, Giles. I'll draw him off, and you squeeze through as soon as he's out of the way.' He started to protest but she went on quickly, 'No, for God's sake don't start arguing. Just do as I say.'

She jumped and caught one of the sloping bars of the roof, near to the perimeter of the cage, then began to swing smoothly from bar to bar, hand over hand, moving round in a wide circle, passing only a few feet from the gorilla. Ozymandias watched. Slowly he became annoyed by the performance. He rose, bellowed, pounded his stomach, and began to lumber after the fast-moving figure. He was very quick on all fours, but slow on the turn and when standing upright. She avoided the clutch of a great hand, drew Ozymandias round to the other side of the small central cage, and called, 'Now, Giles!'

Pennyfeather was at the bars. For a moment she thought he was trapped, but then his head and shoulders were through. She lost sight of him for a second as she swung round, and when she looked again he was clear.

Ozymandias was using the roof bars now. Unlike the smaller monkeys he was no gymnast. He and his brethren climbed seldom, and then slowly. But the vast reach of his arms was a constant danger. Pennyfeather saw that Modesty would never have time to escape unless the gorilla could be distracted for a few seconds. He stumbled round the outside of the cage, picked up a stick and began to rattle it between the bars, screaming insults, but it was not until Ozymandias swung past close to him that he was able to get in a jab with the stick that drew the gorilla's attention.

Furious from the baiting now, Ozymandias dropped to the ground. The terrible drumming began again as he thumped his massive belly, shrieking at Pennyfeather, who kept lunging with the stick and shouting profanities at him. Modesty dropped down by the bar. Her measurements were no larger than Giles' except perhaps for the bust, and that would yield.

She was through, and heard Giles give a choking scream of pain. Ozymandias, one great arm thrust between the bars, had caught him by the wrist. She ran four long strides, caught one of the vertical bars, swung up almost to the horizontal and brought her outer leg scything round so that her booted foot drove straight into the gorilla's great face between the eyes as he pressed it to the bars.

The kick would have killed any man. It may even have hurt Ozymandias. Certainly it startled him. He jerked back, dropping Giles, then lunged forward again, screaming. But Giles had rolled clear. Modesty knelt over him. He drew in a shaky breath and his teeth were chattering as he said, 'Sorry . . he was a bit quick for me. I'm afraid he's bust my wrist.'

He got to his feet, holding his right wrist gingerly. Already it was beginning to swell. She said, 'I'll get some sort of splint on it as soon as we're clear. Come on. The quicker we get into that tangle of valleys beyond the woods the better.'

He nodded. 'All right. She's pretty bad, but if you give her a shot of morphia I expect she can walk as fast as I can manage just now.'

She looked at him, uncomprehending. 'Walk? Who?'

'You know. That girl.' He jerked his head in the direction of the house beyond the acacias.

'*Lisa?* Are you out of your mind?'

'Eh? No, I'm quite all right except for my feet and this wrist, darling. Can't leave her though. She's got acute appendicitis, you see, and they're going to let her die.'

It was unbelievable, and she could feel herself almost shaking with exasperation, yet at the same time something deep within her reached out to him. She said, 'God Almighty. We'll have enough to do, saving ourselves. You can hardly walk and you've broken a wrist. How the hell do you think you can help her?'

'Well, I don't know. But something might turn up. My medical bag's in her room, and I've got all the stuff I used to carry in Kalimba. I mean, we can't just *leave* her. I feel sorry for her, actually. She's not like the others, you see.'

'That's what Willie thought.'

'Yes, but I don't think she could help it. I mean, help

whatever she did that got us in this mess. There's something very rum about her.'

Modesty was aware of seconds and minutes running away. She looked quickly about her. Ozymandias had subsided into a sulk, pawing at his face. Beyond the house the smoke was still thick. It looked as if the fire-party would be busy for some time yet. But with Giles half-crippled, every minute was important.

She said, a snap in her voice, 'It's crazy, Giles. Come on, let's get moving.'

'Yes, you're right, I suppose.' He gave her an effortful grin. 'You go on, darling. But I can't help being a doctor, so I'm stuck with it. We'll try to catch up with you. Don't worry.'

'Don't *worry*?' She could have hit him.

'I mean, it's not your business. But it really is mine. I can guess how you feel about her, but the thing is, I doubt if she could help doing *any* of the bloody awful things she may have done. I think those bastards did to her what they were trying to do to you.'

For a moment her mind seemed to splinter, as if she had run headlong into a brick wall. Then she stood very still, feeling suddenly cold, remembering how close she had come to having her spirit melted down and remoulded to Brunel's design.

She looked at Giles, and then a zany gaiety rose astonishingly within her, an almost drunken recklessness. She remembered him squatting in the cage, gibbering, scratching his chest, saying, '. . . no, it wasn't the *Reader's Digest*, it was the *National Geographic*.' Inward laughter and a strange exuberance bubbled within her. This had become the maddest of all capers, and she might as well play it madly through to the end.

She grinned at him like an urchin accepting a dare, and said, 'All right. But you're not very mobile, so wait here and hide in the trees while I go and get her. If your bag's there, I'll give her a shot of morphia before I bring her down.' Without waiting for an answer she turned and ran for the house.

There was no time for caution or finesse now. The only way was to move in a straight line at top speed, and ride the luck for all it was worth. She crossed the veranda, went through the dining-room windows which still stood open, and was halfway across the room when Mesquita appeared in the open doorway to her left, at the end of the long room, the FN rifle in his hands. She had thought every man would be at the fuel store, but Mesquita was here. It seemed that her luck had run out fast.

Without breaking her stride she swerved towards him, cleared a couch with a long hurdling stride, and lunged on. In the moment that she jumped the couch she had heard the snick of the bolt driving a round into the barrel chamber as Mesquita pressed the release stud. Eight paces still separated them, and he was smiling as he brought the rifle up. Mesquita had shot big game, and his reactions were very fast. He would have ample time to shoot, but there could be no turning back now, she could only go on, closing as fast as her legs would drive her, and hoping. Hoping for one chance in a thousand to aid her. A miss, or a misfire, or—

Behind her Willie's voice said, 'Break right, Princess,' and she dived sideways, low to the floor, forearms slapping down in a breakfall, head turning so that her eyes never left Mesquita, seeing the rifle barrel start to follow her and then swing quickly back, seeing the shock in Mesquita's face, seeing the expected glitter of the knife-blade, the silvery streak that split the air and vanished at Mesquita's throat, hearing the soft thud of impact, seeing the black hilt jutting from the neck as the rifle sagged in limp hands, as the legs folded and Mesquita hit the floor ... all this in the fraction of a second before shock clamped its iron hand upon her.

She lay with fingers digging into the carpet, staring at the tufts of pile only inches from her eyes, unable to turn her head, wondering if this was insanity or nightmare.

Willie Garvin was dead. He had fallen three thousand feet to earth, and there was no way under the sun that he could be alive. Yet she had heard his voice ... could see Mesquita lying there dead, with one of Willie's knives in his throat.

A sound of feet on the carpet. A hand gripping her arm. She was hauled up without ceremony.

Willie Garvin. In a brown and green camouflage shirt and slacks. The shirt unbuttoned, hanging open. Beneath it, the slim leather harness holding twin sheaths on his left breast, one sheath empty.

Willie Garvin. Brown face. Fair hair. Blue eyes, looking at her anxiously. The S-shaped scar on the back of the hand that gripped her arm. Big. Solid. Alive.

Impossible.

His gravelly voice said, 'All right, I know it's a shock, Princess, but it's me.'

She felt her body begin to shake. Felt the muscles of her face begin to twist. He took her by the shoulders, gave her a none too gentle shake, then lifted a finger warningly two inches from her nose. 'You save that till after,' he said sternly. 'Don't you *dare* start grizzling in the middle of a caper.'

She nodded her head in mute acquiescence, fighting inwardly, her mouth open as she dragged in a long shuddering breath. He watched her for moment, then walked over to Mesquita, jerked the knife free and wiped it on the man's trouser leg before slipping it back into the sheath under his shirt. She saw now that he had a small haversack on his hip, a Colt M16 automatic rifle slung on one shoulder, a sheathed machete on his belt. A water bottle. A coil of rope round his waist. A light rucksack on his back.

Willie Garvin. Impossible.

He came back to her and said, 'It's quite a story. Tell you about it later. You okay now?'

She said in a whisper, 'Willie? . . .' and put both hands on his shoulders, uncertainly at first, then gripping hard, feeling the reality of him.

'I *told* you it's me,' he said curtly. 'Christ, who d'you think fired that fuel store, Princess?'

She knew, suddenly she knew, that he was being brusque because he feared she might break down if he was gentle with her, and this more than anything wiped away the dread that she might be dreaming. It was real. This was Willie Garvin, alive. She had to fight back the tears again.

He had taken a belt with a hostered Colt .32 on it from the haversack. 'Brought you a gun,' he said. 'And here's a kongo.'

She slipped the kongo in her pocket and buckled on the belt, not taking her eyes from him, keeping her lower lip gripped between her teeth. He did not smile.

Her fingers closed on the denim of his shirtfront. 'Willie . . .' she said. For a moment nothing more would come. There were no words for the explosion of feeling that shook her, joy so intense that it hurt, unbelief and certainty, exhilaration and a ludicrous sense of outrage. Then, with the shirt scrunched in her fists, she gave him a small fierce shake. In a voice not her own, tremulously, like an adult scolding a child after some narrow escape, she said, 'You . . . you scared me out of my *wits*. You wait till I get you home!'

Willie Garvin began to laugh.

Twenty minutes later they were half a mile into the belt of wooded savannah, carrying Lisa on a crude stretcher. Willie had cut two slender saplings, trimmed them to seven-foot poles, and slipped them through three of the empty sacks by the gorilla's food-store, cutting holes in the bottoms of the sacks. He was carrying the head of the stretcher, Modesty the rear. Pennyfeather's huge shabby medical bag was slung on her back and secured by rope.

Pennyfeather limped along behind them, using a stick Willie had cut for him. He had been astonished to see Willie Garvin alive, but Modesty saw that the impact it made on him was far less than on herself. She realized, perhaps with envy, that Giles Pennyfeather was in some ways blind to physical impossibilities. It showed in his surgical attitude and methods. It had shown in his extraordinary belief that with both feet and one hand injured he might somehow spirit Lisa away to safety on his own, and perform an emergency operation somewhere in the bush. It had shown in his first words after absorbing the shock of seeing Willie emerge in gathering dusk from the house, carrying Lisa in his arms. 'Jesus! I never thought we'd see *you* again, Willie, honestly!'

The burden of the stretcher was nothing to her. She watched Willie's back as he moved steadily on, and the measureless joy that filled her was like champagne. She felt renewed and refreshed, with boundless stores of energy. There were a hundred questions to be asked, but they could wait. For the moment she was content to revel in the immense happiness that possessed her.

The dusk had deepened rapidly, but Willie did not hesitate. He seemed to know exactly where he was going. They came out of the trees, crossed a low ridge and moved along a winding valley for a hundred yards or so. Willie said, 'Okay, Princess. Take five.'

'It's all right, Willie love. I'm not tired.'

'Good. But it's for Lisa. Better let Giles 'ave another look at 'er.'

'Yes, of course. Sorry.' She lowered the stretcher with him, taking herself to task. They were still deep in trouble, and she must be careful not to let euphoria dull her wits. The white-haired girl wore a pale blue wrap and was covered with a blanket. She was conscious, but in a stupor from the shot Modesty had given her. Pennyfeather knelt over her now, feeling her pulse and her brow, talking to her quietly, cheerfully.

'Poor old love, you're having a bit of a rough time, aren't you? Never mind, we'll soon have you fixed up. Just don't worry about anything, eh? I fancy those sods back at *Bonaccord* have played hell with you, one way and another. Still, that's all over now.' She groped for his hand and clung to it, not saying anything. Giles Pennyfeather went on talking.

Modesty moved a few paces away and sat down beside Willie, resting the weight of the medical bag on a rock. He looked up at the sky and said, 'They won't come after us tonight now.'

'No. They haven't any dogs. They'll start a search at crack of dawn, I guess. Have you got a base, Willie?'

'Sure. Only about another mile and a half. I dumped the rest of the gear there.'

'When did you get here?'

'Last night, by 'copter from Tanzania. Hush-hush. Tarrant laid it on. He's got an undercover man in some mineral development survey company there.'

She wanted to know about all the days before last night, but that would keep. She said, 'This caper's all shot to hell, Willie. A dogfight. Give me a quick idea of how we stand.'

'I brought in all the gear I could carry,' he said. 'No good barging in till I'd got the score, so that meant finding a base. I was lucky there. You'll see soon. Then I spent three hours before dawn, making a recce.' He looked at her. 'For all I knew, they'd chucked you out of the Dakota, too.'

She had not realized that, but it was obvious. He had come to *Bonaccord* with the knowledge that she and Giles might have been long dead.

'I didn't see you till this afternoon,' he said. 'I was on that hill overlooking the village, with glasses.'

'When they set me up for the gang-bang?'

He nodded. 'I was 'aving a job not to start shooting when Brunel came an' called it off. I couldn't figure that.'

'Part of his brain-washing campaign. I'll tell you later.'

'Well, at least I knew you were alive then. I saw them take you back to the 'ouse. Didn't know where Giles was, but I thought I'd fire that fuel store a bit before dusk, then come an' find out when they were all busy with it. I saw Giles taken up to the 'ouse about an hour before I set things going, so that fitted in all right. At least, I thought it was going to, but things got confused.'

She nodded. 'I was planning a break tonight myself, hoping to take the Land-Rover. Then everything went crazy.' She glanced towards the stretcher. 'The girl killed Brunel. Giles was brought in and found she's got an appendix that needs taking out quick. Meanwhile Chance got delusions of grandeur and took charge. He'd discovered the Novikov coordinates somehow, so he didn't need Giles any more. Or me. He put us in the cage with Ozymandias. That's the gorilla.'

Willie sat up straight. 'Jesus!'

'Yes. Then the fuel store went up. You were just in time to draw Chance and Jacko away.'

'But!—'

'The gorilla?' She began to laugh, trying to stifle it. 'Sorry, but it's so crazy. I feel a little drunk. Giles had read an article about gorillas somewhere.' She choked and recovered herself. 'He knew a bit of gorilla talk.'

In the gloom, Willie looked at her doubtfully. 'Gorilla talk? You're 'aving me on.'

'Honestly, Willie. I don't mean Tarzan stuff, but a word for food and the way you have to act. Then we got Ozymandias to bend one of the bars for us, and squeezed out. Giles nearly didn't make it. Ozymandias broke a wrist for him.'

'You got Ozymandias to bend one of the bars?' Willie shook his head slowly. His voice was anxious as he said, 'Princess, are you all right?'

'It's true, Willie love. I'll fill you in later on the details. I don't know, but crazy things just seem to happen when Giles is around. Now, back to you.'

'Me? Oh . . .' Willie rubbed his head, trying to collect his thoughts. 'Well, there's not much more. I waited till there was a crowd busy with the fire, then I made for the 'ouse. It took time, because I 'ad to make a big loop round. Just when I got there I saw you. You were running like the clappers, across from the trees and in through those french windows. I was at the corner of the veranda then, but I didn't want to yell out, so I came belting after you. Came in just when you were going for that bloke with the rifle.'

They were silent for a moment, then she said, 'No chance of any transport?'

He shook his head. 'I set fire to all the vehicles in the garage. Sorry. But I reckoned if there was going to be a running fight we'd be better off with everyone on foot than in a car chase. Got more chance of playing sneaky when you're on foot in this kind of terrain.' He shrugged. 'That was all right for you an' me. I didn't figure on Giles being 'alf crippled. Or the girl.'

She sighed. 'I didn't figure on her, either. Giles thinks she's different. Not one of them.'

'Well ...' Willie rubbed his chin with the back of his hand. It was a familiar mannerism, but it made her catch her breath with a stab of pleasure. She had never thought to see him rubbing his chin like that again. He said, 'I dunno, Princess. She conned me all right. But I'm still glad we didn't leave 'er be'ind.'

He got up and walked across to the stretcher, squatting on his haunches beside Giles, looking down at the girl's sweating face. ' 'Allo, Lisa. Feel better for a little rest?'

Still clutching Pennyfeather's hand she said in a whisper, her lips scarcely moving, 'I'm sorry ... so sorry, Willie. They made me. I didn't know. Didn't know what they were going to do.'

'Sure. Don't worry about it.'

'When they . . . killed you, I wanted to die.'

'They only tried, Lisa.' He grinned. 'Can't kill the wicked that easy. *He rode upon a cherub and did fly; yea, he did fly upon the wings of the wind.* Psalm 17, verse 8.'

The faintest of answering smiles touched her eyes. Pennyfeather said, 'Ah, yes. I'm pretty curious about that aeroplane business, you know. Don't quite understand it.'

'Go on?' Willie fumbled in his pocket. 'We'll 'ave to get going in a minute. Like some chocolate, Lisa? Give you a bit of strength, eh?'

'Don't give her that!' Pennyfeather said indignantly. 'She hasn't eaten for hours, thank God, so don't spoil it. Modesty's got to operate as soon as we're settled in somewhere for the night.'

Willie turned his head slowly, staring. 'Modesty?'

'Well, *somebody* has to. I can't hold a scalpel with this.' Pennyfeather drew out his hand from the rough sling supporting it. The hand looked like a shiny bladder, the swollen fingers sticking out of it like teats from an udder.

Willie stood up and went back to Modesty. He jerked a thumb over his shoulder and said, awed, 'Did you hear that? He wants you to take 'er appendix out!'

'I heard. I was hoping I heard wrong.' She drew her hands

down her cheeks, then held them palm-up and looked at them. After a moment she gave a helpless shrug. 'I suppose that's the way it has to be. I told you this caper had gone crazy.'

Forty minutes later they climbed a long pebbly slope which brought them to a grassy plateau where rocks lay scattered. It was not a large plateau, but curved in a crescent round a low rocky bluff a hundred yards away.

'Only a couple of minutes now,' Willie said. 'I got a cave there, in that bluff. It's very nice, with a back exit over a long, twisty sort of valley.' He gave a little chuckle. 'Good place to 'ide out. We'll be right in the crotch of The Impossible Virgin.'

CHAPTER TWELVE

Lisa said dully, 'I'm sorry. They made me do it. The voices.'

It was an hour since they had carried her into the cave. Under Pennyfeather's guidance Modesty had immediately given her a quarter grain of morphia and a one-hundredth grain of atropine. Pennyfeather's right wrist and forearm were now splinted and firmly bound with surgical tape. Sitting beside the girl as she lay on the blankets, holding her hand, he said cheerfully, 'Voices? What voices, old dear?'

She moved her head in distress. 'I didn't say that. I didn't mean to say it. I can't tell you.'

'Certainly you can. I'm your doctor now, so you can tell me anything. Absolutely anything.' He did not speak persuasively but with simple conviction.

After a few moments she said, 'The voices in my head. They tell me what I have to do.'

He showed no surprise. 'How long have they been doing that, Lisa?'

'Ever since . . . I don't know. For years.'

'Really?' He looked genuinely interested. 'Are they telling you now?'

'Not now. They've stopped. A little while ago they said I must find a gun and shoot. Shoot all the Enemies. Make a lot of noise.'

'What enemies?'

'You. Willie. Her.'

'That's a bit odd. We're not your enemies. You know that.'

'Not mine. Theirs.'

'Whose?'

'The voices.'

'Oh.' His voice became austere. 'Well, to be frank with you, old girl, I don't think much of your voices. They seem a pretty bad lot to me. Do they always tell you to do beastly things like shooting people?'

She nodded slowly, her eyes filling with tears, and whispered, 'Yes. Like that. They made me . . . with Brunel . . . the knife. I have to obey, or they never stop. They nearly drive me mad.'

'I see,' Pennyfeather said gently, and pressed her hand. 'Well, we'll get that sorted out later. Simply must whip your grotty old appendix out first.' He drew away the blanket that covered her. She was naked beneath it now. 'You just relax. Modesty's got to shave your tummy a bit.'

He glanced over his shoulder, and saw Willie lift a deep metal cooking pan from the flame of a spirit stove. Carefully he poured warm water into a mug Modesty held. She moved to kneel beside the albino girl, smiled at her, and said, 'Don't worry, I'm pretty good with a razor.'

From a low entrance the cave rose to five feet high and ran deep into the rock, narrowing and twisting in a dog-leg to emerge as a smaller opening on the far side of the narrow bluff, overlooking a deep valley which ended at this point. There were two big containers of equipment in the cave, sausage-shaped canvas packages each three feet long. They told Modesty that at some time Willie had called at her house in Tangier to re-equip before heading south to Rwanda. There were two M16 rifles and twenty magazines

221

of ammunition; grenades, blankets, water, first-aid kit, insect repellent, and all the necessities for survival in wild country.

A small pressure lamp hung suspended from a length of rope slung across the cave and fastened with pitons. Before lighting it Willie had fixed groundsheets over the cave entrances to prevent any light showing.

Pennyfeather had his big medical bag open beside him and was taking out items carefully, laying them on a sheet of oilskin beside him. Strangely, he seemed less clumsy than usual, perhaps because he could use only one hand. When Modesty had finished preparing the girl he said, 'Now do you think you've got it all straight, darling, or do you want me to run over the op again?'

She shook her head, and there was marked abruptness in her voice as she said, 'I'd rather get started. I'm just acting as your hands, and you'll have to tell me what to do as we go along. Is Willie going to give the ether?'

'Yes. I'll put her under myself, then he can take over. I'd rather be at your end for the op.' He looked down at Lisa and said, 'Don't be scared about this, old dear. Modesty's assisted me with heaps of ops, and she'll be terribly good at it.'

'Yes.' The girl spoke wearily, uncaring. 'Make me sleep soon. Please. The voices are speaking to me again . . .'

Willie lifted an eyebrow but said nothing. He moved away with Modesty, and when he had made a cap with a knotted handkerchief to confine her hair she began to scrub her hands in the container of water. It was very hot now. Another pan held instruments, boiled in an antiseptic solution.

Pennyfeather dripped ethyl chloride on a gauze mask and held it close to Lisa's nose and mouth. 'Come on now, old thing. Nice deep breathing. That's the girl. In . . . out. And again. Lovely.' Two minutes later he rested the mask on her face, took up the ether drip-bottle and began to let a single drip at a time fall on to the gauze.

Willie, scrubbing his hands now, said in a troubled whisper, 'I 'aven't 'ad time to think about this bit till now, Princess. No gloves, no masks, a couple of gallons of water and a bottle of Dettol. It's 'ardly Dr Kildare stuff.'

She grimaced, shaking her hands to dry them. 'It's Dr Pennyfeather stuff. I don't think he's ever operated in a proper theatre.'

Five minutes later they swabbed their hands with ethermeth and were ready. Pennyfeather said to Willie, 'Right, you take over at this end. Just one or two drops every fifteen seconds. If she starts grunting or goes blue in the face, lift the mask for a bit till she's breathing normally, then carry on.'

Willie said unhappily, 'Blue in the face. All right.'

Modesty knelt on the girl's right, Pennyfeather on the other side. The container of instruments was beside her now, together with an open packet of swabs on a sheet of oilskin. She knelt with hands held away from her. She had taken off her shirt before scrubbing up, and already the sweat gleamed on her body in the heat of the pressure lamp. Drawing in long deep breaths, remembering what Giles Pennyfeather had told her, she visualized on Lisa's ether-swabbed stomach a line drawn from navel to iliac crest, and a point two-thirds of the way along. McBurney's Point. She took up the scalpel, touched it lightly across the skin, and looked at Pennyfeather. He nodded encouragingly. She held her breath and made the incision, three inches long.

Blood. She swabbed with her left hand and cut down through the layer of fat to the pink muscle. Clamps now. Spencer Wells artery forceps. She had done this for Giles half a dozen times. Pick up a bleeding point, clamp it; the next, and clamp. Again.

A little metallic forest of clamps round the incision now. Dry out with swabs. Start unclamping. Trouble now if a point hasn't clotted – difficult to tie off without assistance. Damn! Giles should have sterilized his one good hand, so he could help her. Too late for that.

Lucky. No bleeding.

Outer muscles now. Tease open the fibres with scissors. Now get in a finger of each hand. Split the muscle for the length of the incision. Fingers . . . hope to God they're sterile.

223

They should be, but why the bloody hell does Giles cart around this mass of gear and nostrums but no surgical gloves? Does he think he can *talk* the bugs to death?

He was talking now, cheerfully and approvingly. He must have been talking all the time, but she had only just registered that her hands were following his instructions.

'Lovely, darling. Now whop a retractor in. That's the ticket. Got to have a decent hole to work in. How's she looking your end, Willie? Good ... good. Now split the inner layer of muscle, darling. The grain runs the other way. That's it. Bloody marvellous. Second retractor. Good, now let's have a squint.'

She knelt back, and he bent over to peer into the cavity, holding his breath. After a moment he looked up at her and grinned. 'Just like the diagram in a text-book. Don't look so fraught, we're doing fine. Now you see that white membrane? That's the whats-it. I forget. Ah yes, the peritonium. Slit that the same way as the first incision. Christ, no! Not the scalpel, or you'll cut the gubbins underneath. Just a nick with the scissors, then get a finger through the hole before you cut.'

Two minutes later she eased out the appendix with her finger, a thin tube half an inch across and three inches long, swollen and inflamed.

'None too bloody soon,' Pennyfeather said, frowning at it. 'Right, get hold of the end in the Baker forceps. I can hold it for you. Now, you see that artery lying in the fat? You've got to tie it off.'

'Wait a minute, I'm getting sweat in my eyes. It's running down my arms, too. Why the hell didn't you tell me to put sweat-bands on? Willie, dry me off. You can leave that drip for half a minute.' She knelt holding her hands up above her head while Willie mopped her face, body and arms with a towel. 'All right.' She lowered her arms and prepared to make the ligature, then paused. 'Oh, God ... my hands have started shaking, Giles.'

He said, unruffled, 'Ignore it. They'll stop as soon as you give them something to do. Go on, get that artery tied off.'

Astonishingly he was right. Under his guidance she completed the ligature, made a purse-string suture, crushed the base of the appendix with a Spencer Wells, made a tight ligature above the crushed portion, then took up the scalpel for the last time and made the final cut.

Scalpel, appendix and forceps dropped together on to her discarded sheet of oilskin. She wanted to relax, but knew that the longest part of the work lay ahead, the sewing up.

Pennyfeather said, 'Super. Now invaginate the stump into the caecum.'

She lifted her head to stare at him. 'Do *what?*'

'Push the stump inside the tube.'

'Well for Christ's sake say so!'

He chuckled. 'Take it easy, darling. Good. Now pull the gut of the purse-string tight and tie off. I'll count the swabs.'

She was slow and awkward with the sewing up. First the white membrane, then the two layers of muscle. As she laid the retractors aside Giles said, 'Take away the mask now, Willie. We won't be much longer.'

She used nylon thread to sew the outer incision with interrupted sutures half an inch apart. As she cut the thread of the last stitch her hands began to tremble again, but it did not matter now.

She put a gauze dressing over the wound, fastening it with adhesive tape, then laid a towel over Lisa's stomach and drew the blanket up over her. When she stood up, crouching a little under the low roof of the cave, she could feel her teeth chattering. Willie Garvin rose and rested his hands on her bare slippery shoulders. 'You know that was illegal?' he said solemnly. 'You got no licence to practise.'

She laughed, and the shivering was swept away by a warm glow of relief. She said, 'Do you think she'll be all right, Giles?'

'Eh? Well I don't suppose she'll thank you for those stitches.' He gave a breathy chuckle. 'They're not much better than mine.'

'I never could sew. Will she come through?'

'I don't see why not.' He wrinkled his brow. 'I'm more worried about her voices than about the op. Don't like that at all.'

'Voices?' She began to wash her hands in the fresh water Willie had poured for her. Vaguely now she remembered hearing something said about voices just before the operation. 'What did she say, Giles? I wasn't listening.'

'Well, I'm afraid she suffers from delusions. Hears voices, like Joan of Arc, except they don't tell her to save France, they tell her to do pretty beastly things. That's why she stuck a knife in Brunel. They told her to.'

'Seems like a good idea to me,' Willie said, wrapping up the discarded swabs.

'I'm not bothered about Brunel. But I gather they've made her do other things, over quite a long time. Years.'

'I remember now,' Willie said thoughtfully. 'She used to listen. Often when she was with me it seemed like she was listening for something.'

Giles nodded. 'Aural delusions,' he said with a touch of gloom. 'Very tricky. I suppose she'll end up in a head-shrinker's hands, for what it's worth. I don't trust those buggers myself, shoving electric shocks through people's brains the way they do. Barbaric sods.'

'You can fret about that later,' Modesty said. 'It doesn't become a question until we get ourselves out of this. Did you have anything in mind, Willie?'

'I fixed for the 'copter to stand by for a pick-up at eighteen 'undred hours tomorrow. It'll touch down about two miles east of 'ere, same place I landed last night. That's if we're there to signal. And it won't come again. I figured if I couldn't get you out in thirty-six hours I wouldn't be going back anyway. So if we miss the pick-up we'll 'ave to get across the border on foot. It was the best I could do, Princess.'

She smiled. 'It's a hell of a lot better than I'd hoped for. Will she be all right to travel a couple of miles on the stretcher, Giles?'

'By tomorrow evening? Oh, yes. She ought to be sitting up a bit after twenty-four hours anyway.'

Willie knelt beside the girl's head, looking down at her, feeling a strange compassion. He noticed that Giles was holding her hand again and gazing at her contemplatively. He said, 'You going to sit with 'er all night? You could do with some rest yourself.'

'Oh, I'm all right. She needs me just now.'

Curious, Willie said, 'Giles, are you sort of *willing* 'er to get better?'

'Eh? Oh, don't be a bloody nit.'

'Well, what then?'

'I'm just thinking about her, that's all.'

'Thinking what?'

'Christ, I don't know. There's so much to a person. I mean, anybody. You can't just take a quick squint and *know* them. She's a mess, poor little bitch. I'm trying to think of her the way she ought to be, all straightened out.'

'You're not a doctor, matey. You're a shaman. A witch-doctor.'

Giles gave a guffaw of amusement.

Willie said, 'You can laugh, but—' He broke off and bent lower. 'Blimey, I can't 'ear 'er breathing!'

'Well, she is. Nice strong pulse. The reason you can't hear her breathing is because she's breathing slowly and without any noise, that's all. It's a healthy sign.'

Willie bent lower till his brow was almost touching the blanket beside Lisa's face, listening. She stirred. Her head turned and her cheek fell against his. Modesty finished drying her hands and said, 'We'd better save this lamp, unless you still need the light for keeping an eye on her, Giles.'

'Uh? No, that's okay. When she starts to come round we'll have to get her well propped up. I'll need a hand for that. But you can put the light out for now. I'll hear her as soon as she stirs. Look, will you stop bloody well nuzzling her, Willie?'

Willie said in a fierce whisper, '*Shut up!*'

They both stared at him. He was still kneeling at Lisa's head, bending low, and now he had a hand to her head, pressing her cheek against his. After a moment or two he straightened up slowly, and looked at them from a face that was pale behind the tan.

'Did you say she 'eard voices?' he said.

Giles blinked at him. 'Yes. Nothing all that strange about it. Aural delusion.'

'All right, I'll tell you something strange, then. *I can 'ear 'em too!*'

There was complete silence in the cave for several seconds. Willie looked at Modesty and motioned with his hand, shuffling back on his knees. 'You got to press your ear right up against 'er cheekbone,' he said. She took his place and bent low.

Tiny, infinitely distant voices in a high-pitched chorus, faint and muffled as if by the flesh and bone of the head that enclosed them, felt rather than heard, yet the words, the chanted words, were just audible.

... Be strong now, Lisa. You are our child and we are pleased with you. The Enemy is dead. Brunel died under your hand and we are pleased with you. Gather your strength Lisa. Forget all pain and weakness. This is the last trial, the last trial before you come to the freedom and peace we have prepared for you. We have placed you among the Last Enemies so that you may destroy them. Be unafraid. You are our child and we are your protectors. Seek for a means, Lisa. You will find weapons to hand. Be skilful, child, for the Last Enemies are cunning. Seek for a gun, and destroy them ...

Modesty straightened up, her face wooden, and motioned for Giles to take her place. A minute later he lifted a drawn, incredulous face from the blanket beside Lisa's head and said with utmost fury, 'There bloody well *are* voices in her head! How the hell are they doing it?'

Modesty looked at Willie, who wiped his face with his hand and said, 'That shook me. That really shook me ... talk about creepy.'

'Creepy?' Pennyfeather raged in a voice that cracked with anger. 'What's creepy about it? It's *people*, by God, not spirits! It's those *bastards*! How the hell are they doing it?' With his rag-bound feet and Robinson Crusoe trousers, his gaunt face, spiky hair and gangling limbs, he looked like a demented scarecrow crouching there, yet somehow there was nothing ludicrous about him. The power of his wrath seemed to fill the cave.

Modesty said, 'A miniature receiver, Willie? How small could it be and still work?'

Willie sat back on his heels, looking at the unconscious white face beneath the white hair. 'You could get down below cherry-stone size as long as the transmitter was punching out a good short-wave signal. These days they give people radio-pills to swallow, with a transmitter inside. Then there's pacemakers. They're pretty small for what they do, and they need a lot more juice than this would.'

'So it's possible?'

'It's been possible in theory ever since micro-circuits. Now someone's done it. Brunel could find the right bloke. You'd need a Mallory cell for power – or better still, a nuclear battery. And a transducer to convert the electrical signal from the micro-circuit.' He nodded. 'It could be small enough all right.'

'Implanted in her skull?'

'No . . . I don't think it's in the skull, Princess. Be a tricky surgical operation, wouldn't it? And you couldn't renew the battery simply.' He pinched his lower lip. 'Wait a minute, though. A few years back I read about a bloke who kept 'earing radio programmes in 'is head. Thought he'd lost 'is marbles, except the programmes were real and coming from the BBC. They found in the end that he'd got fillings in a tooth, with two different metals. That set up a current because of acid in the saliva. Like a battery. And some freak effect made the thing act like a receiver tuned to a BBC wavelength.'

He took a pencil torch from his pocket. 'Steady 'er for a minute, Princess.'

Modesty held the girl's head while he gently eased her mouth open and peered in. After a moment he said, 'There's an upper tooth at the back with a metal crown. No, not just a crown. It's all metal. That could be it.' He swabbed his hand with ether-meth and slipped a finger and thumb into her mouth, but after a few seconds shook his head and said, 'Can't shift it, but I reckon it ought to unscrew. Let's 'ave a pair of forceps.'

Pennyfeather took forceps from his bag. His hands were shaking with the rage that still possessed him. Willie swabbed the forceps and bent over the girl again, peering into her mouth with the torch as he sought a grip on the tooth.

'Ah! ... That's got it moving.' He handed back the forceps, reached in again with finger and thumb. They saw the sinews of his hand moving rhythmically. He brought the thing out and held it up in the light of the hanging lamp. The top of it was the size and shape of a molar, made of hard metal. From where the root of the tooth would normally begin, the metal tapered sharply inwards like a cone for almost half an inch, and the tapering surface was threaded.

'They must've killed the nerve, cut the tooth off at the gumline, and tapped the root so this would screw in tight,' Willie said.

Modesty took the metal tooth and held it to her ear. 'I can't hear anything now.'

'You wouldn't. The jaw-bone acts like an amplifier.' He looked at Giles. 'Jaw-bone's connected with the ear, isn't it? I know you can 'old a lady's watch between your teeth and it sounds like a grandfather clock ticking.'

Modesty slipped the tooth into her mouth, holding it between her back teeth. After a few moments she nodded and took it out again. 'Yes. They're still going on. It's clearer than before.' She looked at the tooth with a grimace of disgust, and handed it to Willie.

Pennyfeather's face was clenched as if he might almost cry with the towering anger that consumed him. Modesty moved round beside him and put her arm about his shoulders. 'Here, steady on, darling,' she said gently.

'It's so . . .' He struggled inarticulately for words to match his feelings. 'It's so bloody crucifyingly *wicked*, Modesty!'

'I know. Brunel was that kind of man.'

'But – but to play God in someone's head, some poor little bitch he'd bought as a kid and hammered into submission anyway!'

'Yes. Like stealing someone's soul. But at least Brunel's dead now.'

'And that's a queer thing,' Willie said thoughtfully. He held the tooth in his palm, gazing at it. 'Let's 'ave a rundown on this. Brunel found some micro-circuit genius to make this gizmo. He'd probably got a tame dental surgeon, too, and took Lisa along for a check-up every six months. New tooth with a new battery gets screwed in while she's under a whiff of gas. He gets the voice effect on tape—'

'It's voices, Willie. A chorus.'

'No problem. You use a throat mike and modulate the voice up to a higher pitch. Then you record 'alf a dozen times from the original, with a micro-second's difference between each run. You end up with that choir-of-angels effect, and when you want Lisa to 'ear voices you plug the tape-recording into a transmitter and switch on. There'd be a limit to range, but two or three miles would be as much as you'd ever need.'

Pennyfeather had recovered a little, but his voice still shook as he said, 'I don't wonder she killed the swine.'

Willie said patiently, 'She didn't know, Giles. She killed 'im because the voices told 'er to. And that's what's queer. Brunel wouldn't 'ave the voices tell Lisa to kill *him*, surely?'

They were all silent for perhaps half a minute. Then Modesty said, 'It was Adrian Chance. Sure as God made little apples, that's who it was. He must have found out about this, maybe only in the last few days. Or maybe he's known about it for a long time, but I don't think so. Remember how he was today, Giles, after Brunel was dead? Hopped-up and riding high. Like a man who'd won a fortune – no, more than that, captured a kingdom. That's just about what he'd done, when you come to think of it. Brunel's kingdom. He'd killed Brunel without any danger to himself or any possible come-back. He just made Lisa do it for him.'

231

Willie nodded. 'It figures. And now little Adrian's broadcasting away, trying to get Lisa to shoot 'oles in us. You can't say 'e doesn't try.'

'She's lived with those voices for years,' Modesty said, and a shiver touched her. 'How in God's name is anybody ever going to straighten her out in the head?' She looked at Giles Pennyfeather. The spasm of rage had passed and he was thinking deeply now. He pulled at his nose and said, 'It's going to take a long time, you know. Never mind. I'll just have to stick with her till she's better.' He held out his hand. 'Let me have the tooth, Willie.'

'You're going to tell 'er?'

'As soon as I think she can take it. Maybe as soon as she wakes. Basically she must be pretty stable, or she'd have gone completely potty by now.'

Willie passed the tooth over, doubtfully. 'I just thought . . .' He glanced at Modesty. 'Well, sorting out this kind of thing is a bit of a specialist job, isn't it?'

Modesty looked down at the girl. 'Yes. But what she needs is healing, Willie. That's Giles' speciality.'

Ten minutes later they had settled down for the night. Willie sat just within the cave entrance, taking the first four-hour watch. Modesty lay wrapped in a blanket. Deeper into the cave, Giles Pennyfeather sat with his back against the wall, holding Lisa's hand, talking to the unconscious girl in a low, chatty voice about some incident from his days as a medical student. 'Fenshaw his name was . . . or was it Henshaw? Something like that, anyway. Very weird patient. Used to eat bits of glass, nuts and bolts. Had a sort of craving. They found nearly half a pound of junk in him when they opened him up. Well, before that, I was taking his pulse and temperature, and suddenly he just bit my thermometer in half and swallowed a great chunk of it.' A whispering guffaw. 'I wish I could have seen my face, old dear. I was scared to sound his chest in case he bit a chunk off my stethoscope. I'd just paid fifty bob for it . . .'

Modesty tuned his voice out. Five minutes later she threw back the blanket, moved to the mouth of the cave and sat down beside Willie, tucking her hand under his arm.

' 'Allo, Princess.'

'Hallo, Willie love. It's no good trying to sleep until I know what happened to you. Come on, tell me.'

'About when they chucked me out of the Dakota?'

'What else? I've been trying to guess, but it's a waste of time. We were at three thousand feet, so you must have reached terminal velocity. It wouldn't matter if you hit trees, water, or the middle of a thirty-foot haystack, you'd still never walk away from it.'

He laughed. 'I did better than that. It's still not a record, though.' There was a touch of regret in his voice. 'Not fair, really, because you can't go faster than terminal speed, even if you start at twenty thousand. So I must've come down just as 'ard as the others.'

'What others?'

'Oh, there was a bloke called Worsfold, tail-gunner in a Lancaster during the war. It blew up over France, and 'e fell over seven thousand feet in the tail section. Only broke a leg and a few ribs.'

She was always intrigued by the way Willie Garvin could recall anything he had ever heard or read. There was hardly a subject on which he could not produce some curious piece of knowledge, usually surprising and sometimes bizarre. She said, 'That was pretty freaky, but I think he was cheating. You weren't wrapped up in a tail section.'

'No. But neither was Alkemade. He baled out over Germany at 18,000. Plane was on fire. No parachute, it got burned up before 'e could strap it on. So Alkemade jumped rather than fry. Fell for nearly two minutes, then went through a lot of fir trees loaded with snow, and down onto a big mound of underbrush covered by a snowdrift. Came out of it with a twisted knee and a strained back.'

She gave his arm an impatient shake. 'There weren't any trees or snow for you. Stop tantalizing, Willie.'

'All right. But there was a bit of snow, only you couldn't see it.'

'We were way below the snow-line, surely?'

'Yes. But there'd been a big fall two nights before. Remember those spurs running from the mountains? Well—' He paused. 'No, I'd better tell it the way it 'appened. Right up to the time I slid out of that strait-jacket I was too busy to be scared. I was still trying to throttle Jacko or pull 'im out of the plane with me. But when the jacket was dragged off an' I just fell, then I was scared all right.'

He gave a dry chuckle. 'It felt like even me feet went white, Princess, honest. Anyway, soon as I fell I slipped into the dereve position. I still don't know why. It was a bit awkward, still strapped to the chair, but I got travelling pretty fast.'

She had used the dereve position in free fall herself when making a delayed parachute-drop. It was a kind of prone semi-crouch which used air resistance to give the faller horizontal motion during the descent. You could achieve up to forty miles an hour of forward movement with it.

Willie said, 'The thing was, I'd already got a hell of an impetus from the speed of the plane, maybe a couple of hundred miles an hour at moment of exit. I could see the crest of a spur ahead, and some'ow I wanted to clear the ridge before I 'it the deck. I dunno why, except that there was only rock straight down below, and maybe I thought there might be something better the other side.'

She felt him shrug. Then, 'God knows what I was 'oping for. I mean, I couldn't see any snow then, and even twenty foot of it wouldn't slow you down much. But ... well, you know, Princess. You just keep trying in case something turns up.' He paused, and went on with a touch of wonder, 'Something did, too. I cleared the crest of the ridge by about two-fifty feet, an' there it was below me.'

'Snow?'

'Not just snow. A drift. The wind 'ad piled it against the east side of the ridge the night before. It was only on the eastern slopes, that's why you couldn't see it, the way we were travelling. You know 'ow it gets freaky sometimes. Only a few inches of fall, but it gets funnelled into a drift in places. Most of it 'ad melted with the temperature coming up overnight, or was well on the way, but there was a deep gully running straight down the slope of this spur, right below me. And I was moving dead in line with it.'

He took out cigarettes, gave her one, and lit them. She said, 'How deep was it, Willie?'

'About twenty or thirty feet, as it turned out. Not enough. When you're doing a hundred and twenty miles an hour, you don't come to a stop in twenty-odd feet without getting bust up a bit. But it was just about then I 'ad an idea.' She saw him smile in the glow of his cigarette. 'I'd been dropping for nearly twenty seconds, so it was 'igh time to start thinking. There was only a couple of seconds left. I was still moving forward, and this long gully sloped down the side of the spur. So I figured that what with the speed I was moving 'orizontally, an' what with the downward slope of the gully, I could maybe sort of skim into the snow at an angle, and get as much as seventy or eighty feet of it to plough through before I 'it the rock underneath.'

'And that was it?'

'Not quite all of it. I nearly broke me back doing a quick flick to bring meself feet forward. Next second I landed with an almighty bloody *whoomp!*, sitting on the chair and drilling into the snow on a line that ran smack down the middle of the gully. I still reckon I might 'ave bust me spine when I struck rock, but I'd got another lucky number waiting to come up.'

She turned her head to peer at him in the darkness. 'Something else?'

He nodded. 'I'm not too clear on this bit, because I pretty well blacked out with the deceleration. I could feel the eyeballs sinking back into me 'ead, an' all the blood was draining down to me feet, but I didn't quite go out. I reckon the chair 'elped. The legs acted as braces for mine, and the seat compressed the snow as I went on down, so it made a tunnel, a sort of square tunnel for me to go through. I only saw that afterwards, though. Next thing I knew there was another big *whoomp!* I'd stopped, and I 'adn't struck rock. I'd struck something soft, and there was all 'ell going on. I was in the middle of a load of struggling, scrabbling bodies, all squawking and baa-ing like they were being driven to the slaughter 'ouse.'

'Sheep?'

She felt his silent laugh. *'He shall come down like the rain into a fleece of wool.* Psalm 72, verse 6. About twenty of 'em there were. I've known 'em do that sort of thing up in Yorkshire. They 'uddle for shelter and get buried in a drift. That's what saves' em, because they keep each other warm, and their breath makes a sort of blow-hole, a little shaft in the snow reaching up to the surface, so they can breathe. That's what they'd done, and now they'd got Willie Garvin for company. The funny thing was, I didn't get a scratch from the fall, but I nearly got suffocated trying to climb out of the drift.'

She drew in a long breath, trying to find something to say. No comment was adequate. At last she said helplessly, 'Well ... that clinches it. You were born to be hanged, Willie love.'

'Looks like it.' He was silent for a few moments, and when he spoke again his voice was very sober. 'When I got out I nearly went crazy. I reckoned they were going to throw you out next. It took nearly five minutes before I remembered the way they'd seated us. You an' Giles strapped in seats, me on the chair. I was the only one set up for a quick exit. That's what I kept telling meself, anyway, and it made me feel a bit better. It looked like they aimed to keep you alive, at least for a bit, and I figured they were taking you to *Bonaccord*, so the quicker I could follow, the better.'

He ground out his cigarette on the floor of the cave. 'That's when the luck ran out.'

She pressed his arm. 'You'd had your share, Willie.'

'I know. But I was afraid it was going to be wasted. I found a farm three miles away, and of all things a French copper on a motor-bike was there to see the farmer about a licence for 'is truck. I'd got no papers, nothing. They'd taken me jacket and cleaned out me pockets before they strapped me to that chair. I started pitching a yarn, but I wasn't on very good form just then. The French cop asked a lot of questions, getting more suspicious all the time, then took me in. I spent a day and a night in jail before they even informed the consulate. It was slow murder.'

She leaned her head against his shoulder. Later his frustration with French red tape would seem funny, but she could well imagine his feelings at the time. 'Poor Willie. I'm sorry.'

He said, 'I thought I'd go berserk. It was two days before they sent a bloke from the consulate. About four times a day I thought of breaking out, but being on the run in France wasn't going to 'elp much. So I sweated it through. I kept telling meself they wanted you alive and you'd manage to stay that way some'ow. In the end I got a message to Réné Vaubois through the consulate bloke, and then things started moving fast. Réné sprung me and staked me for money. I got a plane out to Tangier, and went straight to the villa. I reckoned it was better to get kitted up for a proper job rather than come charging down 'ere on a wing and a prayer.'

It made sense. There was all the equipment needed for any kind of caper in her villa on The Mountain overlooking Tangier. But the restraint Willie had laid upon himself must have been enormous.

'I rang Tarrant from Tangier,' he said, 'and put 'im in the picture. Very blasphemous, Tarrant was. Then I chartered a private plane to Bukoba, and made contact with Tarrant's bloke there, the undercover man with the mineral development company.' He gave a little laugh. 'Everything seemed to take for ever, but there wasn't any better way to play it. I figured if you'd stayed alive for the first two or three days, you'd probably figured a way to get yourself out of trouble anyway.'

'They had me under drugs, Willie. I didn't know until Giles spotted it, and I wasn't getting anywhere until the last couple of days, when I stopped drinking the doped water. If you'd come earlier, I'd have been just a passenger.' She thought of the moment in the dining-room, with Mesquita's finger on the trigger of the rifle. 'I'm glad you didn't come a couple of seconds later, though.'

'Me too.' He exhaled a long breath. 'I'd like to know about that gorilla business sometime.'

'Sometime, but not now. I won't compete against your high-jump story.' She made a sound that was almost a giggle.

'Sorry Willie, I'm feeling a bit light-headed. Like from a little too much champagne. Only a few hours ago . . .' Her voice changed and faltered for a moment, then steadied. 'Only a few hours ago I thought I was alone. It's nice not to be.' She gave his shoulder a little thump with her fist, pulled his head down and pressed her lips hard against his cheek. 'Welcome back, Willie love. And please – don't do it again. I've never felt so lonely.'

Five minutes later she was asleep, the blanket drawn up about her, her head pillowed on his leg. Listening to her slow regular breathing he smiled to himself in the darkness and shook his head wonderingly.

Willie Garvin was a man with enormous confidence in himself and a substantial opinion of his own capacities. This had not always been so, and there was no vanity in it now, for he was convinced that whatever merits he possessed had been created in him by Modesty Blaise. It was a belief she had never been able to dispel, and she had long since given up trying. Very content now, Willie sat meditating gratefully on his luck; not his luck in the three thousand foot high-jump, but the luck he had known these eight or nine years past.

It was marvellously good that he meant a great deal to her. She had just said as much, but he knew it anyway. This was a wonder he never failed to enjoy, for he regarded her as a human being in a class of her own. It was a private view; he did not expect others to share his opinion nor care whether they did so. He had never believed she was perfect and without fault, simply that she was unique in a very special way. He had always called her Princess, but this had never become a meaningless name to him. As far as he was concerned she remained a princess, through all the easy familiarity and closeness, even when they played their zany private games together; even when, very rarely, she turned to him in weariness or hurt to be comforted like a child. As a princess he had first seen her, and still saw her, and he never wanted that to change.

They had given her a bad time, he thought, Brunel and the others. He would hear more about that later. But she had always been able to ride out bad times. Perhaps what had hit her hardest was his own seemingly certain death. After all, they had been together a long time now. Certainly something had hit her badly this time. The little laugh-lines at the corners of her eyes, which made her eyes seem to sparkle when she looked at you, they had gone. Or if not gone, were no longer laugh-lines. They had not been there way back in the early days, when he had first known her. In those days she had hardly known how to laugh. It was Willie's secret pride that laughter had been his gift to her, that the little laugh-lines were of his making. He hoped they would come back again now.

Some time later Pennyfeather called. Modesty woke at once. Willie lit the lamp and they both went to help prop Lisa up as she came to consciousness. When she was settled, Pennyfeather would not let them stay but sent them back to sleep or keep watch, as they pleased. His eyes were red-rimmed with weariness, but he seemed unaware of his own condition.

'Don't fuss and don't get under my feet,' he said with curt authority. 'I'll see to Lisa.'

Modesty said, 'But you need some rest yourself, darling.'

'I'll have time for that later.' He looked up, glaring a little. 'You just worry about getting us out of here. And try to shoot as many of those buggers as you can, if you get the chance. They're just human bloody poison. I'd like to join in, but I'm no use for that, so leave me to look after Lisa. I'm going to get her better if it's the last thing I do.'

He looked at the pale face under the white hair. Her head lay back against a folded towel on one of the canvas containers propped against the wall. She was barely conscious as yet, her eyes still half closed.

Pennyfeather squeezed the limp hand he was holding. 'Poor little sod,' he said with soft compassion.

CHAPTER THIRTEEN

At first light Modesty lay beside Willie on a broad ledge outside the small back entrance of the cave. This was the junction of the two long ridges which formed the legs of The Impossible Virgin. From the ledge, the ground sloped down into the deep valley below. The walls enclosing the valley were high and more than sheer, they leaned inwards in many places. Together with the cliff where the cave lay, they formed a massive and twisting hairpin of rock with the valley lying between the prongs.

Binoculars to her eyes, Modesty studied the grey walls hung with gnarled roots and dark green foliage. The valley bottom was dank with moisture that could come only from heavy condensation between the leaning walls, yet it was sufficient to gather in little puddles and to keep alive the coarse grass and some low, broad-leaved bushes in the thin soil where the underlying rock could be seen breaking through here and there.

On each side were strange fern-like trees which seemed to hug the shade of the walls yet reach up for the light, looking too thin for their straggly fifteen-foot height. A brooding, oppressive atmosphere hung over the valley.

'So that's Novikov's golden mile,' Modesty said, and lowered the glasses. 'You've been down there, Willie?'

'I took a walk right along it yesterday, early morning, checking it as a way out.'

'And found gold?'

'I didn't stop to look. But I knew this was the location marked on that map of Tarrant's, and I found signs. Somebody was down there not so many weeks ago, and they'd been scratching around here an' there quite a bit. Must've been Novikov.' He shook his head slowly. 'It's pretty weird down there, Princess. You get a feeling it's never changed since I don't know when. Like walking on the moon, maybe. It's a place where nobody goes.'

'Why not?'

He turned his head to her and grinned. 'This is the bottom 'alf of The Impossible Virgin, remember? Well, I've found out what the joke is, why she's impossible. She's got a special kind of chastity belt. When you walk down that valley you find yourself 'olding your breath, because it's full of about a million wasps.'

'Wasps? Just ordinary wasps?'

'No, a special kind. And they're like the rest of the place. You feel they've been there since before we started walking upright. Take another look at the walls and those straggly trees.'

She raised the glasses and focused carefully. At once she saw the nest. One . . . two . . . six . . . a dozen. She lost count. Three feet long and half as wide, they hung like blackish bombs from the trees and from the roots and foliage on the inward leaning walls. There were smaller nests hanging from some of the bushes. The valley was full of them, and suddenly it took on a new and more tangible menace.

'A special kind of wasp?' she said, and lowered the glasses. 'How do you know, Willie?'

He grinned again. 'I learnt from an expert. She called them Polybioides, and they're a hell of a sight more vicious even than 'ornets. Less than an inch long, black, thin-bodied, but they've got a nasty temper and a sting to match.'

'And you think that's why nobody ever goes there?'

'I think you'd need a damn good reason, and I don't suppose anyone's ever 'ad one, till Novikov came along.'

She looked at him curiously. 'Who was this she-expert who told you about African wasps?'

'Brenda. Bright girl, about twenty-eight. Very passionate she turned out to be. Liked a romp in the open air. Smell of new-mown grass, the whisper of the breeze, and all that nymph and satyr stuff. She 'ad a little cottage in Devon I went to.'

'About the wasps, Willie.'

'Ah well, she was a hymenopterist.'

'That sounds indecent.'

'I 'ad the same thought, but it's not about hymens. She was a wasp-lady. Studied them. Had a degree and all that. Anyway, we were in a nice warm tangle in the garden one summer afternoon when she told me. First I got stung, and then she told me. She'd got bees and wasps and 'ornets there, so she could study them live.'

'That's a nasty moment to get stung.' Modesty pressed knuckles to her lips to suppress a bubble of laughter. 'Was it very bad?'

'Bloody wicked,' he said feelingly. 'Got me on the rump, and put me right off. After she'd doctored me I 'ad to go and look at all 'er colour-slides. Went on for hours it did, and I was sitting sideways all the time. That's when I saw pictures of these wasps we've got down 'ere. Went rabbiting on about them quite a bit, she did. Seemed to think I'd be fascinated by wasps and their 'abits. I never went back. Told 'er I'd found out one of their 'abits and that was enough for me. Might've given me a complex that ruined my love-life. I think you're laughing, Princess.'

'Just trying not to. I'm sorry, Willie.'

He was pleased to have amused her. Looking down into the valley where time seemed to have died he said, 'I'm not saying they're just waiting to pounce. You can walk through the valley all right. You might even knock a nest down an' get away with a bad stinging if you moved quick enough. But if you went down there and fired a shot I don't reckon you'd come out alive. It's stiff with nests. Anyone who stirs those little black devils up is going to be wearing a wasp overcoat in two minutes. I suppose the natives know it, and they steer clear. Probably been like that for a good few thousand years. Africa doesn't change much.'

She gazed down the twisting length of the silent, dead-looking valley. The insects, the vicious little stinging insects, had perhaps been there before man walked the earth and might well be there long after he had vanished, living and breeding and dying, but never changing over countless millenia.

She said, 'And that's the way you want us to take Lisa out when it's time to go?'

'It's the best way, Princess. I mean, most direct and the easiest terrain. We'll be all right as long as we keep pretty quiet and don't disturb a nest.'

'All right. It's certainly a lot less exposed than going out the front way. What time should we start? I'd like to stay in the cave as long as we can, but don't cut it too fine. We mustn't miss that chopper.'

'Say . . . five o'clock?'

'Yes. Let's hope we don't get into a fight before then.'

He smiled. 'Giles is all for shooting 'em.'

'So am I, but we'll come back for that.' She thought for a moment. 'Chance must be wondering what the hell has happened. He gets back from fighting the fire to find Mesquita dead, Lisa gone, and no dead bodies in the gorilla's cage, just a bent bar.' She looked at Willie. 'He could never guess that you're alive, but he's bound to guess that *somebody* turned up to get us out of trouble, and now he's assuming we've had to hole up because of Lisa. He must be, or he wouldn't have recorded a tape of the voices to make her stir up trouble.'

'So he'll come searching. I don't fancy 'is luck.'

'Neither would I, except that van Pienaar brought in a tracker yesterday for hunting a lion they've seen signs of. He'll probably be a wizard at it.'

They went back into the cave. Lisa seemed to be in a natural sleep now. Giles, more hollow-eyed than ever, said, 'She's going pretty well. I've given her some Omnopon for the pain. Have we got any milk?'

'I've got a tin of condensed,' Willie said.

'Good. She can have a little diluted and warmed up when she wakes next time.'

Lisa opened her eyes slowly and said, 'I'm awake now, Giles.' His eyes wandered, and found Willie. She made a feeble attempt to smile. 'Sorry, Willie.'

'Don't keep saying that, love. You got nothing to be sorry for. It wasn't your fault.' He knelt beside her and looked at Giles, lifting an eyebrow in query.

243

'Yes, I've told her,' Giles said. 'She knows about the voices.'

Watching the girl, Modesty saw tears brim from the pink-tinged eyes and run down her cheeks. She wondered if Giles had been wise to hit Lisa with such a massive shock so soon. She would not have dared to herself. But the tears were a good sign. They were not hysterical, they were sorrowful. And perhaps the impact, the frightful impact of having the false mainspring of her being so abruptly shattered, was better absorbed while she was distracted by physical pain and under sedation.

Mentally Modesty shrugged. Leave it to Giles. It was his kind of miracle.

Lisa closed her eyes again and whispered, 'Hold my hand, please.' Willie started to reach out, but it was for Giles Pennyfeather's hand that she was groping.

Modesty said, 'I'll see to the milk, then we'll all have breakfast. It's going to be a long day.'

Before dawn, Willie had been out on the crescent-shaped plateau, rolling small boulders to various parts of the rim at the top of the pebbly slope. Now the sun was high and the morning past, and still there was no sign of pursuit. He lay fifty feet away from Modesty, looking down the long incline they had mounted during the night. Both lay with heads on the shadowed side of a small boulder, each with an M16 rifle and spare magazines of ammunition. This was the best position for defence, the rim of the plateau. The cave itself would be a death-trap, but here they could cover the whole approach to it at long range.

Willie took a sip from his water-bottle and looked at his watch. Nearly one-thirty. It seemed that Chance and his boys were looking in the wrong direction. He glanced behind him, across the plateau to the cave, then into the distance ahead where the volcanic hills forming the breasts of the Virgin stood out clearly.

He said, 'D'you realize we're lying right on the *mons veneris*, Princess?' He saw her grin without turning her head. Then the grin vanished. He looked down the slope and saw a little group emerge from the broad cleft five hundred yards away, which opened into the far side of the narrow green and brown plain below. A white man, not Chance or Jacko; two Kikuyu in shirts and jeans; and a smaller native in a loin cloth.

Modesty lifted the glasses to her eyes. The white man was van Pienaar. She guessed that the smaller native was the tracker. A pity he had been on hand, for the city Kikuyu would have little bush skill. She saw him trot back and forth, quartering the ground, then go down on one knee. After a moment or two he spoke to one of the Kikuyu, who in turn spoke to van Pienaar. The white man looked slowly round, studied the slope to the bluff for a long time, then gave an order. All four moved back round the shoulder of the cleft.

She lowered the glasses, looked across at Willie and said, 'They're on our trail. Van Pienaar's probably sending back for reinforcements before following up. I don't think he liked the idea of pressing on up this slope.'

Willie rubbed his chin. 'Looks as if Chance didn't just rely on the tracker. That was only a small party. They've probably got four or five parties casting around for us.'

'That's good. If they've split up it'll take them time to get together.'

It took an hour and a half. Then a half-track vehicle from the farms nosed out of the cleft. Chance climbed down from beside the driver, waving Camacho and several Kikuyu into cover. Modesty estimated the range again. Over five hundred yards. Too far for accuracy with this rifle, and bad tactics anyway. Killing Chance was important, but time was of greater importance now. They had not been found yet.

The tracker reappeared. Chance stood half hidden by the vehicle. The tracker set to work. He seemed apprehensive, and kept glancing all about him, but within minutes he had nosed his way to the foot of the slope. He stood there and waved to Chance, pointing up the slope, then ran back across the open ground as fast as he could go.

Modesty said, 'Slip back and warn Giles that we'll be

shooting soon. And tell him to take a look out at the back every five minutes.'

'Right.' Willie moved away, wriggling on his stomach until he was far enough from the rim of the plateau to stand up unseen. Modesty put the glasses to her eyes again. Three Kikuyu, led by Selby, emerged from cover and began to trot across the open ground. Selby carried a sub-machine gun. the Kikuyu carried rifles and had machetes at their belts. They reached the foot of the hundred yard slope and started up. Modesty checked that her M16 was on semi-automatic, adjusted the sight, and put a bullet through Selby's head.

He went rolling down the foot of the slope. The three Kikuyu turned and ran like hares. They were easy targets, but she did not shoot. From beyond the half-track came a burst of fire, single-shot and automatic. She heard a few bullets sing overhead, a few hitting the slope, a single whining ricochet. The firing stopped.

She turned her head and saw Willie wriggling back across the plateau. He eased himself into position behind one of the boulders. There was a good scattering of them, and even with glasses it would be hard for anybody on the far side of the strip of plain to pick out a target.

Modesty said, 'I don't think we'll have too much trouble until we have to disengage. They can't outflank us, and if they try to rush we'll wipe them out on that slope. I guess Chance will aim at keeping us pinned down here till sundown, and then they'll have pretty fair odds.'

'We've got to be gone before then.'

'Yes.' She reflected for a while. 'Willie, can you rig up something to fire a shot once every few minutes after we've gone?'

'You mean *at* them? Blimey, no. You'd need timing devices or some sort of clockwork gadget. I 'aven't got any gear I could modify for that, Princess.'

'Just the sound of a shot would do. Anything to stop them knowing we've snaked away. Think about it, anyway. I'm sure you can figure something.'

Under his breath Willie said, '*Jesus!* . . .' and grinned.

There were times when she displayed an almost alarming faith in his ingenuity. Very flattering, but . . .

He had some fuse and plastic explosive, but not enough slow fuse to make a rig for setting off bullets at longish intervals. And in any case, using p.e. to set off a bullet would produce the wrong sort of noise. Chance and his crew knew what a bullet sounded like. It wasn't on.

He saw that the half-track was moving. Somebody was crouched down out of sight in the seat, driving blind. Half a dozen Kikuyu were bunched behind the half-track, with only a foot or a shoulder showing fleetingly. Presumably they were calling directions to guide the driver.

Modesty said slowly, 'Look, I don't want to kill any Kikuyu unless we have to, Willie. Not that I'm crazy about this lot. They're a vicious bunch and they enjoyed stripping me off and strapping me over that oil-drum. But they're just doing what Chance says, so let's not sign them off while we can avoid it.'

Willie grimaced. Men coming after you with guns and machetes were fair game, he thought, no matter who they were. But she was a bit weird about this sort of thing, and he accepted it without thought of argument. Mind you, if it came to a crunch, God help the lot of them. She would pull no punches then. He said, 'I think it's one of the whites driving.'

'It's Loeb. I saw him through the glasses as he got in. I'll fire three rounds rapid into the cab, trying for a ricochet, and you nail him if he shows.' He had barely sighted when he heard the *crack-crack-crack* of her rifle. One bullet caught the edge of the steel chassis and howled away. He did not see where the others hit, but the half-truck lurched round, exposing the group of Kikuyu, who scrambled frantically to get behind it again. Willie's finger itched. A burst of automatic fire just then would lower the odds drastically. The half-track was still turning. Loeb's head and shoulders showed for a moment as he lifted himself slightly, shouting and waving an arm at the Kikuyu. A hundred and fifty yards. Willie put a bullet into Loeb just under the lifted arm.

The man fell sideways and hung limply over the track-guard. The machine ground on. It was moving away now, back to the point it had started from, driverless. The Kikuyu scampered ahead of it in panic, trying to use it as a shield and at the same time avoid being run down. Again there came a burst of fire from the cleft, and mingled with it was the heavier sound of a hunting rifle.

Modesty said, 'Better change our positions a little—' She broke off, seeing that Willie lay flat with his head bowed on one forearm. 'Willie! Are you all right?'

He looked up, blue eyes bright as the sky, an astonished grin on his face. 'Eh? I'm fine. I just 'ad an idea about that thing you wanted. The bullets after we've gone. Can you manage okay while I go an' see Giles?'

She relaxed, and wiped the back of a hand across dry lips. 'Willie love, don't act dead next time you get an idea.' She looked down at the plain below. The half-track had lumbered straight into the wall near the cleft and stopped. Nothing moved. 'Yes, I can manage.'

Back in the cave Pennyfeather was giving Lisa some more milk. Willie said, 'Giles, you got some permanganate crystals in your case, I saw the jar. Any glycerine?'

'Eh? Yes, there's about half a bottle. What for?'

'Tell you later.' Willie rummaged in the big shabby bag. 'Jesus, you've got 'alf a chemist's shop in 'ere.' He sorted out a plastic jar with a screw cap, and a plastic bottle, both labelled in Pennyfeather's sprawling hand. 'All I want now is a bit of acid. Weak acid 'll do.'

'What sort of acid?'

'Any sort. Like vinegar, or lemon juice.'

'Why the hell would I carry vinegar?'

'Just something like it, Giles,' Willie said patiently. 'Any acid.'

'Sorry, I haven't got anything like that.'

Willie stared. 'Nothing? In all this load of ancient salves and nostrums?'

'Look, would uric acid do?'

'Yes, I suppose so. You got some?'

Pennyfeather grinned tiredly. 'We've all got some, you silly sod. Why d'you think God gave us bladders?'

248

Willie gaped, then gave a hoot of laughter. 'That'll do.'

'It's jolly weak, though,' Giles said doubtfully. 'I mean, the acid content. I don't know if it'll do for what you want. But there's masses of bird-shit on the rocks just outside. That's full of uric acid. If you half fill a pan with the stuff and top it up with water you'll get a decent concentration.'

'Giles . . . you're better than Pasteur ever was.'

For the next half hour Willie was busy with experiments. Three times he heard Modesty fire a few shots, but she did not call for him. Under test, the bird-dung proved to be the most effective medium for providing what he wanted. He crawled back to join Modesty. She said, 'Nothing's happening. I've just been putting a few shots into the half-track now and then, to let them know we're here. Did you work something out?'

As she finished speaking there came the sound of a shot from behind them. Her head snapped round as she searched the empty plateau, then she looked at him with widening eyes. 'Was that you?'

He nodded, pleased. 'Just a single shot for demonstration. I can't guarantee the timing, but it'll be good enough.'

She said wonderingly, 'My God, how on earth have you worked it, Willie? I didn't think it was possible.'

He looked at her open-mouthed for a moment, then laughed. 'I'll show you when we pull out.' He looked at his watch, then up at the sun. 'Only about 'alf an hour now.'

'Yes. Is Giles keeping an eye on the back entrance?'

'Keeps checking every few minutes. I don't suppose he'd remember, but Lisa reminds 'im.'

'Lisa? Is she getting panicky?'

'No, she just looks quiet, Princess. Sort of unwound.' He considered for a moment. 'Can't take 'er eyes off Giles. Maybe he's replaced the voices for 'er. It needs something like that to stop 'er cracking, I reckon. A sort of bridge till she can get 'er bearings.'

Modesty said slowly, 'It's funny. As a doctor Giles hardly knows what he's doing half the time, but what he does has a knack of being right. What about the physical thing, the operation?'

'Giles seems to think she's going on fine.'

'He'd know. I doubt if he remembers what the text-books say, but he'd know.'

They hugged the ground suddenly as there came a long burst of heavy fire from across the strip of plain. Bullets spattered against the screen of rocks in a slow traverse. As the echo faded Willie said, 'They've dug up a machine-gun. Sounded like a Lewis.'

The next move would probably be a rush under prolonged covering fire from the machine-gun. Using a pocket mirror fixed in a split stick as a periscope, Willie surveyed the ground. Modesty watched him, two grenades laid ready in front of her, waiting for his signal. Willie also had grenades ready. If an attack came, he would wait until it was on the slope before he threw his first grenade. Her own would be for use at shorter range if necessary.

There was another long burst of fire, but no figures emerged on to the open ground. Willie said, 'I think they're just getting the range right, so they can fire on a fixed trajectory after dark.'

'That suits us. Better let them know we're still here.' She lifted her rifle.

Every five minutes they threw a few shots towards the cleft or at the half-track, to signal their continued presence. Apart from an occasional burst of fire from the machine-gun, nothing more happened. After twenty minutes Modesty said, 'Let's make a start. That first bit of slope down into the valley isn't too good for a stretcher. You go and carry Lisa down in your arms, Willie, come back, take the poles and sacks down, and fix up the stretcher. Giles can manage his medical bag if you tie it on his back. Leave whatever you think we won't need. When you're all set, come back for me. If we work it like that we can be heading down that valley only a couple of minutes after I've fired the final burst.'

Willie said, 'I'll need about twenty minutes.' He began to wriggle away towards the cave. In fact it was just over seventeen minutes later when she heard him whistle. Sighting carefully, she put three shots into the half-track and three into the shadowed cleft, then turned and snaked away across the little plateau until it was safe to stand up.

Willie was waiting for her by a flat piece of rock a little way from the cave. On the rock, some twenty 7.62 mm cartridges had been stood upright in an irregular circle round a pan containing a dirty grey liquid. Each cartridge was planted in a blob of dark brown mush, like moist Barbados sugar. From the pan radiated long strips of twisted lint of different lengths. One end of each strip rested in the liquid, the other end vanished under a blob of mush. She saw that the liquid had begun to creep along the strips of lint. Since they varied in length, the moisture would reach each blob of mush at a different time.

She paused only for one look, and then she was hurrying on to the cave with Willie beside her. 'What the hell *is* it?' she said, fascinated.

'Permanganate crystals mixed with glycerine. You put a couple of drops of acid on it, and it starts spontaneous combustion. Bubbles up like lava, then bursts into flame. And blimey, it really burns, Princess. Gets practically incandescent. More than 'ot enough to explode a cartridge.'

She ducked through the small aperture at the back of the cave, and he followed her. She said, 'That dirty water – it's acid?'

He grinned. 'From bird-dung. You don't need it strong. That was Giles' idea. Worth a Nobel prize, I reckon.'

There was something about the whole conception that awoke her sense of the absurd. She said, 'Don't tell me some female firework expert taught you that.'

'No, I read it in a book at the orphanage. A Hundred Things a Bright Boy Can Do, or something like that. I used it to set fire to Dicer's bed the night I scarpered.'

She was still giggling as they reached the bottom of the slope. Lisa lay on the stretcher, Giles stood beside her, hunched under the weight of his bag. He said, 'What's the joke?'

'You and Willie and the bird-dung. I'll explain later, darling. Come on, let's go home.' Faintly she heard the sound of the first cartridge exploding, and bent to lift the front of the stretcher. The M16 was slung across her back now. Willie lifted the other end, and they began to move. Giles said, 'Are you sure these wasp things are safe? I can't have Lisa being stung, you know.'

'We can't 'ave anybody being stung, matey,' Willie said. 'They'll be all right if they're not disturbed, and we're not going to march through 'em singing *We Shall Overcome*, are we? Look, you walk be'ind me, and for Christ's sake don't do any of your falling-down tricks, or putting your foot in it.'

Pennyfeather looked baffled. 'That's a bloody extraordinary thing to say.'

The air in the valley was oppressive, but it held something beyond heat and humidity. There was a sullen menace, as if the spirit of some measurelessly ancient god-insect slept within the grey-green walls. Here and there a few darting black bodies danced in the air. No. More than a few. It was like searching the sky at dusk for stars. The longer you looked the more you saw.

Each nest was suspended by a single pedicel which seemed too fragile for the great bulk it carried. They hung from the spindly trees, from the taller bushes, and from the inward-leaning walls, a vast colony of colonies housing the absolute masters of this valley, who lived their complex and mindless lives at a level far below the threshold of any fear, prepared to attack whatever might disturb them, man or beast, large or small. The soft throbbing hum that pervaded the valley might have been the slow heart-beat of a sleeping giant.

Modesty imagined the effect of a shot echoing down the valley, reverberating from wall to wall, building to a crescendo of sound, and felt the sweat run down her body. It was absurd to imagine that voices in ordinary conversation would rouse the fury of the black hordes, yet nobody spoke now, even in a whisper.

They reached the first slight bend, and saw a longish straight stretch ahead before the walls twisted again. The

Virgin's legs, seen in close-up, were hardly shapely. At the head of the stretcher Modesty picked her way with care, keeping to the middle of the valley. It was as they came to the next bend that she heard Willie say urgently, '*Princess!*'

She stopped, lifting her eyes from the ground immediately ahead, and saw the men a hundred yards away. Adrian Chance and Jacko Muktar, Camacho and ten or eleven Kikuyu.

CHAPTER FOURTEEN

She said, 'Put her down, Willie,' and lowered the stretcher, bracing herself against the bitter shock. Van Pienaar must have been left behind with the heavy machine-gun to maintain the pretence of attack, while the rest had been making a looping march for the last hour or more, to bring them round into the far end of the valley.

She felt a wave of anger towards herself. Two hours ago she could have picked off most of the Kikuyu during their running retreats. *Fool*, she told herself. *You'll die for being soft one day. Maybe today. And the others too.*

When she turned to Willie he saw that her eyes had become black as jet. She said, 'All right. We play this for keeps from now on. Put a point on those staves, Willie.' She laid her gun down on the ground. Willie bent and drew out the two poles from the stretcher. They were a little thicker than the normal quarter-staff, and a few inches longer, but they would do. With his machete he began to shape the tips of each staff to a short sharp point.

Modesty was looking along the valley. She saw one of the Kikuyu swing up his rifle, and fancied she could hear Chance's quick yelp of rage as he slammed the barrel sideways with a sweep of his hand. She could see him speaking, gesticulating. The Kikuyu began to stack their rifles in a pile.

Evidently Chance did not trust them to keep their fingers from the trigger in the heat of battle. He was going to send them in with machetes.

Giles said slowly, 'There are too many of them, aren't there?' Without turning to look at him Modesty said, 'It won't take long to find out. You stay here with Lisa. All right, Willie. That patch of bare rock.'

She took one of the staves from him and started to run. Giles watched them go, then he knelt and took Lisa's hand. Her face looked grey with fear. From somewhere he dredged up a haggard smile and said, 'Look, you needn't worry, old dear. Chance's mob can't do any shooting, you see. And Modesty and Willie, they're terribly good at this sort of thing. They'll manage all right.' He did not believe himself.

As he ran, Willie touched the machete at his belt and the knives strapped on his chest under the shirt. The bare patch of rock they were heading for made as good an arena as any. It was clear of nests, and the footing was sound.

Modesty said, 'Better if I meet the first rush and you bowl them out on the flanks. They mustn't get round us.'

He grunted an affirmative, stopped ten paces short of the arena and began to scour the ground for fist-sized rocks. Her briefing had been short, but for him it set out the complete tactics of the coming fight. She ran on another thirty paces and stopped on the far side of the flat stretch of rock, the quarter-staff poised in her hands.

Chance was ready now. She heard him snap a command, and the group of Kikuyu started forward, machetes swinging. The three white men stood fast, watching. At first the Kikuyu came slowly, picking their way with care round a few nest-hung bushes, then they broke into a run. The run became a pounding charge. The sun glinted redly on the long blades. The madness of blood-lust was upon the Kikuyu, she could hear it in the sound of their panting, see it in the gleaming faces and white-rolling eyes.

From well to the rear, Willie Garvin watched. To other eyes she would have looked a pathetically small and lonely figure, without hope of lasting for a second against the frenzied stampede. For a moment Willie himself felt sudden horror at having allowed her to take the first onrush, then he excluded all horror and alarm ruthlessly from his mind and watched with clinical appraisal.

Her plan was right. She could not do the vital job that he was about to do. And he acknowledged without envy that she was better equipped then he was to meet the massed onslaught, even though his ability with the quarter-staff was greater, for among her skills was one he believed unique, one that never failed to fascinate him. He waited for it now almost eagerly. In combat, and providing there was room, she could move backwards in retreat as fast as an opponent could run at her. No doubt she had developed this in childhood and youth, against opponents always much heavier and stronger. It was astonishing to watch and painful to experience, for though she moved back almost at sprinting pace she was on the offensive the whole time, maintaining precise distance for striking, whatever her weapon or even with no weapon at all but hands and feet.

He knew from his own experience in practice combat with her how disconcerting and dangerous this skill was. You kept going on and on but you never quite made contact, because your timing was wrong; yet somehow she kept getting through to you and hammering the starch out of you. And this time she had the long-reaching quarter-staff as a weapon.

He saw her flex her legs, rise on the balls of her feet, and lean forward slightly, the staff poised.

This was it. This was when she suddenly wasn't there . . .

Eleven men brandishing machetes cannot strike in a wedge. The attack had become three irregular lines, one behind the other, spreading out. She was already backing fast when the first men came within distance. The quarter-staff whirled in a controlled blur of motion. Thrust, reverse, parry, chop, parry, thrust again. She slithered back ten paces in the first three seconds, to hold her distance and take advantage of the staff's long reach. She was using only deflection-parries against the machetes, so that the darting, slashing staff was never for an instant stilled.

Some of the Kikuyu were moving wide on her flanks, but she ignored them. One man was down with his larynx stove in, another with a shattered knee. A third was folding forward, a great wound under the heart. On her left now a man was darting in, machete swinging, foam on his lips. From the corner of her eye she saw his face cave in as a two-pound rock hit his cheek with terrible force. Willie Garvin was in action, and his skill in throwing was not limited to the knife; she had once seen him throw a felling-axe, the most clumsy and ill-balanced of missiles, and split a six inch sapling at fifty feet. A second man was down on her right, whimpering, holding a shoulder broken by another rock.

The range for Willie was only fifteen paces now. He hurled his third and last rock. His throwing action had the flickering snap of a whip, and the rock whistled in a flat trajectory to bounce three feet high from a Kikuyu's skull. A broken skull.

But there were five left, and a slashing machete had sliced three feet from one end of Modesty's staff. Willie said, 'Back off, Princess,' and sprinted forward. She ran back, ducking under the swing of his staff as the five Kikuyu came after her.

For several years now Willie had dreamed without hope of testing the quarter-staff in real combat to prove his belief in it, and now, incredibly, because the rolling echoes of a bullet in the valley would bring death to all, the moment had come. He felt intense, eager interest as he launched into the combination moves he had worked out and practised with so much thought and care over the years.

Flank swing, check, parry, reverse and thrust . . . flowing, always flowing in smooth sequence, footwork blending with every move of body and weapon. One of the men had run clear, looping to come in from the rear. Willie ignored him, leaving him to Modesty. In front of him there were only two men left standing. Now one. He heard the scuffle of feet on dry rock behind him, the hiss of a swung blade, a choking grunt and a soft thud.

The lone survivor had frozen in a crouch. He turned and began to run. Willie drew the machete from the sheath at his belt, weighed it briefly in his hand to assess the balance and rate of revolution in relation to distance, then threw. The machete made one revolution in the air and thudded home between the running man's shoulderblades. He went down without a sound, slithering along the ground.

The only movement now came from the man whose knee Modesty had shattered in the first rush, and the man with the broken shoulder. Willie moved forward and swung his staff twice. No more concessions today. Then there was no movement at all.

Fifty yards away, Adrian Chance, Jacko Muktar and Camacho stood like statues. Willie turned, started to speak, then froze. The Kikuyu who had outflanked him lay face up. He was dead. She had got him with the shortened staff in the larynx. But Modesty lay half-sprawled across him, un-moving.

Willie Garvin was beside her in half-a-dozen great strides, kneeling, taking her gently by the shoulders to turn her, dreading to find the frightful wound of a machete blade. Her head fell back on his arm and she whispered, 'Hold that position, Willie. Don't turn round. Got to bring Chance and the others in reach.'

Relief washed over him like a breaking wave, and with it came the old sense of quick admiration. She must have worked it out even as she was dealing with the last Kikuyu, and by God she was dead right. If Chance and the others ran for it now, if they got clear of the wasp-infested valley and waited in hiding with their guns . . .

He laid her down and began to tear off his shirt with frantic haste, as if for a pad to staunch a deep wound. She lay with her head turned sideways, eyes almost closed, and whispered, 'They're coming, Willie. Trying to move fast without making a noise. On clear ground now. Jacko and Camacho have picked up a machete apiece. Chance hasn't bothered, he's just got a knife. You take Jacko first and then Camacho, they're carrying guns and they just might be crazy enough to use them. Wait for it . . . wait. *Now!*'

He came smoothly to his feet, turning, a hand flashing to the twin knives lying in echelon on his left breast. The three men were only ten paces away, coming in fast. The first knife drove into Jacko's heart at eight paces, the second into Camacho's at six. As they went down, Modesty came past him like a sprinter from the starting-blocks. Willie saw that Chance's face beneath the silver hair had the imprint of madness stamped upon it now. The eyes were wild, the lips drawn back in a grotesque, startled grimace, as if he still could not believe that this was really Willie Garvin, alive; that the machete-swinging killers had been put down; that Jacko and Camacho had died in the last second.

He was still moving forward under momentum and there was a knife in his hand, but she was so fast that he had not begun to lift the knife when she reached him in a long striding jump like a hurdler, the toe of her boot driving into his body just under the heart. He quivered with shock, the light going out of his eyes as he took two tottering paces back and folded slowly to his knees. Before he could keel over she swung the kongo in her clenched fist. The scything hammerblow exploded on his temple, and he toppled sideways.

Willie Garvin pushed a hand through his hair and surveyed the scene. A few curious wasps were already investigating open wounds in still bodies. Looking back now, he realized that it had been an eerily soundless battle, like a scene from an old silent film. He did not trouble to go and look at Chance. That blow with the kongo was a killer, and she had meant it. He said, 'Well, it works, Princess. The old quarter-staff. I always said so.'

'That's what you always said, Willie.' She looked about her and made a weary grimace of disgust, then opened her shirt and pulled it down over one shoulder. On her arm was a thin red line from shoulder almost to elbow, the skin sliced as if with a razor. Blood welled slowly from the cut.

Willie gripped her arm and worked the flesh with his thumbs, frowning. 'You were playing the deflections too fine,' he said. 'But it's all right, only a sixteenth deep.' He took an antiseptic field dressing from his thigh pocket and began to pull it apart so that it would spread over the wound. She looked up at the sky. Already three vultures were circling lazily against the red-gold glow of the sun, waiting. She said, 'There won't be much for anybody to find.'

Willie nodded. When the surviving Kikuyu, the two he had stunned, came round and dragged themselves away, the vultures would float down. By dawn there would be only bones left, both here and on the plain where Selby and Loeb had died. The Kikuyu would probably be blamed for everything. They had turned on their masters, perhaps during a hunt, but had disturbed the wasps and paid the penalty. If the injured Kikuyu survived, they would probably disappear into the bush rather than crawl back to *Bonaccord* and face eventual questioning when the ramshackle police force got round to it. In that case the bones in the valley might never be found.

'There's one of 'em left,' Willie said. 'You can still 'ear 'im banging away on the Lewis every now an' then.'

'It's van Pienaar. When he comes here to find out what's happened he won't hang around to be asked questions. He'll just head for somewhere a long way off and hope to be thought dead with the rest.'

Willie finished taping the dressing in place. 'I'll fix it better when we can get at Giles' bag,' he said, and moved to pick up his shirt. Together they walked slowly back to where Giles waited. He still squatted beside Lisa, holding her hand. Her eyes were closed but there was no fear in her face now. He looked up as they drew near, a haggard, red-eyed scarecrow with a grin splitting his grimed face. Though he tried to keep his voice down, it held a muted bay of excitement.

'I say, you didn't half go, you two! I told Lisa those buggers were in for a shock – and that last bit was *jolly* cunning, if you ask me! I really thought you'd copped it, darling. So did that silver-haired sod and his mates.' He drew breath for a guffaw, held it, saw the two pieces of severed pole that Modesty carried, and frowned in exasperation. 'Oh Christ, now look what you've done. We needed that for the stretcher, you know.'

She said gravely, 'I'm sorry. I didn't think.'

Willie laughed. 'I expect we've 'ad worse problems if only we could remember 'em. Tell you what, Giles – suppose I lash the bits together?'

Forty minutes later, and a full mile from the point where the Virgin's splayed legs ended, they rested beside a tangle of bush edging a triangle of flat stony ground which dipped to a small river half a mile away. This was the pick-up area Willie had arranged.

The horizon was lifting to hide the deep red glow in the western sky. Giles sat beside the stretcher. Modesty lay face down on the ground, head pillowed on her forearms, asleep. Willie prowled a little anxiously, ears cocked. He carried a rubber-covered long-beam flash-lamp, ready to signal when he heard the helicopter.

After a while he moved to crouch beside Lisa and said, 'Feeling okay, love?'

'Yes.' Her voice was small.

'Tummy all right?'

'Yes. Thank you.'

Carrying her on the stretcher during the last half hour he had looked down at her from time to time and spoken a word or two of encouragement. It had been difficult to read the look on her face, but he had fancied there was a hint of fear in her eyes whenever she took them from Pennyfeather and looked up at him. Not exactly fear, perhaps, but a shrinking away, a shadowy hint of recoil.

Now he saw it clearly, though she was trying to hide it by forcing a smile to her pallid lips. He had been going to pat her hand or touch her cheek in a simple caress, trying to tell her without words that the past was dead, and that life for her would begin anew tomorrow. Instead he gave her an amiable grin and said, 'Not much longer. We're on the last lap now.' Then he got up and moved slowly away.

Well, there was a thing for you. He thought he understood it now. Lisa had been made to kill. The voices had made her do it. Perhaps already Giles had given her the healing self-absolution she would so desperately need. And good for him. She knew now that Brunel was the killer behind the voices, knew what had been done to her, and hated it. That was good, too. But she had seen the battle in the valley, seen Modesty Blaise and Willie Garvin kill. She must know that there had been no other way, but still it placed them among those capable of such things, even skilled in them, so that in her eyes now they were to some degree tainted as being of the same breed as the enemies they had fought.

He smiled ruefully to himself. Pity about that. The real Lisa was a nice kid. He had enjoyed being with her, sleeping with her, and had hoped vaguely to repeat the pleasure some time. But it would not happen again now. The fairy tales missed a point, he reflected. It was all right rescuing beautiful damsels in distress, but only as long as they didn't see you doing the necessary gory bits, like chopping off the giant's head and so on. That seemed to put them off, even though it saved their lives. They probably couldn't help remembering it whenever they looked at you.

Ah well...

The red glow had gone and the sky was dark purple. He sat cross-legged beside Modesty, close to her, chewing a dry blade of grass, watching her sleeping face. When he heard the distant clatter of the helicopter's rotor he laid a hand on her shoulder and she lifted her head at once.

'The chopper, Princess. On time. I'll go and signal.'

'I'll come with you.' They walked out a little way on to the stony plain and waited. She lifted his arm and put it round her shoulders, slipping her own arm about his waist. Two minutes later they saw the helicopter coming in across the river at three hundred feet.

She said, 'That's a welcome sight. Let's have a big hand for Willie Garvin, folks.'

He said in an earnest, nasal voice, 'I owe it all to Sexpot, the new-formula aftershave lotion that makes a man masterful. Until I started using Sexpot I could never get helicopters to land in Rwanda.' Lifting the flash-lamp he pointed it at the helicopter and switched on the beam, moving his hand in a little circle. In his normal voice he said, 'Are we going to do anything about Novikov's golden mile, Princess?'

He felt her shrug, felt the sudden weariness in her now

that to be weary no longer mattered. 'Let's leave it to the wasps, Willie love. They were there first.'

Six weeks later, in the penthouse, Tarrant said reproachfully, 'After all I've done for you, after all the fascinating experiences I've provided for you, I do feel you might have made contact with me sooner.'

Although it was only mid-afternoon the room was rather dark because the curtains had been partly drawn. On a table at the far end a colour-slide projector had been set up and there was a screen on the wall. When Tarrant arrived, Modesty had been sitting at the projector, writing in an indexed notebook. She was wearing a white towelling bathrobe. Her feet and legs were bare, her hair was down and had been clipped in two loose pigtails which stuck out slightly, giving her the look of a Victorian child.

She said, 'Yes, I'm sorry I didn't get in touch. I've been rather taken up with one thing and another. But I did ask Willie to make a point of seeing you.'

'I spent a very pleasant Sunday with him at The Treadmill soon after you got back.'

'Oh, good. You don't know where he is now?'

'I'm afraid not. He was going off somewhere next day.'

'I see.' She looked disappointed for a moment, then smiled. 'I suppose he told you what happened in Pelissol and Rwanda?'

'He gave me a bare outline, but wasn't inclined to be reminiscent. He described it as a grievous and vexatious caper.'

'He's been reading Winston Churchill again. But it's a fair description. We made a horrible mess of it, but muddled through.'

'Oh, I know all the details,' Tarrant said smugly. 'I went down to your cottage in Wiltshire where Pennyfeather was nursing the albino girl through her convalescence, and had a long chat with him.'

She laughed. 'You've got a nerve. I can't imagine it was a very coherent story. Not from Giles.'

'The salient features were there.' He looked at her. 'You're

262

lucky to be alive. To call Willie lucky isn't enough by half. You'd need to invent a new word. That part of it must have hit you very hard, until he turned up again.'

'Very.' She looked slightly annoyed, he thought. Annoyed with herself. That was strange. The look vanished and she said, 'Sorry to be dressed like this, but I wasn't expecting you. I've been down to the pool for a swim and haven't bothered to change yet.'

'It's for me to apologize for calling unannounced, but I'm not going to. You look enchanting. What's happened to Giles and the girl?'

She said, 'This arrived today,' and took a letter from the pocket of her bathrobe. 'You're welcome to read it. Do you mind if I finish these slides?'

'Please.'

The envelope bore a Peruvian stamp. Tarrant drew out the letter and unfolded it. The writing was neat and regular. The address was simply, *The Hospital*, and the name of a town or village he had never heard of.

Dear Miss Blaise,

We have settled in now, and Giles is very busy. The equipment is rather primitive and there is not much of it, but he does not seem to mind. He is a wonderful person, and all the patients like him. He asks me to send his regards to you and to Willie, and says he will write as soon as he can find time.

I am writing to thank you for the great kindness you have shown me, and to apologize for not being able to express my gratitude on the occasion when you called on me at the cottage you so kindly lent to Giles for my convalescence. I had not fully recovered at the time.

We are very happy here. I hope that you and Willie are in good health. Once again, my thanks to you both.

Yours sincerely,
Lisa.

Tarrant's eyebrows were almost touching his hairline as

he looked up. Seated at the table, Modesty pressed the slide-change switch, looked at the screen, and made a note. He said, 'Good God, you'd think the girl was thanking the vicar for a nice Sunday School outing. "Your great kindness." That's a cool way to sum up taking her appendix out in a cave, quite apart from the rest of it.' He got up and walked to where Modesty sat. 'It's shameful.'

She looked up, amused at his indignation. 'It isn't shameful at all. It's more of a miracle. I think everything that happened in Rwanda, and everything before that, has dwindled almost to a sort of pre-natal memory. She's been reborn, and Giles was the midwife.'

'With a little help from his friends,' Tarrant said drily. 'I should think you and Willie must feel somewhat unappreciated.'

'Oh, don't be stuffy. It all just happened. I'd have left her behind if Giles hadn't insisted. And without the stretcher, we wouldn't have had a quarter-staff apiece when it came to the big crunch. So she doesn't owe us anything.'

Tarrant sighed and put down the letter, wondering at her logic. He said, 'What exactly are they doing in Peru?'

'Dealing with earthquake casualties. Giles is a volunteer with the medical emergency section of the Red Cross now. It was my idea and I'm rather pleased with it. Wherever there's a disaster, he'll go and work as a doctor there.' She switched to another slide. 'It's perfect for him. He's right in his element, working under conditions that would terrify most doctors. And Lisa's acting as a nurse for him. She hasn't any experience, but if you're with Giles you soon learn. I didn't think I could take an appendix out until he made me. I expect they'll marry soon, and I think it'll work out for her. Giles could marry a hundred girls and be happy, but I fancy he's the only possible man for her.'

'It sounds very promising for them. You say he's a volunteer?'

'Yes. He works without pay.'

'Then what do they live on?'

She made a note in the indexed book. 'Well, I used that money we took from Brunel's safe. The Distressed Gentlefolk will have to wait till next time. I bought Giles a ten-year annuity with it, so he'll have about two thousand a year coming in.'

'He didn't protest?'

'Yes, but it was all fixed by then. And I pointed out that it wasn't my money anyway. Another good thing is that Lisa's going to be a pretty rich girl one day. I won't have to worry about Giles being on the bread-line.'

'Why is she going to be rich?'

'Because she's Brunel's legally adopted daughter, and it looks as if she'll inherit whatever they can track down of his estate. Not *Bonaccord*. The Rwanda government is taking that over, but I've had a smart lawyer out there for the last five weeks. He'll screw some compensation out of them. He's also dug up securities and holdings of gold in Swiss banks. And a numbered account passbook. There's going to be plenty, and Lisa's the only one in the field. Nobody else has a claim.'

'I see why you've been busy and elusive,' Tarrant said. He looked at the screen. It showed a small blue flower in close-up. 'That's very pretty. You once told me you didn't like horticulture.'

'Not quite. I said flowers and plants won't grow for me. I don't think they like my aura. These are slides of Maltese wildflowers. That's a blue pimpernel, and very common, but Malta has hundreds of different wildflowers, and some of them are rare.' She stared at the screen. 'It's the best time of year for them just now. I never get tired of roaming over the cliffs and down in the valleys, hunting for them. It's lovely.'

'And you take these photographs?'

'It's a sort of project Willie and I started a year or so ago. We have a little villa out there, and we're trying to find specimens of all the different wildflowers. That means several hundred. I'm just checking what we've got so far.'

'It doesn't really sound like Willie.'

'It probably doesn't sound much like me, either. But we've become highly competitive in finding the rare and the very rare species. The thing's developed into quite a needle match, so we have a gentleman's agreement that we only go hunting together. No stealing a march on the other.'

Tarrant was only mildly surprised. He had long ceased to wonder at the unexpected ways in which Modesty and Willie spent their time, singly or together. He said, 'It sounds a nice healthy and harmless pursuit. When are you going out there again?'

'I don't know. When we get together, I suppose. But I haven't heard from Willie for quite a while. He's probably sunning himself in Bermuda with a gorgeous redhead.'

'You almost sound as if you mind. You've never minded before.'

'No, of course I don't mind. I expect him to. It's just that ... well, we usually take a break somewhere together after we've come through a patch of trouble. We like that. But I spoilt it this time.'

'You?'

She did not answer at once, but switched off the projector, went to the window and drew back the curtains. When she looked at him he saw that her smile was rather crestfallen. 'Yes, it was my fault,' she said. 'For over a week I thought he was dead. I knew he was dead. Then he came back. It was so marvellous. But when we got home I kept fussing over him. I couldn't help it. And it made poor Willie uneasy, because that just isn't the way we are. After a little while he quietly pushed off. To let me get over it, I suppose.'

Her expression changed. She looked puzzled and a little aggrieved. 'But he might have known it would soon pass. Now he's been gone so long I'm beginning to get vexed with him.'

'As intended, I'm sure,' said Tarrant, amused. 'He's goading you back to normal.'

'Yes.' She stood with hands deep in the pockets of her bathrobe, frowning thoughtfully. 'But enough is enough. It's too bad of him. I've a damn good mind to go out to Malta and hunt up a few specimens on my own.'

'My dear,' said Tarrant solemnly, 'you have a gentleman's agreement not to do so. He'd be greatly shocked if you broke it.'

'Willie? Of course he wouldn't. He knows very well I'm not to be trusted. It would just serve him right.'

They heard the sound of the lift, and waited without speaking, watching the doors. The lift stopped and Weng emerged. He said, 'There was a special delivery for you down at the desk, Miss Blaise. It just arrived.' He handed her an envelope, greeted Tarrant politely, and went out along the passage to his room.

She looked at the envelope. It was stiffened with cardboard inside. She said, 'It's from Willie – and sent from Malta!'

Inside there was a single colour-slide but no message. She said nothing, but Tarrant saw indignation suddenly widen her eyes. He thought he detected a hint of pleasurable excitement also. She moved to the projector, switched it on, and put in the slide. On the screen, a small purple trumpet-shaped flower with a hairy stem appeared.

'It's Purple Viper's Bugloss!' she said. 'Classified as Very Rare in Malta. We spent a whole week hunting for it last year.' She turned to Tarrant. 'Oh, he's a crook! Willie Garvin's a double-crossing crook!'

'It's certainly a breach of agreement calling for the severest reprimand,' Tarrant said gravely.

She looked at her watch with narrowed eyes. 'Four-fifteen. There's a plane about five-thirty from Heathrow. I can just make it, if there's a seat.' She started towards her bedroom. 'Will you be an absolute honey and ring the BEA desk for me? I'll only be a few minutes.'

She was gone. Tarrant blinked, then went to the phone.

It was just under seven minutes later when she emerged wearing slacks and a jersey tunic, a camel-hair coat over her arm, a large handbag hanging on a strap from her shoulder. She had plaited her hair in two pigtails and tied the ends with scraps of green ribbon matching the tunic.

Tarrant said, 'You'll only be charged half-fare, looking like that.'

'Did you get me a seat?'

'Yes. The ticket will be at the desk. You have to pick it up by five.'

267

'You're my favourite middle-aged man.' She lifted her voice. 'Weng! Clear all this stuff away, will you. I'll be in Malta from about eight o'clock onwards if you need to ring me about anything.'

Weng appeared, showing no surprise. 'Yes, Miss Blaise.'

'And take a holiday yourself. You can draw on the general account, and just let me know where you are.' She turned to Tarrant. 'I'll take the Jensen. Would you like to come with me and drive it back? Then you could look after it for me while I'm away. Or are you too busy just now?'

'I'm busy, but I'm not going to miss having a Jensen for a while. Where's your luggage?'

'I travel light.' She touched the handbag. 'And I've everything I need at the villa.'

'Transport from the airport at the other end?'

She laughed. 'There are plenty of taxis at Luqa, but Willie's going to be waiting there for me or I'm much mistaken. He knows damn well he's put a squib under me.'

'Give him my best.' They entered the lift. 'And I trust you won't fuss him.'

'Fuss him?' Her frown held dark menace and her foot tapped the floor impatiently. 'I'm going to scorch his ears. I don't mind him toying with a redhead in Bermuda, but when he goes hunting Purple Viper's Bugloss without me it's an outrage.'

Tarrant laughed. 'Have a lovely time,' he said.

If you have enjoyed this PAN Book, you may like to choose your next book from the titles listed on the following pages.

Peter O'Donnell

MODESTY BLAISE   30p

Comparisons of Modesty with James Bond are irresistible. The similarities are marked – the restless changing scenes, the ingenuity of both sides, the violence, the surging confidence in telling' – EVENING STANDARD

SABRE-TOOTH   30p

'I don't recommend anyone to start on it, because the fact is that once you have begun it's very hard to put down'
       – THE DAILY TELEGRAPH

A TASTE FOR DEATH   30p

'No one could fault Peter O'Donnell for excitement, detail and ingenuity' – OXFORD MAIL

PIECES OF MODESTY   25p

Once again, Modesty proves which member of the species is the more deadly, daring and delectable – as well as softer in the clinches. 'She feeds on danger like a starving man-eater' – BIRMINGHAM EVENING MAIL

Victor Canning

THE SCORPIO LETTERS 30p

'Crisp thriller . . . the mysterious blackmailer Scorpio is excitingly and violently unmasked.'
– DAILY EXPRESS

THE GREAT AFFAIR 35p

'A first-rate adventure story . . . high on action' – BOOKS AND BOOKMEN

THE MELTING MAN 30p

'Few more macabre settings for a climax could be imagined than the private waxworks of a mountain chateau . . . Crisp, polished and as tense as they come.' – BRISTOL EVENING NEWS

QUEEN'S PAWN 30p

'Canning at his best . . . a master of invention and suspense.' – TIMES LITERARY SUPPLEMENT

MR. FINCHLEY DISCOVERS HIS ENGLAND 35p

'This is a quite delightful book, with an atmosphere of quiet contentment and humour that cannot fail to charm.' – DAILY TELEGRAPH

Dick Francis

'Dick Francis's novels are probably the best sports detective stories ever written'
— NEW YORK TIMES

'The best thriller writer going'
— SUNDAY TIMES

FORFEIT 25p
Awarded the 1970 Edgar Allan Poe prize by the Mystery Writers of America.

ENQUIRY 25p
'By far the best Francis' — SPORTING LIFE

FOR KICKS 25p
'Jolting action scenes' — FINANCIAL TIMES

ODDS AGAINST 25p
'Dead-cert smash hit' — DAILY MIRROR

BLOOD SPORT 25p
'One of the year's best chillers'
— NEW YORK TIMES

FLYING FINISH 25p
'A highly ingenious story of sadistic criminality that builds to a tremendous climax'
— THE FIELD

RAT RACE 25p
'Impossible to stop reading'
— DAILY TELEGRAPH

These and other PAN Books are obtainable from all booksellers and newsagents. If you have any difficulty please send purchase price plus 7p postage to PO Box 11, Falmouth, Cornwall.
While every effort is made to keep prices low, it is sometimes necessary to increase prices at short notice. PAN Books reserve the right to show new retail prices on covers which may differ from those advertised in the text or elsewhere.